Darkness

Paul Dale Anderson

2AM Publications

Rockford, Illinois

2AM Publications
3211 Broadway
Rockford, IL 61108-5941
www.pauldaleanderson.net

Publisher's Note: This is a work of fiction. Names, characters, places, and incidents are a product of the author's imagination. Locales and public names are sometimes used for atmospheric purposes. Any resemblance to actual people, living or dead, or to businesses, companies, events, institutions, or locales is completely coincidental.

Book Layout © 2014 BookDesignTemplates.com

Darkness/ Paul Dale Anderson. -- 1st ed.
ISBN 978-0-937491-14-0

I owe a debt of gratitude to the forerunners of this novel: To Roger Zelazny, for his brilliant *Lord of Light*; to Elizabeth Cunningham, for her wonderful Magdalen books; to Jim Butcher for the Dresden novels; to J. R. Tolkien, for the Hobbit and the Ring; to C. S. Lewis, for the Wardrobe; to Henry Kuttner and Cathy Moore, for everything they wrote; and to the storytellers of old, for giving us the many myths and legends I have retold here. May the tradition continue forever.

"What's in a name? That which we call a rose by any other name would smell as sweet."

— William Shakespeare, *Romeo and Juliet*, II, ii, 1-2.

BOOK I

"The sun also ariseth, and the sun goeth down, and hasteth to the

place where he arose."

Holy Bible, King James version. Ecclesiastes, 1:5.

CHAPTER ONE

On the morning of that fateful fall equinox, the sun simply disappeared and the world turned dark. In the United States of America it happened at precisely 7:08 Ante Meridian, Central Daylight Savings Time. One minute the sun was there in the sky. The next minute it wasn't.

No eclipse had been predicted. No person anywhere could see—not with high-powered binoculars or the even more powerful refracting telescopes situated in observatories—an alien entity from outer space blocking the sun's light; no giant spaceship nor aberrant asteroid had moved between the earth and the sun to absorb the sun's rays while half the planet slept. Whatever had happened to the sun, it certainly wasn't natural.

Scientists claimed our sun was still there, exactly where it had always been, but human eyes simply couldn't perceive it. It hadn't gone nova overnight and exploded into a billion tiny pieces. There were no black holes tugging at the solar system, dragging the sun and planets into oblivion.

No one had gone blind during the night. No one, said medical authorities on all the morning talk shows, should worry about going blind. People could see perfectly well in artificial light from fluorescents or incandescents, but no one anywhere could see the sun no matter how hard they tried. Go outside, said the scientists, and see for yourself.

Nor should, scientists emphasized, people obsess about new ice ages forming. Temperatures hadn't abruptly changed, No glacial ice would creep down from the frozen north to destroy civilization. Earth was still bombarded with the same amount of solar heat and with the same number of unseen rays as yesterday and the day before that. But the sun had somehow dropped out of the normal visual spectrum, and neither you nor anyone else could see the sun with the naked human eye.

Authorities urged people to remain calm and not to panic, but people had already panicked. Some were hysterical. Some acted irrationally. One well-known televangelist said the battle of Armageddon was about to be waged as prophesied in the sixth chapter of the Book of Revelation. All of the phone lines in the preacher's toll-free telephone bank suddenly became overwhelmed with people who had never seemed religious before calling to charge large donations to credit cards and to shout Halleluja.

New religions sprang up practically overnight. Some were really weird. The world wide web was filled with doomsday prophecies.

In the far north of Sweden, in the country of the Lapps and the land of the midnight sun, an old man with a long white beard, whom many said looked a little like a very tall but skinny Santa Claus, picked up his shaman's drum and chanted jojks.

His aged fingers beat rhythmically on a reindeer-hide drumhead tied around an ancient hoop drum carved from the sacred wood of the World Tree. His name was Biegolmai Davvii, and he was a Saami reindeer herder and the Guardian of the Watchtower of the north wind.

Biegolmai Davvii was the man who sang the sun to sleep every night with ancient songs and Biegolmai woke the sun in the morning with his sacred drum. He had been doing that every day—with the exception of a very few days at the end of June when the sun did not set north of Kiruna, or those few days near the end of December when the sun didn't rise—for as long as anyone could remember, and the sun had never ever failed to rise when it heard his jojks. Now he sang the sunrise song, but the sun refused to show its face.

Something was rotten in Denmark, and Biegolmai could smell it all the way up here some two thousand kilometers to the north of Copenhagen. Whoever had done this was the most powerful magician Biegolmai had ever known, and he had known many magicians and sorcerers over the millenia. None of them were capable of producing a negative hallucination on such a grand scale as this, and no one he knew would even try.

Negative hallucinations, where one doesn't see something that is actually there, were much harder to produce than positive hallucinations. When people thought they saw something that didn't really exist, those people were seeing a posive hallucination. When something real seemed to disappear, that was a negative hallucination. All mass hallucinations were incredibly difficult to produce, if they could be produced at all. Hiding the sun—making every person on earth think the sun had disappeared—required magic. An hallucination of this magnitude depended on real magic to sustain the negative effects over time.

And if a single magician could do this, what else might he be capable of? What else could he do? What else *would* he do? Magic—real magic—was a fine art, and very few practitioners had the expertise and finesse to be called adept. Dabblers, yes. Adepts, no. True adepts maintained a very low profile and remained hidden from public view. From time to time, Biegolmai encountered the more advanced adepts climbing the World Tree, the tree of life that connected all worlds. One had to climb the World Tree to ascend to the spirit realm, and adepts were walkers between worlds. Seven levels of initiation were required just to walk between multiple worlds, and nine levels of initiation were required to become an ascended master and enter the spirit realm. Biegolmai could count the number of ascended masters alive today on the fingers of both hands.

Biegolmai Davvii was one.

Biegolmai left his body behind. His spirit ascended the World Tree to join with the other Guardians of each of the Watchtowers of the Four Winds. There were four primary Guardians plus four who supported spokes of the wheel of life.

All eight spirits merged into one. It was as if he were them, and they were him.

Sara Nelson had recently assumed Guardianship of the West Watchtower, and she was the female element of the earth itself. Though only twelve years old, Sara embodied the attributes of the Great Mother. Like all of the Guardians, Sara had lived many past lives. In one incarnation she was Sa-Ra, in another Quan Yin. In others she was known as Ta-ra, Kubaba, Cybele, Freyja, Sarasvati, and Purple Lotus Flower. Biegolmai became Sara, and Sara was Biegolmai.

Lokesvara Sailendravarman was Guardian of the East Watchtower, and he was said to be the reincarnation of Manjusri Bodhisattva. Lokesvara was a Lama at the temples of Angkor Wat in northern Cambodia. Lokesvara was slightly taller than the average oriental, but he was slight of frame and looked ancient and fragile. Lokesvara was soft-spoken, very wise, and the kindest man Biegolmai had ever known. Now Beigolmai was also Lokesvara, and Lokesvara was Biegolmai.

La Curandera was Guardian of the South Watchtower. She was once known as Ixchel, and in another life she was called Ix Tzutz Nik and in another Tunupa. She was a Bruja and healer from the Chilean Andes, and she often appeared as a beautiful young woman or a wrinkled old hag. She had recently reincarnated as a twenty-year-old man named Jerry Walker whose hair and beard had turned white after he nearly died when a volcano erupted in Chile and he was badly burned by molten lava. Biegolmai was La Curandera, and La Curandera was Biegolmai.

Biegolmai, himself, was Guardian of the North Watchtower. He was once known as Wiracochan, Horagalles, Torrekall, and Aijeke. To so very many he had always been known simply as "Grandfather" or "Grandfather Winter" and no one ever recalled Biegolmai being young. He was very tall, nearly seven feet tall, and he had a bushy white beard that made him look a lot like Santa Claus or Oddin, father of the gods in the Norse mythology.

There were four new Guardians of the Crossquarters, the spokes of the wheel that reinfored the primary directions: a U. S. Marine Corps drill instructor from San Diego, California, named Jonathan Roy Fish who was the latest reincarnation of Akashagarbha, the Boundless Space Bodhisattva with the ability to appear any place at any time; Kisikil Lilake—sometimes called Kisi, sometimes Lily, sometimes Nanshe, sometimes Lakshmi, sometimes Shakti—lived in a tree outside the Zagros caves beside the banks of the Great Zab river a few miles north of where the Zab flowed into the Tigris, and Kisi possessed the powers of the earth itself; red-haired Bryn Helgasdottir— sometimes called Nott or Sigrdrifa or Brynhildr or Gudrun— who had a home on a rock near Hlymdale, not far from Biegolmai's own home in northern Scandinavia and was thought to be a norn or the reincarnation of a valkyrie; and Shachar Hadad Elman, twin brother of Shalim Yam Elman, who lived not far from Idlib in modern Syria and who could move mountains with his mind. Shachar's brother had relocated to America many years ago, and the brothers had not seen each other in years.

These four crossquarter Guardians replaced former Guardians who had recently been killed when an adept named Philip Ashur sought ultimate power by destroying the polarities that kept balance in the universe. Polarity was what made magic possible, and the union of opposite polarities created life, generated energy, and shifted subtle energies from one point in space and time to another. Four of the Guardians had to be male and four had to be female to balance polarities.

"How could this happen?" asked Lokesvara Sailendravarman. "It was not something I sensed in advance."

"Nor I," said La Curandera. "Whoever did this has acquired incredible power."

"Sacrifice," said Sara Nelson. "He or she acquired power from human sacrifice."

"How many sacrifices would it take to produce such power?" asked Bryn. "And who would voluntarily relinquish his or her life energy in this day and age? Perhaps one or two people, but to build up such power would take thousands of people willing to sacrifice their lives. I simply don't see that happening. Self-sacrifice isn't in style these days."

"Would animal sacrifice work?" asked Jon Fish.

"No," said Biegolmai. "Where would those human sacrifices have to be made to affect the sun in this way?"

"Machu Picchu," said La Curandera, sounding absolutely certain. "It is the only place on earth where such sacrifices would have this affect on the sun. The Incas were a blood-thirsty civilization. They built their empire on human sacrifice. And the Intihuatana is there for a reason."

"What is the Intihuatana?" asked Shachar Elman.

"It is a ritual rock where the Incas tied the sun itself to the mountain so they could harness the sun's power. To do so required sacrifice, primarily of virgins between the ages of six and nineteen. The Aztecs also made human sacrifices— beheading and extracting the still-beating hearts and the brains and working memories of victims and eating them raw—but none of the Aztec sites have the Intihuatana. So the sacrifices must have taken place at Machu Picchu near the top of the great mountain where the Intihuatana still exists."

"They sacrificed children?" said Sara Nelson, shuddering at the thought. Sara was little more than a child herself.

"The ceremony," said La Curandera, "called *capacocha* in Quechua, captured the immense power of the sun. Men who ate the hearts of female sacrificial victims acquired the power to move the sun. Or so the Incas believed. The Incas called themselves Sons of the Sun. They believed they were the sons of Inti, their Sun god."

"Belief is a powerful tool," said Biegolmai.

"Amen to that," said Sara Nelson.

"We can send Akashagarbha to Machu Picchu to see if our adversary is there," suggested Lokesvara. "I would go myself, except climbing mountains is the province of younger folk than I. Jon, will you please go there now in spirit form and report back?"

Jon's spirit left the World Tree and circled over the mountains of Peru like a bird. Within minutes, he was back.

"I saw long lines of women and children climbing up the west side of the mountain," said Jon Fish. "So great was the accumulated power at the peak, however, that not even Akashagarbha could penetrate the darkness."

"Now," said Lokesvara, "we know where our adversary is located."

"But how do we get to him and make him reverse what he has done?" asked La Curandera.

"And who is he?" asked Shachar Hadad Elman. "Who is this adept that knows what to do and isn't one of us?"

"And why has he done this? Why has he hidden the sun?" wondered Kisi Lalake.

"Two reasons," said Biegolmai. "He hides in darkness, and he thrives on chaos. We must find him quickly before this magician becomes so powerful not even the Guardians can stop him."

CHAPTER TWO

T he Lone Ranger had hung up his guns for good. Now the Ranger—the sole surviving member of an elite squad of U. S. Army Rangers massacred by Taliban in Afghanistan—lived the simple life of a humble Buddhist monk, one of many at Angkor Wat, the ancient temples constructed by the Khmer kings in the northeastern part of what became known as Cambodia. And he was happier than he had ever been in his entire life.

Though he still sometimes thought of himself as the Lone Ranger, he was no longer the same man. The embittered ex-soldier who had sought revenge and who had hired out his guns to the highest bidder was dead and buried.

Money meant absolutely nothing to him now, and he had given all of the blood money he had acquired as a hired assassin, close to two million dollars hidden in Swiss and Cayman bank accounts under the fictitious name of Albert Schweitzer, to the poor. Now he owned nothing but the clothes on his back, the traditional red and safron robes of the dedicant. On his feet were well-worn sandals he had constructed himself of woven bamboo. He had relinquished everything he owned. Finally, the Lone Ranger felt free to become truly enlightened.

He had done terrible things. He had lost his mind, as well as his men, in Afghanistan, and he had killed hundreds of innocent civilians in retaliation. After the Army discharged him as mentally unqualified for retention, he had hired out as an assassin and killed again. Now, at last, he was done with killing. He had vowed to never kill again.

After completing his novitiate, the Ranger had continued studies at the lamasery. He had asked the Abbott to be intitiated into the mysteries of the Pho-wa, the ways of continuing consciousness after death. Lama Lokesvara had granted his request, and the Ranger was preparing to receive his first instruction into the Pho-wa mysteries when suddenly Lokesvara's spirit departed the Lama's body. The Ranger waited patiently for the master's spirit to return.

When the master did return to his mortal body, he brought Jon Fish with him.

Fish materialized in physical form, wearing familiar camouflage-patterned battledress. The Ranger would have been very much surprised by that sudden appearance if he didn't know who Jon Fish really was.

"Jon," he acknowledged with a nod of his head. "Good to see you again."

"And you, my friend," said the Marine as he warmly clasped the Ranger's hand.

"I thought you were back in the saddle at San Diego. What he hell are you doing here? Please don't tell me you left the Corps because you got religion and decided to become a monk like me."

"I'm on emergency leave from the Corps. They'll survive without me for a week or two, and I'll straighten the troops out when I get back."

"Your instruction in Pho-wa must wait, my son," Lokesvara sadly informed the Ranger. "In a few hours when the sun would normally rise above the mountains to the east, the world will remain in darkness. We Guardians suspect the work of a rogue adept, and Jon located this adept atop a mountain in Peru. But the magician is already very powerful and grows even more powerful. We must immediately intervene. Are you willing to help?"

"What do you want me to do?" asked the Ranger.

"Accompany Jon to Peru. We cannot teleport in or out because of the natural vortex at Machu Picchu, and we can't get close enough in spirit to see what's happening on the mountain top. We have to send someone up the mountain on foot. Jon has volunteered to go. Will you volunteer to go with him?"

"I've renounced killing. I will not take the life of another sentient being."

"I, too, have made the vow of ahimsa," said Lokesvara. "I do not ask you to break your vows, my son. As Vajrapani, you have no need to kill. You will find other means to accomplish your mission. These may help." Lokesvara rose from lotus and walked across the room to a table containing holy relics. He returned with the Vajra, the magic lasso, and the sacred Kris. Lokesvara handed them to the Ranger.

Power infused every muscle, nerve, fiber, and cell of the Ranger's being as the Vajra—two symmetrical spheres with a compass point at each end to direct polarized energy and joined together by an ornate cyllindrical shaft—fit neatly into his right hand. The Vajra was said to have been forged of two magic metals by Tvastar, the weapons-maker of the gods. The Kris— an asymmetrical wavy blade that looked like a crawling serpent—was forged of magical magnetic iron ores and blessed nickel from fallen meteorites. The Kris, along with the magic lasso—a braided rope of hemp and cotton similar to ropes Sufi Faqirs used to climb to the heavens and disappear from sight— fit his left hand. Vajrapani was fully present now, and it was Vajrapani—the protector and guide of all the buddhas—who said, "I will do as Manjusri asks."

"Very good," said Lokesvara. "Vajrapani and Akashagarbha, is there anything else you need? Are you ready to go?"

"We can teleport directly to the base of the mountain," said Jon, the reincarnation of Akashagarbha Bodhisattva. "But we'll have to walk the rest of the way to the top." He stood and removed his uniform cap, his battledress blouse with insignia, and his wrist watch. He was dressed now only in combat boots, camouflage trousers with belt, and a light brown t-shirt. It was springtime in the Andes, and he wouldn't need a coat.

"I'm too conspicuous in robes," said the Ranger. "But I no longer own civilian clothes."

"One moment," said Lokesvara. He left the room and returned with jeans, boots, and a black shirt. "These may fit," said the Lama.

"Now I'm ready," said the Ranger when he was dressed in the new outfit.

Both men blinked out of existence in Cambodia and flashed back into existence in Peru, on the east bank of the Urubamba River near the base of Machu Picchu. From there, they ascended the mountain on the Old Inca Trail, cut rocks laid down nearly seven centuries ago to form a cobblestone road where men could easily walk two abreast. But the trail was winding and sometimes difficult, especially in total darkness. And, because moonlight was merely the reflected light of the sun, no moon was visible to guide their way up the mountain.

"You are already more than 10,000 feet above sea level," spoke La Curandera's voice in their minds. "As flatlanders, you may feel lightheaded, but there is no time to rest and acclimatize."

"Where are you?" asked Jon.

"High overhead," answered La Curandera. "You cannot see me. My spirit joined with the spirit and body of a condor, and condor eyes can see even in the dark. I cannot fly near the peak, but I will remain with you to guide you more than half-way up the mountain. Then you will be on your own."

"Don't worry about me," said the Ranger. "I was Army Airborne. I can handle heights."

"The road narrows, and you have to cross several deep gorges on rickety rope bridges."

"How do you know so much about this place?" asked Jon.

"I lived on this mountain in many past lives. I was here before the Incas. My people knew the heavens intimately because we lived so close to the heavens every day of our lives. And we could see, from the tops of these mountains, the movement of the stars. We knew how to read messages from the stars, and we recorded those messages in stone effigies carved into these very mountains. As above, so below. What happens in the heavens affeccts what happens here on earth, and vice versa. It was true then, and it is true now."

"What happened when the Incas came?"

"Instead of reading the stars, they sought to alter the course of the stars to control events on earth. They built Machu Picchu to conduct rituals for that purpose. At the top of the mountain, they sacrificed unblemished children at propitious times. Children were their gifts to the gods, and children carried a message from the Incas to the gods. Show us how to change time and space, they begged, and we will honor you forever."

"Did the Incas learn how to alter time and space?"

"Yes. They learned much. They believed their leaders had become as gods themselves before the Spaniards came and decimated the Inca civilization, not with superior weapons but with smallpox and plague. The Incas became master alchemists, and they knew how to melt rock and reform it. This they learned from watching volcanoes at work. They cut rock in quaries. Master metalsmiths also melted rock down, moving molton rock from one place to another and reforming it to meet their needs. The Incas could do this because they knew the secrets of fire and ice."

"The secrets of fire and ice?"

"Used in alchemy to temper metal. I learned the secrets of fire and ice from Biegolmai when he visited me on this very mountain eons ago. The Incas learned it by watching what happened when the molton lava that belched from active volcanoes ran into icy glaciers."

"Biegolmai was here many centuries ago? At Machu Picchu?"

"Yes. And at Lake Titicaca and Tiwanaku. You can see his image carved into the rock face a few miles from here."

"What is so special about this place that brought two adepts together on this mountain?"

"The confluence of three sacred rivers: Rio Ahobamba, Rio Urubamba, and Rio Tambo. The Urubamba, which my people called Wilcamayu or sacred river, encircles Machu Picchu on three sides like a horseshoe magnet, something very auspicious to the Incas. The Tambo links the Urubamba to the Amazon River. The Incas became masters of air, earth, fire, and water. They sought to capture the spirits of the condor, the rock, the volcano, and the river through their works and their icons. Heads up, now. You are about to run into a long line of people on the trail just ahead of you."

Jon and the Ranger could hear them now, not too far ahead, hundreds of bare or sandaled feet pounding the ground, pulverizing what little grass grazing llamas left between slabs of rock. The human herd moved up the mountain in reverential silence; no one spoke. Jon and the Ranger could tell that many of those feet were tiny and belonged to children or young women. Their walk was purposeful, deliberate. It was as if they were in a hurry to get to the top of the mountain.

And now the trail began to fill in behind them, too. Jon heard a baby cry somewhere in the distance.

Jon and the Ranger became boxed in. There were people ahead of them, people behind them, a solid rock cliff to the right, a nasty drop off on the left. In one sense being boxed in was good. As long as they could sense the person in front of them, they knew they were still on the trail. If the person in front of them suddenly disappeared, which sometimes happened, they knew they walked too close to the edge.

They continued on in the dark, climbing higher and higher, ascending now at a 60 degree angle as the trail became almost too steep to climb. They walked for hours, and no one stopped to take a break or catch their breath. The people behind them pressed closer. They wedged together, one solid stream of sweating humanity climbing a trecherous trail into the clouds.

"How much farther to the top?" Jon's mind asked the spirit of La Curandera.

"Another day," came the answer. "Maybe a half day at the pace you are going. Only twenty miles remain. But they are mostly uphill miles, and you will walk slower than normal, especially as you go higher and the atmosphere thins."

"A whole day? You got to be kidding!"

"You have only begun the trek to the top. The Incas chose this place for many reasons, one of which was they could see ememies approaching on foot or horseback long before they reached the citadel. The Incas had plenty of time to prepare for battle, and they sent out *chasqui*—runners—to cut the ropes made of ichu grass holding two suspension bridges over the *pongo* or canyon. There is a 1900 foot drop to the Urubamba if the bridge is cut. There is also a bridge yet ahead of you made of two logs. The Incas rolled the logs over the side of the canyon to render the trail impassible. There is also ahead a very long tunnel cut through the mountain that could be blocked or barricaded."

"Can you see if the bridges are intact?"

"The one who is at the top left everything intact. He or she wants the sacrifices to arrive unharmed and unblemished."

"These people have volunteered to be sacrifices?"

"All except you."

"Why?"

"That is for you to find out."

Jon reached out and touched the Ranger's shoulder. "Let's stop someone behind us and ask where they're going in such a hurry," said Jon.

"Do you speak Spanish?"

"No, but La Curandera does. And she speaks Aymaran. It's her native language. She'll translate for us."

Jon turned around and waited for a woman to bump into him. Then he walked side by side with her while trying to strike up a convesation.

"Where are we going?" he asked in perfect Spanish. When the woman didn't reply, he tried Aymaran.

"To the top of the mountain," replied the woman who was around seventeen or eighteen, to judge from her voice. "We have been called."

"Who called you?"

"The Q'ero."

"Who are the Q'ero?"

"You know."

"No, I don't."

"Q'ero are the descendents of the Inca, the sons of the sun."

"How did they call you?"

"Through the Apus."

"The Apus?"

"The spirits of the mountains. You can see their faces in the rocks. They call to us, and we must come. We must do as they say."

"You hear the carved stone faces speak to you?"

"Yes."

"You hear them with your ears?"

"Yes."

"And what did they tell you when they spoke to you?"

"That the time is upon us. It is the time of the *mastay*, the gathering. It has been prophesied for 15,000 years. And now the time has come."

"The time for what?"

"The time for *despachos*, for sacrifice."

"Why? Why must there be sacrifice and what will this sacrifice accomplish?"

"The eagle from the north has joined the condor of the south at long last, and the *Mosoq Karpay* or Great Rite opens doors between worlds that we may step through and join the gods. We willingly and joyously sacrifice our bodies that our spirits may pass through the door to the heavens. We know this is true because the sun and the moon have already gone through those doors to light our way."

"Ask her to tell you more about the eagle from the north," said La Curandera.

"The eagle from the north is the white *apu*, a white man with a curly black beard, that the prophecies said would come at the final hour. It is he that guides us through the door."

"An Americano? A yanqui?"

"Si. He has much power."

"And gaining more with every sacrifice," said La Curandera within Jon's head. "Now we know it is an American doing this. And the American is male, at least in this lifetime. But how could an American have acquired such knowledge? Who is he? And why is he doing this?"

"He's opening portals between worlds?"

"Yes. His power increases with every willing sacrifice."

"Can't we stop the sacrifices?"

"Yes. Vajrapani can stop them, for Vajrapani is like Viracocha, the Incan god of action and the shaper of worlds. Though Vajrapani is without a beard, he is a white man. And he carries the Vajra and the Kris. They may think you are Viracocha's brother, the god of thunder."

"What can I do without harming anyone?" asked the Ranger who posessed the reincarnated spirit of Vajrapani.

"Use the power of the Vajra and the Kris to call down lightning from the heavens. For the brother of Viracocha was said to command the rains and the winds."

The Ranger turned to face the people coming up the trail behind them. He raised the Kris in his left hand and the Vajra in his right, and he called down fire from the heavens. Instantly, clouds formed above the valley of the Urubamba, lightning flashed and thunder boomed, raindrops began falling.

All those on the trail behind them and many of those immediately ahead of them saw, in the flashes of light from the lightning, a tall, powerfully-built white man holding his hands to the sky and calling down the wrath of heaven. The man they saw resembled icons of Viracocha, for he held in his left hand what appeared to be a short sword and in his right hand a scepter. Some actually swore he looked exactly like Viracocha, for they saw a beard on his face and, in truth, he did have a slight beard since he hadn't shaved in more than twelve hours and his facial hair was dark. Overhead, they saw the sacred condor, another sign of Viracocha.

"Go back!" he commanded in a voice as loud as thunder, and his words were spoken not in Aymaran but Quechua, the sacred language of the Q'ero. "The time is not yet come. Go back!"

And they went back, returning to their homes enthralled. The god of the Incas had actually spoken to them personally. And even many of those who were in front of the two Americans turned around and went back down the mountain, averting their eyes as they passed the man who held the sword and the scepter. For it was said that those who dared to look directly at the face of a god often went blind. Those who did look did indeed see the face of a god. And one or two actually did go blind when they looked at the lightning.

But there were still thousands of people lined up on the trail, enraptured people who paid no attention to the lightning nor the voice of yet another god. So the Ranger lowered his arms and the lighning stopped, the clouds cleared.

And the two men continued the climb to the top of the mountain, falling in behind the long line of people who were deliberately hurrying to their deaths.

CHAPTER THREE

N o one was ever born a god. One *became* a god.

It was a long process, one that took millenia and many multiples of births and re-births. Perhaps that was true even of the one true God, blessed be his name, but no one was around now who knew and could say for certain.

Shachar Hadad Elman, and his twin brother Shalim Yam Elman, had known many gods during their multiple lives. Shachar preferred to be called Hadad, for that was the name of the god he recalled from his earliest remembered past life.

Hadad's first remembered incarnation was in Ebla—a once great semitic city built entirely on a massive table of white sandstone rock in the middle of a desert in what eventually became modern-day Syria—some seven thousand years ago. It was there, in the fifth millenium before the common era, that he learned the many semitic dialects he still spoke. It was also in Ebla that he learned to read and write in the cuneiform script of the Sumerians. His native languages were Akkadian and Aramaic, but he spoke many languages like a native.

In a later life Hadad would become Sargon of Akkad, known as Sargon the Great or Sargon the sorcerer. His brother would become Sargon II of Assyria.

The major gods of Ebla included El, sometimes called An or Anu, sometimes called Ea or Enlil, the supreme god and creator; Ishtar, goddess of the moon and night and beloved consort of El; Shapsh or Shayla, goddess of the sun and day; Dagon, god of grain and all growing things; Mot, god of death; and various other male and female deities, some major and some minor. It didn't take long for Hadad to notice that powerful men often assumed the names of their god, wearing those names like mantles for protection. Thus did Shachar become Hadad.

Hadad or Addad or Haddu, was the god of the west wind and god of rain and storms. His twin brother Yam, or Lotan, was the god of the untamed sea and of wildly rushing rivers. Yam was wild and uncontrollable, irresponsible, unpredictable. Yam was also known as Apep in ancient Egypt, Vritra in India, Jörmungandr in scandinavia, and Yam was the prodigal son of El. Sometimes he was called Ya or Yaw instead of Yam. He was the sea serpent, the leviathan. Yam was a fire-breathing dragon, the Loch Ness monster, and he was the serpent of the garden of Eden.

Hadad and Yam both wanted to become gods. Hadad wanted to become omniscient, and Yam wanted to become omnipotent.

The twins fought incessantly, and in each of their many incarnations they had vied for power. Hadad had grown in knowledge and acquired wisdom when he embraced both his masculine and feminine attributes equally. He remembered well the times he had lived as a woman, for it was as a woman that he learned the true meaning of magic. Magic was a "Ma" word, and all Ma words were power words. Other "Ma" words included magnetism, make, mathematics, magister, master, material, mandala, and even man. Man was a "Ma" word because every man was born of a woman.

The keepers of magic were women. Without women, there could be no magic.

All true mages had to embrace their feminine sides to tap into power, for magic only happened when interacting male and female polarities merged. Magic—real magic—required the two hemispheres of the human brain to synchronize, for neurons to fire across the corpus callosum. Men who didn't do that remained mere illusionists, spellcasters. It took great feeling—raw emotion—along with clear vision and words of intention to make magic real.

Magic was born of marriage—the hierogamos—that brought male and female polarities together. Marriage was a "Ma" word. Marriage yoked the male and female polarities into something very powerful.

Women were able to free their emotions, to loose them on the world, and emotions were absolutely essential to making magic. When women reached menarche and female hormones flooded their bodies and brains, their emotions became a powerful force, driving them to create and procreate. When male and female met after menarche, magic naturally happened.

After more than fifty centuries of learning, Shachar Hadad Elman became a master of magic, a hidden Imam, a true adept. He was like unto a god.

If power corrupts and absolute power corrupts absolutely, Hadad would have become corrupted long ago if not for his feminine side. Hadad was first and foremost a scholar who loved learning for learning's sake, and there was always so much more to learn that he seldom had time to think of himself. Instead, he thought of the effects his actions had on others, and he had never deliberately hurt another sentient being in order to acquire power or even knowledge. He was always willing to work with others for the common good, and Hadad knew it was that trait and that trait alone that enabled him, and not his brother, to become an Ascended Master and one of the eight Guardians of the Watchtowers.

Yam had never been female. He had to steal feminine energy to make magic.

Many men may be called magicians or sorcerers or alchemists, and some men are even good enough at their craft to be called adept. Many men learn the secrets of magic, and some even become practitioners of the Great Art equal to or greater than their female counterparts. But few are those who possess compassion. Compassion allows ascenscion to the very top of the World Tree where the physical and spiritual realms meet and marry.

Hadad had great compassion. He remained at the summit of the World Tree after the others had left because he worried about his brother. He was his brother's keeper. Of all the men Hadad knew who had the power to hide the sun, only Yam would dare to do such a thing. Yam cared little about others.

There remained a connection between Hadad and his brother that brought them together in many of the lives they lived. Hadad had lost track of his brother when Yam went to America, and the few times he had searched for his brother's spirit, Yam had hidden from him. After each failed attempt to re-connect with his brother, Hadad had felt more separated, more alone.

Now Hadad allowed his spirit to search the entire United States of America, from sea to shining sea. Yam wouldn't be far from water, and he was most likely to abide near an ocean or a raging river. When Hadad could not locate his brother along either the Pacific or Atlantic coasts—nor near the Mississippi, the Colorado, the Missouri, or the Ohio—Hadad searched the shores of South America. He found traces of his brother's energy signature near the Amazon River. But Yam wasn't hiding in the rain forest nor along the banks of the Amazon. Where on earth was he?

Now Hadad was seriously concerned. If Yam were indeed at Machu Picchu and Yam was involved with the disappearance of the sun, Hadad would have to stop him, perhaps even kill him.

Hadad recognized two men among a throng of women ascending the mountain. Overhead, he sensed the spirit of La Curandera in the form of a condor.

Hadad allowed his spirit to speak directly to the mind of Jon Fish, the incarnation of the spirit of Akashagarbha. "Jon, it's Hadad. I think my brother Yam is doing this. He has the knowledge and will."

"Do you know why?"

"He has always sought power for power's sake. He wants to be more powerful than me. Maybe it's sibling rivalry. I don't know him that well anymore. I'm not sure I ever did."

"Thanks, Hadad."

"I will remain with you in spirit for as long as I can. But there's a vortex at the top of the mountain I can't penetrate."

"We know. That's why we're climbing this hill on foot. If we could flash in and flash out, we would."

"Luck be with you."

Luck, Hadad knew, was a beautiful woman, and like so many of the gods and goddesses of myth and legend, Lady Fortuna was fickle and constantly switched sides. Those who played the god game and fought deadly battles gambling on their god or Lady Fortuna to take their side were often disappointed when luck sided with their opponent. Such men carried their bitter disappointments to their graves, and sometimes even beyond.

*   *   *

Kisikil Lilake—sometimes called Kisi, sometimes Lily, sometimes Lakshmi, sometimes Shakti, sometimes Huaco, sometimes Lachesis—was a Neanderthal. She lived in a tree outside the Zagros caves beside the banks of the Great Zab River a few miles north of where the Zab flowed into the Tigris. Kisi possessed the powers of the earth itself. Over the millennia, Kisi became as fully human as anyone else, but her Neanderthal blood gave her special powers that no one else had. She was always in contact with the earth, grounded, as if her tree had roots that went deep into the heart of the Great Mother herself. Kisi was as much at home in a tree or a rock as she was in a tent or house.

Kisi's gods and goddesses were all natural, and she never visualized them with faces or human-like personalities. The sun, moon, earth, and stars were part of her pantheon, as were rocks, and rivers, and trees, and blades of grass. Her mother was the earth, and her father the sun. Her brothers and sisters were the stars.

Kisi was much older than Hadad, but in this incarnation she looked much younger. People thought she was no more than seventeen or eighteen, and often that presented a problem. No one took anyone that young very seriously.

So Kisi manifested another persona that she showed from time to time. Sometimes she appeared as Baba Yaga, the wise old babushka; sometimes she was Kali or Durga. She was maiden, mother, and crone wrapped into one, for she had been all of those things many times in the past.

Though all magic comes from the mother, Kisi's magic was different than Hadad's. Kisi had learned from wise women in Anatolia, the Valley of the Nile, the Valley of the Indus, and in the mountainous regions of southern France and northern Italy. She was a strega, and she talked to the lares. Lares were everywhere, and there was a lar in every rock, every blade of grass. And every lar had its genius, its purpose, its raison d'etre.

These things she understood intuitively, for her intuition was great. She could sense things that others couldn't. Like all stregas, Kisi possessed a well-developed ajna, or third eye, and like the reptiles and amphibians she was descended from, Kisi could sense objects in the dark.

Kisi had met both Hadad and his brother Yam in several past lives, and she, too, suspected Yam might be behind the disappearance of the sun. She remembered meeting Yam in the city of Ashur, near the confluence of the Little Zab and Tigris rivers, north of Babylon and Ur, more than four millennia ago. She was a priestess of Ishtar, and Yam was a sorcerer in the service of the Akkadian king. The temple of Ishtar adjoined the palace, and Kisi and Yam were literally neighbors. She had sensed a power in him even then that made her afraid. No man could have acquired such magical power without stealing it from a woman.

And he had. From two women. From Tiamat and from Anath, both of whom Yam had seduced. From Tiamat, a priestess of Ishtar and keeper of the Tablets of Destiny, he stole the Tablets of Destiny and the knowledge of chaos magic, and from Anath, the warrior wife of his brother Hadad, he stole a magic bow that fired the arrows of the wind. It was suspected that Yam hit Tiamat over the head with a club while she slept, cut Tiamat first in half and then into small pieces, and dumped Tiamat's remains into the Tigris. Because Yam had the blessings of the Akkadian king, and may even have acted at the direction of the king, no one wanted to know the truth of what happened to Tiamat. She had simply disappeared from the face of the earth, and the only one who seemed to care was Kisi.

Without her magic bow, Anath was unable to protect her scholarly husband, and Yam slew his brother with a sword while Hadad translated a cuneiform tablet— comparable today to burying one's nose in a book—in the library of the king. After covering her husband's mutilated body with earth so that Hadad might someday be reborn, Anath set out for vengeance. Blinded by hatred, she mistakenly killed a man named Mot, named for the god of death, slaying him in a fit of rage that so disfigured the man's body that he was completely unrecognizable. Anath compounded the mistake by boasting that she slew Yam, which she honestly thought she had, and the king ordered Yam's sister-in-law put to death in a public execution. She was drawn and quartered while Yam and Kisi and the entire city watched the spectacle. Yam gloated with glee as Anath was torn asunder.

Yam was not a nice man.

In another life, Kisi fought for the Free French Resistance during World War II. Yam had been an SS officer named Hermann Steinschneider, and he carried an ornate wooden staff embedded with Vril energy and engraved with occult symbols and mystic runes. Prior to the war, Steinschneider had been a stage hypnotist, magician, and mentalist in Berlin. It was rumored that he was the one, not Paul Josef Goebbels, who had taught Hitler hypnotism and mind control. Yam worked directly for Heinrich Himmler, who was said to be the reincarnation of an Akkadian king. Yam was one of Himmler's Schutzstaffel and he wore double-s sig runes that looked like ragged bolts of lightning on his uniform's lapels. Yam was under strict orders from Hitler himself to root out occult activity in France. No one could use the occult—astrology, clairvoyance, mind reading, or runic power—except the Nazis, and Yam was ordered to uncover and steal all occult knowledge in Europe, then kill those who possessed such knowledge and power so no one else could use it against the Third Reich.

Yam began a book-burning rampage throughout France, creating chaos everywhere he went. He murdered thousands of innocent men, women, and children indiscriminately. He sought out gypsies and Kabbalists, alchemists and astrologers, rune masters and monks. He violated the sanctity of churches and synagogues, burned holy books and rabbinical texts, and killed rabbis, priests, and nuns without mercy.

Too late to save the clerics, Kisi invoked the Shekhinah, the feminine energy of creation itself, and hid herself and the few remaining resistance fighters camped in the woods under a cloud of Shekhinic protection. The Shekhinah—the feminine aspect of the divine presence—spread a blanket of protection over all those dwelling in a certain place so evil couldn't see them, couldn't find them, couldn't touch them. Yam could smell her magic, and he sniffed about for days trying to find the source. Finally, he gave her an ultimatum: "Reveal yourself or I will line up every man, woman, and child I can find and have them tortured and then shot."

Kisi knew what Yam was capable of, and she couldn't allow innocents to die because of her. When she stepped out from under the protection of the Shekhinah, Yam hit her with a spell that would have decimated any mere mortal. Though Kisi's body perished instantly, she had sensed what Yam was about to do before he did it and she had already transferred her spirit into the body of a falcon. She dove straight down at Yam's face with both talons extended like claws, and she tore off chunks of raw flesh and gouged out one eye before Yam could protect himself with a spell. Kisi called upon the lares, and the very earth herself opened up beneath Yam's feet. Unable to keep his balance, he fell to the ground and released the magical Vril-infused staff from his left hand.

Kisi swooped down once again, and she picked up the wooden staff in her beak and flew off with it. As the bird containing her spirit ascended to the heavens, Kisi could hear Yam's curses until they faded in the distance.

And now they were both back in mortal form. Kisi had been reborn in her homeland in 1947, after a brief time in the spiritual realm where her memories were stored away in a part of her spirit that took years to access again. But nothing is ever really forgotten, and those memories came back to her first in the form of dreams, and then as vividly recalled events from the past. All of the knowledge and wisdom she had acquired over the centuries were hers again.

But Yam had not progressed to the spirit realm where the lessons he had learned from his past lives could be examined and reflected upon. Perhaps he continued to live in the physical world. Perhaps his memories were still intact and he hadn't changed any since the last time they had met.

If that were true, then Yam was more dangerous now than ever. One of the blessings of entering into the spirit realm was reflection on the life just past and learning how your actions had impacted others. Then, when you were reborn, you could start anew. You could work to cleanse the karmic debt incurred by your actions in your past life. It was in the spirit realm that one learned the true meaning of compassion, for if your actions had caused any to suffer, you would experience every bit of that suffering yourself before rebirth. Then, in future incarnations, you would take care not to cause that kind of suffering again.

In all of history, there had only been a few adepts who were able to keep their bodies alive almost indefinitely, and they were able to amass knowledge and wealth beyond anyone's dreams. Eventually, they also died, for no one lives forever. And when they did eventually die and entered the spiritual realm, their suffering was as great as all of the suffering they had caused over the length of their extended lives. It was not something that anyone would wish for.

But if Yam Elman had prolonged his life, he had accumulated the knowledge and power of an additional three-quarters of a century. And that potentially made him the most dangerous man alive.

Now Kisi dropped to the ground and sat in lotus, her buttocks and thighs in touch with Mother Earth. She allowed her eyes to close, and opened her third eye.

Yes, she could sense him now. Yam was still alive. He didn't die in France.

She released her spirit, and her spirit soared to the World Tree and called to Hadad. "Do you know where your brother might be?" she asked.

Hadad's spirit came to her and answered, "I think he is at Machu Picchu."

"He is the one who has hidden the sun?"

"I suspect. I have relayed my suspicions to Jon and his companion, and warned them to be wary."

"How soon will they reach the top of the mountain?"

"Less than four hours now."

"What can we do to help?"

"Nothing. I stayed with them as long as I could, but the vortex prevented my spirit from remaining with them the rest of the way to the top of the mountain."

"Then we must wait?"

"Yes. Now we must wait."

"But will the spirit of Akashagarbha be able to penetrate the vortex? Can Akashagarbha stay with Jon all the way to the top? Will Jon be able to access the power of Akashagarbha when he needs it?"

"Vajrapani is with him. He has the Vajra and the Kris."

"I'm afraid, Hadad. My intuition tells me it won't be enough."

"Then let us pray, Kisi. Let us pray to all of the gods we know. Because, at this stage of the game, if prayer doesn't work then we are completely out of luck. There is nothing else we can do."

*   *   *

They were in the clouds, literally walking through clouds, and the rarefied air took their breath away and drained their strength. Every step now was pure torture. They had been going up and up for hours on end, pausing only long enough to relieve themselves over the edge of the mountain. Up higher and higher. Their calves and shins screamed for rest, and they could barely lift their feet to continue the climb. So they shuffled along as best they could.

"I wish we had brought a canteen," said Jon. "Or bottles of water."

"We're almost there," said the Ranger. "What's the matter, Marine? I thought you did twenty mile hikes in your sleep."

"Not uphill."

"Up the hill, down the hill, over the hill, under the hill. It's all the same to us Airborne Rangers."

"I thought you gave all that up when you became a monk."

"Once a Ranger, always a Ranger."

"Yeah. Semper Fi."

"C'mon, DI. Pick 'em up. Put 'em down. If I can do it, you can do it."

Suddenly, the people ahead of them stopped, and they nearly collided with two women.

"Can you see anything?" asked the Ranger.

"Not a thing. We lost contact with La Curandera a few miles back. Hadad, too. We're on our own."

"Shhhhhh. Someone is coming down the mountain."

They could hear footsteps coming closer now, and then someone was standing right next to them, one person on each side, offering them drinks from golden chalices. The drink was ice-cold water, flavored with something extra. Jon put his finger in the chalice and discovered leaves soaking in the bottom of the cup.

"Coca leaves," said the Ranger. "Don't drink it, it's a drug."

Both men pretended to drink, then handed the chalices back to the bearers.

Since Jon and the Ranger were the last people in line, the bearers turned around and went back up to wherever they had come from, and the line began moving forward again.

Now the trail opened up, and they could see the ruins of Machu Picchu spread out before them. All along the trail through the ruins were native women holding lit torches to light the way, and the procession progressed upward past wide agricultural terraces, past dozens of stone buildings without roofs, all the way to the end of a central plaza where they waited in a long line again before climbing up to the sacred plaza—the holiest of holies—where more people were lined up eagerly waiting to be sacrificed.

Near the perfectly-aligned stone walls of what looked to once have been a storeroom for grain, behind which could be seen the very peak of the mountain and additional rows of terraces, was a solid basalt slab shaped like a modern bed. Before

Jon or the Ranger could intervene, a fat old man wearing a golden ceremonial mask plunged a sharp knife the size of a short sword into the heart of a naked woman reclining on the stone and plucked out her still-beating heart.

Four other men standing near the stone bed removed the body, carrying it to the other side of the sacred plaza where other bodies were stacked like cordwood inside a three-sided enclosure.

The next woman in line had already removed her clothes and was walking toward the basalt bed.

"Stop!" commanded the Ranger as he raised the Vajra and Kris high into the air. But nothing happened. Vajrapani did not come, did not manifest in the physical world, did not fill the Ranger with awesome power. No storm clouds formed high overhead. No thunder boomed. No lightning raced out of the night sky to pummel the evil-doers.

"Oh, shit!" said the Ranger as all eyes turned to him and hundreds of voices raised the alarm of interlopers in their midst. "The vortex is sealed. Vajrapani can't get past the seal."

Jon called upon the spirit of Akashagarbha, the Boundless Space Matrix, but no cosmic energy flowed into his mortal body to fill him with the unlimited power of boundless time and space. He felt alone and naked and vulnerable.

"Seize them!" commanded the man with the golden mask. He spoke in American English with what sounded like a mid-western accent. Some of his henchmen who understood the

American tongue translated "Seize them!" into Spanish and Aymaran and Quechua.

It took a minute for the crowd to react. So stunned were most of the people that anyone would challenge their god that they remained frozen to the spot. The concoction of Inca tea— coca leaves steeped in water—designed to alleviate their altitude sickness and to drug them into submission, made them sluggish and slow to respond. But when they did respond, they were angry.

"Let's get the hell out of here!" shouted the Ranger as the angry crowd closed in on the two interlopers.

Fortunately, both Jon and the Ranger were no strangers to hand-to-hand combat. They whirled and kicked, threw and tossed, pivoted and punched, but the sheer numbers of angry Peruvians threatened to overwhelm them. Still, they fought on until all but a handful of men were immobilized with concussions or broken bones. But there were hundreds of angry women to contend with, and neither American wanted to strike a woman.

Finally, when they were surrounded and had no hope of escape, the Ranger placed his lasso on the ground and stepped into the protective circle made by the rope and asked Jon to join him. Though none of Vajrapani's other magic had worked, the lasso kept their attackers at bay. Casting a circle on sacred ground had power of its own.

For no one could step inside a magic circle unless they were invited. And the circle generated a cone of power that would repel knives and bullets the way wax repelled water.

"What we have here is a Mexican stand-off," said the man with the golden mask, seeming to understand the magic involved. "You can't go anywhere or do anything. And my people can't get to you or destroy you. It's a stand-off."

"We know who you are, Yam," shouted the Ranger. "Your days are numbered."

"There are no more days," said the man in the golden mask. "Nor nights. All is darkness."

"Be gone," said Jon. But without the power of Akashagarbha, his words were only wishful thinking. Instead of being banished to the farthest regions of boundless space, the man in the mask still stood in the same place holding the same sword.

"They have no power to interfere," said the man in the golden mask. "Let the sacrifices continue."

And the people lined up again. They began removing their clothing.

And the man in the golden mask ripped out their hearts and cut off their heads, and Jon and the Ranger were trapped within a sacred magic circle of their own making and helpless to interfere.

CHAPTER FOUR

B ryn Helgasdottir—sometimes called Nott or Sigrdrifa or Brynhildr or Raua—who had a home built on basalt rock near Hlymdale, not far from Biegolmai's own home in northern Scandinavia, was thought to be the reincarnation of a Viking Valkyrie, a warrior woman, and a witch. In 1783, Bryn Helgasdottir lived close to the southern coast of Iceland, near a small farming village called Kirkjubæjarklaustur. She had lived there in a former lifetime as well, way back in 1186 when she was an Irish Benedictine nun at the Kirkjubaejar Abbey. She kept being drawn back to this spot by the power ley lines created where the eternal fires of the Lakagígar and Grimsvotn volcanoes married the eternal ice of the Vatnajökull glaciers.

In 1783, the Laki volcano erupted, sending plumes of acrid smoke and miles of molten lava over much of the land, killing a quarter of the population of Iceland. As the poisonous mist, filled with ash and fluorine and sulfur dioxide gases, belched from fissures and craters for nearly a year to spread clouds of death over half the planet, millions of people died from asphyxiation and famine. People as far away as India and the Mississippi valley of the fledgling United States of America were adversely affected by the polluted air. Crops died on the vine, and livestock choked to death, and those that didn't die were sickly and malnourished and had few offspring that survived.

Bryn had been powerless to help. She had not yet achieved mastery of her craft, and her fighting skills proved useless against the fierce forces of nature. She had died then, too, her lungs filled with choking gasses and particles of ash.

It wasn't until a later rebirth that she discovered the volcanic eruptions in Iceland had been deliberately caused by a bearded man, an evil sorcerer from the south, who thrived on chaos. He was said to have piercing brown eyes that appeared coal black under bushy black eyebrows.

Bryn Helgasdottir met the man with bushy eyebrows and piercing black eyes face to face in northern Wisconsin in 1836. Wisconsin had just become a legal territory of the expanding United States of America when mighty Michigan, preparing to enter the union as a separate state, bequeathed the remaining Northwest Territory to Wisconsin. Bryn was born of mixed blood, the great granddaughter of a Scandinavian adventurer-explorer named Siggurdson and a native American wise woman named Willow, and Bryn's fiery-red hair attested to her mixed heritage. A former member of the Fox tribe, cousin to the Sac and Kickapoo, Bryn and her mother had settled along the banks of the Fox and Wisconsin rivers. After White Cloud and Black Hawk surrendered in 1832, the territory was overrun by thousands of diggers of valuable lead ore. They ruthlessly killed red-skins right and left, including Bryn's mother. Bryn fled north to the lands of the Ojibwe and the Menominee and the Chippewa where there were still old-growth forests with plenty of deer and cranberry bogs in the marshlands. Native men and women fished the flowage and the rivers at night and lived in peace with the hearty Swedes and Norwegians who settled the grasslands, tilled the soil, and survived the harsh winters.

Bryn befriended Emma Wells, a young white woman who lived in a log cabin in the heart of the north woods with her single mother and three sisters. Though they had no man to defend their household or provide for their livelihood, they managed to thrive. Emma's mother had changed her name from Brunnar to Wells when she came to America from Sweden, and she acquired land from the Chippewa in a fair trade, nearly two-thousand acres of old-growth forest in exchange for produce from her garden, two healthy plow horses, and a string of beautiful pearls she had inherited from her grandmother. Miss Wells had traveled down to the new capital at Belmont and recorded the deed, and the land was legally hers to have and to hold.

Yam Elman appeared on horseback one day, riding in from the southwest. He was a big man, not tall but broad of shoulders and wide of girth like a glutton. Bryn pitied the poor horse that had to carry such weight. Elman was wearing buck-skin breeches, high leather boots, a dyed cotton shirt, and a black topcoat covered with dirt and dust. He had a full black beard, and curly black hair down past his shoulders. He looked to be about forty, and he had extremely bushy eyebrows over two sunken hollows hidden in shadow. His eyes didn't look at you but through you, pierced your heart like a knife, for under those bushy eyebrows were two orbs the color of night.

The trouble began shortly after Elman arrived. Elman offered to buy the Wells property from Emma's mother, but the woman refused to sell. Elman raised the price, but the woman still refused. He tried one more time, but she said she wouldn't sell at any price.

Bryn was in the woods hunting deer with Emma one morning when the bad white men came to kill Emma's mother and her four daughters. Bryn and Emma were armed only with bows and arrows and hunting knives, and the ten men carried firearms. Some had flintlock pistols and some had cap and ball rifles, but all ten were heavily armed and they were heading in the direction of Emma's house. They waded downstream in the shallow creek that ran the length of the property, then began sneaking through the trees as if they, too, were hunting deer.

They were all dressed as Indians, but they weren't Indians. Most of them had beards. And no Indian that Bryn knew ever grew a beard or carried a gun.

Bryn and Emma followed the men, trailing them as they would trail a buck through the underbrush, silently, stealthily, downwind. When the ten men reached the log cabin and opened fire on the building where Emma's mother and Emma's sisters lived, Bryn and Emma silently shot each of those men in the back with flint-tipped arrows. Then they carried the bodies off the property in five trips and left the bodies to rot in a ravine on the far side of the creek.

When Elman learned his men had been killed, he was furious. His next attack involved magic, and even two centuries ago Yam was a powerful magician, well-versed in spellcraft. But he didn't expect two teenaged girls to be almost equally adept. Bryn knew counterspells for every spell Yam threw at them.

But Yam didn't give up. He wanted that land for reasons of his own, and he would stop at nothing to get it.

When he tried to step on the property to burn the old-growth trees, he discovered a blanket of protection over the land that prevented him from personally entering the woods. He tried snakes next, calling in poisonous reptiles from as far west as South Dakota. Rattlesnakes, mostly timber rattlers but a few big diamondbacks and some sidewinders, cottonmouths, even a copperhead or two, and they answered his call and came as quickly as they could crawl.

But they couldn't penetrate the blanket of protection. Not a single snake entered those woods.

Now Yam was so furious that he revealed himself and his true nature. He attacked Emma's family with all the power at his disposal, invoking the forces of nature. He made it rain for forty days and forty nights, and the earth itself became a swamp.

He called the four winds, and the winds howled and shrieked and tore through the trees with hurricane force. He caused the earth to quake, and he opened new fault lines in Missouri and Canada that caused major damage to towns all around.

Bryn and Emma had climbed two 80 foot-tall white pines and watched Elman's antics from the safety of the forest. They were well-protected because the earth here formed a natural vortex, part of powerful magnetic ley lines that circumvented the globe, and Emma's family knew how to utilize that vortex to cast a magic circle around the entire property. In retrospect, Bryn realized that was one of the reasons she had been drawn to this time and place: she had unconsciously followed the ley lines here to the vortex.

When Yam continued his abominable assault on the earth herself, Bryn raised her bow and shot an arrow at one of Yam's eyes. But Elman had disappeared before the arrowhead reached its mark. Instead of ripping out Elman's brains and shattering the back of his skll, the arrow continued until it lodged in the trunk of a tree.

Bryn thought that was the last she'd ever see of Yam Elman, but she was wrong.

CHAPTER FIVE ·

J on's anger grew with every sacrifice. He was bristling mad and growing madder with every passing moment.

After the heart was cut out of each victim's body, the man with the mask would take a small bite. Then he would whack off the victim's head with the short sword he held in his hand, extract the brains, and sample those. Besides increasing his power by absorbing the life force of each victim, Yam seemed to be searching for something.

As Jon's anger increased, so did his personal power increase exponentially, for magic is linked to emotion. Although Jon still couldn't manifest Akashagarbha within a sealed vortex, all of his senses were heightened. Now Jon could see clearly even into the darkest shadows, and he noticed several of the men standing around the edge of the area carried conventional weapons. One had an AR-15 semi-automatic rifle, and one carried a shotgun. Two others had pistols holstered at their hips.

As a trained Marine, Jon knew how to take guns away from people, and he was familiar with how all of the weapons the men wore operated. The AR-15 had a magazine with twenty 5.56 millimeter rounds, and he assumed the magazine was still full. The shotgun was a pump-action with four rounds plus one in the chamber. Each of the handguns held eight to nine rounds. If he and the Ranger could get to those guns, they had a chance of stopping the last of the sacrifices.

Keeping his voice low, he related his plan to the Ranger.

"I took a vow not to kill anyone," the Ranger whispered. "I won't harm another sentient being."

"If you don't help stop the sacrifices," argued Jon, "it's the same as killing those people lined up to be sacrificed. If we can get to those guns, we can prevent the deaths of dozens of innocent people."

"Okay," agreed the Ranger after a moment of hesitation. "I'll grab a gun. But I won't shoot to kill."

"When everyone's attention is riveted on the next naked woman, we'll make our move. I'll take the shotgun and the guy on the right with a Beretta. You get the AR-15 and the guy on the left with the Smith and Wesson."

As the attendants removed the latest mutilated body from the basalt table and the next naked woman stepped forward to meet her fate, Jon jumped out of the magic circle and raced across the square to disarm the henchman with the shotgun, ripping the shotgun from the man's hands before he could fire, smashing the steel barrel of the shotgun hard against the man's unprotected skull, instantly whirling to take out the henchman next to him who was reaching for his Beretta, executing maneuvers he had used many times before in combat and taught fresh recruits each new cycle in Marine bootcamp. The Ranger hit the guy holding the AR-15 on both sides of the neck with fast karate chops designed to rupture the carotid arteries, rendering the man instantly unconscious but not killing him. As the man fell, the Ranger retrieved the rifle and swung the butt of the AR-15 up into the jaw of the man with the Smith and Wesson, shattering the man's jawbone.

"Stop!" the Ranger commanded once again when he had the Smith and Wesson firmly in his hand, and all eyes were once again upon him as he turned to face the man with the mask. This time, instead of holding the Vajra and the Kris, which he had tucked into his belt before leaving the circle, he held an assault rifle and a pistol aimed at the man in the golden mask.

The man in the mask stopped. Obviously, he had no spell of protection in place that would deflect bullets.

Jon ran up to the man with the mask and ripped the golden disk from his face. The upper half of the entire left side of that face appeared hideously disfigured as if something long ago had ripped huge chunks of flesh from the left cheek and gouged out the left eye. The face had healed but the skin was horribly wrinkled and scarred, and the empty eye socket made the man look like a nightmarish monster. The other eye, beneath a single bushy white eyebrow, was dark and piercing and filled with hate. If looks could kill, Jon would already be dead.

The monstrous sight took everyone by surprise. Several of the women screamed, and most of the men turned their eyes away.

Face to face with pure evil, Jon hesitated the barest fraction of a second, but that was enough time for Yam to disappear like a puff of smoke floating away on the wind. The mutilated visage simply faded out of existence in the blink of an eye. One moment the man was there, the next moment he was gone. Simply gone. When the monster left, he took with him the golden mask and all of the accumulated power he had acquired from the sacrifices at Machu Picchu.

As if awakening from a dream, Yam's remaining henchmen suddenly came alive. Guns materialized in their hands and they opened fire at Jon and the Ranger. Jon took one round in his left shoulder and one in the right hip. As he fell to the ground, he raised the shotgun and returned fire.

The Ranger reacted without thinking. Years of training took over and he reflexively raised the AR-15 one-handed and shot the first gunman in the groin, another man in the stomach, and a third in the forehead. He killed two more before he realized what he had done.

Now Jon had the Beretta in his hand and took careful aim from a prone position. He killed the remaining eight men with expertly placed shots before passing out from loss of blood. The Beretta fell from his hand and he lay still as death.

The Ranger threw his own guns away and knelt next to Jon. Jon phased in and out of consciousness as the Ranger tied a tourniquet of black cloth, ripped from the Ranger's borrowed shirt, around Jon's arm and shoulder. Both bullets had gone straight through without hitting bone, leaving painful holes in Jon's shoulder and hip. The Ranger tore the rest of his shirt apart, folded the cloth into two squares, and pressed one against the entry wound and one to the exit wound on the hip to prevent Jon from bleeding out.

The women who were still alive were all heavily drugged. After Yam disappeared, they stood there like statues carved from the surrounding stones, their eyes glazed over, their expressions placid and emotionless, unaware their eagerly awaited appointments with death had been cancelled.

"You need a doctor," said the Ranger. "Can you walk?"

"No," said Jon, grimacing and biting his lower lip to control pain. "I'm busted up pretty bad. I'd never make it down the mountain. But something changed when the evil guy pulled out. He doesn't control the vortex anymore. Can you sense the difference? See if you can contact La Curandera. Maybe she can get through the vortex."

"I am already here," whispered La Curandera's voice in their minds as a giant condor swept down from the skies with outstretched wings. "This was my vortex once before, and I claim it again now. Yam broke the seal to escape. Give me a moment, and I will be with you in body as well as spirit."

As the condor landed on the basalt table, one of the women standing in line to be sacrificed suddenly snapped out of her drug-induced daze. She was a very beautiful Peruvian woman, somewhere between sixteen and nineteen, barefoot and small of frame, with large brown eyes and very long and very shiny black hair, wearing a plain alpaca shift dyed magenta. She stepped out of her place in line and approached the two men as the condor returned to the sky.

"Now I have a new body," said the girl in English. "This little one was more than willing to sacrifice herself to help her people, and she has allowed me to share her body for as long as I need it. I promised to take good care of her while we are together, and I shall."

"Can you help Jon?" asked the Ranger.

La Curandera placed one hand over Jon's left shoulder and the other hand over the hole in Jon's hip. Sparks flew from her fingers, and the frayed edges of Jon's t-shirt, where bullets had passed mere moments ago, actually caught fire as heat from the flames cauterized the open wounds. Jon lost consciousness again.

"What did you do?" asked the Ranger.

"All of the universe is composed of energy," said La Curandera. "I simply transferred a quantum of life-force energy from one place to another. Jon's body is now filled with healing energy, and healing has already begun from the inside out. Jon will be well tomorrow."

"How did you do that?"

"I am La Curandera. I am a healer. It is what I do. Someday I will teach you, and you can be a healer, too. Someday, but not now. Now is not the time."

"Thank you," said the Ranger.

"Now we must take care of the dead. Will you help me?"

Together, they piled the remaining bodies in the rock enclosure, including the bodies of Yam's henchmen. La Curandera raised her arms, said a few words in a language the Ranger didn't understand, and the bodies burst into flame.

The smell was terrible. Black smoke rose from the piles of burning flesh and the Ranger thought he saw disembodied spirits rise up along with the flames and smoke.

"Those that Yam ate will remain trapped in the physical realm until Yam's death," explained La Curandera. "But the others have been freed to continue their journey."

"I killed five men today. I didn't choose to kill them. It just happened."

"You chose to save the life of your friend. And to save your own life. You were forced to make a choice, and I believe it was the correct one."

"I also made a sacred vow not to take the life of another sentient being. I have broken that vow."

"But you are alive now, and so is your friend. That would not be true if you had kept your vow."

"I took five lives to save two. Where is the balance in that?"

"You also saved the lives of all those women and children waiting to be sacrificed, and you saved the body I wear now. They would all be dead if you had kept your vow. In a sense, you kept your vow by breaking it."

La Curandera left the Ranger to ponder her words while she walked to the drugged women and revived each of them with a single tap to the center of the forehead. She spoke to the women in their own language, and some of the women cried while others simply turned away and began the long walk down the mountain in silence.

When La Curandera came back, she said, "The girl's name is Kiyari. It means moonlight in Quechua. She lived near Cusco with her parents and two sisters. Both of her sisters were sacrificed here tonight. She is filled with sorrow that she was not sacrificed with them."

"I'm sorry we couldn't stop the sacrifices sooner," said the Ranger. "Those people shouldn't have perished."

"Most will be reborn. Their journeys will continue. Death is not the end but a new beginning."

"But they suffered."

"They were drugged. They felt nothing when the knife entered their bodies."

"Where did Yam go?"

"To America," said Hadad, appearing in front of them in physical form. "He went to the United States. I have been tracking him."

"Where in the United States?" asked the Ranger.

"To Wisconsin. He found another ley line in northern Wisconsin. He is there now."

"Then let's go get him," said the Ranger.

"When the time is right," said la Curandera. "Meanwhile, we have much to do here."

"What can we do here?" asked the Ranger.

"Seal the vortex with wards so Yam cannot return," said La Curandera. "He will return if we let him. I do not intend to let Yam get anywhere close."

"He was looking for something in each of the sacrificial victims," the Ranger said. "He tasted their essences and rejected them. Whatever he was looking for, he didn't find it."

"Then it is assured he will be back," said La Curandera. "There is something here he needs."

"What could be so special about this place that Yam would risk coming back here?" asked Hadad. "He already acquired all the power he needs."

"I don't know," said La Curandera. "But whatever it is, he will come back to get it. And we must be ready for him."

"When you figure it out," said the Ranger, "let me know. Meanwhile, I'm taking Jon with me and returning to Angkor Wat."

"Go in peace," said La Curandera.

The Ranger picked up Jon in a modified fireman's carry with Jon's arms dangling on either side of the Ranger's neck and the full weight on his back, and the two men blinked out of existence on Machu Picchu and teleported to the other side of the world.

CHAPTER SIX

S ara Nelson lived on a small farm in northern Wisconsin, adjacent to major ley lines—natural lines of electro-magnetic flux—emanating from the heart of mother earth herself like blood flowing through arteries and veins. This ley line flowed from the arctic circle through Wisconsin, down through Rockford in Illinois, down through Cancun in Mexico, down through Machu Picchu in Peru, down through the south-ernmost mountains of Patagonian Chile, and came back up the other side of the world. Other ley lines—lines of magical pow-er—circled the world in different directions, connecting Easter Island with Machu Picchu, connecting Angkor Wat with Mo-henjo Daro, Gobekli Tepe with Delphi, Tibet with Egypt. Ley lines were constantly in flux.

Where ley lines crossed running water, a natural vortex emerged. Such a vortex was created at Machu Picchu where a major north-south ley line was crossed thrice by the sacred Urubamba River. Other vortices emerged in Egypt where the Nile crossed several key ley lines, in India where the Indus river and the Ganges crossed another ley line, in the mountains of southwestern China where the mouth of the Mekong crossed similar lines of power, and in Cambodia where the Mekong joined the Tonle Sap and Siem Reap rivers on yet another major line of power. It was there that the temples of Angkor Wat were built near what was once a great and powerful vortex, and it was at Angkor Wat that Lokesvara Sailendravarman served as the Guardian of the Watchtower of the East.

The central jagoti in the main temple at Angkor Wat represented mythical Mount Meru, the sacred mountain described with great reverence in Hindu and Buddhist texts. Temples were built on mountains near vortices to magnify the power of the vortex, and if there were no mountain nearby to build a temple upon, then ancient peoples often built their own mountains from earth and stone. Native American cultures built mounds along rivers where vortices were present, and ancient Egyptians built pyramids.

Here in northern Wisconsin, near the confluence of the north and south forks of the Flambeau River, not far from where the Flambeau flowed into the Chippewa River, there existed a natural vortex that had existed since the time of the glaciers. Here, instead of a mountain, the trees of an old-growth forest fulfilled the same function. There were mounds here, too, built by indigenous peoples many centuries ago, and in one part of the old-growth forest still standing there was a sacred mound and a rock formation. And a vortex.

This was the vortex where twelve-year-old Sara Nelson served as Guardian of the Watchtower of the West. Sara had been born into her present life, the daughter of Herman and Deborah Nelson, on a tiny farm adjoining the forest. Ellen Groves and Daisy May Martindale, two midwives who delivered Sara, had trained young Sara from an early age in the workings of magic and had helped Sara remember what she had learned in previous lives. When Sara reached puberty and experienced menarche, the memories of all her past lives flooded over her and she was able to recall all she had learned in thousands of incarnations. Sara was now an Ascended Master, one of a handful of true magicians who knew and worked real magic. Sara was a natural magician, and her sorcery came to her from the Great Mother herself. She was in touch with the earth, and all that grew from the womb of the earth was Sara's to command: wind, water, fire, and minerals of all kinds; trees, grass, all flowering plants; insects, birds, and reptiles. As long as she remained grounded to the earth, each and every time Sara touched wood she could make magic happen.

And because Sara wore a piece of cedar from a fallen branch tied to a soft deerskin cord around her neck, Sara was always in touch with magic.

Though Herman Nelson had finally rebuilt the farm house that fierce winds had destroyed late last year, Sara now lived in a house owned by Diane Groves. Diane's house was surrounded by 1800 acres of old-growth and second-growth trees, and a hundred yards east of that house was a sacred circle containing an ancient Indian mound and a fire pit surrounded by granite and basalt boulders left behind by retreating glaciers. The mound was the center of a powerful natural vortex on a major north-south ley line.

Diane Groves and her sister-in-law Sheila Ryan had constructed their new two-story wooden house out of oak and pine on the exact same spot where Diane's mother's house once stood. Diane's mother, Ellen Groves, had inherited the former house and more than 1800 acres of remaining old-growth forest from a great aunt named Emma Wells. Emma's mother had acquired the property from Chippewa Indians, and she had registered the title with the state before Wisconsin even became a state. Emma had built the original wood-frame house adjacent to the log cabin where she and her sisters had been born. Emma Wells lived in that original house until she passed away in 1950 at the age of 138.

There were twelve rooms in the new house. Beneath the house was Emma's original root cellar which doubled as a tornado shelter. The house had an entrance foyer near the front door, a huge living room with a granite fireplace, an equally-big kitchen and dining room with a four-burner cast-iron cooking stove along one wall, a kitchen pantry filled with cooking utensils and stairs down to the root cellar, a rear door that led to a utility shed a hundred feet from the house where snowmobiles and axes and shovels were stored. The stairs to the second floor led from the foyer to six bedrooms. There was no indoor plumbing, nor any electricity anywhere near the house. Water came from a well, and there was an outhouse behind the utility shed. The house itself stood in a clearing where a long firebreak cut through the trees from the two-lane County Road O on the north to a four-lane state highway a mile south of the property. The firebreak was the only way in by car and the only way anyone was allowed on the property, but Diane's Prius was now parked several hundred miles south in Madison where Diane Groves was an assistant professor of history at the state university, and Sheila Ryan's Subaru Forester was parked near Sheila's law office at the Sawyer County seat in Hayward. Sheila had given up a lucrative private practice in Chicago to become an assistant state's attorney in rural Wisconsin after she married Tom Groves, Diane's older brother. The husbands of both women were active duty army officers stationed in other states, and they visited the house only twice a year when they were on leave from the army.

Sara had the whole house to herself today, and she sat naked in lotus position in front of a roaring fire she'd built in the huge stone fireplace as much for light as warmth, her haunches in contact with the bare oak floor in the pine-paneled living room. Sara Nelson ascended the World Tree where her spirit met the spirits of Biegolmai Davvii and Lokesvara Sailendravarman.

"Hadad tells us Yam is now in Wisconsin," said Biegolmai. "Beware. He will attempt to reach your vortex and steal its power."

"I have protected the site with wards," said Sara. "He cannot get close."

"Nonetheless, he will try. Don't underestimate him."

"What can I do to prepare, grandfather?"

"Find him before he finds you. His energy signature, bloated by sacrifices, is far too powerful to hide. If he is somewhere near you, your spirit can locate him. But be careful. If he senses your spirit self, he will know your body is unoccupied and vulnerable. Right now he has not the power of a vortex of his own. But he is still a very powerful sorcerer. If he learns about you, he will find a way to come for you and attempt to kill you and claim your life-force."

"I can take care of myself. Despite my appearance, I am not a child."

"That is true," agreed Biegolmai. "You are almost as old as I. We can discuss our incarnations another time. Go now, and find Yam. See what he is up to."

"Why have you not done that already? You can spirit travel as easily as any of us."

"Male energy cannot get close to him," said Biegolmai. "Like repels like. I can sense where he is, but I cannot get close enough to see what he is doing."

"I understand about polarities," said Sara. "My female energy can go where your male energy cannot, and vice versa."

"Now go. We must find a way to return sunshine to the world before the world becomes more chaotic than it already is. People were not meant to remain in darkness for long periods of time. If Yam's intent is to create chaos, he has succeeded."

* * *

Sheila Ryan ran a small law office in Hayward, Wisconsin, and she worked part-time, and only occasionally, for the District Attorney's office in the Sawyer County courthouse across the street. Unlike her previous office in Chicago, Sheila had no staff, no partners, no secretary, no legal assistants to help her. She had to do all of the work herself.

At 32, Sheila Ryan was not only a very beautiful natural redhead, she was also a very competent attorney. She had graduated cum laude from DePaul University's prestigious law school, and she had learned her trade as a successful litigator in Cook County courts, working legal magic on behalf of some of the largest corporate clients in America. She had come to the north woods originally only to steal 1800 acres of land from the heirs of Ellen Groves after Ellen had been brutally murdered by Philip Ashur and his hired thugs, but she had fallen in love with both the land and its people and hadn't returned to her former life as a high-priced corporate attorney. Instead, she had purchased a small office building in downtown Hayward and hung out her shingle on Main Street where she now practiced law. She worked part-time for the District Attorney's office as, alternately, an assistant prosecutor and a public defender. Sawyer County had very little serious crime, so there was very little part-time work.

Normally, Sheila's personal clients were few and far between. Other than DWI—driving while intoxicated—cases or hunting out of season or taking more fish than the DNR—Department of Natural Resources—allowed or the occasional probate case that came her way, Sheila had too little work and very little income. That was okay with her. She no longer had a taste for designer clothes and expensive automobiles, and she didn't need to pay thousands of dollars a month in rent for a luxurious apartment in a lakefront highrise and thousands more for an office on LaSalle Street. Burt Ryan's little girl had gone back to her humble beginnings, and she was very comfortable with that.

But today she had more clients than she could handle. The phone hadn't stopped ringing since she had arrived at the office, and the DA's office needed her to consult on two murder investigations and more than a dozen new battery cases. In the last two days since the sun had disappeared from sight, crime in the county had escalated to epidemic proportions.

And then some asshole had called to say he had a prior claim to the 1800-plus acres Emma Wells had deeded to Ellen

Groves. He said his name was Sam Elman, and an ancestor of his had legally purchased the land from an Ojibwe chief. He claimed the land originally belonged to the Ojibwe and not the Chippewa, and Emma Wells and her mother had fraudulently registered the land in their name when they couldn't possibly own that land. He asked for a cease and desist order effective immediately and a restraining order keeping the descendants of Ellen Groves from occupying the property.

Sheila asked for the man's name and phone number and told him she would call him back after she investigated the legitimacy of his claim.

Elman, however, was insistent. He said time was of the essence and if Sheila didn't represent him, he would find someone else who would.

Sheila was equally insistent. She had dealt with assholes before, and she wasn't about to be intimidated by a man—any man—ever again. She told the asshole she was too busy to talk with him today, but if he left his name and number she would get back to him as soon as she could.

He gave her his name and phone number. He said he would wait for her call. If she didn't call him back soon, however, he would find someone else to represent him.

Sheila put all other calls on hold while she began researching Elman's claims in county records. She quickly discovered that the Ojibwe sold most of their land rights in 1837, a year after Emma Wells' mother had registered the deed with the state. When Ms. Wells acquired the property in 1836, the land was still owned by the Ojibwe.

But the Ojibwe band was one of the tribes of the Chippewa nation. They called themselves the Anishinaabe people, and the Betonukeengainubejig band of the Chippewa were the ones who had settled this area and sold the property to Ms. Wells. Chippewa was the name whites had given to the Ojibwe who had remained in this region instead of migrating to Canada. Today, they preferred to be called Ho-Chunk instead of Chippewa or Ojibwe.

There was indeed a claim made in 1847 by one Samuel Elman that he was the legal owner of the Wells property, but Elman had left Wisconsin for Missouri before the case came to court. When Elman failed to appear before the magistrate, the court should have ruled in favor of Ms. Wells. But since Ms. Wells was not married—and there was no evidence that she had ever been married—the court had ruled in favor of Mr. Elman. The judge had declared that an unmarried woman had no right to own land in this state or any other. Both federal and state homesteading acts were clear on the matter. He cited the Northwest Ordinance of 1787, the Public Land Ordinance of 1785, the Land Law of 1800, the Land Act of 1820, the preemption acts of 1830 and 1841, and the federal Government Land Office public lands surveys of 1832. Since Miss Wells could not prove she had been legally married and her husband had died after the marriage was consummated, she didn't qualify to hold lands as head of household. Therefore, her claim to the land was null and void.

Sheila was stunned. Every feminist bone in her body screamed foul. It was something that Sheila was sure to win in any court in America today, but only after a lengthy court battle that might take months or even years to be resolved.

Meanwhile, Sam Elman had a legal right to claim that property and kick Diane Groves and her houseguests off, at least . until the issue finally resolved itself in court.

This was terrible. Not only would the Groves family lose their home and the house they had recently rebuilt, but they would lose the old-growth forest they had protected religiously against loggers for so long that it seemed like a crusade.

And they would lose control of the vortex and the magic circle to Elman.

Sheila picked up her phone and dialed Diane Groves' office telephone number in the history department at the University of Wisconsin. When the call went to voice mail, Sheila said, "Diane, it's Sheila. Call me back. We have a problem. A very big problem."

*   *   *

Diane Groves was too young and too good-looking to be a tenured professor of history. She was tall, slender, raven-haired, and articulate. Even without makeup, Diane's natural beauty made men think of only one thing. But Diane Groves had three earned doctorates from prestigious universities, and her colleagues and peers considered Diane Groves a leading authority in the study of ancient religious rituals. Those who read her published papers and didn't know what she looked like were amazed by her brilliant research.

Most of her graduate students were women, accepted into the program only after Diane was sure they were serious about scholarship. The few males who were accepted into the program were intensely dedicated researchers. Any man who wanted to get close to Diane Groves couldn't do it simply by taking her classes.

Today's seminar was a discussion of the role of the sun in archaic religious rituals. Besides Stonehenge, there were thousands of monuments in all parts of the world dedicated to tracking the sun's movements, and it was obvious the sun played an important role in the religious lives of ancient peoples: Ra, Khepi, and Atum in Egypt; Helios and Apollo in Greece; Mithras in Persia; Shamash in Ur; Inti in Peru; and Ri Gong Yang Xing Jun in China.

And it was evident from the chaos in the world today that the sun still played an important role in human affairs. The disappearance of the sun two days ago had generated a resurgence of religious fervor that hadn't been seen since human beings witnessed the first total eclipse many millennia ago. Diane thought the discussion topic was timely and of great importance. She was disappointed to discover her students didn't feel the same way.

Despite Diane's strict policy of mandatory attendance at all scheduled seminars, few of her students had showed up today. And Diane could tell that those who did were too distracted to participate with any vigor. She dismissed the class early.

When she returned to her office, she found a message on her voice mail. She immediately called Sheila Ryan back and said, "What's the problem?"

Diane listened while Sheila explained about the law and the validity of Elman's claim. Diane said, "I'm on my way. I'll be there in four hours. Don't do anything until I get there." Then she remembered Sara was alone in the house. "I'll meet you at the house. Can you close up your office right now and go to the house and stay with Sara until I get there?"

When Sheila agreed, Diane hung up and called her department secretary and cancelled all her scheduled classes and graduate seminars for the rest of the week. The secretary said other professors had also cancelled most of their classes because of the current crisis. Diane promised to call back in a week, or sooner if they saw the sun. Then she hung up the phone, walked to the door and locked it, and returned to her desk and removed all her clothes. She placed her skirt, panties, blouse, and bra on the desk and prepared to meditate.

Diane sat naked on the floor in a modified lotus position, her thumbs touching the middle fingers of each hand to form closed circles. One by one, she sealed each of the twelve external openings of her body: Eyes, both nostrils, mouth, both ears, both nipples, her anus, her urethra, her vagina. If she were going to leave her body, she wouldn't leave it vulnerable to intrusion.

She opened her crown chakra and her spirit soared.

In the space of a heartbeat, she was inside her house in the woods. She saw Sara Nelson sitting naked on the floor in front of the fireplace, saw the sacred circle in the woods a few hundred yards outside the house, saw the firebreak leading from the road to the house, saw headlights from a lone vehicle driving down the firebreak toward the house. Inside the vehicle were two men. One man was dressed in hunting camouflage clothing and he held a high-powered rifle between his legs like a phallus. The older man driving the car had a white beard and wore a black eye patch covering one eye.

His face looked horribly scarred.

In her disembodied form, Diane could do nothing to prevent the two men from walking in on Sara. So Diane located a body to occupy, a lone hawk she found perched on a high branch of one of the 80-foot-tall white pines, and she swooped down straight at the car. The driver saw the bird coming directly at him, and he swerved to the left. The man in the passenger seat rolled the window down and fired the rifle from the open window. But the car was still swerving, and the sky was dark, and the bullet went high and wide and missed its mark.

The sight of the hawk in the headlights seemed to unnerve the driver, and the car continued to swerve wildly, the front tires jumping in and out of wheel ruts worn into the firebreak. The car spun sideways as it slammed to a stop. The passenger jumped out of the vehicle before it came to a full stop, and he fired at the hawk. Bang! Once. Bang! Twice. Diane swooped left and up, then she came around behind the man with the gun so he couldn't get a bead on her and he was still trying to turn the rifle all the way around when the hawk hit the side of his face and ripped the face wide open. Blood gushed from holes torn in his cheek, and the man screamed and dropped the rifle.

Diane circled again and came straight down at him with talons on both feet outstretched and speared his eyes, and both eyeballs ruptured and sprayed fluid and blood. Long stings of muscle and nerves dangled down into the man's open mouth and stifled his screams.

The man driving the car whipped the car all the way around and drove back up the firebreak as fast as he could go. He didn't look back even once to see if his passenger were still alive.

"Thank you," whispered Sara Nelson's voice inside Diane's mind.

"You saw?"

"I've been observing Yam for two hours. I heard what he told Sheila."

"Sheila says Elman will try to force us off the property while the case is in court."

"Can he do that?"

"He'll try. Sheila says he has a strong case."

"We've got to stop him. We can't let him have this property."

"We will stop him, I promise you. In the meantime, protect yourself. I'm going back to my body so I can drive home. I'll be back in four hours."

Before Diane left the hawk, she saw Sheila's Subaru enter the firebreak from the county trunk. With Sheila and Sara together, Diane felt certain they would be safe until she could return.

She didn't know how wrong she could be.

CHAPTER SEVEN

Hadad Elman found his brother hiding in northern Wisconsin. Yam had changed so much in the intervening years that Hadad barely recognized him in physical form, but the energy signature was exactly right and Hadad knew the man with half a face was indeed Yam Elman.

Yam had grown fat with power, his bloated physical body reflecting the corrupt spirit within. He was old, ugly, scarred, corpulent, and very angry.

Not only had he been thwarted at Machu Picchu, he had been frightened half to death by a hawk. Yam was an old man in an old body, and his heart—overburdened by his physical bulk and weakened with the passage of time—had nearly stopped when that hawk had swooped down directly at Yam's remaining eye. It didn't matter that he was protected by the thick safety glass of the car's windshield. All he could see was a pair of taloned claws aimed at his face, and he had panicked.

And then, when those talons had shredded the face of the hunter Yam had hired to kill the women on the Groves' property, Yam's panic escalated and all Yam could think about was escaping.

Yam had used his power to extend his life in the physical realm, and his birth body was wearing out so fast he had to exert more and more power to keep it functioning. He possessed magic, but he used most of his magic to keep a body that had endured much longer than nature intended functioning.

Somewhere near Machu Picchu was a woman with the magic to make Yam young again, to heal his wounds, restore his face, and extend his life almost indefinitely. He was so very close to finding her that he thought he could actually taste her, but she had slipped through his fingers when he had been forced to flee for his life after two armed men threatened him with guns.

He wanted to go back to Machu Picchu and search for that woman again, but he couldn't. Not yet. Another sorcerer had taken possession of the vortex and prevented his return.

In order to go back to Machu Picchu and battle that sorcerer in a place she now owned, Yam needed to acquire the full power of another vortex. He had three to choose from: The vortex of the north near a rock formation called the Seita in the frozen lands of northern Scandinavia; the vortex of the east near the temples of Angkor Wat in Cambodia; and the vortex of the west in the north woods of Wisconsin. There were other vortexes, too, but none nearly as powerful as those three.

Yam had been in Wisconsin before, nearly two hundred years ago, wearing another body. He knew the territory well enough, and he had a prior claim to the land where the vortex resided. So Wisconsin had been his first choice.

But now he had second thoughts.

As long as Yam had control of the sun, his power would continue to grow. He thrived on chaos, and chaos was running rampant throughout the world. People everywhere were restless, worried, unable to cope. Thousands if not hundreds of thousands of people had already acted irrationally, resorting to physical violence as their bodies filled with adrenalin from the natural flight or fight response that always kicked in when human beings confronted the unknown. Soon there would be millions of people panicking or losing their minds. He fed off their fear and confusion the way a vampire feeds on blood.

Angkor Wat was his second choice, and he prepared to go there now while the legal machinations he had set in place wound their way through the court system. When Sheila Ryan hadn't called him back immediately, he had retained another lawyer to press his claim. If he were unsuccessful at Angkor Wat, he would come back here and wait for control of the local vortex to cede to him.

Suddenly, Yam sensed another spirit presence that had invaded his innermost mind and knew his secret thoughts. Only one person in all the world was capable of doing that without Yam's express permission, and that person was his twin brother

Hadad. Even as children five thousand years ago, they had been able to enter each other's minds without the other knowing it. One of the reasons both had become as powerful as they now were was because both had shared the secrets they had learned when one entered the other's mind.

Hadad had always been a scholar, someone who was more interested in learning about magic than using what he had learned in the real world, and what Hadad had learned from Yam in the past had not appreciably interfered with Yam's plans. Yam was the doer, the one who stole magic from others and used it to steal more, and Yam had stolen everything his brother knew and more. It was Hadad that Yam had been searching for in France in 1942 when a falcon had swooped down and ripped his face away. Though Yam knew it was a woman in the falcon's body that attacked him and not his brother's spirit, Yam blamed his brother for the loss of an eye and half of his face.

An eye for an eye—*lex talionis*, the law of like retribution—had been Hammurabi's code of justice when Yam had been an advisor to that king back in Babylonia nearly five millennia go, and Yam hungered to have his eye back or another in retribution. As it said in Deuteronomy 18: "Then you shall do to him as he plotted to do to his brother....You shall not have pity: life for life, eye for eye, tooth for tooth, hand for hand, foot for foot."

Yam attacked Hadad's spirit with all the power at his immediate disposal. A disembodied spirit was vulnerable, and Yam hit Hadad's spirit with a double whammy that blinded Hadad and would keep his spirit from being able to return to his human body, wherever that body might physically be located. Yam quickly excised Hadad's wounded spirit from his mind, and left Hadad's spirit to wander aimlessly until the physical body eventually deteriorated and died from lack of spirit. For the human body required spirit to perform routine functions like drinking and eating and defecating. Death by dehydration normally occurred within a week or two when a body had no spirit.

Yam had no pity, and he was glad to be done with his brother once and for all. Hadad would be reborn into another body after a time, but far too late to interfere with Yam's current plans. With Hadad out of the way, Yam was free to proceed as he pleased.

He blinked his one good eye and instantly he flashed out of existence in northern Wisconsin.

And blinked back into existence on the banks of the Siem Reap River, not far from the temples at Angkor Wat.

*   *   *

Lokesvara was worried. The aged Lama was normally very serene, and it was extremely unusual to see him worried. Because he remembered each of the many lives he had lived in the past and knew with certainty that he would be reborn yet again, he felt there was little worth worrying about. Now Lokesvara's students were worried because the master was worried. What could possibly be so dire that might cause Lokesvara Sailendravarman to worry?

True, the sun's familiar face had been hidden for nearly three days, and the moon had been absent for as long. But Lokesvara had assured his students that the sun was still there and daylight would soon return. He told them they shouldn't worry. Also true was the fact that one of the men the master had sent on a secret mission had returned gravely wounded. But his wounds were nearly healed, and he was already walking and talking as if nothing had happened.

Only one of the students at Angkor Wat knew what worried the master, because he appeared to be worried, too. Though that man was one of the newer monks, he seemed to know more than all of the other monks combined. He was a master of meditation, and he could recite most of the Sutras and ancient Tantras from memory. And, though he was an American, he spoke Mandarin and Mongolian like a native, and he spoke fluent Tibetan, Hindi, Thai, Lao, and Khmer with barely any accent. He read sacred texts in Sanskrit, Pali, Mandarin, and English. And he knew history, both modern and ancient, as if he had lived it.

One of the things that worried the newcomer was his broken vow. He had taken human life in order to save his own life and the life of his American friend, and that obviously troubled him greatly. Immediately after his return, after he had seen to the comfort of his friend and spoke with Lokesvara in private for almost an hour, he had changed into his robes and secluded himself in meditation. All of his fellow students were praying for him, and incense and prayer flags carried their prayers to heaven on the four winds.

When the stranger from America—who was no longer a stranger because he was accepted as one of their community of monks and scholars—had first arrived at the temple complex more than a year ago, he was almost as troubled as he appeared now. He simply materialized one day unannounced, speaking perfect Khmer Surin, and saying, "I take refuge in the Buddha, the dharma, and the sangha." The doors were opened unto him, and he was admitted to the sangha, the community of believers. It wasn't until much later that it was learned that the American was well-known to Lokesvara, who welcomed the stranger like a brother as soon as he saw him.

As the American, who took the name of the Bodhisattva Vajrapani after his initiation, continued to meditate, his burden seemed to lift. All of the bad karma he had brought with him eventually dissipated, and Vajrapani's soul now seemed as clean as the pure snows of Mount Meru.

That is, it was until he returned from Peru where he had killed five people.

Now the American Vajrapani was deeply troubled again, and his excessive worry may have infected the master. Lama

Lokesvara had also retreated into secluded meditation, and he had cancelled all of his classes until further notice.

Monks and students alike were surprised to hear the very same mantra emanating from two separate places in the main temple: "Om, Vajrapani, hummmmmmmmmm." Over and over again. "Om, Vajrapani, hummmmmmmmmm." The mantra repeated, and repeated, and repeated, droning on and on, over and over. Again and again. Louder and louder. "Ommmmmm, Vajraaaaaaaapani hummmmmmmmmmmmmm." On and on it went, seemingly forever. Repeating over and over, again and again. Echoing through all the hallways and corridors and chambers of the temple. Increasing in volume. Increasing in tempo. Droning on and on. Shaking the walls. Shaking the very foundations of the temple itself, through the lakes and reflection ponds and moats surrounding the temples and the waters lying deep beneath the sandy soil, creating ripple after ripple in the once serene surfaces of those waters. Until, finally, the two separate voices—now joined by a third voice coming from the direction of the sick room—merged into one sound, perfectly synchronized, perfectly entrained. On and on went that incredible sound, building in volume and intensity. "Oooommmmmm, Vajraaaaaaapani, hummmmmmmmmmmmmmmm." Reaching crescendo.

And the students could feel the energies building up within the walls of the main temple, an incredible energy that was far from subtle and increased more and more as the droning went on and on.

Suddenly, there was silence.

Then, from the American, they heard, "Pāṇātipātā veramaṇī sikkhāpadaṃ samādiyāmi. Adinnādānā veramaṇī sikkhāpadaṃ samādiyāmi." In English, it meant, "I undertake the training principle of abstaining from taking life. I undertake the training principle of abstaining from taking the not-given."

Then all three voices, the voice of Lokesvara and the voice of Vajrapani and the voice of the American Marine, said, in unison, "Sadhu," which means "Good," or "It is done," or "So mote it be."

And then Vajrapani stepped out of his meditation chamber and all the monks and all the students immediately prostrated themselves. For it was not the American called Vajrapani who stepped out of that chamber, but Vajrapani himself, the mahabodhisattva, the wielder of the thunderbolt, the protector of all Buddhas. In his right hand he carried the sacred Vajra, and in his left hand he carried the ancient Kris and the mighty lasso. This was not the peaceful Vajrasattva, but the wrathful Vajrapani, fierce warrior, slayer of dragons and demons.

And out of the office of the Lama stepped not Lokesvara Sailendravarman, their beloved teacher, but Manjusri Bodhisattva, the manifestation of the Buddha's wisdom, and in his right hand he held high the flaming sword of wisdom. This was not the peaceful Manjusri depicted in icons and sacred texts, but the

Youthful Manjusri, the wrathful Manjusri, fierce warrior and eternal youth, the Yamantaka or terminator of death.

And out of the sick room stepped not the American Marine, but Akashagarbha, the Boundless Space Matrix, whose powers were said to be as great as time and space itself. He carried no weapon, for he needed no weapon.

Three of the eight great Bodhisattvas manifested in their most fearsome aspects in one place and time! It was a miracle beyond belief. Those who dared open their eyes to look upon those glorious and terrible figures considered themselves blessed. Those who dared not open their eyes wondered what danger could be threatening enough to bring these three great protectors of the dharma into the physical realm to interact with ordinary mortals.

It wasn't long before they had the answer. The walls began to shake, the ceilings started to crack. It felt like a massive earthquake had begun at the very center of Angkor Wat and spread through the entire temple complex like shock waves from an atomic bomb blast.

This time it was not sounds that shook the world, but blasts of incredible power from some outside source. Blasts that threatened to crumble the ancient laterite and sandstone stones to dust.

But temple walls had been protected by the magic of sound, and the energy of the two vibrations of equal and opposite polarity simply cancelled each other out, the frequency of the sound waves perfectly offsetting the destructive vibrations of outside energy. What otherwise would have meant the total destruction of the Temple City became little more than a minor disturbance. It was as if the three Great Bodhisattvas had known the attack was immanent and they constructed a magic circle and cone of protection with the Vajrapani mantra just in time to prevent catastrophe.

Now the students of Angkor Wat watched in shock and awe as the three Great Bodhisattvas rushed outside to confront their mysterious attacker. Vajrapani held the Vajra high, and thunder boomed, lightning flashed. Manjusri waved the flaming sword of wisdom, and night seemed to turn into day even without the help of the sun. Where Akashagarbha walked, doorways to other worlds opened and closed.

Within minutes, all three Bodhisattvas were back, but not for long. Once again, the students couldn't believe their eyes as the fierce visage of the Yamantaka melted away, and Lokesvara Sailendravarman—the kindly old teacher they all knew and loved—stood in his place.

So, too, did the formidable figures of Vajrapani and Akashagarbha fade, and the American monk and the American Marine appeared in the hallway of the temple where the two Bodhisattvas had been.

"Yam returned to Wisconsin," said the Marine who still possessed Akashagarbha's boundless insight "We should go after him."

"No," said Lokesvara. "We must stay to guard the vortex. Let others do their part. Come, brothers, we shall inform Biegolmai of the attack on this temple."

As the three men moved through the corridors of the temple, monks and students greeted them with traditional wais of respect.

"Namaste," said Lokesvara as he placed the palms of both hands together and bowed, returning the wais. "Namaste."

Namaste: I honor the manifestation of the holy, the god or goddess, that exists within you. That word, and the Anjali mudra that went with it, had taken on new meaning for monks and students who had seen with their very own eyes the enlightened god-like beings that existed within three ordinary-seeming mortal men who now passed before them through the halls of the hallowed.

And more than one of the students wondered if such a god-like being also existed within himself.

*   *   *

Hadad's mortal body was still at Machu Picchu, and he had to find a way back into his own body before decrepitation began and that mortal shell died of neglect. He had less than 72 hours to return his spirit to the flesh or his current life would abruptly end. He would someday be reborn in a new body, of course, but he would be born with a memory wiped clean like a blackboard erased by the teacher at the end of each class period. It might take many years for him to recover all he had learned from previous lifetimes and rewrite those precious memories on that blank slate. His mind rebelled at the thought of the damage Yam could do in those intervening years.

Spirit travel had its benefits: One could journey anywhere in the blink of an eye in discarnate form and observe, but not alter, current and past events. If one were psychically attuned to another spirit, one could even speak to that spirit or simply listen in to the other's thoughts. The psychic connection between polar opposites was always very strong, and the connection between Hadad and his brother was even stronger. Getting inside Yam's mind had been easy until Yam discovered the connection and abruptly severed it.

But the perils of spirit travel were often overlooked: The body that was left behind became vulnerable without spirit motivation, and the body was subject to wandering spirits walking in and taking over unless the body was properly sealed against all intruders. But the physical body was little more than a vehicle for spirit, and just like other vehicles left abandoned, bodies would naturally deteriorate over time. All bodies needed fuel to operate, and they needed periodic care and maintenance or sludge would accumulate, fuel lines would become clogged and inoperable, and the body itself would rust and begin to break down.

Hadad had properly sealed his body before leaving it, and he wasn't worried about other spirits or discarnate entities walking in and possessing the body while his spirit was gone. What concerned him now was getting back to his body in time to prevent cells from breaking down and that body became completely uninhabitable by anything but worms.

Wandering around in total darkness, Hadad's spirit had no idea where in space and time Yam had sent it. He could be all the way at the other side of the universe or back in time to ancient Egypt for all he knew, or he could still be in northern Wisconsin or Timbuktu or anywhere or anywhen.

He was literally flying blind, and none of his senses worked. There was no way to orient himself in space and time so he could edge his way back to Machu Picchu and the human body he had left behind. Was he doomed to wander about in this wilderness for forty days and forty nights before the spirit realm called him home after his body simply perished from neglect?

Filled with despair, Hadad began to ruminate on the regrets of a thousand lifetimes. In each of those lives, Hadad had done things he sorely regretted doing. And, so too, he had not done many things that he knew he should have done. But what he regretted most was that he had no way to stop his brother from gaining access to all the vortexes on earth and, thus, acquiring total power over all worlds.

Hadad had no way to alert the other Guardians to Yam's diabolical desires. If only there were some method to communicate, he could die happy. But there was no way he could think of. Yam's double whammy had depleted all of Hadad's psychic energy and he was left speechless as well as blind.

Though Yam's double whammy had knocked him senseless, Hadad thought he could feel something happening around him. It wasn't exactly a sound that he could actually hear, for he could hear nothing, but a vibration that reverberated through the subtle energies of the universe—the aether itself—and touched his spirit, and his spirit interpreted the shift in energy as a sound.

"Ommmmm, Vajrapani, hummmmmmmmmmm!"

As the vibrations increased in tempo and intensity, his spirit tuned into the subtle shifts much as a radio tunes in to the high frequency energies generated by broadcast network transmitters. "Ommmmmm, Vajraaaaaapani, hummmmmmmmmm!"

Could he follow those subtle energies back to the source like a jetliner following the homing beacon sent out from an air traffic control tower? "Ommmmm, Vajrapani, hummmmmmmmmm!"

Now his spirit became entrained with the vibrations, and his spirit automatically repeated the mantra: "Ommmm, Vajrapani, hummmmmmmmmm!"

He recognized the work of Akashagarbha, the Boundless Space Matrix, who had the power to reach effortlessly through all time and space. He could visualize with his third eye, the mind's eye, Jon Fish sitting in lotus. Though he still couldn't see, he could imagine.

And now his powerful imagination took over, and Hadad's spirit imagined he was one with Akashagarbha. And the power of the imagination caused subtle shifts in the energy of the universe and Hadad's spirit ceased to exist in one place and time to emerge in another.

And now his senses began to return as he found himself in a dark cave in the Phnom Kong Rei Mountain in central Cambodia, near the other end of the large Tonle Sap Lake directly opposite Angkor Wat. Hadad remembered living, during one of his many previous incarnations, here in this cave long ago. His name then was Sen Putthisen.

Sen's mother and her eleven sisters were all pregnant when they had been blinded and imprisoned in this cave by Queen Santema, an evil sorceress, who demanded their eyes be plucked out so she could devour the eyeballs. Though Sen's mother had been spared one eye, she had remained in the dark cave to help her sisters. All twelve women give birth in this cave, but eleven of the children died and only Sen survived. After Sen grew to manhood in the darkness of the cave, Santema pretended to befriend Sen, and she asked Sen to do her a favor. She gave Sen a letter and asked him to deliver it to her adopted daughter, Neang Kang Rei. She also gave Sen a letter of safe passage through the forest of the giants which surrounded the cave and threatened to devour anyone who tried to leave. Santema, however, lied about one of the letters. The letter to her daughter instructed Neang Kang Rei to kill Sen and eat him.

Fortunately, Sen had met a hermit in the forest and showed the letters to the hermit so the hermit would permit Sen to pass. The hermit changed the instructions to Neang Kang Rei, telling her to marry Sen instead of killing him, and to devour him only with kisses. After they were married, Santema's daughter showed Sen the many secrets of magic herbs and magic potions, and Sen learned how to restore sight to his blinded mother and her eleven sisters with an aromatic herb called ma-am that grew on the side of the mountain.

But that had been so very long ago, and Hadad had forgotten all about it.

Hadad's spirit was still weak from the double whammy that threw him for a loop, but he was back in the world, back in the present, and he could see and hear and feel.

Hadad willed his spirit to speak to the spirits of Akashagarbha and Manjusri at Ankor, and he informed both them and Vajrapani of Yam's plans.

Then he returned to his body at Machu Picchu to make himself whole again.

CHAPTER EIGHT

K isikil Lilake and Bryn Helgasdottir appeared in Wisconsin nearly simultaneously, drawn to the vortex by a sense of impending doom.

Bryn had been there before, and she quickly oriented herself to the familiar landscape. Little had changed in the heart of the old-growth forest in nearly two centuries, and she felt right at home among the tall trees.

Kisi, too, had been there before in another body, but that was long, long ago when the land was still very young and almost all of the land had trees, many even larger than these. This land had then belonged to the predecessors of the Anishkinaabe, who later became the Ojibwe, and Kisi was a Jissakiwinini of the Ojibwe, a Ninth Degree Midewikwe or spiritual healer, an Anishinaabeg medicine woman. According to Ojibwe legend, four Midew Manidoowag or Manitous, had long ago visited the Anishinaabe people in spirit form and communicated both the mystery of the sacred medicine bundle and the seven fires prophecies. Kisi now knew that the four Manidoowag spirits were Biegolmai, La Curandera, Lokesvara, and Sara in previous incarnations, but she didn't know that then. They had come from the four directions to teach her people to cure illness, and to save the land from total destruction. They foretold of great sheets of ice that would soon come down from the north to envelop all the land of the Anishinaabe, and that only the trees of this one special place would survive. They directed her people to build an earthen mound and a sacred circle atop that earthen mound, and they gave the people words of power to speak over the land to protect the land and the trees. If the people did as they were told, the land and all that was upon it would survive, just as turtles managed to survive in the midst of chaotic seas by crawling up on land and planting their eggs in the earth of an island in the middle of the sea.

Kisi did as the white elders prescribed, a tradition passed down to her by her mother. Her mother had built the mound and created the sacred circle, and she spoke the words of power exactly as she had been taught and those were the words she taught to her daughter.

Kisi's name then was Wininwaa, daughter of Nookomis, and she was known as the Maiden of the West Wind. Her medicine was strong because she had learned much from the white Manitous who had come from afar, especially the two women who were wondrous healers. She used herbs to heal her people and to cure many illnesses, and she used the magic they taught her to extend her own life so that she might fulfill the first two of the seven prophecies. She lived through many of the harshest of winters that grew worse and worse as the ever-advancing ice sheets became larger and larger until they finally engulfed the land of the Anishkinaabe. Every day and every night Wininwaa repeated the magic words that could save her beloved trees.

And when the ice finally came, with the power of moving the very earth itself as it came ever closer and closer, the sheet of ice split in two as if some mysterious wedge were suddenly driven deep into the frozen heart of the ice mountain. Part of that massive sheet of ice flowed to the east, and part diverted to the west. Not far to the south, the two parts joined together again into a solid sheet of ice. In the middle was an island of undisturbed land, and on that land still grew hundreds of tall trees.

Wininwaa lived a long time, and during her long life she gave birth to ten children, eight girls and two boys.

They carried on the sacred traditions, and they passed those traditions on to their own children and to their children's children. And the people of the Anishkinaabe still endured today, thanks to the wisdom of the elders.

Kisi, who was always at home among trees and rocks, greeted the Lares in their own languages and they welcomed her to share their humble abodes as if she were kin. After tens of thousands of years, Kisi felt as though she had finally come home.

The two women walked together from the woods to the house, and Bryn was amazed to see a modern two-story wood-framed building now occupying the same spot where once Emma Wells had lived with her mother and sisters in a cabin made of rough-hewn logs.

Sara Nelson was expecting them both, and Sara opened the front door and the women embraced before entering the house. Sara introduced Bryn and Kisi to Sheila Ryan, explaining that Sheila was the wife of Tom Groves. Sheila and Tom had known each other in hundreds of past lives, and they had loved each other forever and a day.

Sheila possessed her own magic, acquired over many lifetimes, and Sheila could do some things the other women couldn't. Together, they would be a formidable force allied against the power of Yam Elman.

Diane Groves, said Sara, was on her way up from Madison, and they expected her shortly. Diane, the daughter of Ellen Groves, was an adept who came from a long line of adepts. Diane's mother had been one of the Guardians, Sara's predecessor and teacher, and Diane's aunts and great aunts were masters of magic and advanced spiritual adepts. Her great-great aunt was Emma Wells.

"Where is Yam Elman now?" asked Bryn Helgasdottir. Bryn was bristling for battle, and she wanted to take Elman on before he did any more damage.

"Close by," said Sara. "He has tried once already to get on the property and take possession of the vortex, but Diane's spirit drove him off."

"He is an evil man," said Kisi Lalake. "He has no compassion, no conscience."

"How can that be?" asked Sara. "Each time one enters the spirit realm, one becomes more compassionate."

"He does not go to the spirit realm between lives. He uses magic to extend his life almost indefinitely, and he remains in the physical world to accumulate power. If his body wears out or he sustains serious injuries that cannot be healed, I believe he takes possession of other bodies when it pleases him to do so."

"How does he do that?" asked Sheila.

"He simply walks in when he finds a body that is vulnerable," explained Bryn. "All bodies become vulnerable when the spirit travels. Spontaneous spirit travel happens to everyone, although most people don't recognize it for what it is. It can happen when one is driving a car or playing a piano or singing or listening to music or experiencing an orgasm during coitus or masturbation. When one experiences a feeling of ecstasy, one's spirit soars and momentarily becomes detached from the body. The word ecstasy is derived from two Latin words meaning to stand outside of the self or to stand apart from the body, but the body continues to operate without the spirit being present. The heart continues to beat, the lungs inflate and deflate. Walkers between worlds use rhythmic chants or the beat of a drum to create a feeling of ecstasy that allows them to travel quickly and easily between worlds. Biegolmai does that all the time, and so do Lokesvara and Akashagarbha. But they seal their bodies against intruders before they begin chanting or singing or drumming. Take care that you do the same."

"But doesn't the body die without the spirit being present?"

"The body keeps on functioning as it normally would. The heart continues to beat, the lungs continue to inflate and deflate, the metabolic processes go on the same as always. After a while, those processes do slow down, as if the body were going into hibernation. But the body doesn't move—isn't able to move—unless there is a spirit present to motivate it. Wandering spirits can simply walk into an unprotected body and take possession. It happens all the time."

"Sometimes," added Sara, "several spirits occupy the same body. There may be a wandering spirit or discarnate entity that has taken possession and doesn't know to seal the body to prevent other spirits from also entering. Often, a spirit will return to its own body and not notice others who may have taken up residence while that spirit was gone. It is only later, when the original spirit attempts to do something that is in conflict with what an invading spirit desires, that the original spirit notices it is no longer in complete control. Such divided minds lead to erratic behavior that psychiatrists attempt to fix with mood-altering and mind-numbing drugs. Drugs can be used to effectively sedate one or more spirits, but they cannot fix the basic problem."

"When a body is sealed by a walk-in," continued Bryn, "the original spirit cannot re-enter. Then that spirit becomes a wandering spirit that looks for another body to occupy."

"Trauma, too, can separate the spirit from the body," said Sara. "Battlefields around the world are filled with discarnate spirits that were shocked from the body by concussions from bomb blasts or as a result of sudden violence such as a bullet or a blade striking the body. You always know where battles have taken place on earth by the number of discarnate spirits wandering around. If a spirit is out of the body when the body dies, that spirit does not automatically progress to the spirit realm where it will eventually be reborn into a new body. It wanders around, sometimes forever, looking for a way back into its former body. If it cannot find its own body, it may try to take possession of another. Be especially careful to protect yourself around battlefields, both ancient and modern. There are spirits out there who have been looking for a body for millennia."

"If Elman doesn't go to the spirit realm to be cleansed before he reincarnates," said Kisi, "then he carries with him all the accumulated karma of several lifetimes and that may slow him down a little. But he also carries with him all of the memories and all of the knowledge and all of the power he has accumulated over many generations, and that makes him very dangerous."

"So what can we do about him?" asked Sheila.

"Kill him," said Bryn.

"Do we have to?" asked Sheila.

"We have to," said Bryn. "He'll eventually be reborn, but first he'll have to go to the spirit realm where his memories will be purged. Plus, he'll have to relive all of the pain he's caused others since the last time his spirit was cleansed. If that doesn't teach him compassion, nothing will."

"But if he's so powerful, how do we kill him?"

"That's the sixty-four dollar question."

"Keeping yourself alive long after your body has burned itself out uses up lots and lots of energy," said Kisi. "I had to do it once or twice myself, and it really takes a toll. Elman needs the power of a vortex to sustain his old worn-out body, and for some reason I don't know or can't understand he doesn't want to trade it in on a new model."

"He only has half a face and one eye is completely missing," said Sara. "You'd think he would want to walk into a whole body, maybe pick someone younger and better looking. We know it's not his conscience holding him back. Why does he want to keep that body when it's costing incredible amounts of energy to do so?"

"It's got to be draining him," said Bryn. "He's already using energy to hide the sun and energy to keep his body from falling apart. He used up a lot of energy today on a futile attack of Angkor Wat. Whatever energy he stole from Machu Picchu will soon be depleted, and then he'll become desperate to re-place it. He's getting some energy from the chaos he created by hiding the sun, but not nearly enough yet. He plans to get more as time goes on and panic spreads. But he can't attack us here, in this protected place, with the energy he has left. He'll go some-where else to replenish what he's lost and get what additional he needs before he tries to come here again."

"Where else can he go?" asked Sheila.

"You don't think he'd be stupid enough to try to get past Biegolmai and take the Seita, do you?" asked Kisi.

"I wouldn't put anything past him," said Sara. "Especial-ly if he's desperate."

"We should alert Biegolmai to be wary," suggested Bryn.

"Do that," said Sara. "I'm going to see if I can find Elman."

"Watch our bodies," said Kisi. "I'm going to Machu Pic-chu to speak with Hadad. If anyone knows what Yam plans to next, it's his twin brother."

* * *

La Curandera watched Hadad's body suddenly return to life. It always amazed her to see both eyes blink open, both arms and both legs twitch slightly as nerves and muscles reconnected, the head begin to lift up and breathing returned to normal. A moment ago that body sat totally inanimate, looking quite life-less. Now it moved, and it moved deliberately, and it moved with purpose.

"Anything happen while I was gone?" asked Hadad.

"I've been cleaning up," said La Curandera. "Yam left a mess behind."

"Do you know where he is now?"

"Wisconsin," said La Curandera.

"I wonder what he wants in Wisconsin."

"He wants the vortex, but you already knew that. Didn't you? Yam seeks power over everyone and everything. If he can't have this vortex, he'll go after another of the power centers. While you were gone, he attacked Lokesvara at Angkor Wat. But Lokesvara knew he was coming, and Yam's spells didn't stand a chance against the combined power of Manjusri, Vajrapani, and Akashagarbha."

"How did Lokesvara know Yam was coming?"

"I thought you told him."

"No," said Hadad. "How would I know what Yam planned?"

"Are you okay? You don't sound quite right. Is your memory intact?"

"Yam hit me with a double whammy when he discovered I was worming my way into his mind. I'm still trying to get my bearings back."

"I can help restore your memory," said La Curandera. "May I touch your forehead?"

"No," said Hadad, quickly turning his head away from her hand before she could make contact. "That's all right. Just give me some time to orient myself. I'll be fine."

"You sure?"

"I'm sure."

La Curandera went back to her housekeeping and left Hadad to sort out his thoughts. Whatever Yam had hit his brother with, it had definitely changed him.

La Curandera was pleasantly surprised when Kisi Lilake popped in. She and Kisi had shared several previous lifetimes, and they were more than just friends. Kisi was like a little sister to her.

"I came to speak with Hadad," Kisi said. "Where is he?"

"He just got back. You'll find him in the Temple of the Condor. Come, I'll show you where that is."

La Curandera guided Kisi across the central plaza and down some steps to the small enclosure at the east end of the ruins called the Temple of the Condor.

There sat Hadad, next to a stone slab cut in the idealized shape of a condor. The condor's head was at one end and the folded wings along its sides. It took a real leap of the imagination to see a condor within, but the image was there if one looked for it. The beak and eyes were well-defined.

"We need to know about Yam," said Kisi. "Where does he get his power?"

"I haven't seen my brother in a long time," said Hadad. "I tried to find him, but he threw a spell at me that blocked my vision. I know nothing about him."

"But you know him from past lives," said Kisi. "You are twins. You are opposite sides of the same coin."

"He gets his power by creating chaos," said Hadad. "He is completely unpredictable. You should avoid him."

"Where is he now?"

"Somewhere in the United States. Wisconsin, I think."

"Twins have a psychic link through all lifetimes," said Kisi. "Didn't you try to track him?"

"I did," said Hadad. "And he whammied me. He hit me so hard, I couldn't get inside his mind."

"Can you try again? It's really important."

"I'm afraid to try. He hit me so damn hard, I still haven't recovered."

"Did you know he attacked Lokesvara at Angkor Wat?"

"La Curandera told me."

"We think he'll try for the Watchtower of the West next, or perhaps even the Watchtower of the North. With you and La Curandera here, we don't have to worry about the south. And Lokesvara has secured the east. Yam is running out of energy, and we think he's desperate to get more."

"Yam isn't stupid. He learned a lesson at Angkor Wat."

"No," said Kisi, "he isn't stupid. But he is dangerous."

"That he is," said Hadad.

"Protect yourself. Both of you. He may try to come back here."

"Why would he do that?" asked Hadad.

"Jon thought he was looking for something at Machu Picchu. Power, yes. And control of the sun. But there was something else he looked for here that he didn't find. The man is ruthless and relentless. He will stop at nothing until he finds whatever it is he wants or needs."

"And what could that be?" asked Hadad.

"An essence of some kind. Or a memory. Jon said Yam tasted the hearts and minds of each of the sacrifices. None of the willing victims had exactly what he looked for and he kept looking, but he didn't find it. Maybe it doesn't exist. Or maybe one of the women or children he didn't taste sill has it."

"And that's why you think he'll come back here?"

"Yes."

"The remaining women and children have gone back home," said La Curandera. "If Yam does come back here and somehow wrestles control of the vortex away from me, it will take time to bring the sacrifices back. We can stop them before they get half-way up the mountain. He won't find what he's looking for here."

"Don't underestimate Yam," said Hadad. "He can be tricky."

"He is, indeed, a trickster," said La Curandera. "He is brother to the coyote and the snake."

"He can be charming and seductive, and then he'll stab you in the back," said Kisi. "Be careful, Hadad. He has killed you before in other lives, and he'll kill you again if he gets a chance."

"Don't worry about me," said Hadad. "I can take care of myself."

"Then, I'm off to warn the others," said Kisi. "Biegolmai next. Then Lokesvara. Then back to Wisconsin. If Yam comes at us, we'll be ready."

"Yes," said Hadad. "We'll all be ready."

*   *   *

Yam was waiting with another double whammy when Hadad tried to return to his own body. The spell hit Hadad hard, twice as powerful as the last time, and Hadad's spirit hurtled through time and space, flying, tumbling, falling, failing to find purchase with anything physical. Finally, the disembodied spirit came to rest in a dark place somewhere on the other side of the universe, far from anywhere.

While Hadad's spirit was traveling in Cambodia, Yam had secretly invaded Hadad's mortal shell at Machu Picchu and taken over Hadad's physical self. Though Hadad had sealed his body against walk-ins, Yam's energy signature was a twin to

Hadad's. The human body, unable to differentiate between the good twin and the evil twin, accepted Yam's spirit as its own.

As long as Yam's spirit inhabited Hadad's physical form, Hadad didn't need to worry about his mortal shell deteriorating from lack of spirit. Yam could, of course, place Hadad's human body in harm's way, and that body might be killed or otherwise damaged beyond repair. But the body wouldn't die of simple neglect.

What did worry Hadad was what Yam intended to do while residing inside Hadad's physical form. Yam now had access to the power of the vortex at Machu Picchu, and he would be entrusted with the secrets of the Guardians as long as La Curandera believed Yam was Hadad. Yam's next move would be to take La Curandera unawares, killing the mortal body she now occupied before she realized what was happening and could transfer her spirit elsewhere, perhaps into a passing condor or a serpent. If La Curandera had an inkling of what Yam was about to do, she could move her spirit to another body, human or animal, and survive in the physical realm even though her mortal shell might perish. But if her spirit were trapped within Kiyari's body at the very moment of death, her spirit would fly to the spirit realm to be cleansed, and then to wait for eventual rebirth into the physical realm in a newborn's body. But it took time for the body to give up the spirit after death. Sometimes spirits remained attached to the decaying body for as long as seventy-two hours.

So the worst-case scenario would be if La Curandera's essence remained trapped in Kiyari's body while her heart and brain were extracted and ingested by Yam. Then Yam could consume La Curandera's incredible knowledge and power and make it all his. Not only would he have access to all her thoughts and female energy, Yam's actions would delay La Curandera's entry to the spirit realm until her trapped spirit could be released from within Yam's own body. And that could only happen if Yam were killed. Until Yam died in the body he currently occupied—Hadad's body—Yam would be in complete control of the vortex at Machu Picchu, and he could continue with his former plans, undetected by the Guardians.

This time Hadad doubted he would find any beacon in the wilderness—any guiding light or sacred sound—to lead him back to his own time and place. He was lost in a space beyond the stars, literally in the middle of nowhere, and he was certain his spirit would remain trapped here in this vast emptiness and darkness until the very end of time.

But this time he did not despair. Maybe, he reasoned, if he tried hard enough for long enough he might discover some way to communicate with the Guardians back on earth.

And tell them they had to kill Hadad's mortal body if they wanted to stop Hadad's evil twin from gaining enough power to take control of the universe and live forever.

CHAPTER NINE

Kisi was uncomfortable. She had left Machu Picchu feeling something wasn't quite right, but she couldn't exactly put her finger on it although the uneasy feeling endured, became stronger. Her feminine intuition was sounding alarm bells that made the hair on the back of her neck stand straight up.

When she visited Biegolmai at the Seita, a pile of ancient rocks standing silent sentinel amid frozen tundras that covered the land of the Lapps in the northernmost reaches of Sweden near the Finnish border, she spoke of her feelings.

"First, tell me about Hadad," said Biegolmai. "Is he all right?"

"He'll be fine. He's still a little shaken up by a double whammy Yam threw at his spirit."

"Perhaps you were disturbed by the residue of evil Yam may have left behind at Machu Picchu."

"Perhaps. But what I sensed was not something old but something new, something current. Not a residue. Not something left behind, but something that was present in physical form. It was a resident evil that I sensed."

"Who else was there?"

"Hadad, myself, and La Curandera in her new body."

"Tell me about this new body of hers."

"Very pretty. Young."

"Did you sense the evil within her?"

"No. I sensed something else. Not evil, but strange. Something ancient and mystical. Very powerful."

"Perhaps you sensed La Curandera's spirit inside her."

"This was something different, something separate. I can't explain the feeling. It wasn't bad, just...different."

"What do we know about this girl?"

"Her name is Kiyari. La Curandera said Kiyari means moonlight in Quechua. The girl lived near Cusco with her parents and two sisters. Both of her younger sisters were sacrificed at Machu Picchu, but Kiyari was older, and she kept being shoved farther back in line. Fortunately, Jon and the Ranger stopped the sacrifices before Kiyari was killed."

"Let me ponder on this while you confer with Lokesvara. Tell him what you told me."

"You want me to go to Angkor Wat?"

"Yes. And say hi to Jon for me while you are there. Make it a point to talk to both Jon and Vajrapani. They may have noticed something helpful when they confronted Yam at Machu Picchu. Ask them."

"I will."

Kisi had known Jon Fish well in several previous lifetimes, and in some of those lifetimes she had also encountered and come to admire the man who now embodied the spirit of Vajrapani. Both men had long ago been warriors—brothers in arms—in the service of the Licchavi republic, residing in the capitol city called Vaishali in northeastern India on the north bank of the Ganges, not too far from modern-day Varanasi. Vaishali was capital of the Vajji Alliance, a confederation of eight great ruling clans, of which the Licchavi rajas were the most influential leaders of the Vajji Alliance. The year was 483 BCE, and Kisi's name had been Amrapali back then, more than 25 centuries ago. Because of her extraordinary beauty and many talents, the royal court made her the state courtesan and she was given the rare title *Vaishali Janpad Kalayani*. Her duties were to entertain at state dinners and other royal social functions. She was an accomplished dancer and a singer of great renown, and it was said her voice could charm the pants off any man. She spoke six languages, and she could read and write in all of them.

Amrapali was the glue that held the alliance together, for she had made the rulers of the warring clans promise peace in exchange for her smiles, and it was said men would do anything to see her smile. The chief Raja of the Licchavi considered Amrapali a national treasure. When visiting kings came to Vaishali,

Amrapali was sent to greet them. So it was that Amrapali met Prince Siddhartha Gautama of the Shakya clan, beloved son of King Suddhodana. The Prince and his entire retinue of 300 saffron-robed monks were invited to stay at Amrapali's mango grove estate, for Amrapali was also known as the Lady of the Mango Grove, and the estate had been given to her by grateful admirers.

Jon and the Ranger worked for the Senapati, the chief general of the Licchavi armies, and the Senapati had pledged loyalty to the Chief Raja of the Licchavi, King Chetaka Prasenajit, and the nine members of the ruling council. Only the most courageous and loyal of the Senapati's troops were assigned to guard the royal court and play bodyguard to the royal courtesan, and Jon and the Ranger were among those chosen to be Amrapali's bodyguards. Their residence became the mango grove at Kotagrama where Amrapali lived. Thus, it came to pass, that they also were present when Prince Siddhartha came to stay at the mango grove during the season of monsoons.

Jon's name at the time was Kripa Shestra, and the Ranger's name was Drona Bharadwaja.

It was no surprise that Amrapali and Kripa fell in love. They spent so much time together, talking and walking alone in the beautiful groves of ripening fruits, that love between two such accomplished and beautiful minds was inevitable. Drona, who was married to Kripa's sister Kripi, was happy for the couple, but he also was very worried they would be found out. For it was the duty of the royal courtesan to smile at all men, and to favor none. She was considered *nararvadhu*, the wife of the whole city of Vaishali, and she had been married to the state in a formal ceremony that declared her virginity was public property forever. If the Senapati or the Raja knew of the secret romance between Kripa and Amrapali, Kripa's life would immediately be forfeit and Amrapali disgraced, her estates forfeit.

When Prince Ajatasatru Kunika—whose very name meant "enemy yet to be born" and who was known as "the child with a sore finger"—of the neighboring Magadha Kingdom imprisoned his aging father King Bimbisara and mercilessly tortured the old man into revealing all the secrets of the kingdom and of the neighboring Vaishali Republic, Ajatasatru—who was Yam Elman in another incarnation—devised ways to divide and conquer the adjacent Vajji confederacy. He was aided in this coup by Devadatta, a cousin of Siddhartha Gautama. Ajatasatru knew from torturing his father, slashing the old man's arms and legs and pouring salt and boiling oil on the open wounds, that Amrapali was the key to unlocking the Alliance. For King Bimbisara had once been in love with Amrapali, and it was the charming and beautiful Amrapali who had elicited the promise of peace from Ajatasatru's father. In order to break the peace treaty between Magadha and Vajji, Ajatasatru searched for ways to discredit Amrapali.

Ajatasatru's spies watched the courtesan day and night until they uncovered not only the secret ongoing relationship between Amrapali and Kripa, but also the fact that the lovers had been influenced by the teachings of the Enlightened One, now known as Sakyamuni Buddha, during his recurring stays in the sacred mango grove at Kotagama. Though Amrapali continued to sing and dance and entertain visiting royalty the same as always, she had changed dramatically. Now she harbored thoughts of the emancipation of women—all women, including herself—and the equality of all sentient beings regardless of caste. Such thoughts were considered dangerous to the male rulers of India, for they threatened the very fabric of society and contradicted the teachings of the Vedas.

When Ajatasatru brought this to the attention of the Chief Raja and the Senapati, they refused to believe him. They called him a liar, and they initiated preparations for war between the two neighboring states by making alliances with Ajatasatru's brothers.

So Ajatasatru got the war he had wanted. He attacked Vaishali, and fierce battles ensued on both sides of the Ganges. Each side mustered more than 30,000 men, 3,000 elephants, 3,000 horses, and 3,000 war chariots complete with swinging maces and spinning wheels with sharp blades that rent asunder the Licchavi infantry as the chariots charged through the Licchavi ranks. The Magadhalean troops were likewise decimated and dismembered as the war went on and on.

Kripa and Drona, both renowned archers, were recalled into general service and sent to fight against the armies of

Magadha. Both Kripa and Drona were killed when Magadha's war elephants crossed the Ganges with thousands of troops following in the chariots of death as they charged through the Licchavi ranks and advanced on Vaishali itself.

After Kripa was killed, but before Ajatasatru could take the city of Vaishali, Amrapali renounced her royal titles and became a Buddhist nun, seeking sanctuary in the sangha, donating her lands and the fruiting mango groves to Gautama during his last visit to the city. Shortly after, Gautama achieved nirvana and it was said Amrapali pined away for all that she had lost.

Now, once again, Kisi and Jon were physically reunited. And, once again, they faced, in the present time and place, the common enemy that was the evil spirit now known as Yam Elman.

"Tell me more about this uneasy feeling you had at Machu Picchu," urged Lokesvara.

"I'm unable to describe it," said Kisi. "Something wasn't right. I have no idea what."

"Did you discuss this with La Curandera?"

"No."

"Why not?"

"It didn't seem important at the time."

"Tell me about Hadad. What was he like?"

"Not himself. Yam hit him with a double whammy."

"A double what?"

"It's a term western sorcerers use to describe a blow of incredible spiritual and physical power that knocks an opponent completely off his feet. It comes as such a shock that the opponent's senses are temporarily wiped out and the opponent is left helpless and vulnerable."

"That's what Yam did to Hadad?"

"Yes. And then Yam sent him away to the nether regions."

"How did he get back?"

"I don't know."

"I do," said Jon. "He said he heard our chant. He followed the vibrations back here. That's how he managed to warn us about Yam's attack. Fortunately, the Vajrapani mantra protected the vortex. Unfortunately, we were not ready in time to catch Yam before he escaped."

"Hadad was here? You spoke with him? He warned you about Yam's attack?"

"Yes. His spirit was here."

"That's not what Hadad said. He said he learned about the attack from La Curandera after he returned."

"Are you certain?" asked Lokesvara.

"Yes."

"Return to Machu Picchu immediately. Take Akashagarbha and Vajrapani with you. Hurry. Yam is in Hadad's body, and La Curandera is in danger. Go! Go!"

Kisi flashed out, and so did Jon and the Ranger. One minute they were there, and the next moment they were elsewhere.

*   *   *

La Curandera knew. She had suspected something was terribly wrong when Hadad said he didn't know what Yam was doing in Wisconsin, didn't know Yam coveted the vortex of the west. He said he hadn't seen his brother in years after telling her Yam had just hit him with a double whammy. Either Hadad's memory was radically altered by severe trauma, or the man was lying through his teeth. But when he said he hadn't informed Lokesvara about Yam's planned attack on Angkor Wat, she was fairly certain Hadad wasn't who he appeared to be.

Since Hadad was an Ascended Master and spiritual adept, she knew Hadad would never neglect to protect his body against walk-ins. Therefore, it had to be Yam's spirit in possession of Hadad's body because no other spirit could gain access. The psychic connection between twins made possession possible, especially when one of the twins was as powerful as Yam Elman and the other twin had been hit with a double whammy.

But La Curandera now faced a real dilemma. She possessed the power and the will to kill Hadad's body. That would trap Yam's spirit within Hadad's mortal shell until the physical body deteriorated and Yam's spirit fled to the spirit world. But

Yam's death wouldn't lift the spell of invisibility he had placed on the sun, and no one else but Yam knew how to do that.

So La Curandera waited and watched. She watched Hadad's body carefully for confirmation of her suspicions, she watched for any false move that might betray his intentions, and she watched closely for indications she was about to be attacked. But Hadad's body hadn't moved since Kisi had left. Yam just sat there in lotus, his eyes closed, his breathing regular. It was as if he were communing with the spirit of the condor that infused the rock he sat upon.

La Curandera suddenly knew what Yam was up to, and she instantly flashed out of there barely a moment before a huge condor swept down from the sky, passing harmlessly through the space where her body had been. La Curandera's spirit, and the nineteen-year-old body of Kiyari it now occupied, disappeared from Machu Picchu and reappeared in the living room of Diane Groves' house in Wisconsin.

Sara Nelson, Sheila Ryan, and Bryn Helgasdottir sat naked on the hardwood floor in front of the massive fireplace. Though one needn't be naked to spirit travel or work simple magic, allowing the bare flesh to come into contact with the earth or with bare wood or with certain metals or crystals potentiated magic and magnified one's power. When women— and men who were truly adept—did serious magic, they preferred to be naked.

Certain apparel performed similar functions. Magicians devised elaborate costumes that worked almost as well. Cone-shaped hats, especially ones decorated with rows of sun and moon symbols or runic inscriptions or Hebrew letters or pentagrams or hexagrams or eyes of Horus, were sometimes efficacious, and so were headdresses that contained feathers or crystals or precious jewels and stones. Robes made of pure cotton or lamb's wool or pure silk sometimes worked. But naked was best.

"Yam is at Machu Picchu. Yam now occupies Hadad's body, and he controls the vortex and the Intihuatana," said La Curandera.

"Why did you leave?" asked Sara. "Why did you not stay and fight? Why did you abandon the vortex to Yam?"

"I had to save the girl," said La Curandera. "If I had stayed and battled Yam, Kiyari's body would certainly have been damaged or killed."

"You could easily choose another body," said Sara. "What is so special about this one?"

"I'm not certain. Yam kept looking at Kiyari as if he wanted her."

"Perhaps it was lust. She is very young, and very beautiful."

"It was indeed lust, but not of the flesh. I believe Kiyari's essence was what he was looking for at Machu Picchu. I could not let him obtain it."

"At the expense of abandoning the vortex?"

"Yes."

"Tell us exactly what happened," said Bryn.

"I grew suspicious of Yam when he just sat there in the Temple of the Condor without moving. He was physically there but he wasn't really there because his spirit was in communication with the power of the condor. He called down a giant condor to attack me, and I barely escaped in time."

"Then he is more powerful than we suspected," said Bryn. "Men do not have the natural ability to commune with birds."

"He has stolen power from women," said La Curandera. "Over the millennia he has acquired feminine energy from many sources. The sacrifices at Machu Picchu gave a tremendous boost to that power."

"I still can't believe so many women voluntarily relinquished their life force energies to him. How could he get them to do that?"

"He played God," said Sara. "Women are spiritual beings who seek sacred union with the divine energy. The women who sacrificed themselves at Machu Picchu saw Yam as the manifestation of that divine masculine energy and were drawn to him like moths to a flame."

"I wouldn't do that," said Bryn. "Not in a million years. I wouldn't surrender my life energy to any man, not even a god."

"Nor I," said Sheila.

"Don't be too sure of that," said Sara. "Polarity rules all forces in nature. Opposites attract. Male energy attracts female energy and vice versa. Opposite polarities can exert incredible influence over each other, as you have seen often in each of your own lives. Polarity is what makes magic possible, because polarity is the underlying creative force of the universe. Male and female. Yin and Yang. Light and dark. Fire and ice. Positive and negative. Good and evil. Matter and ant-matter. Neither pole could exist without the other, and where their energies meet magic happens."

"When opposite polarities actually come in contact with each other," said La Curandera, "energy is altered—energy becomes matter or matter becomes energy—and the resultant shift in potential affects the entire universe. Our job, as Guardians, is to maintain a delicate balance between polarities so the dance of creation can continue. If energy shifts too far in one direction or the other for long periods of time, chaos results."

"That's what happened when Yam hid the sun," said Sara. "Without light to balance dark, many things on earth became unbalanced. Sleep patterns were disrupted, people lost track of time, some people lost their minds."

"As above, so below," said La Curandera. "Chaos here on earth is a reflection of things happening throughout the universe. That chaos feeds Yam's power."

"Every day until light returns to the earth, Yam's power increases," said Sara. "We must find a way to restore the sun."

"How can we do that?" asked Sheila. "Must we capture Yam and force him to bring the sun back?"

"Impossible," said La Curandera. "We must find another way."

"Anyone have any suggestions?" asked Sara.

"I believe Kiyari is the key," said La Curandera. "There is something inside her that can help return the sun, and that something is very powerful."

"What is it?" asked Bryn.

"I don't know yet," said La Curandera. "But I will search her memories until I find it."

*   *   *

Kisi hit what seemed like a stone wall, and she immediately bounced back to Angkor Wat. When she opened her eyes, she saw Jon, and the Ranger had returned to Angkor Wat, too.

"Something bad has happened," said Jon. "La Curandera no longer controls the vortex. We can't get through to Machu Picchu."

"Lokesvara is communicating with La Curandera," said the Ranger. "His spirit has left his body."

Kisi released her spirit and soared to the World Tree. There she found the spirits of La Curandera, Biegolmai, and Lokesvara.

"We couldn't get through," said Kisi.

"We know," said Biegolmai. "La Curandera had to abandon the vortex. Yam is now in control of Machu Picchu."

"And he controls Hadad's body," said La Curandera. "We are trying to locate Hadad's spirit, but his whereabouts eludes us."

"Akashagarbha can help," said Kisi. "He is master of time and space. If anyone can find Hadad, it is Akashagarbha."

"I will speak with Jon when I return to Angkor," said Lokesvara. "I'm sure Jon will want to help."

"Will Yam begin the sacrifices again?"

"Unless we stop him," said Biegolmai.

"The sacrifices will feed his power," said La Curandera. "But he will not find what he seeks at Machu Picchu. The real power is inside a girl called Kiyari. Her body is safely watched over by Sara and Bryn in Wisconsin."

"What is so special about Kiyari?"

"I have known her before," said La Curandera.

"Where?" asked Kisi. "And when?"

"Her name then was Uqllu. She was my sister. We lived in a cave called Pacaritambo, in the Tambotoco hills near Lake Titicaca. It was the time before the great flood, the Unu Pacha-cuti. There were eight of us: four brothers and four sisters. Kisi was also there."

"There have been so many lifetimes," said Kisi. "It takes time to remember them all."

"I will help you remember," said La Curandera. "See our father, the great Viracocha, dressed in a white robe and carrying a golden staff called Tapac-yauri. He is a tall white man with a white beard, and he may remind you of Biegolmai."

"I see him," said Kisi.

"Now see your brothers and sisters. There is Uqllu, a beautiful girl, not unlike you. That is Kiyari in a past life. Your name in that life is Huaco, mine is Cura, and Bryn's is Raua. Our brothers are called Ayar Cachi, Ayar Anca, Ayar Uchu, and Ayar Manco. Cachi is the Ranger, Anca is Jon, Uchu is Hadad, and Manco is Yam."

"Yam is our brother?"

"Yes. In this life and in many others. Yam was called either Ayar Manco or Urco in those days. Hadad was known as Ayar Uchu or Cusi Yupanqui. He was given the name Pachacutec, which means the one who changes the world. Because Ayar Uchu was a scholar of great intellect who preferred study over military training, Ayar Uchu became a teacher, and Ayar Manco became Capac, or warlord."

"I do remember," said Kisi. "Manco was mean and a bully."

"He hasn't changed much in ten millennia."

"But that was so very long ago, long before the Inca empire began."

"*We* were the beginnings of the Inca. The Inca were our descendants."

"Uqllu was a real treasure," said Kisi. "I do remember her now. She was a living doll. So sweet."

"Yes, she was."

"It's all coming back to me now," said Kisi.

"Then let the memories flow," said La Curandera.

And they did. Kisi was back there now, fully present in the highland valley at the very foot of the Andes. Her name was Huaco, and she was the daughter of Viracocha, and she had inherited her father's golden staff when her father left to walk across the sea. She lived in a cave in the hills above the valley, and she had three sisters and four brothers. Two of the sisters, one brother, and herself were dabblers in the mystic arts, and they traveled far and wide studying and learning and performing magic. Sister Cura was a healer, and she often went into the Amazon jungle for long periods of time where she discovered trees and herbs with miraculous curative powers, and even some plants that could poison and kill instead of heal. Sister Uqllu was mistress of the Pururaucas, and she knew the mystery of making living men from solid stone. Brother Uchu had left the sacred valley, and like his father before him, had walked over the big waters to the many lands far to the west where he had studied with the Lao Tsu, great master-teachers of the orient. It was there that he learned to move mountains, and to turn lead and tin into gold. On his return, he would teach the natives on many of the islands to carve apu from stone to honor Con-Tici

Viracocha. Sometimes he also taught those natives how to move those stones with their minds.

Huaco spoke to the spirits of the stones and the spirits in the rivers and lakes, and she and sister Uqllu, were made Coya, leaders of women, and they were priestesses of the moon goddess and they oversaw the magic of the Moon Temple. They faithfully performed the sacraments of Mama Quilla, Mother Moon, and they supervised the plantings of corn and the husbanding of animals according to the divinings of the moon. They taught women how to cook and preserve food, to spin thread from alpaca wool and to weave that thread into cloth, and they taught women to midwife and all about menstruation and when to get pregnant and how to prevent pregnancy and how to heal the sick or injured. Huaco and Uqllu and Cura were known far and wide as miracle workers.

And they taught women to fight. Sister Raua was a warrior born, and she fought alongside men and won many battles. It was said she was as fierce a warrior as two of her valiant brothers, Ayar Cachi and Ayar Anca. Brother Ayar Ucho was an Amawtakuna, a philosopher and scholar, too much of an intellectual to be bothered with fighting. And brother Ayar Manco was a coward and a thief.

Raua was captain of her own army, and she was renowned for her ability with the ayllo or haybinto, three stone balls tied with alpaca thread that was a precursor to the boleadoras. She was also an excellent archer, and she could handle a sword as well as any man.

One fateful day Raua rushed into the Temple of the Moon and asked her three sisters for help. "Quickly, my sisters," Raua begged. "Manco has allied our enemies against us. He seeks to subjugate us and steal our secrets. Cachi and Anca are fighting valiantly, but they are being overwhelmed by sheer numbers."

"Is there none that will fight with us?" asked Cura.

"None. Manco has stolen the Tapac-yauri and uses the golden staff to put the fear of Viracocha in them. All our neighbors fight against us."

"Then I will organize the women," said Cura. "And dress them for battle."

"Uqllu and I will speak to the stones," said Huaco. "Raua, can you gather up all of the army uniforms you can find? All of the colorful cloth that we have woven and dyed and embroidered? Bring them to the standing rocks on the plain where we will be talking to the stones."

"Why?" asked Raua. "Why waste time while the battle rages?"

"Because," said Huaco, "we are going to build an army, an invincible army. Uqllu, bring those pots. The ones Cura just brewed from plants she brought from the Amazon."

"But they are filled with poison," protested Uqllu.

"Precisely," said Huaco. "We shall dip our swords and arrows in the poison pots."

Surrounding the field of battle were hundreds of standing stones. Each of those stones contained an Apu, a spirit of the holy mountain from which they had come. Raua and the women warriors dressed the stones in the battledress uniforms of the day while Cura dipped arrows and swords in pots of poison.

Then Huaco and Uqllu spoke to the spirits of the mountain residing in the stones, and the stones came alive. Dressed in military uniforms and carrying swords and bows, they obeyed Huaco's orders to march forth into battle.

The women warriors joined Anca and Cachi fighting to protect the temple. Cachi, wearing the copper mask of Illapa, roared like thunder as he valiantly charged into the foe and slew enemy right and left. Anca seemed to be everywhere, moving in and out of enemy formations like a wraith, leaving a train of death and destruction in his path. Raua entered the fray with her bolas and sword, followed by dozens of women warriors who fought like men.

Huaco and Uqllu directed the stone warriors at the wave of advancing enemy soldiers. Though they moved stiffly and awkwardly, the warriors of stone could not be killed, and they slowly cut a path through enemy ranks so Anca and Cachi and Raua could reach the tribal leaders directing the battle from the rear. Hearing Cachi's mighty roar, seeing throngs of advancing stone soldiers armed with poisoned weapons, the leaders fled. First among those to flee was Ayar Manco.

The enemy troops, those still able, followed their leaders. They threw down their weapons and ran as fast as their legs could carry them. The stone army pursued the enemy, chasing them past the banks of the Urubamba into the hills beyond.

That night there was a great celebration in the Temple of the Moon where brews of barley and corn were consumed in large amounts and brothers and sisters, husbands and wives, embraced. Cura and her apprentices had tended to the wounded, and the spirits of the dead had been released when their bodies were consumed by fire on the sacred pyre.

"You did well today, my sisters," said Ayar Anca. He embraced each of his sisters in turn, kissing them full on the lips. "How did you learn to fight like that?"

"We women have many secrets," said Cura.

"Apparently," said Anca.

"Manco has betrayed us," said Huaco. "What shall we do with him should we find him?"

"He is too dangerous to let live," said Ayar Cachi.

"He is our brother," said Cura. "I cannot kill my brother."

"He is no longer a brother to me," said Cachi.

"Nor to me," said Anca.

"We should let Ucho decide," said Huaco. "When he returns from his travels, he will be impartial. He was not here to experience the hatred."

"And he is wise," said Uqllu. "He can see things we cannot."

"Then we will wait," said Cachi. "Now put Manco from your minds. Tonight we celebrate our victory."

They danced the night away, drinking and embracing and frolicking. Many babies were conceived that night.

When dawn came, the revelers walked—if they were able to walk—to their homes in the hills. They were still cave dwellers in those days, and Ayar Cachi lived in a cave not far from his ancestral home. From the mouth of the cave, he could see the sun rise over the mountains, casting ominous shadows over the entire valley.

Tired and sore from the ferocious battles he had fought the day before, half-drunk from consuming more brew than he had intended, he fell into a deep and dreamless sleep. When he awoke, he discovered the cave entrance was blocked with heavy stones, boulders from the hills that had been moved down in the night with great stealth. After Cachi entered the cave at dawn, hundreds of men pulled those rocks into place with ropes, sealing Cachi inside. His home had now become his tomb, and he was alone in the darkness with no hope of ever seeing the sun again.

Meanwhile, sister Huaco and brother Anca were embracing in the fields as was the custom of their people. Love between brother and sister was not only condoned but encouraged.

Suddenly, Ayar Anca stiffened and went rigid. His entire body became hard as a rock. Ayar had turned to stone, and Huaco's caresses went unnoticed.

Because she could talk to spirits trapped in stone, Huaco heard her brother's voice telling her he was alone in the darkness. "I am here, my love," she replied. "I am still with you."

"I cannot see you. I can hear your sweet voice, but I cannot see you."

"Who did this to you?"

"Only one man has the power."

"Manco?"

"It must be Manco. Somehow, he has stolen magic from the temple and uses it against us. He wants to create an empire and become king, and he sees us as all that stands in his way."

"How do we undo what he has done?"

"We cannot."

"Your spirit is trapped within the stone?"

"Forever."

"No!" cried Huaco. "I will find a way to free you."

"There is no way."

"There must be. I will find a way. If it takes forever, I will find a way to free you."

Suddenly, the scene faded from Kisi's mind's eye, and Kisi was fully back in the present. The memory remained, but the emotional intensity gradually faded, along with the images.

"Manco, I mean Yam," Kisi told La Curandera, "imprisoned Jon's spirit in stone. We've got to do something!"

"Relax," said La Curandera. "Hadad released Jon and the Ranger more than ten millennia ago. Hadad learned much during his sojourn in the orient, and when he returned from his travels he was a very powerful magician. He, with help from his sisters, tracked down Yam and killed him. Yam has never forgiven his brother for that."

"You recovered those memories?" asked Kisi.

"Only recently. Like you, I have some memories that are very ancient and more difficult to recall. Kiyari helped me remember."

"I was about to remember when something drew me back to the present," said Kisi.

"You felt a subtle shift in energies," said Biegolmai. "As did we. The universe is changing again. Yam's power has just increased exponentially."

"How? What has happened that made Yam more powerful?"

"Chaos," said Biegolmai. "Chaos is replacing order in the universe. Yam has disrupted human perception of order by hiding the sun, and it has taken days to build momentum. But now people doubt what they once knew to be true. The sun no longer rises and sets, the moon has become divorced from the sun, and darkness rules the earth. Human beliefs have been shattered, people distrust other people, hopes have become fears. All this feeds Yam's power."

"And," added La Curandera, "Yam has begun taking sacrifices again at Machu Picchu. He has called women and children back to the mountain to take their life-force energies."

"Can we stop him?" asked Kisi. "Surely, there must be some way to stop him."

"Perhaps," said Lokesvara. "I am returning to Angkor Wat. Send Bryn to me. It is time to put a stop to this madness."

"What can you do?" asked Kisi.

"Watch me," said Lokesvara. "And learn."

BOOK II

"Quis custodiet ipsos custodies?"

"Who watches the Watchmen?"

"Who guards the Guardians?"

--Juvenal. Satire 6. 346-348

"Turning and turning in the widening gyre
The falcon cannot hear the falconer;
Things fall apart; the centre cannot hold;
Mere anarchy is loosed upon the world,
The blood-dimmed tide is loosed, and everywhere
The ceremony of innocence is drowned;
The best lack all conviction, while the worst
Are full of passionate intensity."

--William Butler Yeats. *The Second Coming.*

CHAPTER TEN

B ryn Helgasdottir and the Lone Ranger dropped out of the sky at 28,000 feet. They descended on the wind, buoyed up by nylon parachute canopies that they had deployed shortly after they had materialized over the Andes.

This was old hat for the Ranger. He had been trained to jump out of perfectly good airplanes, and he had successfully completed hundreds of such jumps in the past. Some of them had been night jumps, and he knew what to do in the dark.

But this was something new for Bryn. The Ranger had given her expert instructions, and she had practiced her landings by jumping off the third story balcony of the main temple at Angkor and rolling to the ground. She was proud of the way she handled the riggings during the actual descent, and proud of her courage. She was reminded that great pride often preceded a great fall, and suddenly she was unsure of herself.

Kisi had appeared in Wisconsin and said Lokesvara wanted Bryn in Cambodia, and Bryn had gone immediately to Angkor Wat where Lokesvara explained what he wanted her to do. Lokesvara had already sent Akashagarbha to search for Hadad's spirit in the far reaches of outer space, and the Ranger needed a battle-ready companion to attack Yam in his stronghold at Machu Picchu. Because Yam's control of the vortex shielded the top of the mountain from other spirits teleporting in or out, they had to materialize outside of the cone of protection and glide in from the north. Lokesvara had procured parachutes and weapons.

Bryn and the Ranger were armed with two each Heckler and Koch P2000 semi-automatic pistols in nine millimeter carried in leather holsters, and they each had a Heckler and Koch MP5K submachine gun slung across their chests. They carried additional magazines with more than enough ammunition to stop an army.

Bryn was a warrior born, and she knew how to fire the weapons. Unlike the Ranger, she had no compunction about killing. If she had a chance to kill Yam, she wouldn't hesitate.

She couldn't see the peak of Machu Picchu coming up at her from below in the darkness, but she followed the Ranger's instructions and toggled the steering lines to glide silently in through the clouds. She trusted in her instinct and her intuition to direct her to the landing site.

Now she could see the central plaza and the terraces of Machu Picchu, lit by torchlight, and she guided the chute to put her down in the plaza. She hit the ground hard, and for a moment she was disoriented. She dropped and rolled, and came up in a fighting stance looking for opposition.

When no one came at her, she unbuckled the chute, folded it as best she could, and tucked it behind a wall of rocks.

"This way," said the Ranger. He was out of his chute, and he held the Heckler and Koch submachine gun in his huge hands. He was dressed in camouflage fatigues and combat boots, and he seemed perfectly at home carrying weapons.

"It was as exhilarating as you said it would be," Bryn admitted.

"The jump? You must be an adrenalin junkie like me," said the Ranger.

"I guess I am," said Bryn.

"Good," said the Ranger. "Everything we do today involves risk. You'll get your fill before we're done. Just don't let it go to your head. Okay?"

"Don't worry. I know how to watch my back."

"I need you to watch mine," said the Ranger. "Lokesvara put me in charge, and I expect you to follow orders."

Bryn bristled. She wasn't used to taking orders from a man.

"C'mon, then," said the Ranger. "We have to climb up to reach the sacred plaza where Yam is doing the sacrifices."

Bryn unstrapped the machine gun from across her chest and followed the Ranger up the hill. She was surprised how hard it was to catch her breath, and each step uphill seemed harder than the last. If her muscles ached for rest already, what would it be like when she had to exert herself in combat?

Now they could see torches and long lines of women and children slowly advancing across the central plaza to jam the stone stairs that led up to the sacred altar. Realizing he'd never get through that bottleneck, the Ranger cut straight across the closely-cropped grass—grass chewed almost to the roots by grazing llamas—and dashed straight into the sacred plaza. Above them rose the stone stairs leading to the Temple of the Sun and the Intihuatana.

This time the Ranger rushed in with his guns blazing, bullets ricocheting off stones behind where the man in the golden mask stood holding a dagger raised above the chest of a naked woman. Other women were lined up on the stairs coming into the plaza, and a dozen or so women were standing at the head of the line eagerly removing their clothing. To Bryn, these women looked little different than women she had seen waiting in doctors' offices or free clinics to get mammograms.

Bryn followed the Ranger into the enclosure, looking for targets. She saw no armed men, and she held her fire.

"You again!" shouted the man in the golden mask, dropping his knife.

"We have to stop meeting like this," said the Ranger. "Surrender, or you're toast."

"You would kill an unarmed man?"

"If I had to. I have done it before, and I will do it again."

"Then be damned!" shouted the man in the golden mask, and he disappeared.

Suddenly, Bryn was attacked by dozens of angry women. They swarmed around her like ants around a half-empty Pepsi can left behind after a picnic in the woods. Though she was well armed, she didn't want to kill innocent women. She tried valiantly to fend them off with her fists.

But there were far too many of them. They tore at her hair, at her face, at her clothing. They wrestled the Heckler and Koch from her hands and turned it against her.

The Ranger shot the woman holding Bryn's gun. He fired a short burst that peppered the woman's arm and made her drop the gun. Blood spattered the torsos of other women, and several of the women screamed.

Bryn broke free. She hit one woman in the face and kicked another in the knee.

Suddenly, La Curandera materialized inside the sacred plaza in the form of Kiyari. She spoke a few words in Quechua, and the women backed off.

"What did you say?" asked Bryn.

"I told them the Ranger was the true eagle of the north, and that you were the condor of the south. You came to save them from false gods."

"They believed you?" asked the Ranger.

"I created a doubt in their minds. It was enough." La Curandera said some more words to the women, and they looked to the Ranger for confirmation.

"Let Vajrapani appear," said La Curandera. "Show them your power and they will go home peaceably."

Suddenly, the Ranger seemed to grow to gigantic proportions. Gone now were the camouflage garments and boots of the soldier, replaced with the robes and sandals of the Bodhisattva. In his right hand he held the Vajra and in his left hand the Kris.

Winds howled. Thunder boomed and lightning flashed. Dark clouds rolled in from the north and the entire mountain was deluged with pelting rain that extinguished the torches and drove the women back down the mountain.

"Illapa," whispered the women as they retreated. "Illapa."

"What does Illapa mean?" asked the Ranger as he resumed his human shape.

"Illapa was the Incan god of weather," said La Curandera. "The son of Viracocha and the brother of Inti, ruler of the sun."

"I want to thank you," said Bryn. "Both of you. Thank you for saving me from those harpies."

"No, thank *you* for giving me back the vortex."

"Where did Yam go?" asked the Ranger.

"Back to Wisconsin," said La Curandera. "Bryn should follow him. I have the feeling Sara and the others will need her help."

"Any word yet on Hadad?" asked the Ranger.

"No," said La Curandera. "He's out there somewhere, and Akashagarbha is searching for him."

"Wherever he is, Akashagarbha will find him," said the Ranger. "It may take time, but Akashagarbha will find him."

"We may not have much time left," said La Curandera. "The sun has been hidden for more than three days, and many people are at their breaking points already."

*   *   *

People were starting to act really crazy. The Public Defender's office had asked Sheila to represent a man who had killed his wife and four children, and another man who had taken his deer rifle and set up a hunting blind over the expressway to fire hundreds of 30-30 rounds at passing cars, killing three people and causing dozens of accidents. She had heard stories of mothers who had poisoned their infants and then themselves, neighbors who had butchered neighbors, and people who had driven their automobiles off cliffs. Several people were arrested for public indecency—they had removed all their clothes and paraded naked through downtown streets—and other people were walking around speaking gibberish. Sanity was a tenuous thing. When sanity lost its moorings to common, everyday events that defined reality, sanity drifted away on the waves of repressed emotions, floated away on the tides of despair.

Sheila had telephoned Sam Elman back and left a message in his voice mail, telling him she would not be able to represent him. Elman had not yet returned her call.

On this fifth day of darkness, Sheila had encountered little or no traffic on the drive into town. Many of the stores were closed, and people appeared fearful of the few people they did encounter. It seemed the absence of daylight had eroded human trust, and life-long friends barely spoke a civil word to each other, if they spoke at all.

Sheila had a television in her office, and she spent an hour or two flipping through cable news networks. People were acting strange all over the world, and large city police departments were unable to cope with the rashes of violence that were erupting daily. Political hotspots had heated up to the boiling point, and places like the middle-east and some parts of Africa were engaging in open warfare. The United Nations had declared a state of emergency in Palestine.

Scientists still had no reasonable explanation for what had happened to the sun, and they cautioned people not to jump to conclusions.

Some religious leaders and a few fringe cults prophesized the end of the world or visits by aliens—some friendly, some not so friendly—from the darkest regions of outer space. Fox news did an entire segment on theories of alien invasions, interviewing psychiatrists who debunked such theories as pure paranoia and conspiracy theorists who claimed the government was covering up the fact that aliens had visited us many times in the past.

The world had always been a scary place for a lot of people, but the rules of civilization had made that scary place appear manageable. Now some of those rules seemed no longer to apply, and people had become so afraid of the dark that they were acting irrationally.

Sheila was about to close up the office and go home when two men entered and pointed guns at her. Both men were big, dressed in camouflage hunting jackets and matching caps. One had a hunting rifle and the other a shotgun. Sheila knew better than to move.

"We're going to take a little ride," said the shorter of the two men. He had a week's growth of brown beard on his face, and he had a thick neck like a man who lifted weights. "Stand up so my friend can tie your hands."

Sheila didn't try to argue. She stood and held out both hands. The taller man—not much more than a teenager—took a length of clothesline from his jacket pocket and wrapped it tightly around Sheila's wrists, fastening the ends with double square knots like a Boy Scout or a sailor might do. Then he tied another length of rope around her neck like a leash and practically dragged her outside to a waiting pick-up truck, a blue Dodge Ram 3500. She got into the front seat between the two men.

They drove southeast out of town, heading towards Park Falls on a state highway. After about eight or nine miles, they left the highway and followed an old fire trail deep into the woods. The fire trail dead-ended in front of an old moss-encrusted log cabin. Sheila saw the glow of a kerosene lamp through the window.

The men hauled her inside the cabin, and shoved her into a chair next to a small wooden table. Two other men were seated on the other side of the table.

"Welcome, Sheila Ryan," said one of the men sitting at the table. Sheila recognized the voice as Sam Elman's. His face was badly scarred, and one eye was missing.

The other man looked dead or asleep.

"I'm Sam Elman, and this is my brother Hadad. Hadad is traveling right now, and he left his body with me for safekeeping."

"What do you want with me?" asked Sheila.

"You made me angry," said Elman. "I was told you were the best attorney in the county, and you hurt my feelings when you refused to represent me."

"So you kidnapped me because I hurt your feelings?"

"Yes," said Elman. "And because I know who you are."

"Who am I?"

"You are the beloved sister-in-law of Diane Groves, aren't you? I didn't know that when I asked you to represent me, but I know it now. You live in the same house with Diane Groves, and you share her secrets."

"Yes, I do live in the same house with Diane."

"What do you suppose she would be willing to give up to get you back?"

"You want that property bad enough to kidnap me?"

"Oh, yes. Bad enough to kill you if she doesn't turn the property over to me within twenty-four hours."

Sheila believed him. She had heard many men testify in court, and she could usually tell when a man was lying. Elman wasn't lying. She knew she would be dead within twenty-four hours. But Elman would kill her even if Diane gave him the vortex. He had already made up his mind. She was a dead woman walking.

Death didn't particularly worry her. She knew she would someday be reborn in a new body, and she knew she could recover her memories in a new life. She had done it many times in the past, and she expected to do it many times in the future.

She would regret leaving this life behind. She had only recently found the man of her dreams, and she knew Tom would be devastated to lose her. But she also knew they would meet again, as they had in the past. They were soul mates, and their spirits were linked in love through all eternity. Not even death could keep them apart.

"Now here's the plan," said Elman. "You behave your-self, and you get to go back to your office as soon as Diane vacates and I'm ensconced on the property. But if you make trouble, I'll make you so sorry you'll wish you were never born. Do you understand me?"

"Yes."

"Good. Henry?" Elman beckoned to one of the other men, and the younger man came forward. "Will you please de-liver my message to Ms. Groves? The only way you can get on the property is to drive up the firebreak. Drive all the way up to the house and give the message to Ms. Groves."

"Then what?" asked Henry.

"Then get the hell out of there."

"Come back here?"

"Yes."

"What if they follow me?"

Elman laughed. "Let them. They can find us whenever they want. In fact, I expect they'll find me before you get back. They can watch us and we won't know they're there. But they can't touch us."

"Why not?"

"Because I am far too powerful. If they try to get close to me, I'll whammy them. I'll knock them for a loop that will send them so far away they'll never find their way back."

"You can do that?"

"I can. Do you see my brother sitting there? That's just his body. His real self went bye-bye."

"Jeez!"

"Now, be a good boy and go deliver the message. Come back when it's done."

After Henry left, Elman showed Sheila where she could sleep. "When you need to visit the outhouse, George will go with you. He'll wait outside the door. You know I can find you if you try to escape, so don't even try. Be a good girl and you'll go home in one piece. Cause trouble, and you'll go home in pieces. Oh, and I'll keep a piece of you as a souvenir, a trophy. I'll eat your heart and suck out your brains. You know what that means, don't you?"

"No. What does it mean?"

"It means I'll take your life force and keep you from ever reincarnating."

"You can do that?" Sheila asked, not wanting to believe it could be true.

"I can, and I will," said Elman. "I can, and I will."

*　*　*

Bryn had rejoined Kisi, Sara, and Diane in front of the fireplace. She had just finished relating the events at Machu Picchu when they heard a vehicle drive down the firebreak toward the house.

There was a lone man behind the wheel, and he didn't appear armed. He parked the Dodge pick-up ten feet from the door, left the motor running and the headlights on, and walked up to the porch. Diane opened the door before he could knock.

"Ms. Groves?" asked the man.

"Yes?" said Diane.

"I've been asked by a Mr. Samuel Elman to deliver a message. Sheila Ryan is Mr. Elman's guest and will remain his guest for the next twenty-four hours. He promises to deliver Ms. Ryan to you, unharmed, in exchange for this property. He instructed me to give you this pre-paid cell phone to contact him with your response. Should you decline, or decide to ignore Mr. Elman's kind offer, Mr. Elman will deliver parts of Ms. Ryan to you at the place and time of his choosing. He invites you to verify that Ms. Ryan is indeed his guest."

"Cell phones don't work on this land."

"Mr. Elman is aware of that. He says you will need to leave the property to call him. He promises you that he will allow you to do that, but he will monitor your movements. Do you understand what I have just told you?"

"Yes," said Diane. "I understand that Elman has abducted Sheila and is holding her hostage to get my land. I also understand that Elman will kill her if I don't give him my land. Did I get that right?"

"Yes, Ma'am. You have twenty-four hours from right now to get off the property."

"Tell Mr. Elman that he'll have my answer in twenty-four hours. Now you get off my property, you little piece of shit, before I tear you apart."

"I'm only the messenger," said the boy, backing off the porch. "Don't kill the messenger."

Diane remained on the porch until the Ram's taillights faded in the distance. Then she calmly reentered the house and told the others.

Sara immediately scouted out Elman's energy signature, while Kisi went to the World Tree to inform Biegolmai, La Curandera, and Lokesvara. Bryn tried to comfort Diane with words, but words didn't work.

"I can't let Sheila die," said Diane. "I can't!"

"We won't let her die," said Bryn. "We'll get her back safe and sound."

"How? How can we do that?"

"Sara and Biegolmai and Lokesvara and La Curandera will think of something."

"What about Hadad? What did Yam do with Hadad?"

"Akashagarbha is looking for him. If anyone can find Hadad, it's Jon."

"I can't give up this land," said Diane. "There's too much at stake."

"Sheila wouldn't want you to do that. She'd rather die than let Yam have the vortex."

"But it's not just death. Yam will cut her up, eat her heart, and steal her essence. She'll never come back, Bryn. She'll be gone for good. She's family, Bryn. She's *my* family. I'd never forgive myself if I let that happen. My brother would never forgive me, either."

Sara returned to her body. "Yam has Sheila in a cabin about twenty-five miles from here," said Sara. "Sheila is unharmed. Yam has set wards and cast a spell of protection. I couldn't penetrate that cone of power to reach Sheila's mind to reassure her we would rescue her. But she's alive. And she looks calm. She's a brave woman."

"I think she knows," said Bryn.

"She knows," said Diane. "She is a strong spirit. She'd rather die than have us surrender the vortex."

"Tell us about this cabin in the woods where Yam holds Sheila," asked Bryn.

"It's an old cabin, recently rebuilt and reinforced. I think it is where Yam lived two hundred years ago when he tried to get this property from Emma Wells and her mother. The cabin is set back in the woods at the end of a fire trail. It's mid-growth forest, mixed pine and hardwood."

"How many men does Yam have with him?"

"I saw one. Plus the messenger who is on his way back to the cabin."

"Are they armed?"

"A few rifles and shotguns."

"Then the Ranger and I could take them."

"No," said Sara. "You surprised Yam at Machu Picchu, and he wasn't prepared to defend himself against bullets from the two of you. Yam expects to be attacked at the cabin. It's a trap. He has spells already in place, and all he needs to do is say the word and the spells activate. He can defend that place against an army. If we try to go in, he'll whammy us to kingdom come."

"And he holds Sheila hostage," said Diane. "He may have set a spell in place particularly for her, or she might be caught in a crossfire. We don't dare attack him with bullets or magic. We'll have to think of something else."

"What else is there?" asked Bryn.

"Hadad," said Sara. "Yam is back in his own body, and Hadad's empty body is just sitting there waiting for Hadad's spirit to return. If Akashagarbha can find Hadad in time, Hadad can fight Yam from inside the cone of power."

"But where is Hadad's spirit? And how will Akashagarbha find him in the vastness of time and space?"

"I don't know," said Sara. "We can only pray that he does."

* * *

Jon Fish was awed by the complexity of the universe. Akashagarbha could see both the macro and the micro universes, much as a scientist could see inside living cells with the help of electron microscopes and astronomers could penetrate the incredible distances between star systems with refracting telescopes. Matter and energy interacted on multiple levels, and vibrations begun billions of years ago still reverberated somewhere. Every action had a cause and every action had an effect, and this universe and many others were intimately interrelated. What happened in one place and time affected what happened in many other places and times.

Yam's actions on earth had far-reaching effects in every corner of the universe. Akashagarbha found Yam's influences reverberating from ancient Peru, Mesopotamia, India, Tibet, China. Egypt. Turkey. Iceland. The United States. Hadad's influences were less obvious, less earth-shattering, but they were also there. Hadad was reluctant to exercise power, and his reticence had often led to his death.

Yet he had made contributions that often offset Yam's intrusions with more subtle changes in the fabric of creation. He had mended holes and tears his brother had caused, blended together colors and shapes, and woven a design that was both meaningful and utilitarian. Hadad had acquired many of the secrets of the universe and he had left behind a message and a permanent record.

It was written in cuneiform, the wedge-shaped symbols of Sumeria and Akkadia. Unfortunately, neither Akashagarbha nor Jon Fish could read ancient Akkadian.

Akashagarbha continued the search for Hadad across time and space, following energy trails that were as old as time itself. Where, oh where, has the little lost lamb gone?

Akashabarbha had systematically scoured the known universe, and now he headed for the farthest reaches of space and time itself. Matter did not exist here, only energy in its purest forms. It was filled with potential, but none of that potential had yet been actualized.

This was a part of the universe where light hadn't yet penetrated. It was the land of perpetual primordial darkness. It was a land totally without form. It was the void, the ein sof, the limitless nothing.

For this was a place without spirit. It was an unfertilized egg, a stem cell, a place without reason or purpose.

Theoretically, it didn't yet exist but only had the potential of existence. And nothing that did exist could enter that space without changing it forever and being changed by it.

If Hadad's spirit were trapped in that void, it had lost all memory. It wouldn't be able to recall any of its past lives, and all that Hadad had learned over the millennia would be gone, wiped clean like a blackboard at the end of class. Only Akashagarbha had the power to enter that place and not be forever changed. For he was the Boundless Space Matrix, the mother and father of nothingness, and his spirit was kin to the void. The darkness and despair that existed there existed also inside him, and Jon Fish had experienced it personally after his brother died in Afghanistan, his mother had died of cancer, and his father had deserted the family. Jon had left the Corps to take care of his mother, and he was unable to find a job—any job—in Rockford, Illinois where unemployment was constantly in the double digits. Evicted from his family home for failure to pay the mortgage, Jon was reduced to committing burglaries and robbing pedestrians in order to survive. And survive was all he had done, allowing himself to slide into a deep depression that destroyed his self-esteem and pushed him to the brink of suicide.

Lokesvara had saved him. Lokesvara had taught Jon Fish how to meditate and how to recall past lives. Jon learned from Lokesvara how to astral-travel, to teleport, and to manifest the spirit of Askashagarbha.

Jon Fish eventually returned to the Marine Corps he loved so much, and he became a drill instructor of new recruits at the San Diego recruit station. But if it hadn't been for Lokesvara, Jon Fish would today be a derelict drunk or dead.

Lokesvara embodied the spirit of Manjusri, the Bodhisattva of Wisdom. When Manjusri went into battle, he carried the flaming sword of transcendent wisdom in his right hand and the sutras in his left. It was said that Manjusri and his companion Samantabhadra had together conquered death, and Samantabhadra had gone on to a pure land and had become a Buddha, while Manjusri returned to earth as a Bodhisattva in order to teach the dharma to all who would hear.

Jon wished Manjusri were here now. He could easily summon Lokesvara across time and space, but Lokesvara had assigned this mission to Akashagarbha, and it was Jon's mission to complete.

So he ventured into the void, disturbing the previously undisturbed primal soup. Even in his discarnate form, Jon could feel the fear formlessness caused. For here, there was no order, no direction, no up or down, no right or left. Everything was new and unknown, and not even Akashagarbha had experienced anything like it before.

Darkness went on forever. There was no beginning and no end to it.

But Akashagarbha's patience was boundless, and he continued to search every square inch of nothingness. If Hadad's spirit wasn't here, it wasn't anywhere.

Could immortal spirits disappear completely? Jon didn't think so.

Hadad had to be here someplace. If his body had died, Hadad's spirit would have gone directly to the spirit realm where it would be cleansed and prepared for rebirth. But Yam had kept the body alive by possessing it, and Hadad's body still breathed, his blood still circulated, his heart still beat. So Hadad's spirit had to be here, hidden in the darkness.

Akashagarbha continued on relentlessly, his spirit searching out another eternal spirit in the total darkness of the void. If two soul mates could find each other again after centuries of separation, surely two kindred spirits could find each other in the dark.

Or perhaps not. Just as opposites could attract, so could likes repel. Even in the void at the far end of the universe, polarity played a role. If Akashagarbha could reverse his polarity, he might be guided straight to Hadad like a compass pointing north.

Jon went deep inside himself and recalled the many times he had lived as a woman. Balanced spirits had nearly equal amounts of masculine and feminine life force, and they often alternated between male and female bodies in successive lives. What they learned as a man remained with them forever, and so did what they learned as a woman.

As Akashagarbha slowly reversed polarities, he felt a gradual pull drawing him across the void toward an undisclosed destination.

And there was Hadad's spirit.

Akashagarbha attached Hadad's spirit to his own, and in less than a heartbeat they were back in the real world, in Lokesvara's chamber at Angkor Wat.

As Jon returned to his body, he released Hadad's spirit. But the freed spirit did not return to Hadad's body. It remained in the room with Jon and Lokesvara.

"Why is he still here?" asked Jon.

"He has been changed," said the old monk. "He is not the same Hadad we knew. He has lost all reference to what he once was."

"How can that be?"

"He was in the void much too long, and the void drained him of all substance."

"What can we do to restore his substance?"

"We would need a way to re-implant his memories, to return knowledge to his spirit of who he was and what he accomplished. We can tell him what we remember of him, and that will be a start. But what we need is a way to give him back the knowledge that he had acquired over the millennia. That would take something like a written record of his accomplishments. Of course, such a record doesn't exist."

"But it does exist. I saw it."

"Where?"

"On the wall of time. It was written in cuneiform."

"Show me."

"Can we leave him? Will he be okay?"

"We'll take him with us." Lokesvara became pure spirit and touched Hadad's spirit, linking it to him. "Now show me."

Together they went to the wall of time and read what was written there.

CHAPTER ELEVEN

S heila Ryan waited for the inevitable to happen. She knew she needed to be ready to move instantly when her friends came for her, as they surely would, and she prepared for their arrival. She closed her eyes, focused on the breath, and went inside herself to find the strength she would need for the coming confrontation.

Sheila wasn't adept with magic. She hadn't been born into an entire family of adepts like her husband had, where every woman had been taught the female mysteries from the time they could walk. Sheila had been born the youngest of three children. The other two were boys, and they were bullies. Her mother had died when Sheila was three, and she had been raised by her drunken father and her older brothers. Any magic there might have been in that family disappeared with the death of Sheila's mother.

But Sheila had lived many previous lives where she had known magic, and Diane had helped Sheila recall a few of those lives. Though Sheila had been female in most of her lives, she had also been a male. She knew a few of the male mysteries her husband had revealed to her in secret, and she remembered some things she had learned from her own lives as a bard in pre-Stonehenge Britain, as a student of Thoth in ancient Egypt, as a member of Pythagoras' inner circle at Croton, as an apprentice to Abou Moussah Djfar-Al Sell who was also known as the alchemist Geber, as an acolyte of Artephius in Spain, and as a life-long friend of Roger Bacon. She had also been a close friend of the Irish poet William Butler Yeats, and she had been a member of the Golden Dawn society and a freemason when she was a man.

And Sheila had been a close friend of Diane Groves and Sara Nelson for almost a year. She had watched them do magic, and she had participated in circles around the mound of power in the old-growth forest.

Sheila had observed Yam Elman closely when he had left his body to travel elsewhere, and she had watched him when he performed one of many rituals he used to preserve his life. Much of Elman's magic was resident in the body he now wore. That answered Kisi's question about why Elman was reluctant to trade his body in on a new model. If he did, he would lose much of his magic.

Sheila knew the effects of magic were accumulative, building up like static charges in a body waiting to be released only when that body came into contact with another body of differing potential. Many mages were so electrified that they could fry an opponent just by looking at him.

Magic accumulated in physical places as well as bodies. Places where magic rituals had been performed for centuries retained a portion of that magic each time a ritual was performed. The Isle of Isis in the middle of the Nile was one of those magical places. The Temple of Delphi was another. Stonehenge was yet another.

And so were Machu Picchu, Angkor Wat, the Seita, and the vortex on Diane's property.

All of those places were centers of magic, and rituals performed there over the millennia had increased the natural power of ley lines and rivers a thousand-fold. Beneath Diane's property there flowed an underground river that fed natural springs along the property line and made the shallow creek running across the property into a bubbling brook of constantly running water with a transformative power all its own. For magic and water always worked together. And great magic required a great river or ocean to be effective.

Water was the elixir of life, and the human body was two-thirds water. Elman regularly replaced the water in his body with fresh water pumped from a well. That well tapped into the aquifer that fed the river that ran under Diane's property.

Sheila reached out with her mind to touch that underground river, to tap directly into it, and she felt a mighty pulse of surging power fill her being anew. Water contained mostly feminine energies, though there were always some masculine components also present in running water, and Sheila felt refreshed and replenished.

Elman had grilled Henry for nearly half an hour after Henry returned from delivering Elman's message, and Sheila had actually felt sorry for the young man. Henry appeared to be very intelligent, soft-spoken, and enthralled by Elman's dominant personality. He was way out of his element here, and things didn't bode well for Henry's future.

But Sheila had to think of herself, and things didn't bode well for her, either. Sheila had overheard Henry and Elman discussing what would happen if Diane didn't vacate the property. Sheila didn't mind dying, but she did mind Elman keeping part of her body as a trophy. She knew she would never be reborn as long as one part of her former self remained trapped in the physical world. She would never see her beloved husband again in this life or any other, and that would be pure hell.

So Sheila formulated a plan. She would build up her energies and wait for an opportunity to break free. Maybe—just maybe—she could generate enough energy to burn the ropes off her wrists.

Time was running out. She had already been held half a day, and she had less than twelve hours to escape or she would surely die.

And she didn't think Elman would make her death either easy or quick.

*   *   *

Diane didn't know what to do. She didn't want Sheila to die, but she didn't dare let Elman have the vortex, either. Diane's mother had considered herself a caretaker of the trees—it was a sacred trust, Ma always said—and she was killed when she wouldn't sell those trees and the land they grew on. Ellen Groves had been Guardian of the West, and she took her responsibilities very seriously. Now Sara, Ellen's one-time apprentice and protégé, was the Guardian of the West Winds, and she, too, took her responsibility seriously. Sara would never relinquish the vortex voluntarily.

Nor would Kisi nor Bryn.

And that meant that Sheila would die. Diane had no doubt Elman would keep his word. He'd cut Sheila's body into pieces and throw away the pieces. All except one.

That one he'd keep as a trophy, a souvenir, something to re-member her by. And as long as that single piece remained alive in any way, Sheila would never be able to be re-membered by anyone else, not even herself. Her spirit would remain attached to that piece of flesh, and her spirit couldn't enter another body. She would never be reborn.

Her spirit would belong to Elman for as long as he lived.

Diane watched Kisi's spirit return to Kisi's body, followed by Sara and Bryn returning to their own respective shells.

They had been to the World Tree where they had conferred with La Curandera and Biegolmai far longer than expected, but now they were back.

"What are we going to do?" asked Diane. "What did Biegolmai decide?"

"Akashabarbha found Hadad," said Kisi.

"That's wonderful! Is Hadad okay?"

"No, he isn't," answered Bryn. "His spirit resided too long in the void. His memory has been wiped clean. He has no memory. None."

"Then his spirit has lost all connection with his body."

"Yes. His spirit can't remember the way back."

"It's hopeless then," said Diane, sounding thoroughly disappointed. "Without Hadad, what can we do?"

"It's not hopeless," said Bryn. "Lokesvara thinks he can restore Hadad's memory."

"How?" asked Diane.

"Hadad left behind a written record," said Kisi. "But it's written in cuneiform on the wall of time. It needs to be translated into Akkadian before Hadad can remember."

"How long will that take?"

"No one knows. However, once Hadad's spirit remembers who he is, Hadad will be able to return to his body."

"And then what?"

"Then he'll confront Yam from inside the cone of protection. Yam won't be anticipating that. By the time Yam knows

Hadad's spirit has returned to his body, Hadad will be back in control of his physical body. Hadad can dismiss the cone and let us in."

"And we can free Sheila," added Diane.

"Yes. We can free Sheila."

"Will it work?" asked Diane.

"It will have to," said Sara. "We have no other options."

Diane breathed a sigh of relief. "It *will* work," she said confidently. "I know it will."

"How much time do we have left?" asked Bryn.

"Two hours," said Diane.

"That's not much time."

"No," said Diane. "It isn't."

*   *   *

Hadad's memories gradually returned as Lokesvara spoke slowly and precisely to Hadad's spirit, translating first from the wedge-shaped cuneiform symbols to Greek, then into ancient Akkadian. It was the way Lokesvara had learned to read cuneiform. He had studied many languages over the centuries, but Greek seemed to be the Rosetta stone that made other languages understandable.

Because Lokesvara and Hadad shared a love of learning, their kindred spirits could communicate on many levels. When Hadad first returned from the void, he was as a child. He had no familiarity with written or spoken languages, and he had to learn to recognize words all over again. Lokesvara had been patient and kind, and he had taught Hadad slowly and systematically in a place that existed outside of normal time. Eventually, some of Hadad's memories began to return and Hadad could once again understand what he heard. And then he remembered how to speak.

"I know you," said Hadad's spirit.

"My name is Lokesvara."

"I know you as something else. Manjusri. Yes, Manjusri. That's your name. Manjusri."

"I am also Manjusri."

"Yes. You are Guardian of the East."

"I am."

"I know who you are. But I don't know who I am. Who am I?"

"You are Schacar Hadad Elman, and you are also a Guardian."

"I am?"

"You are. And you are the one who wrote these words on the wall of time. They are your words, from your own mind. They are an enduring record of who you have been, and what you have done."

"I have been all those people? I have done all those things?"

"Yes."

"It seems impossible."

"Each of us lives many lifetimes, Hadad."

"You said I had a brother. What is he like?"

"His name is Shalim Yam Elman, and you have been soul brothers in a number of lifetimes. Although you are alike in many ways, Yam is also your complete opposite, Hadad. He fears you and hates you. He has killed you many times, and you have killed him before, too. You must kill him again."

"But why? I thought brothers were supposed to love and help each other. Isn't that the way it should be?"

"Yes," said Lokesvara. "That is the way it should be."

"But things are not always the way they should be, are they?"

"No, Hadad, they aren't."

"And that's why you need me, isn't it? You need me to counter Yam's actions with my own actions."

"Yes."

"What can I do?"

"You can help us free a woman Yam holds captive in a cabin in Wisconsin. No one else but you can do this, and Yam will kill the woman if you don't help."

"Why would he kill her?"

"He wants her land. Rather, he wants her sister-in-law's land. He has threatened to kill the woman, Sheila Ryan, unless Diane Groves gives him the land."

"Why doesn't she give him what he wants?"

"Because there is more at stake here than just the land. Yam wants the power that lies within the land and the magic of the trees that grow upon it. If he gets that power, there's no telling how much damage he can cause. Will you help us stop him?"

"Yes."

"Good. Now I want you to remember. Picture in your mind's eye all that has happened to you. It may appear as a motion picture on a screen, perhaps a television screen, and you can speed the images up or slow them down by pushing the fast forward on a remote that I am handing you now. Begin at the beginning and view all of the events that happen in each of the many lifetimes you see on the screen. When you are ready, press the fast forward button on your remote and allow your memory to fill in any blanks between frames. You can go through an entire lifetime in ten seconds, recalling everything that happened in that lifetime. Now rewind the tape and play it through again. Keep doing that until you remember ....remember ....remember ...."

As the events of a thousand lifetimes flashed in front of his mind's eye, Hadad did indeed remember. He remembered his first birth in Africa, his rebirths in Ebla, Anatolia, Akkadia, Lake Titicaca, India, Tibet, China, Egypt, Greece, Rome, Britain, France, and his current lifetime in Syria. He remembered his brother in all of Yam's incarnations, though Yam had not reincarnated the last few times Hadad had; how they had been tied together by a psychic connection far stronger than blood, how Yam had lied and cheated, and stole, and slaughtered, how Yam had hit Hadad with a double-whammy and sent him reeling into the void....

And then Hadad was suddenly back in his body, sitting in a chair in a log cabin, and Yam was sitting opposite him at a wooden table. Yam's face was hideously scarred, and one of his eyes was missing.

When Hadad asked, "What happened to your face?" Yam acted like he had just seen a ghost.

*   *   *

Sheila didn't expect Hadad to come alive. She was as surprised as Yam when Hadad opened his mouth and asked, "What happened to your face?"

Sheila recovered before Yam did, and she sent a surge of power from the very center of her being racing down both arms and into her wrists where it pooled and intensified. She could smell the cotton fibers of the eighth-inch clothesline heating up, burning, searing her flesh, creating blisters; and then the strands began to separate until, one by one, they popped apart and her hands were finally freed. Henry and George stood guard nearby, but they were so fascinated by the effect Hadad's words had on their leader that they didn't notice Sheila lunge from the chair until it was too late to stop her. She plowed head-first into

George, knocking him into the wall so hard that she heard the back of his head crack like an eggshell. The shotgun fell from George's hands and clattered to the floor without discharging.

Henry didn't react quick enough to stop her, and the momentum of Sheila's lunge carried her past the younger man and Sheila was half-way out the door and into the night before Henry could think to shout, "Hey! Come back here!"

Yam tried to whammy Hadad, but this time Hadad was anticipating the attack. With a flick of his wrist, Hadad deflected the blast of pure energy and sent it hurtling harmlessly skyward, ripping a large hole in the ceiling as it veered off toward Mars.

Hadad countered with a spell Bon shamans used to bind evil spirits, and Yam imagined iron chains wrapping around his arms and anchoring him to the chair. Yam inflated his lungs and burst the chains, sending broken links flying about the room.

Now it was adept versus adept, brother against brother, good versus evil, light versus dark. Yam turned into a huge hooded serpent, its triangular head towering over Hadad with foot-long fangs dripping venom as its coils wrapped tighter than a spring and the serpent prepared to strike. Hadad instantly changed into an eagle and flew up off his chair and pecked at the serpent's one good eye as the coiled serpent struck at Hadad's empty chair.

Sheila made it all the way through the door and ran for the woods with Henry following close enough behind that Sheila thought she could smell his fear. She knew he had witnessed, as had she, Yam's transformation into a gigantic snake and Hadad's manifestation of a taloned bird of prey. Was Henry trying to catch her, or was he fleeing for his life?

He raced past her in the dark. Either he couldn't see her or he wanted nothing more than to get as far away as possible from the fierce supernatural battle that decimated the tiny cabin in the woods.

The roof blew off and cabin walls tumbled down as opposing energies met and merged and split apart. Light and dark attacked each other, and the sky lit up like the fourth of July then went blacker than ever before. Sheila had seen dog fights where two alpha males went for each other's throats, and she imagined that happening now. Horrible gut-wrenching sounds filled the woods as trees fell and the earth itself seemed to split apart. Lightning arced in the night sky, weird lights appeared and were smothered or swallowed up, and Sheila thought she saw demons dancing.

She knew it was more than her imagination at work. The very fabric of the universe was being torn asunder as two equally-powerful opposing forces clashed, reeled, clashed again, and spun out of control. A tree fell where Sheila had been standing only moments ago, and the ground beneath her own two feet opened up and geysers erupted, filling the air with steam and frost from water that was alternately boiling hot and icy cold. She heard Henry, somewhere off in the woods, scream and scream and scream, and then the screams abruptly stopped.

There was no place to run, no place to hide. Like Henry, Sheila was caught out in the open in the middle of a battlefield, and she felt vulnerable, unprotected, and doomed. More trees toppled around her, and it was only a matter of time before one landed on Sheila's head.

On and on the battle raged, first Yam gained the upper hand, and then Hadad. Eventually, the struggle had to take its inevitable toll on both opponents. Hadad's spirit had been recently traumatized, but his memories of sorcery were freshly recalled and he had spells at his fingertips that his brother had long forgotten. Yam was augmented by thousands of recent sacrifices, and his power remained formidable despite the drain of energy that kept him alive and kept the sun from being seen. He countered every spell Hadad threw at him, and he threw enough back that Hadad couldn't get the upper hand and keep it. They fought, they grappled; they were like two brothers acting mean to each other when their parents weren't around.

Sheila suddenly found herself snatched by the strong arms of Bryn Helgasdottir and whisked off the battlefield the way Valkyries dragged dead warriors away to Valhalla. Within seconds, Sheila was back in Diane's house and surrounded by women.

"Are you all right?" asked Diane, worry etched on her face.

"I'm alive," whispered Sheila. "I didn't think I would be."

"What's happening now?" Bryn asked Kisi.

"Both men are weakening," replied Kisi. "This can't continue much longer. Yam is running out of steam, and Hadad is barely holding his own."

"What can we do to end it?" asked Diane.

"Nothing. Biegolmai says the battle must play out by itself. If we try to interfere, we could only make things worse."

"How could things get any worse?"

"Yam could win," said Sara. "And then things could get a lot worse."

* * *

Hadad knew it was merely a matter of time. His strength had already ebbed considerably, and yet Yam continued to hammer away at him as if Yam had unlimited reserves and could keep at this forever.

This was a fight to the death, and neither brother held back. If Yam died, all of his accumulated knowledge and power would be gone. He would be reborn, of course, but he would have to start over. And starting over was something Yam didn't want to do.

Before rebirth, Yam would have to endure the memories of all of the pain and suffering he had caused through innumerable lifetimes. He would be personally confronted by every person he hurt, and then he would experience that hurt himself as if he were that other person. Physical pain was never as bad as emotional pain, and Yam had thrived on creating emotional chaos and distress for millennia. He had a lot to answer for, and he fought ferociously to avoid having to answer for any of it.

But Hadad fought with the fervency of righteousness, and he had faith that right would conquer might. He knew his actions were right as surely as he knew his brother's actions were wrong. Anyone who caused as much chaos and destruction as Yam had caused deserved to die, and die Yam must. Hadad would continue the good fight until his brother were dead or his own energy ran completely out.

If it meant he had to die, too, then so be it. He had died many times before, and death—even spiritual death—no longer frightened him as it once had. He had left behind a written record of all he had learned, and he knew he could learn it all over again if he had to. Or others could, and that was almost as good.

Finally, Hadad threw a spell that had absolutely no effect. It simply fizzled out before it got anywhere close to Yam. Yam laughed at his brother's weakness.

"It's over, brother," said Yam. "You have lost and I have won."

Hadad steeled himself for Yam's next blow which would certainly be a killer, but Yam, too, had run out of energy. That blow never came.

The two bothers faced each other and waited for one or the other to regain his strength, but that didn't happen, either. Yam only had energy enough to keep the sun hidden.

Both were completely drained, and neither had the upper hand. Finally, Yam turned his back on his brother. He simply walked away and disappeared into darkness.

Exhausted and spent, Hadad had no energy to pursue Yam. Hadad fell to the ground, stretched out his arms and legs, and drew strength from mother earth. Above him, clouds obscured the stars. He was alone with his thoughts and his memories.

He had learned much today from Lokesvara, including things that he had forgotten because he thought those events were long done with and had no further importance to him or to anyone. But one memory seemed particularly significant to him now, and he sought to recover the details by examining past events.

His name was Ayar Ucho, and he had returned from his wanderings across the great sea. He expected to be greeted by his brothers and sisters with great joy upon his return. He had learned much he wanted to share with them, and he had eagerly looked forward to this reunion with years of anticipation.

But things had changed drastically in the sacred valley of the Urubamba, and Ucho barely recognized the place or the people. Ayar Cachi and Ayar Anca were nowhere to be found. Ayar Manco had taken control of the various tribes though fear, and he had used that fear to build a city high up in the mountains, an impregnable fortress, where Ayar Manco made sacrifices to the sun to increase his power.

Hadad found his sisters hiding in the Moon Temple. "Manco has killed Cachi and Anca," sobbed sister Huaco, "and he has permanently imprisoned their spirits in stone."

"What have you done to counter his evil magic?" asked Ucho.

"Nothing," said Huaco.

"Why not?"

"The moon is only a reflection of the sun. Our moon magic is not as powerful as his sun magic. The moon draws its power from the sun."

"Then combine moon magic with earth magic. Together, they should be more than enough."

"Such a thing has never been done. Is it not sacrilege?"

"It is done all the time in the valley of the Indus," said Ucho. "And in the mountains of Tibet by Bon shamans. And in the frozen north where, for half the year, the sun has no power. It is called the hieros gamos, the marriage of the heavens and the earth, and nothing is more powerful."

"How is it done?"

"On an earthen mound—an altar—in a circle of trees on the night of the new moon when the sun has no influence. It requires an equal number of men and women. Call the other sisters, and I will show all of you how it is done."

So Ucho married eastern magic with western, teaching the women of the Moon Temple to dance naked in the woods. On the night of the new moon, when the bulk of the earth came between the sun and the moon, their husbands joined the women dancing around the earthen altar with arms raised skyward and their bare feet touching the ground. After an hour of dancing and incantations, they raised sufficient energy to move mountains, and they rolled away the rocks from the entrance to Ayar Cachi's tomb, and they split the rock imprisoning Ayar Anca and released his spirit so it might someday be reborn.

Then they set about rearranging the stones of Ayar Manco's mountain retreat. They toppled the Temple of the Sun, and they destroyed the precursor to the Intihuatana so it no longer controlled the sun.

When the sun rose the next day, Ayar Manco was devastated. His power had been stolen from him during the night, and the tribes that had once supported him now deserted him.

And then his brother, Ayar Ucho, regrouped those same tribes and led them against Ayar Manco to kill him. The scholar had proved to be an able soldier after all.

But Yam's spirit had been reborn. Sometimes, when he knew he was about to die, he took possession of another body. Ayar Manco came back again and again to the sacred valley to reestablish the empire of the sun, and eventually—when his siblings had died of old age—he succeeded. The Incan empire ruled the region for more than two hundred years. He was later known as Manco Capac, and he ruled the Incas with an iron fist.

It was in another life, when Hadad and Yam had been born once again in the Valley of the Urubamba, not long before the Incas had built an empire, that Hadad discovered Yam's terrible secret. In order to control the sun, Yam required an influx of female energy to marry with his male energy. And the only way he could get it was through the voluntary sacrifice of women and children.

But the women of the Temple of the Moon rebelled against Manco's demands for sacrifice. None of *them* voluntarily relinquished their life force, or the life force of any of their children, to Yam, who was once again known as Manco Capac. And they urged other women to rebel, too. They granted asylum at the temple to any woman who asked for protection. Soon, the temple was filled to overflowing, and the number of voluntary sacrifices had dwindled to next to nothing.

It wasn't long before Manco and his henchmen attacked the Temple of the Moon to destroy the temple and capture the women and children. They made the mistake of coming late at night, on the night when there was no moon, attempting to sneak up on the three-walled stone structure from the blind side, but Kisi, Kiyari, and Bryn saw them coming through three secret windows cut into the stone.

Bryn and her women warriors were ready for them, and as the men advanced from the woods at the foot of the mountain,

188 · PAUL DALE ANDERSON

hundreds of ayllos snaked out of the darkness and knocked the men off their feet, the strong natural fibers woven into rope wrapping around ankles and legs as the three round stones at the end of the rope entangled and knotted. Now the women were upon the men, cutting their throats with sharp obsidian blades or stabbing them in the heart or gut. The night air was filled with screams, some from the dying men and some from the women warriors who claimed victory with shrill battle cries.

Manco Capac put on the golden sun mask and called upon the sun to aid him, and suddenly the night sky was filled with bright light as if night had turned into midday. Manco used the power of the golden mask and his magic spells to magnify, concentrate, and manipulate the sun's most powerful rays so they became virtual death rays that fried each person he pointed a finger at.

Now women's screams became not battle cries but death cries, as one by one the flesh melted off their faces and frames to puddle around skeletal remains. As Bryn charged Manco, he hit her full in the face with a blast of energy that ripped her apart.

One woman emerged from the three-sided stone structure of the temple and walked fearlessly toward Manco. She wore a silver moon mask over her face and a magenta-dyed loose-fitting robe of woven alpaca wool. Magenta was the color of the moon goddess herself, and this priestess of Mother Moon was called Uqllu, mistress of the Pururaucas, and she was reputed to possess special powers, a gift of the goddess.

Manco directed the rays of the sun at her face, expecting the mask to melt and the face to explode, but instead, like the moon itself, the mask reflected the light of the sun and directed it back, minus the lime-green colors of the spectrum, in a fushine flood that enveloped Manco Capac and turned him to stone.

These things Hadad had witnessed from afar, for he was traveling again on the astral plane and his detached spirit could observe but not intervene. Though he was adept at many things, he had only recently learned to separate his spirit from his body and travel in spirit form. He had not yet learned the secret of physical teleportation.

Yam's spirit remained trapped within that stone for generations, and it was not until an earthquake toppled the stone and split it apart that his spirit was finally freed.

By then, the Incan civilization had collapsed.

Recalling these events gave Hadad hope. There was something special about Uqllu that could stand up to Yam at his most powerful, and there was something special about that mask. Just as Yam had worn the golden mask of the face of the sun when he had made sacrifices at Machu Picchu, so had Uqllu worn the silver mask of the face of the moon when she had conquered Manco Capac and entrapped Yam's spirit in stone.

Hadad knew where to find Uqllu. Today she was known as Kiyari, and she shared her body with La Curandera.

Now if only Hadad could find the silver mask of the moon goddess and return it to Kiyari, maybe they could make history repeat itself and defeat Yam by entrapping his spirit in stone.

CHAPTER TWELVE

"I remember that mask," said La Curandera. "And so does Kiyari."

"Where is it now?" asked Hadad. After he had recovered sufficient energy, he had immediately teleported to Machu Picchu to tell La Curandera of his revelation.

"Neither of us knows where it is. When Kiyari died, whoever became high priestess of the Moon Temple would have inherited it. But the Moon Temple was destroyed even before the Spaniards came. There is a cave on Huayna Picchu that is now called the Moon Temple, but the temple I remember was in the valley near the river. The temple of the sun was high up in the mountains, but the women's temple was at the base of the mountains near the Urubamba, very close to the confluence of the Urubamba and the Patacancha rivers."

"That's what I remember, too. It was close to the confluence of the Urubamba and the Patacancha rivers."

"If the real Moon Temple was destroyed before the Spaniards came in the 16th century, then there is no written record of what happened."

"We need to find that mask."

"If it still exists. It may have been found by someone. People have been looking for Inca gold and silver for hundreds of years. The mask may be in a private collection, in a museum, or it may have been melted down for the silver content."

"Where did the mask come from originally? Who made it?"

"I don't know. It was always in the temple of the moon whenever I was there, and legend says the mask was made by the moon goddess and given to women for protection against men."

"It certainly worked as protection against Yam in the scene I remembered. Uqllu wore it, and the mask reflected Yam's spell right back at him. Where were you when that happened?"

"I was in the Amazon gathering plants," said La Curandera. "Since I must remain here to guard the vortex, I will search for the silver mask at Machu Picchu. Many of the Inca treasures were brought here after the Spaniards looted Cusco and decimated Ollantaytambo."

"Haven't archaeologists gone over every inch of this place?"

"Yes. But there are places they haven't thought to look."

"While you're searching here, I'll go to a university library and research museum holdings. If archaeologists unearthed the mask, it will be listed in one of the museum catalogs."

"Silver is *qullqi* in Quechua," said La Curandera.

"Thanks. I'll remember that."

Hadad told the librarian at the University of Wisconsin library that he was a visiting scholar sent by Diane Groves to do research into pre-columbian artifacts for Professor Groves, and he was given a temporary ID and password to access the university's databases. He searched the Museo de Arte Precolumbino at Cusco, Gallery 357 at the Metropolitan Museum of Art in New York, the Miguel Mujica Gallo Foundation's Gold Museum of Peru in Lima, the Larco Museum in Lima, and the Museo de Metales Preciosas Pre-Colombino in La Paz. He learned that the constant duality or polarity of the sun and moon—day and night, light and dark, male and female—was represented by gold and silver in pre-Incan civilizations, particularly the Chavan and Sican cultures, and that the silver masks of the type worn by Coya, the priestesses of the moon goddess, predated the Incas by more than a thousand years.

There was a silver Incan mask at the Brooklyn Museum, but that didn't look anything like what Hadad remembered. The Museo Larco in Lima had a silver mask, too. But that wasn't it.

The mask he remembered was a sheet of hammered silver, slightly larger than a human face, with eye and nose and mouth indentations but no holes in the eyes to see through. The Coya held the mask in front of her face, unlike the golden masks men wore that were fastened over the face with fiber strings and that usually had holes or slits in the eye indentations.

Suddenly, Hadad remembered another mask he had once seen, a mask made of hammered copper instead of silver or gold. It was the mask of Illapa, the god of thunder and lightning. It was the mask brother Ayar Cachi wore when he went into battle. It had slits for eyes, a defined nose and mouth, and what looked like a beard below the mouth. All around Illapa's mask were jagged bolts of lightning shooting out from the face to terminate in razor-sharp points. The jagged edges and razor-sharp points of those lightning bolts reminded Hadad of Vajrapani, for each bolt looked exactly like a miniature Kris.

Most of the masks in museums were merely funerary masks, made of gold for the ruling class and wooden or ceramic masks for their trusted warlords and principal servants. Those death masks needed no holes or slits for eyes, for the dead knew the way and did not need to be able to see to go on to the afterlife that awaited. The few ceremonial masks on display in museums were not the masks of power Hadad searched for.

There was no mention of either the silver moon mask or the copper Illapa mask in any of the archaeological records Hadad could access, and either the masks were still hidden in the foothills of the Andes or they were equally-well hidden in the hands of looters or private collectors. Either way, they wouldn't be easy to find.

Hadad left the University of Wisconsin library and walked through the streets of downtown Madison in the dark. Many of the streetlights were missing, either shot out with bullets or BBs, or shattered by hurled rocks or bottles. About a third of the stores along State Street were closed or boarded up, and those that remained open didn't seem to be very busy. A handful of scattered pedestrians, most acting dazed and disoriented, dotted the sidewalks. No one seemed to be in a hurry to get anywhere quickly, and there was little conversation taking place even among couples. No one greeted passersby or even acknowledged their presence with a nod. The world had dramatically changed, and civilization was slowly changing with it.

Hadad sat down on a bench at a bus stop and checked his wristwatch. It was midday on a weekday, and normal human activity was practically non-existent. There were none of the usual buses or bicycles on State Street, and traffic on side streets was intermittent at best. At the east end of State Street, Hadad saw a few lights on in the domed state capital building. There were armed National Guard soldiers standing guard around the building, and most of the businesses around capital square looked dark and deserted. Some were boarded up with graffiti spray-painted in day-glo colors that read, "Repent! The end is near!" One read, "Repent! The end is here!"

Hadad had been out of touch with normal human existence for the past week, and he still felt out of touch. His
experience with the void had altered his perception, and he was
still getting used to being back in his body. The world itself had
changed practically overnight, and everything felt strange and
alien. He could only imagine the dread others must sense. Man
wasn't meant to live in the dark forever. If civilization was going to hell in a handbasket after only a week without sunlight,
what would happen if the world remained dark for a month? Or
an entire year?

He flashed out of existence in Madison, Wisconsin, and
flashed back into existence again atop Machu Picchu. La
Curandera had searched the secret passages inside the mountain
to no avail. Now she was searching her memories for details that
might help.

"It was pure silver," she said. "Not an alloy. No nickel,
no copper. It was smelted from quartz and pounded into a solid
rectangle about twelve inches high and nine or ten inches wide.
It was the most perfect mirror I've ever seen."

"That's the way I remember it, too," said Hadad.

"There was no nose or mouth. Only indentations for
eyes."

"And no holes or slits for eyes to look through."

"The Coya held it in her hands in front of her face. Two
acolytes guided her in ceremonies because the Coya couldn't
see. She who wore the mask of the goddess was blind to this

world but could see all other worlds. She was the only one of us who could see the future."

"If that were true, do you suppose she may have hidden the mask where she could find it in the future?"

"That is a possibility."

"What does Kiyari remember?"

"Little more than you or I."

"May I borrow her? I know you cannot leave the vortex unoccupied, but your spirit will suffice. Enter one of the stones, and let Kiyari come with me to find what remains of the Temple of the Moon."

"She speaks no English."

"I remember some Quechua. And I know Spanish."

"Then take her with you," said La Curandera, and her spirit left the girl's body.

*　　*　　*

Lokesvara watched the Ranger and Jon Fish fight. It had been many years since Lokesvara had trained his muscles and senses to react together, but his body remembered and he found his own muscles responding as if he, and not the two younger men, were engaged in mock combat.

Lokesvara had trained differently, first mastering the forms, or taolu, of Taijiquan—the boundless fist—and then coordinating the neijia with the waijia. He had devoted three incarnations to perfecting the art of battle.

These western warriors did things the hard way. Instead of dedicating themselves to study with a master, as Lokesvara had studied naijia with Zhang Junbao in the Wudang mountains and swordsmanship with Xu Xuanping, they studied not at all. Instead, they exercised vigorously, performing hundreds of sit-ups and push-ups daily, running uphill carrying rocks in their backpacks, and kicking at their opponents with all their might. They knew nothing of the theories of alchemy, the science of prolonging one's qi and therefore life, the gates of the breath, the yin and the yang, refining the spirit and returning to the state of selflessness. They had not read the great classics nor recited poetry nor meditated on the art of war. They were pragmatists: They dashed right in and got the job done. Everything else to them was wasted energy.

And who was to say they were wrong? There were many paths to the top of the mountain, and only those who had never been to the very top claimed there was but one way up.

They were good men, the best. They had good hearts. Both had gone far astray, and both had returned to their own true path. They had proven their steadfastness, and they had redeemed themselves.

Though Lokesvara knew many things, there was much he had yet to learn about the way the universe worked. Why or how the spirits of the great Bodhisattvas manifested in these men—and in himself—was still beyond his meager understanding. He knew from his own experiences that he and Manjusri were one, and the spirit of Manjusri lived inside him. They had traveled together for many lifetimes, he and Manjusri. But Lokesvara was entirely mortal, and he had the same limits as other mortals. He suffered and caused suffering. He made mistakes. And someday he would die.

He knew, of course, that he would be born again because it had happened many times before. And he had reduced his desires so that his own suffering and the sufferings he caused others was minimal, even negligible. He had devoted himself to the Buddha, the dharma, and the sangha for more than two millennia. He didn't want to die, but when death came for him once more he was prepared to face his old enemy and embrace him.

So, too, were the two mortal men sparring on the grass outside the temple no longer frightened of death because they were also cognizant of reincarnation.

Normally, this area outside the main temple would be filled with thousands of tourists, but tourists, unable to see the splendor of Angkor in the dark, no longer came. Despite Lokesvara's advanced age, he could sense very well in the dark even on days like today. Master Zhang had taught students to fight blindfolded, and Lokesvara remembered the difficulties he had experienced trying to keep balance without visual orientation, sensing movement which one could not see, and judging distance without perspective. But with time and patience he had learned to do all those things and more.

When blindfolds were removed and sight restored to Zhang's students, one found all of one's senses heightened. Instead of depending mainly on the sense of sight as men were wont to do, one integrated the other senses so one could see with the ears, taste with the eyes, feel with the nose, smell with the mouth, and hear with the fingers.

These things the Americans seemed to do intuitively, and their will to survive and to win gave them an important edge. They knew they fought with right on their side, and right often overcame might.

"The battlefields of history are littered with the mutilated bodies and wandering spirits of men far nobler than you," Master Zhang had taught. "The universe doesn't take sides in battle, doesn't protect good from bad, right from wrong. The universe respects only balance, and balance is what I shall teach you."

Lokesvara had tried to teach the two Americans balance, and they had learned to meditate and to both separate the self from the non-self, the "other," and to integrate the self and the other. He had shown them how to fire the dan-tien, how to awaken the sleeping Kundalini. He had taught them to recall the lessons of previous lives, and he had re-introduced them to the Bodhisattvas they had become.

Vajrapani, the ultimate warrior, was the protector of all Buddhas. He could control the weather and the elements—wind, water, fire, and stone—and he wielded the awesome power of the thunder and the lightning with his two outstretched hands.

He was a fierce warrior, but his compassion was as great as his heart.

To the Incas, he was known as Apocatequil, and before that he was called Catequil and Illapa. He was one of the guardians of the Chakana, the Incan tree of life, by which shamans could crawl up to reach the spirit realm—the Hana Pacha—or down into the underworld—the Uco Pacha—and communicate with the spirits of the dead.

It was said that he was in love with a maiden named Chasca Coyllur. She was the morning star, the link between the moon and the sun.

The legend of Akashagarbha said that he was the twin brother of Ksitigarbha, the Earth Store Matrix, who was also known as Sacred Girl. In China, Akashagarbha was called Na Mu Xu Kong Zang Pu Sa, in Japan he was known as Kokuso, in Tibet he was Namkhai Nyingpo, and he was Aruna in India. It was said Akashagarbha embodied the wisdom of emptiness, of selfless love and giving.

He was a walker between worlds, and his spirit was spawned of stardust. He could travel instantaneously from one end of the universe to another, outracing light rays from earth that took centuries or millennia to reach where Akashagarbha patiently waited to view them. And viewing events in their entirety gave him a unique perspective. He could see everything that happened, not only his own part in the events but all the other parts, too. And he wasn't limited to seeing just events that he had been part of, he could view any event from any time and from any place.

It had been truly said that Akashagarbha had witnessed the creation of the world, because he had.

Bodhisattvas were spiritual beings who had once been mortal men. They had suffered through innumerable rebirths until they were able to transcend suffering and desire and even death by means of their own compassion and selflessness. They were now pure spirit, enlightened beings, and they had earned the right to rest in a Pure Land, to remain in nirvana forever. But so great was their compassion that each Bodhisattva had vowed to return to the physical realm to help alleviate pain and suffering until that day when *all* sentient beings were finally freed from samsara, when the immutable laws of karma and the inevitable cycles of birth and death and rebirth came to an end, when all beings became enlightened and liberated.

Akashagarbha, like Manjusri and Vajrapani, had returned to the physical world to share bodies with kindred spirits. Now the three of them—three mortal men and their spiritual companions—prepared to do battle with a man who feared death so much he wanted desperately to become immortal, who had no compassion for others, not even his own brothers and sisters; a man so selfish he would drive the entire world mad to gain the power to live forever.

Such evil was beyond even Lokesvara's vast comprehension. He knew and accepted the fact that evil had always been an integral part of the universe, a twin to goodness; the universe required balance. But the darkness that now enveloped the earth had disrupted the delicate balance of this world and possibly others, and it could not be allowed to endure.

Lokesvara left his body and his spirit merged with Biegolmai's spirit at the World Tree. Biegolmai came from a different tradition, and he interpreted the universe from the shaman's perspective. Lokesvara had studied with Bon shamans in Tibet so he understood that Biegolmai saw the entire universe as something alive, that the earth had a living, beating heart, that trees and rocks and blades of grass had spirits, too; sacred totem animals, who often embodied the spirits of one's ancestors, acted as spirit guides in the three realms of existence: The spirit realm above, the physical realm here and now, and the underworlds beneath our normal perception. Biegolmai's totem animals were the raven, the reindeer, and the wolf. It was the raven who guided him into the spirit realm, the reindeer who guided him here on earth, and the wolf who guided him below.

"What do your guides tell you?" asked Lokesvara.

"If the sun is not restored soon, Yam's power will be unstoppable. Even now, he continues to absorb female life force. He has founded a religious cult at the ancient mounds near the confluence of the Missouri and Mississippi rivers. He tells people that the sacrifice of women and children is necessary to restore the sun, and he has convinced his followers to voluntarily give up their life force."

"At Monks Mound in Cahokia?"

"On the other side of the Mississippi, just north of Saint Louis. North of Saint Charles. Where the Missouri flows into the Mississippi."

"There are no mounds there of any consequence."

"But there are. It was once a place of great power for the indigenous peoples, and residual energies remain."

"It lies in the heart of an enormous metropolitan area. How can anything magical be left after all these years?"

"Yam was there in the 1830s. He took steps to protect this one place from desecration. He bought the land, and he still owns it."

"That took foresight."

"Yes, it did. Yam is very knowledgeable. He has remained in his current body or in bodies he has stolen for hundreds of years, and his memories continue unaltered."

"Tell me more about these sacrifices. How does he find willing victims?"

"He has a website. And he has a page on Facebook that asks for volunteers. His Facebook page has more than twenty thousand likes."

"How did you learn he has a website and a Facebook page? You have no electricity at the Seita, and the vortex naturally interferes with electronics and radio signals. You don't have access to an internet connection, at least not a working internet connection, and you can't use a cell phone anywhere near a vortex. So how did you learn about his website?"

"My spirit guides are always watching and listening. I have stationed a flock of ravens around Yam's property in Missouri. They keep me informed of everything he does."

"So how does this work? This false religion that Yam invented and his internet website? How does he use that to attract willing victims?"

"People are desperate for a solution to their current problems, and religion has always offered solutions to desperate people seeking salvation. People are more and more desperate to escape darkness with every passing day, and some people are willing to accept almost anything. Many see this as an easy way to reach the afterlife, to leave behind all their fears and worries and problems for others to deal with after they're gone. Yam promises eternal life and eternal light to those who believe in him. And it seems thousands of people do believe in him and his message of salvation."

"And they are willing to give him their life force? Voluntarily?"

"Yes."

"Why doesn't the government stop him? Shut down his website? Isn't human sacrifice illegal? Surely, the FBI or some other agency of government must be aware of what Yam is doing. Why don't they stop him?"

"Americans believe in freedom of religion and freedom of speech, and both are protected by the First Amendment to the Constitution of the United States. Besides, law enforcement has more than they can handle right now, and they aren't particularly concerned when some crackpot advocates sacrificing oneself for one's religious beliefs. After all, Christianity was built on sacrifice, and many Amricans call themselves Christians."

"But he's killing people!"

"None of his victims have complained. Nor have the victims' families. Not yet, anyway."

"We must stop him."

"Yes. Three times have I used magic to knock his servers offline, and three times has he countered my spells. We must go there and stop him in person."

"Send Kisi and Bryn. I will send Jon and the Ranger."

"There is a vortex at Cahokia, seventeen miles from where Yam is located. Yam is in a place of power connected by an east-west ley line to Cahokia, and Monks Mound at Cahokia is on the main north-south ley line from Wisconsin to Machu Picchu. That complicates matters. Yam has set wards and we can't teleport into his cone of protection."

"Then our people will teleport into Saint Louis. They can rent a car and drive the rest of the way."

"Sounds like a plan," said Biegolmai. "I'll ask my ravens to keep us informed of their progress."

CHAPTER THIRTEEN

H adad and Kiyari walked up and down the banks of the Urubamba looking for the site they remembered. Not only had the the Incas torn down older sites and moved many of the stones elsewhere to build fortifications and temples to the sun and their god Inti, Spanish Conquistadores turned most of the old structures into ruins. An ancient temple of the moon stood no chance of surviving the vicissitudes of time in a place such as this.

Still they continued to look. If they could find the temple's location, they could search for the masks in nearby caves and crevasses.

"I remember that turn in the river," said Kiyari in Quechua.

"The Temple of the Moon was on the east bank," said Hadad. "We are near, I think."

"Over there," said Kiyari, pointing. "That is where the temple stood."

"Are you sure?"

"There are only scattered rocks. No large stones remain. But that is where I remember the temple once stood."

"I see."

There was lots of debris, but nothing substantial remained of what was once a magnificent edifice dedicated to the goddess. The temple walls had stood nine feet tall, constructed of solid rock slabs taken from the side of the holy mountain as Eve was said to have been taken from the side of Adam, and the walls themselves extended in a semi-circular arc around an open courtyard that was at least forty feet in diameter. In the center of that arc had stood a bubbling fountain with the purest drinking water Hadad had ever tasted, brought down from inside the mountains in a series of aqueducts that were a marvel of ancient engineering. For the women of the temple were mathematicians and magnificent engineers, as well as astronomers and astrologers, soothsayers and magicians. They were spinners and weavers, planters and sowers, tillers of the soil and warriors of the night. Their community was completely self-sustaining, and they had little need for men except for breeding.

Men were welcome, so long as they came in peace and friendship. But men were never invited to stay the night, with the exception of the solstices and the equinoxes and the new moons. On those nights the women of the moon reveled till dawn, sleeping the next day away with the man or men of their choosing. Men would come from miles around to partake of the revelries, and often those men offered to help the women with many of the heavier labors, like moving larger stones, but the women always declined their help. For the women knew the secret of moving stones with the power of the mind that Hadad had shared with his sisters on return from his travels.

"If the mask was hidden here, it is long gone," said Hadad.

"Where else would it be?"

"It could be anywhere. If the Spaniards found the silver mask, they would have melted it down into a silver ingot. If the Incans had it, it may be in a private collection and unlisted. If looters found it, heaven only knows where it might be."

"I know it still exists," said Kiyari. "I can feel it."

"You can?"

"Yes. It is very powerful. Anyone who has worn that mask is linked to it."

"Can you find it? Can you follow your senses and track it down?"

"In time."

"We don't have a lot of time."

"I know."

"Let's go back to Machu Picchu. You will be safe with La Curandera. Take as much time as you need, and try to locate that mask. Please. Our lives may depend on it."

"Is it really that important?"

"Yes," said Hadad. "It is really that important."

*　*　*

Bryn and Kisi met Jon and the Ranger at the Hertz desk at Lambert Field, better known as Saint Louis International Airport. Jon used his California Drivers License and his Visa credit card to rent a mid-sized black Chevy Camero. When the Ranger suggested it might be wise to take the extra insurance, Jon agreed. If the car were damaged or destroyed, the extra insurance would pay for repairs or a replacement.

Hertz was nice enough to supply several free maps of the area, and they took Interstate 70 from the airport west to US 67, then US 67 north.

Elman's property was near high bluffs overlooking the Missouri River. Native Americans had constructed magnificent cities on both sides of the Mississippi and along the Missouri, but little remained of their handiwork after white men came, first with plows and then with bulldozers, and reshaped the earth. Ceremonial sites at Cahokia had been linked to other sites north, east, south, and west of the main mound, and here, on the banks of the river that connected the Mississippi and the mountains far to the west, was one of the last undisturbed points of power in North America. Elman had acquired the land in 1831, decades before the building booms of the pre-and-post civil war periods destroyed the earthen works of native mound builders and rendered them useless.

Here, on the southern bank of the mighty Missouri, near the confluence of two great rivers, Yam Elman had consolidated his power. This had been a place of sacrifice for millennia, and native medicine men had performed some of the same rituals that Elman now performed. At the very edge of the property was an ancient burial mound where the decapitated skeletons of sacrificial victims had been interred for centuries.

While waiting for Bryn and Kisi to arrive, Jon had borrowed a laptop computer from a young Marine making delayed connections at Lambert, and he had used the airport's wi-fi to check out Elman's website and Facebook page. Elman's website urged people to "Enter the light" and said that Elman would help people find the light again if only they would put their complete trust in him and come to his "Center of Light" in Missouri to receive his blessing. There was a photograph of Elman wearing the golden mask of the Incas, and the hammered gold gleamed and glistened with the flash from the camera, making his masked face seem radiant and magnificent. If only, thought Jon, people could see the scarred visage behind that mask they would know the man for what he really was: A liar, a thief, and a man with no conscience or compasion.

His Facebook page had glowing comments about how Elman was the new savior of mankind, a prophet, a visionary, a miracle worker.

"What fools these mortals be," Jon had said as he slammed the laptop closed with disgust.

"Huh?" asked the young Marine.

"A quote from Shakespeare's *Tempest* ," said Jon. "Thanks, Marine. You have been a big help. I owe you."

"Semper Fi," said the Marine.

"Semper Fi," said Jon. "I got your back, Marine. You get to San Diego, you look me up, hear? I owe you a beer."

Even in civilian clothes, Jon Fish looked every inch the Marine. He was tall and muscular, his shoulders broad and his neck thick and corded and blue-veined. His sandy-blonde hair was cut high and tight, his blue eyes constantly alert. It was said you may take the man out of the uniform, but you could never take the Marine out of the man. That was certainly true of Jon Fish.

And something similar was true of Jon's traveling companions. Though the Ranger had the shaved head of a Buddhist monk, he had the muscular physique of an Army Ranger. His shoulders and neck were identical to Jon's, the results of innumerable daily pushups and pull-ups and military presses. Though not quite as tall as the Marine, the ex-Ranger was built like a bull.

Bryn, too, was tall, especially for a woman. Her fiery hair was bright red, the color of blood, and it was tied up in Celtic knots with a long braid down the back. She was also muscular and hard-bodied, and her tiny breasts were shielded by a bronze breastplate she wore beneath an oversized sweatshirt.

Kisi, on the other hand, was very much a picture of femininity. Her hair was long and silken, naturally blonde, and her breasts were full and round. She wore a fuscia-colored cotton blouse and designer jeans. Her face needed no make-up, and her eyebrows were thin and her eyelashes were long. But she wore the same determined look on her face as the others, and she could be a fierce warrior when she wanted to be.

"We're getting close," said Kisi. "Can you sense the power coming from over there, just to the left?"

Jon pulled off the road and parked the Camero in a ditch. They would have to go the rest of the way on foot, passing through a plowed farmer's field to get to Elman's wooded property overlooking the river. They would be sitting ducks out in the open for nearly half a mile, but there was no other way to get onto the protected property and they had the cover of darkness and the knowledge that electronic devices such as infra-red rifle scopes and night vision goggles wouldn't work within a cone of power. There was a gravel driveway that extended from the road to a house and barn, but the driveway was guarded by armed men. And the northern side of the property faced a 40-foot high bluff overlooking the south side of the river, a climb up a sheer rock cliff that would surely leave them more exposed than crossing an open field.

Besides, Elman had set wards around most of the property, and only one small section at the end of the farmer's field where a creek cut through the land all the way to the river was open for trespass.

It had started to rain shortly after they left Lambert Field, and rain continued coming down as they drove north in the Camero. At first, that rain was little more than a light drizzle, barely noticeable, but as they shouldered the automatic weapons Jon and the Ranger had brought with when they teleported from Angkor and they began walking through the freshly-plowed farmer's field, that rain started to come down in earnest. Cool winds from the northwest seemed to increase in velocity now as they crossed the open space between the road and the trees, driving raindrops straight into their eyes and making it almost impossible to see in the darkness.

As the rain soaked into the plowed furrows, leather boots made loud sucking noises every time one of the four picked up a foot. It took them a long time to work their way more than halfway across the plowed field, and they were already tired and sore. And cold. And wet. Their clothes were soaked completely through, and the winds plastered the wet material against their bodies and stole body heat and chilled them to the bone.

Cold and wet, they plodded on until they reached the creek. Jon took the lead, and he stepped into the running water and continued north, followed by the Ranger, Kisi, and Bryn. At the boundary of Elman's property, they felt the cone of power that Elman had constructed around and above the land he owned. But the running water ran under the cone, and the four—

already cold and wet—dropped down into the even colder water and let the current carry them across the boundary without any problem.

They saw four buildings on the property: A big wooden house, two wooden outbuildings, and a barn twice as big as the house. Beyond the barn, in a clearing near the edge of the cliff, was an earthen mound thirty feet in diameter. West of the mound was a circular fire pit, surrounded by rocks, with a huge bonfire blazing in the center of that circle, sparks shooting high up into the sky as drops of rain pelted the smoldering logs and made them sizzle. Plumes of black smoke obscured whatever activity was taking place on top of the mound, but Jon could see women being escorted one at a time from the barn to the mound. Then the men, and only the men, returned to the barn for another woman to escort to the mound, but none of those women went back to the barn with their escorts.

"That mound is Elman's sacrificial altar," whispered Jon.

"Can you manifest Akashagarbha?" whispered Bryn.

"Not inside the cone," Jon whispered back.

"Then we'll have to do this the old-fashioned way," said Bryn. She pulled the Heckler and Koch from her shoulder and checked the magazine.

"I'll go to the left," said Jon. "Ranger, you take the right flank. Bryn, you have the center. We'll meet at the mound."

"What about me?" asked Kisi.

"Cover us from here. You see anyone come out of the barn, shoot them. Don't let them get anywhere close to us. Understood?"

"Understood," said Kisi.

"On the count of three. One...two...three!"

Jon and the Ranger raced toward the mound with Bryn close behind, the automatic H & K submachine guns ready to do some serious damage. Jon circled around to the west, coming in at the mound from the direction of the bonfire. His nostrils filled with smoke, and the smoke burned his eyes and seared his lungs. But he charged forward, up the hill and onto the mound where Elman stood. Elman wore the golden mask, but this time he held not a sacrificial knife in his hand but a wand.

Jon didn't hesitate. He opened fire at the man in the golden mask, but the bullets bounced off the protective shield Elman had cast over his person, and Jon heard the sound of hundreds of ricochets as both the Ranger and Bryn fired their weapons.

Elman waved the wand and Jon felt like he'd been hit in the gut with a sledgehammer. He doubled over and dropped his weapon. He fell to the ground and rolled into a ball to protect himself.

Now Elman waved the wand at the Ranger, and Jon saw his friend fly backwards and slam into a tree. Bryn charged at Elman and met the same fate.

Agonizing pain spread through Jon's body as Elman aimed the wand again in his direction.

"This time I prepared," said Elman. "I knew you would come, and I set a trap for you."

Elman pointed the wand at the Ranger and Jon heard his friend scream as the crushing force of Elman's power splintered each of the Ranger's fingers and shattered the bones in his arms and legs.

Then it was Bryn's turn to scream as Elman aimed the wand at her and the metal breastplate beneath her sweatshirt exploded. Jagged pieces of metal punctured her chest and abdomen, and blood poured from gaping holes in the knotted muscles where her stomach had been.

"I won't kill you," said Elman. "Not yet, anyway. Not until you beg me to take your life force." He turned the wand on Jon and Jon saw the skin on both hands begin to blister. He felt like he was on fire, as if his blood itself were boiling, and now the blisters on his forehead and cheeks broke and blood and puss streamed down his face and clouded his vision. No part of his body was left unscathed, and even his genitals blistered and split apart like hot dogs left too long on a charcoal grill.

He heard himself screaming then, his screams rising to crescendo. He willed himself to lose consciousness, but the pain endured.

"Beg," said Elman. "You can do it. I know you can."

It would be so easy to comply, to allow Elman to end this misery, to give up now and save himself from the excruciating pain that ripped through every part of Jon's mutilated body. Surely, death was preferable to the continuing torture Elman had planned.

Jon remembered the torture his mother had endured at the hands of the doctors as cancer ate away at her body and doctors removed first one tumor and then another, sometimes removing infected internal organs along with the tumors. The pain-filled weeks and months of radiation and chemo, then more surgery and more chemo, being completely debilitated and dependent on others for everything, connected to bottles and bags and machines that functioned in place of her missing organs. And finally her body had simply given up the fight and she passed peacefully into oblivion, a shadow of her former self.

And he remembered the many times, after the death of his mother and the death of his brother, when he had thought about ending his own life by putting the barrel of a gun into his open mouth and swallowing a bullet.

But he hadn't actually done that, and he had survived for a reason. He had gone on to save countless lives by his selfless actions, and he had returned to the Corps where he had trained others to save lives even if it meant killing. He was, after all, a Marine.

And Marines never gave up.

Semper Fi, he told himself as the pain increased. Semper Fi.

BOOK III

All the souls had now chosen their lives, and they went in the order of their choice to Lachesis, who sent with them the genius whom they had severally chosen, to be the guardian of their lives and the fulfiller of the choice: this genius led the souls first to Clotho, and drew them within the revolution of the spindle impelled by her hand, thus ratifying the destiny of each; and then, when they were fastened to this, carried them to Atropos, who spun the threads and made them irreversible, whence without turning round they passed beneath the throne of Necessity; and when they had all passed, they marched on in a scorching heat to the plain of Forgetfulness, which was a barren waste destitute of trees and verdure; and then towards evening they encamped by the river of Unmindfulness, whose water no vessel can hold; of this they were all obliged to drink a certain quantity, and those who were not saved by wisdom drank more than was necessary; and each one as he drank forgot all things. Now after they had gone to rest, about the middle of the night there was a thunderstorm and earthquake, and then in an instant they were driven upwards in all manner of ways to their birth, like stars shooting.

--Plato. *The Republic*. Book X. The Myth of Er.

CHAPTER FOURTEEN

K isi heard gunshots, and then she heard screams. She had never heard Bryn or the Ranger or Jon scream before, and she barely recognized their voices. But she knew it was them that still filled the air with their blood-curdling cries of pain, and she knew they were already beyond her help.

But she had to do something, so she crawled forward on her belly until she could see the mound and Elman standing atop the mound wearing the golden mask and waving his hands like the conductor of a symphony orchestra directing a command performance of Beethoven's Fifth.

Elman danced about with glee, actually giggling like a little girl. Bryn lay sprawled on the ground half-way up the mound, writhing in pain. The Ranger was fifteen meters off to the right, curled up like a fetus at the base of a tree, screaming his fool head off. Jon was on the other side of the mound, rolling on the ground like he was trying to put out a fire.

All three were screaming.

Whatever Elman was doing to them wasn't real, though it must seem real to all three of Kisi's companions. They were experiencing real pain, and that was evident by the expressions on their faces and the screams coming from their mouths.

Elman was a master of illusion, and Kisi remembered seeing Yam perform illusions on stage in Berlin before the outbreak of the Second World War. His name then had been Hermann Steinschneider, and he was a master magician and illusionist. He had created illusions with the help of a "magic" wand, a wooden stick infused with earth magic and decorated with runes. He used the wand to focus the attention of the audience while he chanted "spells" infused with embedded commands. The rhythmic rising and falling cadences of his voice, the gestures he made with the wand, had entranced the audience and created powerful hallucinations. She remembered Hermann Steinschneider sawing a woman in half, separating the two halves of the woman's body and turning them around so the audience could see her red, raw internal organs spilling out of the severed flesh like meat from a meat grinder. Members of the audience had screamed, as Jon and the Ranger and Bryn were screaming now, and several women in that audience had fainted dead away until they were revived with smelling salts held beneath their flared nostrils. But then Steinschneider had pushed the severed parts back together, waved his magic wand over the woman's body, and the woman had risen up from the table whole and complete, smiling, bowing from the center of her body where she had previously been cut in two, joining hands with her tormentor as both took a final bow to thunderous applause.

Kisi remembered the Vril-infused wooden staff Hermann Steinschneider had carried in France, and her mind flashed back to a previous life when she was known in Zagreb as Maria Orsic, and Bryn was known as Sigrune, and Kiyari was known as Gudrun. The year was 1917, and the First World War was ending badly for Germany. Maria and Sigrune were psychic mediums and channelers in Vienna, and both young women were incredibly beautiful with waist-length hair that had never been cut. One day when Maria was channeling the spirit of the brother of a Hungarian count, another spirit took possession of her. She was driven to put pen to paper, and an incredible thing happened. Without any conscious control, her hand automatically filled four pages with cuneiform writing. Maria knew nothing of cuneiform, but the Hungarian count knew a professor at the university who was an expert in Sumerian culture. The professor translated the writing as a favor to the count, and Maria was surprised to learn that what she had written described the power of Vril and how to harness it. Vril was the power of the universe— some called it prana, or life-force energy—and it was controlled with intended thought and could be directed through wood. That is, wood took the energy of thought and will and focused it so it could be directed to heal or destroy.

And it could also be directed to control men's minds.

"You have lived before," said Sigrune. "In ancient Sumeria, in the land between rivers called Mesopotania. I know, because I lived then, too."

"Is that how I would know to write in a foreign language?"

"Yes, dear. That's how you knew."

"But I don't remember."

"Maybe not consciously. But you *do* remember. Memories of everything you have ever done, seen, heard, smelled, or tasted in this lifetime and all other lifetimes are part of your essence. Those memories remain inside you, buried deep inside your mind. When we go into trance to contact the spirit world, those memories sometimes surface. I think that's what happened to you. There's something important in what you wrote that you were meant to remember."

"Do you really think so?"

"I know so."

Now Kisi remembered. She remembered not only what she had written about Vril in Vienna, but she remembered all that she had learned in ancient Sumer. Vril was a gift of the Elohim, the gods of Sumer, or Shumer in the Akkadian language, or Shin'ar in Hebrew, or Ta Neter in ancient Egyptian. The Elohim were the Watchers, sometimes called the Guardians of the Four Winds, and Sumer or Shumer or Shin'ar or Ta Neter meant "Land of the Watchers" in all known languages.

And the gods of Sumer who had taught Kisi—and Bryn and Hadad and Kiyari, too—about the Vril were now known to her as Biegolmai, Lokesvara, La Curandera, and Sara Nelson.

Vril energy, they said, infused the entire universe. It was the essential power of creation, and it resided in the imagination and in the breath of sentient beings. Though the power of Vril depended on the power of opposites—of polarities—to make magic happen, Vril could also create the illusion of magic. Great magicians who knew how to control the imagination need not waste valuable resources making real magic. There were times when illusion alone accomplished one's goals.

Such was the power of positive and negative hallucinations, and all that was required was an active imagination and a wand or a staff or a crystal to attract and hold a subject's attetion. Vril energy focused the power of the imagination and transfered thoughts from the mind of the Magician to the mind of the target subject. It had been used successfully in India and Tibet for millennia, and it was one of the most closely guarded secrets of adepts in the west.

Kisi had never used Vril energy to control minds, because she was in touch with the earth, and earth magic was always real, never an illusion. But here, within Yam's cone of power, Kisi's magic was contained. She couldn't draw upon the feminine energies of the Great Mother. She felt totally helpless.

But if Yam could use Vril energy to create illusions in the minds of Kisi's companions, perhaps Kisi could create illusions in Yam's mind.Vril energy was everywhere and anyone coud use it. All one needed was a point of focus and to touch wood.

She reached out and touched a tree with her left hand. Kisi focused her own mind on intent, on what she wanted to accomplish. She imagined she was a falcon. She saw herself diving straight down at Yam's face with both talons outstretched like claws, and she saw herself tearing off chunks of raw flesh and gouging out one eye—Yam's last good eye—before Yam could protect himself with a spell.

Kisi saw herself swooping down to snatch the wooden wand, as she had before with the staff, and fly off with it.

She repeated those thoughts over and over again in her mind, projecting those images at Elman on the mound. She saw him as blind and helpless. She repeated those thoughts again and again until they became reality for Yam Elman.

Elman clutched at the mask covering his face, tore the mask completely off and tried to shield his eyes with his bare hands. In his mind he saw the falcon snatch the wand and fly off, and he cursed and cursed and staggered about as if he were blind and could no longer see.

Kisi maintained the illusion, feeling the pain that Elman must feel, the confusion and the despair and the helplessness he felt. She envisioned blood spouting from the empty eye socket where Elman's right eye had been, and Elman screamed.

She could taste the blood now, Elman's blood, running down his right cheek and into his mouth. She could smell the iron-rich odor of fresh blood, and the fear of pending death it induced. Nauseated herself, she fought the need to escape.

When Elman could no longer stand the pain or endure the thoughts filling his mind, he fled in panic. Elman blinked out of existence on the mound in Missouri and went elsewhere.

And he took the mask with him.

Kisi took a deep breath, and she allowed the scene to slowly fade from her own mind. Gradually, she returned to ordinary consciousness.

And so did her companions. Jon moved first, his eyes opening wide as he tried to focus on his hands. He looked at his hands as if he had never seen them before, flexed his fingers into fists, and turned the hands over to inspect the palms. Then he moved his hands over his entire body, feeling for broken bones and open wounds. Then he touched his face as if expecting the flesh to be gone. When he found his entire body was intact, he smiled.

Bryn moved next. She clutched her stomach as if she were trying to force the intestines back inside. Then she felt her breasts, and found them whole and hearty. There were no holes in her rounded flesh, no punctured lungs. She, too, was whole and intact. She looked too weak to stand, and she just sat there as if waiting patiently for her strength to return.

But the Ranger was neither whole nor intact. His head had hit the tree much too hard, and his skull had actually cracked open. He had suffered a terrible concussion that scattered his brains. He tried to think, but he couldn't focus. The world was spinning, and he was spinning with it.

He tried to come back to the here and now, but his brain simply wouldn't cooperate. His synapses were scrambled, and he had lost all touch with reality. His short term memory had been badly damaged.

He was back in Afghanistan, leading his men into a Taliban ambush. Because they had no clue that the Afghan troops they had been training in a base camp outside Kabul were secretly Taliban sympathizers, their midnight raid on a Taliban stronghold was known well in advance by the enemy. Taliban troops ambushed the entire squad of U. S. Army Rangers, killing and mutilating all except one. That one barely survived, thanks to his iron will and the miracles of modern medicine, but he returned to duty as a changed man. Now he hated all Afghans, and he intended to kill every one of them he could find. At first, his superiors had rewarded him for his initiative, for his fierce determination and combat skills, but when they learned he had crawled out of camp in the middle of the night and indiscriminately murdered helpless civilians—men, women, and children—they had cashiered him out of the service with a medical discharge. He had hired himself out then to the highest bidder, and he became a paid mercenary who would kill anyone for a buck. And he had killed a dozen or more men for the money his employers deposited into Swiss and Cayman bank accounts.

Lokesvara had saved him. The old monk had come to America to save the world, and he needed the Ranger's help. Lokesvara had shown the Ranger how to meditate, and Lokesvara had re-introduced him to Vajrapani. And the rest was history.

But the Ranger didn't remember meeting Lokesvara. His brain no longer functioned normally. Nor did he remember Vajrapani. He was the Lone Ranger, the only survivor of that traitorous ambush in Afghanistan, and the hired assassin who killed because it was all he knew and because he was good at it.

He found the Heckler and Koch submachine gun next to the base of the tree, and he clutched the cold metal close to his chest. It was as good a weapon as any to use, and he fully intended to use it.

He got to his feet very slowly, unsure of which bones would still support him. He remembered he had been wounded, his body broken. But he still had a mission to accomplish.

He remembered his mission: to kill, to kill, and to kill some more. The Army had taught him that, and he would never ever forget it.

As he walked away from the tree, he failed to notice in the dark two women and a man sprawled on the wet ground near the mound. If he had noticed them, he would have shot them.

Somewhere near here, he knew in his heart, there had to be enemy soldiers, and his job was to find them and wipe them out. If a few civilians were killed as collateral damage, so be it. He would allow no one and nothing to stop him from completing his primary mission.

He thought about testing the submachine gun on a flock of ravens sitting in a tree, their black bodies barely visible in the flickering firelight. But he didn't want to waste the ammunition on non-essential targets, and he sure as hell didn't want to give away his current position to the enemy.

He walked toward the barn with the submachine gun at the ready. Because he was ready.

Ready to kill, to kill, and to kill some more.

*　　*　　*

Biegolmai's spirit occupied the body of one of those ravens in the tree at the edge of Elman's property that Kisi had touched to acquire Vril, and Biegolmai had observed all that happened at the mound. Had Kisi failed to vanquish Yam, Biegolmai would have found some other way to intervene. But Kisi had done very well on her own.

Now that Yam had physically vacated the property, Biegolmai was able to send his spirit to check on the well-being of his four protégés. Jon was recovering quickly, and so was Bryn.

Kisi was mentally and physically exhausted, but she was all right.

The Ranger, however, was mentally unbalanced. He had suffered real physical damage as well as mental torture, and his mind wasn't functioning normally. Biegolmai's spirit was unable to enter an unreceptive psyche, so he couldn't communicate directly with the Ranger's spirit.

But he could communicate with Jon Fish. "You must stop the Ranger from hurting anyone," Biegolmai whispered inside Jon's mind. "He's not himself. If he goes on a rampage and kills someone, we'll lose Vajrapani forever."

"What do you mean he's not himself?" asked Jon.

"He thinks he's back in a combat zone. I don't believe he'll recognize you, and I don't think he'll listen to reason. He may even see you as an enemy and try to kill you."

"I'm on it," said Jon, leaping to his feet. "If I can't handle it, I'll call Akashagarbha in to help."

Biegolmai watched Jon race across the grounds toward the barn. There were thirty-two people in that barn, and fourteen more people inside the house. Thirty of the people in the barn were unarmed women, and two were Elman's hired gunmen.

While Biegolmai watched, the Ranger circled the barn to the side door. He was about to open the door and rush in with his gun blazing when the buildings—the entire barn, the house, and the two outbuildings—simply disappeared.

Only Akashagarbha, the Boundless Space Matrix, had the power to actually do such a thing, but the Ranger no longer knew who Akashagarbha was. Nor did the Ranger know Jon, who must have asked Akashagarbha to send the buildings elsewhere—perhaps to the middle of a farmer's field or perhaps to a far-off desert—where the Ranger couldn't kill the people inside.

Now the Ranger heard Jon running toward him, and he opened fire with the submachine gun. Jon hit the ground and rolled out of the way before a stream of bullets passed through the space where he had been standing moments before. Jon was on his feet again, rushing forward, the instant the firing stopped. Not only did Jon have finely-tuned combat skills, but he had Askashagarbha's insight to guide him.

Even in the dark, the Ranger's aim was deadly accurate and another burst of bullets passed through the space where Jon had been but a moment ago. Jon managed to stay one step ahead of his opponent. The Ranger's reflexes seemed slower than normal and Biegolmai surmised the man's brain injuries were partly responsible.

Jon was still closing fast as the Ranger's H & K ran out of ammunition. Jon was right on him, wrenching the weapon from the Ranger's hands before the Ranger could reload. The Ranger kicked at Jon's legs, missing his kneecap but connecting with the front of Jon's calf and cracking the tibia. Jon went down, and the Ranger was on him in a heartbeat, smashing both fists into Jon's face.

"I'm a Marine!" Jon shouted. "And I'm your friend, ass-hole. We're on the same side."

"That's what the Afghans said. They lied."

Jon slammed an elbow against the Ranger's cheekbone, but the blow seemed to have little effect. The Ranger raised one massive fist and brought the side of the hand down toward Jon's vulnerable neck in what would have been a killing karate blow had it landed.

But Jon had already transformed into Akashagarbha and tansported out of the way. Now the bodisattva stood ten feet away on both legs as if both tibia were intact. An eerie glow surrounded his transformed body like a neon aura. The Marine seemed to be much taller and broader than before. He looked like a giant.

"What the fuck..." said the Ranger.

"Enough!" boomed the mighty voice of Akashagarbha.

Bryn and Kisi had retrieved their weapons, and they stood a respectable distance from the Ranger and aimed their Heckler and Koch submachine guns directly at his midsection.

"Believe it or not," said Kisi, "we are your friends. We want to help you, not hurt you."

"I have no friends," said the Ranger. "My friends died in Afghanistan."

"You are loved," said Kisi. "Will you not accept that in lieu of friendship?"

"Who the fuck are you people?" asked the Ranger. "And what happened to the Marine I was about to finish?"

"I am that Marine," said Akashagarbha. "If you want to fight, fight me."

"Okay," said the Ranger. "I will."

"Hold your fire," Akashagarbha told Bryn and Kisi as the Ranger leapt to his feet. "Let him come."

The Ranger swung a fist at the giant and Akashagarbha grabbed the fist in his huge hand. As soon as the Ranger and Akashagarbha touched, both men blinked out of existence in Missouri and blinked back into existence at Machu Picchu. Biegeolmai followed then to Machu Picchu in spirit form.

"Where the fuck are we?" demanded the Ranger. "We're high up, aren't we? I can't catch my breath."

"More than ten thousand feet above sea level," said Akashagarbha. "On top of a mountain in Peru."

"How the hell did we get here?"

"I willed us here."

"Both of us?"

"When you touched me, we became linked. I was able to teleport both of us."

"I don't understand what just heppened," said the Ranger, sitting down on a stone slab and holding his aching head.

Akashagarbha called to La Curandera. Both Kiyari and Hadad came carrying torches.

"The Ranger and Jon both need your help," said Akash-agarbha. "The Ranger hit his head and Jon has a broken leg. Will you help?"

"Of course," said La Curandera in Kiyari's voice.

"You ain't gonna touch me," said the Ranger, getting up from his rock and backing away.

"I don't need to touch you," said Kiyari. "But you aren't going anywhere because there's a thousand foot drop behind you." She raised her hands and light shot out of the ring fingers of both hands and infused the Ranger's body with healing energy. "Just relax, and let mama do her work."

Biegolmai watched the proceedings from a condor circling high overhead. He witnessed the burst of radiant light that infused the Ranger's aura as La Curandera drew prana from the heavens and healing energy from the earth. Where they merged inside the Ranger's aura, wheels of light began spinning, spinning, spinning. Up and down the meridians they ran full force, marrying the Ida and the Pingala in a ritual as ancient as time. Healing energy poured into the Ranger's body, and the cracks in his skull mended and the neural pathways that retained the Ranger's memories reconnected and new axions grew and sent signals to old dendrites across synaptical gaps. A flood of memories overwhelmed the Ranger, and he fell to his knees and openly wept.

"Now Jon," said Kiyari. As Akashagarbha's spirit released Jon's body, the Marine returned to his normal appearance and fell to the ground.

Once again Kiyari held up her hands and stretched out all her fingers, and once again healing energy and pure white light poured forth from both ring fingers to envelope his entire body. Within seconds, the tibia knitted together and Jon Fish felt healthy and whole.

"What about the Ranger?" Jon asked La Curandera. "Did you fix him up as good as new?"

"His body is already healing," said Kiyari. "But his spirit needs time to mend. He is no longer linked to Vajrapani."

"Where did Vajrapani go?"

"I don't know. Maybe Loksvara does, but I don't."

"Is the Ranger well enough to travel?"

"Akashagarbha can take him back to Angkor. His body and mind will continue to heal for the next seventy-two hours. Spiritual healing may take considerably longer."

"If anyone can help heal his spirit, it's Lokesvara."

"It's entirely up to the Ranger himself what direction his spirit travels. He is, after all, a free spirit. He rejected violence before, and he may do so again. But circumstances have forced him to break his vows. I don't know what effect that might have on his future actions."

"You think he'll return to violence?"

"He did tonight. It is still inside him."

"Do you think he's dangerous?"

La Curandera laughed. "Yes," she said. "Don't you?"

*   *   *

Kisi and Bryn drove the Camero back to Saint Louis and returned it to Hertz. Then they teleported to Wisconsin and looked for Yam, but they couldn't find him anywhere.

"He has switched bodies," said Sara. "He finally discarded the old one-eyed shell and invaded someone else's body. I think Kisi scared the hell out of him."

"What about his accumulated power?" asked Bryn. "Did he lose it when he gave up the old body?"

"Some," said Sara. "That's why we can't pin-point his energy signature. It's different now than it was."

"He'll need to replenish his lost power," said Kisi. "What do you think he'll try next?"

"He will come here," said Sara, sounding certain. "He has no place else to go. He needs the power of a vortex to hide the sun. He can't touch Angkor with Lokesvara there. He can't touch Machu Picchu with La Curandera there. None of the other vortexes are powerful enough for him. What else is left? The Seita and here. He'll come here, because Biegolmai is at the Seita. Yam isn't stupid enough to try to take on Biegolmai."

"But he's stupid enough to try to take on four women?" asked Kisi.

"Yes," said Sara. "He is."

CHAPTER FIFTEEN

B iegolmai watched Akashagarbha pick up the Ranger, and the two men flashed out of existence on Machu Picchu to return to Angkor Wat. Then Biegolmai willed his spirit to contact La Curandera and thank her for healing the two men.

"It is what I do," she said. "I have always been a healer."

"And a good one," said Biegolmai. "I have always depended on you. You have never failed to heal when asked."

"I want to train some others," said La Curandera. "Is that all right with you?"

"Of course," said Biegolmai. "The world always needs healers. Who do you have in mind?"

"Kiyari," said La Curandera. "And Kisi."

"Good choices," said Biegolmai.

"And the Ranger. When he is ready."

"A man? Can a man be a healer?"

"If he can get in touch with his feminine side."

"And you think the Ranger has a feminine side?"

"Everyone does. You, included."

"Well, yes. I suppose that's true."

"You were a wonderful healer once, Grandfather. I imagine you still are."

"I have other duties that require my attention."

"Like guarding the Seita?"

"Yes."

"The Ranger is still wounded, Grandfather," said La Curnadera, using the honorific she knew Biegolmai treasured, and he knew she only called him Grandfather when she wanted something from him. "I have healed his body, but his spirit remains broken. Does that remind you of anyone?"

"Are you speaking of me, perhaps, La Curandera?"

"Yes, Grandfather, I am. Wasn't that why you began the healer's journey? To heal yourself?"

"Those were dark days, Granddaughter. I was not then who I am now."

"*These* are dark days, Grandfather. As dark or darker than were those."

"How did you get to be so wise?"

"Wisdom comes with time, Grandfather. You taught me that."

"What is it that you want?"

"I want you to be a healer again, Grandfather. I want you to heal the Ranger's spirit. I want you to send him on the shaman's journey into darkness and the underworld and give him a

challenge that awakens the good in him. Can you do that? Will
you do that? For me? And for him?"

"How do you propose we do that, Granddaughter?"

"By abandoning the Seita."

"What! And let Yam have it?"

"Yes."

"Do you realize what damage Yam could do if he gains
control of the Seita?"

"Yes. The challenge must be real."

"No. It is far too risky. I am custodian of the Seita, and I
have a sacred responsibility to protect the World Tree. What you
ask is too much!"

"Where is your faith, old man? Have you forgotten what
the human spirit is capable of?"

"I have forgotten nothing, woman. Least of all have I
forgotten how you try to wrap me around your little finger."

"Discuss it with Lokesvara. You will see that I am
right."

"I have left the Seita unattended too long already. I must
return."

"Then go, Grandfather. And know my love goes with
you."

*   *   *

In the frozen wastelands north of the arctic circle, the land of the Lapps stretched across international boundaries to occupy parts of what is now Norway, Sweden, Finland, and Russia. For tens of thousands of years, the Saami people, like their Komsa cousins for countless generations before them, had followed meandering reindeer herds across the frozen tundra. The reindeer was their totem animal, the spirit guides of the people of the far north, and for the Saami reindeer meant life.

Biegolmai Davvii was a Fjeld Saami. He had long white hair and a bushy white beard and he looked like Santa Claus in an old Coca-Cola commercial, only thinner. He was a giant of a man, nearly seven feet tall and weighed three hundred pounds. His own people called him "Grandfather Winter" and treated him with tremendous respect. No one knew how old Biegolmei was, for he had always been there, near the Seita, through the lifetimes of all who lived now. Some said he was older than the hills. If that were true, he had lived here before the last ice age came and went.

The man called Biegolmai Davvii resided in a plain reindeer-hide hut near the Tornetrask river, somewhere between Karesuando and Kiruna, north of the Arctic Circle in the land of the Midnight Sun, and after the fall equinox the sun virtually disappeared from his part of the world. For half the year the land remained in near total darkness, and for half the year it flourished in full daylight. When the sun was visible to the human eye, that is, which it wasn't now.

Biegolmai's family had been reindeer herders, following the versatile animals up into the mountains during the summer, returning to pasture along the rivers in the winter. Reindeer provided the Saami transportation, were the primary souce of protein in their diets, and furnished hides for coats, shoes, hats, and gloves. But the old man no longer followed the herds, preferring to remain close to the Seita—an ancient artificial rock formation not too far from the town of Karesuando, near the Swedish border with Finland. Local legends claimed this so-called Seita possessed magical powers, and some historians had speculated that the Seita—and other man-made rock formations like it in Sweden, Norway, and Finland—had been the scenes of bloody ritual sacrifices some 11,000 years ago, around the end of the last ice age.

Biegolmai believed he was the guardian of the rocks, and he took his custodianship seriously. He had established wards around the entire area to keep trespassers out, and he had disguised the rock as a simple birch tree, frail and scragly and of no interest to anybody. When his spirit traveled—on his many shamanic journeys into the underworlds or the spirit worlds via the World Tree, or even to Missouri or Machu Picchu—his body remained behind in that tree in the form of a raven. And he had a flock of other ravens nearby keeping constant watch.

Now Biegolmai returned to his body and sat in the tree that was the Seita and contemplated La Curandera's request. She had risked everything twice before to redeem the spirits of Jerry

Walker and Kiyari, and she had been right in doing that. Was she right in asking Biegolmai to risk everything to save the spirit of a man like the Ranger?

Was there no other way?

Biegolmai would indeed need to consult with Lokesvara. Something like this required the concurrance of at least three of the Guardians. He knew where La Curandera stood. What would Lokesvara choose to do?

Biegolmai took down his wards, leaving the Seita unprotected. He dismissed his ravens as watchers. Then he changed his body back into human form and blinked out of existence in Lappland and into existence simultaneously in Angkor Wat.

Lokesvara was tending to the wounded Ranger in the temple's sick room. Jon was there, too, and they looked surpised to see the seven-foot-tall white-bearded Santa suddenly appear next to them as if he had just come down the chimney on Christmas Eve.

"I need to speak with you privately," said Biegolmai.

"What could be so important to bring you here in person?" asked Lokesvara.

"That's why I need to speak with you. In private, please."

"We'll go to my chambers. Jon, please see that the Ranger continues to rest comfortably. Now come with me down the hall, Grandfather. We can talk as we walk."

Biegolmai explained what he had done as they strolled toward Lokesvara's meditation chamber adjacent to the Lama's administrative offices. "Yam will sense that the Seita is unprotected. He will expect a trap, of course. It may take him a while to determine there is no trap in place."

"Of all the vortexes in the world, the Seita is perhaps the most powerful. He can use the Seita to access both the spirit realms and the underworlds. The Seita connects to the World Tree itself."

"I know."

"And yet you left the Seita unprotected that Yam might walk in and take possession?"

"Yes."

"Surely, you have a reason."

Biegolmai reminded Lokesvara that the Ranger's spirit had suffered severe trauma. "La Curandera convinced me the man is worth saving," Biegolmai said, "and I agree with her."

"But what has that to do with the Seita?"

"Everything," said Biegolmai. "The Ranger needs a challenge worthy of his abilities. Something that will tax him beyond his limits. Giving Yam control of the Seita provides such a challenge. Don't you think?"

Lokesvara was silent. "What's the matter?" asked Biegolmai. "Cat got your tongue?"

Lokesvara smiled. He placed the palms of both hands together and bowed.

"Namaste," he said. "I acknowledge the wisdom of your actions."

"It is a risk," admitted Biegolmai.

"All life is a risk," said Lokesvara.

"Indeed," said Biegolmai.

*   *   *

Time didn't exist for the Lone Ranger. His mind was still reeling, and he felt totally disoriented. He remembered his lives as Ayar Cachi. He remebered dying in his cave near the Urubamba, and he remembered being reborn. He remembered being a soldier of Rome, of long marches on foot in Gaul and Britain. He remembered being Drona Bharadwaja and fighting for the Licchavi on the banks of the Ganges. He remembered being a German soldier during the First World War and dying when machine gun bullets ripped his body apart in the trenches in France. He remembered being a non-commissioned American Army Ranger in Iraq and Afghanistan and nearly dying in an amsush. And he remebered being a Buddhist monk named Vajrapani.

How could he remember being all those things?

He was absolutely certain he had been all those people and done all those things, because he could remember the details so clearly as if they had happened yesterday. What he couldn't remember was yesterday. Yesterday was gone from his memory.

He remembered going to Missouri and driving from the Saint Louis airport north to find Yam Elman. He remembered Jon was driving a rented car, he was riding shotgun, and Bryn and Kisi were in the back seat. He remembered leaving the Camero in a ditch in the rain, crossing ruts of the recently plowed field, ducking down in the running water of a creek to get past Elman's wards. He remembered crawling to the edge of the indian mound and confronting Elman in his golden mask. He remembered Elman pointing a wooden stick at him. Everything after that was a blank.

He was lying in a bed in what he recognized as the lamasery's sickroom. He didn't remember how he got there or why he was there. The back of his head hurt as if someone had clubbed him, and when he tried to sit up the room began spinning. Either he was standing still and the world was moving awfullly fast around him, or he was spinning around real fast like a Dervish and the world was standing still. He wasn't sure which.

The world was dark except for a single lit candle flickering yellow and orange on a table by the bedside. He could smell burning incense, and he knew someone had recently been in the room who had been praying.

When he squinted his eyes, he could barely make out the shape of a man sitting in lotus on the floor near the foot of the bed. He recognized his friend Jon by the Marine's muscular neck, broad shoulders, and high and tight haircut.

"What happened?" he asked. "How did I get here? How long have I been in bed?"

"You're supposed to rest," said the voice of Jon Fish. "You're safe now, we're all safe, but you were injured in Missouri. Akashagarbha brought you here two days ago."

"Two days? I've been out for two days?"

"We woke you a few times to force feed you soup and tea," Jon said, rising from lotus and moving closer to the head of the bed. "But, yes. You have been out of it for two entire days."

"Did we get him? Did we get Yam?"

"No."

"What happened to me?"

"You really don't remember?"

"The last I remember is approaching the mound from the east while you came at it from the west. Bryn had the south. Yam was on the mound wearing that damned mask. And he had a pointed stick in his hand."

"That was a wand. He used it to direct energy at us. He whammied all three of us with a spell that sent us flying. You cracked your head on a tree hard enough to scramble your brains."

"I remember he pointed that stick at me. But that's the last I remember."

"It'll all come back to you in time. You're still healing. La Curandera mended your cracked skull, and she rewired your brains. For awhile there, though, you thought you were back in

Afghanistan. You knew you had to complete your mission, but you were mixed up which mission you were on."

"I didn't kill anyone, did I?"

"No, you didn't."

"Good. I've killed enough. I'm done with killing."

Lokesvara and Biegolmai entered the sickroom, and the Ranger couldn't help but stare at the giant. It was the first time the two had met in person.

"You're Biegolmai Davvii," said the Ranger.

"That's correct," said Biegolmai. "And you're the Lone Ranger, sometimes called Vajrapani. How are you feeling?"

"Wobbly," replied the Ranger.

"That's to be expected. You're still healing. You may feel wobbly and not quite yourself for a few days yet."

"I understand I have you to thank for saving me."

"You should thank Kisi for vanquishing Yam, and Akashagarbha for taking you to La Curandera for healing."

"What happened?"

"Yam used Vril energy to affect your minds. Yours, Jon's, and Bryn's. He created a powerful illusion that you believed was real. He tortured the three of you in order to break you down so you would voluntarily relinquish your life force to him. Despite excruciating torture, none of you broke."

"And then what happened?"

"Kisi turned the Vril force against Yam. He imagined a bird attacked his face and tore out his good eye. He fled like the coward he is."

"Kisi did that?"

"She did. She remembered what I had taught her about Vril in a past life, and she vanquished Yam with the same energies he had used to try to vanqusih you."

"What about Yam?"

"He escaped," said Biegolmai. "He is now at the Seita."

"You left the Seita unguarded? Why?"

"For reasons you wouldn't understand. I couldn't leave the wards intact if I intended to aid you. I had to choose between protecting the Seita or aiding you. I chose to aid you. Now I need your help to get the Seita back. Will you help?"

"What can I do?"

"Rest. When you have healed, Jon will bring you to Machu Picchu. I'll meet you there and give you further instructions. Are you willing to help?"

"Yes," said the Ranger.

"Good," said Biegolmai. "The journey of a thousand miles begins with the first step, and you have just taken the first step."

* * *

"Yam went to the Seita," said Sara. "He just walked in and claimed possession. Nothing stood in his way."

"Where was Biegolmai?" asked Bryn.

"At Angkor Wat."

"Why weren't there wards in place?"

"Biegolmai took down his wards before he left for Angkor."

"What! Why would he do such a thing?"

"I'm sure he had a reason. A good reason."

"Perhaps he wanted Yam to physically relocate to the Seita," said Kisi. "The Seita is entirely cut off from most of the rest of the world this time of the year. No one can get to it except on skis or by reindeer-pulled sled. Even the Saami have migrated away from the area, seeking warmth and winter grazing for their herds in the hills. Yam will be totally isolated up there, so far away from everyone and everything. He wil have no way to get humans to make sacrifice. If he teleports away for any reason, Biegolmai may come back and occupy the Seita again. Yam won't take that chance."

"Then what good does the Seita do him?" asked Sheila.

"Besides being a source of nearly unlimited energy, the Seita provides direct access to the World Tree."

"I still don't understand," said Sheila. "Why is the World Tree so important?"

"Because," answered Sara, "the World Tree has roots and branches that lead to other worlds. If one is adept, one can climb the World Tree and enter the spirit realm. Or one can use it to descend to the underworlds. In the underworlds, Yam will find kindred spirits to aid him. And if he frees those kindred spirits and allows them to leave the underworlds to infest the earth, the evil spirits will seek human bodies to possess and use."

"Anyone," added Bryn, "who steps outside his body for any reason might find his body no longer his, possessed by an evil spirit. Spirits who are sent to the underworlds have no compassion, no redeeming qualities. They have no hope of being reborn."

"So," said Sara, "if they reach our world, they will be like an infestation of parasites. They will leech onto any body that is available. The world will be overrun with disembodied spirits occupying himan shells."

"And that," said Bryn, "means chaos. And Yam thrives on chaos."

"If we think things have been bad since the sun disappeared," said Sara, "wait until you see how bad things get if Yam releases spirits from the underworlds. Yam's power will grow exponentially, even without willing sacrifices. When things get bad enough, people will line up to give away their life force just to make the nighmares go away."

"Then why," asked Sheila, "did Begolmai let Yam gain access to the World Tree?"

"Because," offered Kisi, "Biegolmai may have a plan to stop Yam from releasing those spirits from the underworlds. He's sending Kiyari, the Ranger, and me into the underworlds to trap Yam in darkness and keep him there until he restores the sun. I've been summoned to Machu Picchu where Biegolmai will brief us and show us another way to descend the World Tree."

"When are you leaving?" asked Sara.

"Right now," said Kisi. "Pray for us."

And then Kisikil Lilake blinked out of existence in Wisconsin and began the perilous journey to hell and back.

"Wait," said Bryn. "I'm going with you." And Bryn blinked out of existence and followed her sister on her date with death.

CHAPTER SIXTEEN

"Y am is known in the underworlds as Rahu," said Hadad. "and I am known there as Ketu. Yam has been to the underworlds many times. In the underworlds, Rahu has the head of a snake and the illusion of a human body."

"Rahu," added Biegolmai, "is a master of avidya, or illusion. Beware, he may appear in the underworlds as anyone or anything. He is also king of the Nagas, snakes and giant serpent-like creatures. He has absolute power over them in their domain, and he may command them as he desires. Nagas live in Patala, the seventh underworld, but you may find them anwhere in the underworlds. Beware of the Nagas. They will poison your spirits if they bite you."

"You cannot enter the underworld in a physical body," said La Curandera. "This is a spiritual journey, and you must leave your human bodies behind. Before you leave, seal your bodies so no wandering spirits can walk in and take possession. After all openings are sealed, sit comfortably in lotus, and release your spirits through thte crown chakras. As your spirits pass through each of the underworlds, you may manifest spirit bodies to reflect your spiritual development at that phase of the journey. Do not be surpirsed if your bodies suddenly change for the better or for the worse. Expect the unexpected. Nothing in any of the underworld realms is what it seems. You must decipher the hidden meanings behind every revelation. As you pass through each of the underworlds, you will confront different challenges. Each challenge becomes greater than the one previously encountered. If you survive, your spirits will emerge stronger. If you do not survive, your spirits will be trapped in the underworlds forever. Your human bodies left behind here will die of neglect, and you will never again be reborn."

"Yam has already descended the World Tree at the Seita," said Biegolmai. "His spirit waits for you in the underworlds. He has the advantage because he knows the underworlds and you do not. Not yet. But you will learn."

"Your spiritual journey begins now," said La Curandera. "There are nine underworlds and all nine underworlds are frought with unbelievable dangers. I wish you all good luck."

"I'm going with," said Hadad.

"Me, too," said Askashagarbha.

"No," said Biegolmai. "I have allowed Bryn to accompany Kisi, Kiyari, and the Ranger. No more, please."

"Why not?" protested Hadad.

"Because you have other tasks to perform if we are to restore the sun to its rightful place in the heavens."

"But I can help," protested Hadad.

"You can help more by continuing to search for the two masks," said Biegolmai.

"How did you know I was looking for the masks?"

"La Curandera told me. We have no secrets from each other."

"But why not me?" asked Jon.

"Lokesvara may have need for you here," answered Biegolmai. "This time the Ranger must survive or perish without your assistance."

"The Incan gateway to the underworld is there," said La Curandera, pointing to an opening in the rocks. "Once you enter, you must progress through all nine worlds before you can emerge at the Seita. Are you ready?"

"I'll go first," said the Ranger.

"Ladies go first," said Bryn, pushing his spirit aside and entering in front of him.

Bryn entered first, followed by Kisi, Kiyari, and the Ranger. As they descended to the heart of the mountain in absolute darkness, they heard running water, the sounds of a mighty river rushing to the sea.

And then they were falling. It was as if all of the ground around them had been eroded by running water from that river, leaving a bottomless pit into which they plunged. Spirits used to soaring aloft on the winds found themselves caught in a downdraft so powerful that they had no control over which direction they went. They were pushed and shoved downward, accelerating at an incredible speed. Faster and faster. Falling. Tumbling head over heels. Now they felt their spirit bodies being pulled downward even faster, sucked into the maelstrom between Scylla and Charybdis where the daughter of Poseidon and the daughter of Hecate fought each other for the privilege of swallowing them whole and then spitting them out.

Finally, they *were* spit out. They arrived in the first underworld, battered and beaten and a lot worse for wear, finding themselves on the floor of what looked to be a huge underground cavern with solid rock walls and no ceiling. But all four arrived there together and conscious of their surroundings. And all four spirits were surprised to find they wore bodies that looked identical to the bodies they had left behind. They even wore the same clothes.

"It is because our spirits have not yet changed," said Kisi. "We look no different than we did before."

"This is not what I expected," said the Ranger. "I thought there were supposed to be fierce guardians blocking the gates of hell who would challenge us as soon as we arrived."

"Hellhounds keep spirits from getting out, not from getting in," said Bryn. "Getting in is easy. Getting out will be pure hell."

"How come you know so much about it?" asked Kisi.

"Like Hadad, I, too, have been here before," said Bryn. "and so has Kiyari."

"Is that true?" Kisi asked Kiyari.

"Yes," said the girl. "Now that I am in spirit form, I am able to remember all of my past lives as each of you may remember your past lives. My name long ago was Kore, the daugher of Demeter. I was raped and carried off to one of the underworlds by Aidoneus, Lord of the Dead. But before that I was known as Innana, and I came here once to visit my twin sister after her husband was murdered. My sister, Ereshkigal, is a queen here, and she rules one of the underworlds called Irkalla."

"Will she help guide us through the underworlds?" asked the Ranger.

"Alas, no," said Kiyari. "She is jealous of me and hates me. Two of my former husbands are here, also. And they would force me to stay here with them if they could. We can expect no help from any of them."

"Well, then," said the Ranger, "forewarned is forearmed. Shall we proceed?"

"This way," said Bryn.

Though this underworld appeared dark and desolate, there were flickering lights far ahead. As they got closer, they could see that those lights were the flames of a burning sea, an ocean of oil, and that sea bubbled and boiled and emitted noxious sulphuric fumes that smelled like rotten eggs.

Standing on the nearest bank of the sea was a female figure. She held in her hands two torches by which she kept the sea ignited. She had three bodies and three faces, and she had by her side her familiar, one of the hellhounds, a huge dog-like beast with three heads.

"Hecate, Great Mother," Kiyari addressed the woman on the shore, "it is I, Kore, who you knew as Persephone, that asks a favor, a boon."

"Oh, child," responded the crone, and all three of her faces lit up and all three mouths smiled. "I see it is indeed you, the goodly daughter of Demeter. I once promised you that I would be your friend and counselor forever. What is it you ask that I might grant it unto you?"

"The key, Great Mother. I wish to borrow the key to the underworlds that I and my companions may pass through the many gates."

"Alas, my child. That I cannot grant you. The key never leaves my possession."

"Oh, Great Mother, we are on a quest of vital importance. Can you not make an exception for me, for the love and friendship we once had?"

"No, child, I cannot," said Hecate. "But out of the love and friendship I have always for you and your mother, I will offer to accompany you on your quest. Will that be accceptable to you?"

"Oh, yes!" exclaimed Kiyari and threw her arms around the triple goddess.

"Then I shall accompany you. Cerebrus," she called to the hellhound, "take my torches and stir the pot in my absence. Keep the fires burning until my return."

"As you command, Mistress," growled all three heads of the dog at once.

"Now, child,"said the goddess as she embraced Kiyari with two of her arms, "you must introduce me to your companions and tell me about your quest."

"Gladly," said Kiyari. "You may have met Kisikil Lilake and Bryn Helgasdottir before. And this is the Ranger. Hecate is my godmother, and she is keeper of the keys to the gates of hell."

"Goddess," they all said, bowing.

"I do indeed know Kisi and Bryn. They have called upon my powers many times, and I aided them when I could. But I have never before met this Mister Ranger. Is that indeed your given name?"

"No," replied the Ranger. "But it will have to do."

"Are you afraid to let anyone know your true name?"

"Yes," said the Ranger. "I am."

"And rightly so. Names have power, young man. You are wise for a mortal."

"Thank you."

"I remember," said Hecate, "when Isis tricked Ra into revealing his true names. Ra was old, and as sometimes happens with men when they become old he drooled like a baby when he slept. Isis took the spittle of her father, the sun god, and mixed it with the black earth of the Nile, and she formed a deadly serpent out of the moist black earth. When Ra passed by, the serpent struck at his ankles. Poison seeped through the god's body because the serpent's fangs and poison sacs had been formed from fluids of that same body. As he lay dying, the sun god called all his children to aid him but none knew what afflicted their father. None, except Isis, for it was she who had created the serpent and made the poison that now polluted the old man's body. 'Tell me your names, O Ra,' said Isis, 'for it is written that speaking one's true and full name might cure any illness. Such is the power of names.' At first the old god was reluctant to reveal his true names, but as the fire of the poison continued to burn within his body he whispered his full name to Isis. And Isis repeated the name aloud and lifted the spell. Isis entrusted the true name of Ra to no one. None except her most trusted handmaiden. She was said to be a small slip of a girl, a priestess of the moon and a practitioner of He-ket, the sacred magic of the Nile. No one, reasoned Isis, would ever suspect one so innocent could possess the power to name names and control the sun."

"Who was this girl?" asked Bryn.

"She stands next to you now. Her many names are legion: Ushas, Gudrun, and Uqllu. Huitaco, Hina Hine, Juno, and Sarpandit. Ina, Kore, Persephone, and Lasya, to mention but a few. But you know her better as Kiyari."

"Kiyari knows the true names of Ra?" asked Kisi incredulously.

"She does. She may not remember them in this incarnation, but she does know them."

"And knowing those names gaves her power over the sun?"

"Only when she speaks the names of Ra while looking directly into the face of the sun."

"That's the problem," said the Ranger. "No one can see the face of the sun. Not anyone. Not anymore. Someone hid the sun from mortal eyes."

"So I have heard," said Hecate.

"That's why we are here, Great Mother," said Kiyari. "Our quest is to vanquish the man who hid the sun and force him to restore light to the earth."

"And who is this man you seek?"

"His name is Yam Elman," said the Ranger. "I understand he is also sometimes known as Rahu."

Hecate's three faces turned dark. "If it is Rahu you seek, Rahu you shall find. But beware, things are seldom as they seem. Especially, here in the underworld."

"That's the second time today I have heard that," said the Ranger.

"Come," said Hecate. She led the way forward, and the others followed. They circled around the flaming lake, for now they could see that it was merely a large lake that only seemed like a sea, until they arrived at a huge iron door that blocked their way. Hecate reached inside her smock and extracted a silver key on a long silver chain from between her breasts. She inserted the key into a brass lock and turned the key clockwise. The door swung inward slowly on rusted hinges that screeched louder than a thousand birds of prey.

Behind that door lay an endless sea, not like the lake of flames in the previous world, but a true and immense sea that churned and writhed with monsters in its midst. For here there were indeed monsters, vile and filthy leviathons with tails like serpents and mouths that could swallow a man whole. As one surfaced, another dove into the depths. The surface of that sea was seething with activity.

"This be the second underworld," said Hecate. "Here you may find answers to some, though not all, of your questions. Each of you must go your separate ways, for there is only room for one of you at a time to cross this sea. It is called the Sea of Discovery for reasons that will soon become obvious to you."

"How do we cross?" asked Kisi. "I see no boat, no bridge."

"But there *is* a bridge," insisted Hecate. "A narrow land bridge exists just below the surface. It is kept hidden by the constant turmoil of the waters, but it does exist. If you would cross this sea by bridge, you must feel the bridge with your bare feet, for it cannot be seen."

"It'll take us forever to walk across that sea on foot," said the Ranger.

"Here time does not matter," said Hecate. "Here you have forever."

"Ladies first," said Bryn once again, removing her shoes.

"After you," said the Ranger, bowing graciously. "But watch your step."

"Next time," said Bryn, "you get to go first. Sound fair?"

"Fair enough," said the Ranger.

As Bryn began her journey across the vast sea, spiders fell from the roof of the cave to engulf the Valkyrie. She fought valiantly, but to no avail.

As the venomous spiders began to overwhelm Bryn, the Ranger raced to rescue her. He had neither gun nor sword to fight with, but he sought to rescue her anyway. For he still had his wits about him, and he had more brains than a hundred spiders. He brushed them off her with a mighty sweep of his arms, and he trampled them beneath his feet.

Still they came. Thousands of them. Filled with poison. First they bit Bryn. Then they sunk their fangs into the Ranger.

Both fought until their strength ran out. Bryn collapsed first, since she had been bitten first. Then the Ranger collapsed. Both disappeared beneath the waters.

Kisi ran onto the land bridge and began stomping on arachnids. She crushed carapaces, smashed heads, and kicked broken carcasses off the bridge. But it wasn't enough, never enough, and she too was soon overwhelmed. Beasts of the sea— giant sea serpents—came to the surface and fed. Bryn, Kisi, and the Ranger were swallowed whole, along with the debris of a thousand spiders.

"How come we didn't die?" asked the Ranger from within the belly of the beast.

"Maybe we did and just don't know it," suggested Kisi.

"We are in the land of the dead," said Bryn. "We can't die here because everything and everyone in this place is already dead. We are here only in spirit, and the spirit bodies we inhabit don't die because they don't really exist. They are merely representations of how we are used to seeing each other."

"So we can't die?" asked the Ranger.

"No," said Bryn. "But we can be trapped. And if we are trapped or delayed so our spirits cannot return to our human bodies back at Machu Picchu within a dozen days, then those bodies will surely die and we'll be trapped here forever. We'll never be reborn."

"Then we better get moving," said the Ranger. "Right now we're trapped in the belly of this beast, and time is running out."

"What do you propose we do?" asked Bryn.

"We find something to make this half-fish, half-snake throw up. Crawl around and feel for something—anything—that might work. Maybe if we irritate its belly enough, it'll want to get rid of us."

"Nothing here but spider parts," reported Bryn. "Oh, wait a moment. I just found something that feels like a tree branch."

"Break it in three pieces. Give me one part and a part to Kisi. We'll all start poking together. Maybe we can get some kind of reaction out of this thing."

"Here," said Bryn. She handed pieces of wood to both of them. "On the count of three. One. Two. Three!"

They poked and prodded, shoved and pierced. The ground beneath them convulsed. They poked and poked some more. They jabbed. Finally, the floor and walls of their prison began expanding and contracting, churning the waters within and without, until the beast belched bigtime and the three prisoners flew out the open yaw like hurtling canonballs to land faces-first on the hard rocks of the far shore.

Hecate and Kiyari were already there on that far shore waiting for them. Hecate was laughing.

"How did the two of you get here ahead of us?" asked the Ranger when he regained his senses.

"We walked," said Hecate.

"On water," added Kiyari. "We crossed the sea by walking on water."

"You walked on water? Not on the land bridge?"

"That's correct," said Kiyari. "You could have walked on water, too, if you had wanted. It's easy!"

"Why didn't you tell us we could walk on water?" the Ranger asked Hecate accusingly. "Why didn't you show us how we could do that?"

"You didn't ask before," said Hecate. "You set off on your own path of discovery without thinking of other possibilities. But I am certain you learned something very valuable during your long ride in the belly of the beast. What did you learn that you didn't know before?"

"We learned that we can't die," said the Ranger. "Not here, anyway."

"Very good," said Hecate. "Anything else?"

"But we learned we can be trapped here," said Kisi. "And if we can't get out of the trap, our bodies will deteriorate and die when we don't return to them in time. If our bodies die, our spirits will remain trapped here forever and we'll never be reborn."

"Good," said Hecate. "Then your journey across the Sea of Discovery was fruitful."

"Now show us how to walk on water," said the Ranger.

"Come, then," said Hecate. "All of you. Step onto the water and walk upon it. Believe you can do it, and you can."

This time the Ranger went first and Bryn didn't protest. He placed one foot on the water and then the other. Neither foot sank below the surface. He took a tentative step, then another. And another. And another. Finally, he walked across the surface of the sea as if he had done it all his life.

Bryn went next. She did the same thing as the Ranger, stepping tentatively onto the water first with one foot, then the other. When she didn't sink, either, Kisi tried it.

"See?" said Kiyari. "It's easy."

"If you believe," said Hecate, "all things are possible."

"I believe!" shouted the Ranger. "I believe!" He began running across the waters, skipping like a rock thrown sideways so it bounced across the water's surface rather than sinking.

Bryn and Kisi giggled like schoolgirls.

"Tempus fugit," announced Hecate. "Time always flies when you are having fun, and you've had enough fun for now. Are you ready to enter the third underworld? But beware. The temptations of the third world are many and alluring. There are all kinds of traps in this next world, and none look as dangerous as they are. Do not allow yourselves to be easily ensnared while sampling sweet treats."

Once again Hecate removed the silver key from between her bosoms and inserted it into a lock. Again the key turned and the door opened inward.

This world, too, possessed a sea, the bright blue of the cloudless sky reflecting on the calm surface of clear waters. Here there was lots of light, natural light, as if coming from the sun but there was no sun in the underworld, not a real one anyway. All around that vast sea stretched idyllic sandy beaches dotted with shady palm trees that were filled with lush fruits; and apple trees and pears and pomegranets and figs were clearly in abundance in green groves scattered around the beach like oases in the desert. Naked men and women lounged upon those golden beaches, eating and drinking and openly fornicating. Beyond could be seen verdant fields of ripening corn and wheat, and vineyards filled with fruits and berries.

"What is this place?" asked Bryn.

"Here be Elysium," said Hecate. "Here be your hearts' desires."

"It looks peaceful enough," said the Ranger.

"Looks can be deceiving," warned Hecate.

"I don't know about you," said Kisi, "but I could use a bath. I still smell like dead spiders and rotten fish. I'm going to take a swim."

"Go, then," said Hecate. "Bathe and refresh yourselves. But tary not too long. Other worlds await."

Kisi stripped off her clothes and ran for the water. Bryn was right behind her.

Kiyari and the Ranger seemed shy around each other, as if neither were willing to strip off his or her clothes in front of the opposite sex. Finally, the Ranger said, "What the hell," turned his back to Kiyari, and took off all his clothes. He walked determinedly toward the water, glancing once over his shoulder to see if Kiyari would join him.

Then she, too, took off her clothes and ran for the shore. She dove head-first into the water and looked like a water-nymph frolicking in the foam of the sea. She was, at that moment, the most beautiful woman the Ranger had ever seen, for beauty existed in the mind of the beholder and the mind of the Ranger was so attracted by her incredible beauty that he couldn't take his eyes off her.

Soon all four were playing childish games and foolish pranks on each other, splashing water in laughing faces, ducking beneath the surface, and pinching posteriors. After a time, they reluctantly emerged from the water and stetched out on the fine-grained sand, feasting on figs, feeling the warmth of the sun lulling them to sleep. Somewhere in the distance they heard gulls singing as waves gently caressed the shore. The whisper of soft winds through the leaves and branches of faraway trees lulled them like the strings of a harp. The odor of orange blossoms filled the air, and if one bothered to take notice one might smell roses and poppies and hollyhocks in full bloom.

The Ranger looked upon the naked form of Kiyari with great admiration, and he felt himself growing erect. Fortunately, he lay face-down on the sand so none of his companions could see his present condition. When Kiyari rolled over and opened her legs to the warmth of the sun, he spilled his seed into the sand.

Now he saw Bryn and Kisi reach out to touch each other, gently caressing breasts and stomachs, their fingers dancing lightly over contours and mounds. Bryn moved her lush lips to Kisi's erect nipples, and her tongue flicked lightly, very gently, around the tender edges of each areola in turn, making each nipple so moist with her saliva it glistened in the sunlight like a diamond. Kisi moaned and opened both legs to give Bryn better access.

Kiyari, too, opened her legs wider, and the Ranger felt privileged to peer directly into the maiden's heart. She was so beautiful he couldn't turn his eyes away, and he was completely mesmerized by the light down that circled her center like little curlicues of delicate lace. He felt his erection return, harder than ever.

Bryn and Kisi were coupled now, each with her head bobbing frantically between her companion's legs. Bryn moaned softly and Kisi squeeled loudly, and they thrashed wildly about, bucking their hips and clamping their legs and digging firey fingernails into bare breasts and backsides.

Kiyari's eyes were open now, and she looked into the Ranger's hungry eyes as if she could read what was written there. And then, very slowly and sensuously, Kiyari rose from the sand, brushing away stray grains of sand from her shapely buttocks as she paraded past the Ranger's face and his eyes followed her every move. Kiyari lifted one leg, affording him a close-up view of her sex, as she turned very slowly around to face him. She stood directly over his center with one foot placed to each side of his hips, and she said, "Turn over."

And when he did roll over and Kiyari saw his hardness, she sat straight down on top of him and guided him into her own secretmost place, and she was already slippery wet, and his hardness easily slid inside that welcoming warmth and wetness. Her lust-filled eyes locked onto his own, and they rutted like animals until he was entirely spent and she had gasped and screamed so much her voice finally failed her. Then her limp body collapsed on top of his, and they lay quietly together until Bryn and Kisi joined them and all four slept the sleep of the dead.

The Ranger awakened with dreams that haunted him even after he opened his eyes. In one dream, he saw himself killing innocent men and women and chidren by slitting their throats as they slept, blood spurting from opened jugulars and carotids like wine from a tapped cask. In another, he shot an unarmed man in cold blood because he had been paid to do so. In yet another, he saw himself fighting with a man he recognized as his friend Jon, intending to kill anyone and everyone who stood in his way.

The Ranger saw himself circling around the front of an old barn to access an unlocked side door. He was about to kick open that door and rush in with his submachine gun blazing when the buildings—the entire barn, the house, and the two outbuildings—simply disappeared. Now the Ranger saw Jon Fish running straight toward him, and he opened fire with the submachine gun. The Marine hit the ground and rolled out of the way before a stream of bullets passed through the exact same space his body had occupied moments before. Jon was on his feet again, rushing forward, as soon as the Ranger let up on the trigger.

Even in the dark, the Ranger's aim was deadly accurate, and another burst of bullets passed through the space where Jon had been but a moment ago. Jon was managing to stay one step ahead only because the Ranger's reflexes seemed slower than normal.

The Heckler and Koch ran out of ammunition, the last shell casings hitting the ground, the chamber now empty with the bolt locked completely to the rear. But before he could re-load, Jon was right on top of him, wrenching the weapon from the Ranger's hands. The Ranger kicked out at Jon's legs, miss-ing the kneecap but cracking the tibia in two. Jon went down, and the Ranger was on him in a heartbeat, smashing both fists into the man's face.

"I'm a Marine!" Jon shouted. "And I'm your friend, asshole. We're on the same side."

"That's what those Afghan soldiers told me. They lied, and my men are all dead because I believed the lies."

Jon slammed his elbow against the Ranger's cheekbone, but the Ranger barely noticed. The Ranger raised one massive fist above Jon's head and brought it down toward Jon's carotid in what would have been a killing blow had it landed.

And then the Ranger awakened from the dreams. His entire body was drenched with sweat and his legs intimately entangled with the legs of three naked women.

When he tried to get up, he couldn't. It was as if his ankles and wrists had been shackled with cuffs and iron chains while he slept.

He nudged Bryn's shoulder, but Bryn didn't stir. He tried to wake Kisi, but she only smiled at him, turned over, and went back to sleep. Kiyari looked far too beautiful to disturb, but he had to try. "Wake up," he said, kissing her neck. She moaned in her sleep. He nibbled her ear. "Wake up, hon. C'mon, please. Wake up."

Her hand reached for him in her sleep, raking his inner thigh.

"Hey!" he yelled. "Wake the fuck up!"

Neither Kiyari nor Kisi stirred, but Bryn's eyes finally snapped open. "Huh? Whazzz?"

Bryn tried to sit up, but it was as if her spine were broken and her body paralyzed from the neck down. The Ranger could see she was really struggling, her muscles bulging as the cords in her neck strained to lift her shoulders off the ground. "Get the fuck off of me!" she screamed at his face.

"I'm not on you," said the Ranger.

"Well, someone is. Someone is sitting on my chest."

"There's no one on top of you."

"Then why do I feel like there is?"

"I don't know. I feel like someone shackled my arms and legs to the ground."

"You can't move either?"

"Not very far."

"What about Kisi and Kiyari?"

"I can't wake them. I tried. They're dead to the world."

"We're trapped? What the hell happened to us?"

"We let our guard down. We lost control in more ways than one. While we were caught up in ecstasy, someone or something imprisioned our spirit bodies."

Bryn was silent for a moment. "What about Kisi and Kiyari? Why did we wake up and they won't?"

"I woke because I had bad dreams. You woke up because I yelled. Otherwise, we'd all still be asleep."

"You yelled loud enough to wake the dead. How come Kisi and Kiyari are still sleeping?"

"Maybe they have clearer consciences than you and me."

"They sure as hell aren't innocent. But they probably haven't killed one tenth as many people as you and I have over the centuries. And they aren't trained to wake up, like we are, ready to do battle at the slightest noise."

"So how do we wake them? Any ideas?"

"No." Bryn shouted "Wake up!" at both women repeatedly, but neither responded. "I guess it's up to the two of us to figure this thing out. What's holding you captive?"

"It feels like old–fashioned iron manacles and chains binding my ankles and wrists. I can move my hands and arms a little, but not my legs. The chains seem secured to the sand like the sand was cement."

"Can you sit up?"

"Yes." The Ranger performed hudreds of crunches every day during training, and his abdominal muscles were able to raise his upper body without the need of his lower body intervening.

"I can't sit up," said Bryn. "It feels like something really heavy is sitting on my chest and abdomen. I can breathe, but even that takes an effort."

"Stop struggling. Let's think about this rationally for a few minutes. All of us got carried away with our passions, and we let our guards down. Why did we do that?"

"It's this place," said Bryn. "We've all been so stressed out for such a very long time that we jumped at the first opportunity to let our hair down. The four of us are soul mates, kindred spirits, and we're naturally attracted to each other. So when we got to this place where we felt there was no pressure to behave as we usually do, we let our passions take over."

"And when we were in ecstasy, we lost control. Makes sense. We were too busy having orgasms to notice. We didn't begin to notice until we woke up."

"That's what I think happened. I think it is our passions, and only our passions, that bind us. We're held prisoner by our passions."

The Ranger thought about that. "I think you're right," he said. "So how do we get free?"

"We release our passions, and they will release us. Kiss me and we'll see if I'm right. Kiss me. On the lips, like you mean it. Like you want to."

The Ranger moved his upper body over Bryn, and his chest brushed her breasts. He bent down and placed his lips on hers, and he was surprised when her tongue shot straight into his mouth like an arrow. He felt a familiar stirring in his groin as his own tongue met hers in an intimate dance that took his breath away. He had known this woman for millennia, and he had loved her like a sister. But now he saw her for the first time as a woman, beautiful, lush, willing. He moved a hand to her breast and caressed a nipple with his fingers, and his hands moved freely. He was no longer shackled.

Nor was Bryn any longer burdened with an invisible weight that rendered her immobile. Her body writhed beneath his, responding to his touch with passion and ardor. His fingers moved lower, caressing the hard muscles around her navel, and she spread her legs for him and she took his hand in hers and dragged it down to where she wanted it. Now her undulating hips slapped against the palm of his hand as the Ranger's frantic fingers probed her warmth and wetness, exploring her passion, and he felt her other hand on him, pulling him toward her center, guiding him, helping him enter. He was inside her now, and they moved together as if each knew what the other wanted.

Suddenly, she pushed him off. She had amazing strength, and when he tried to reenter, she clamped her legs shut and refused him admittance.

"I don't understand," he gasped, feeling his erection shrinking. "I thought you wanted this."

"I do," she said, trying hard to regain her breath. "But not here, not now. If I allow you to climax, you'll be trapped again. And if I climax, too, we'll both be trapped. Try to awaken Kiyari with kisses. I'll do the same with Kisi. If we awaken their passions, we'll free them. But if we don't learn to control our passions, we'll all be trapped here permanently. You can move now, can't you? You're no longer shacked by your passions?"

"Yes," he said. "I can move. We can both move."

"Then free Kiyari and I'll free Kisi."

As the Ranger moved his hands over Kiyari's body, he felt his erection return. And she felt it, too, stirring in her sleep to reach for him. He rained kisses all over her breasts, her neck, her lips, her ears, her eyes. She moaned, and her eyes flickered, then slowly opened. She smiled at him, and he smiled back.

He opened her legs and rolled his body on top of hers, rubbing against her until she was ready for him to enter. She moaned again, and he slipped inside, thrusting in rhythm with her hips. Her breath quickened, and he could feel the muscles in her legs and abdomen tighten beneath him as she wrapped her legs around his buttocks and urged him to go faster.

He pulled out and rolled away from her.

"Come back," she begged. "Don't leave me! You can't just leave me! Not like this! Please! Come back!"

"I want to, but I can't," he said.

"What did I do wrong?"

"Nothing," he said. "But we have to stay in control of our senses if we ever want to get out of the underworlds and back to our real bodies."

"I don't understand," said Kiyari.

"I think I do, and I'll try to explain," said Bryn. She had revived Kisi, and the two women lay nearby, watching and listening. "Our passions will trap us here if we let them. When the Ranger woke up this morning, his arms and legs felt chained to this place and he couldn't move. When he woke me up, I couldn't move either. I felt like I had a huge weight holding me down. Neither you nor Kisi wanted to wake at all, no matter how hard we tried to wake you. If we stay here in this beautiful setting any longer and indulge our passions the way we'd like, we'll wind up prisoners of our passions and be trapped here forever. That may seem appealing now, but later we'll regret it."

"What do you mean you couldn't wake us?" asked Kisi. "I'm awake now, and so is Kiyari."

"You woke only because we aroused your passions," said Bryn. "If we allowed your passions to be sated, you would have fallen asleep again. So the Ranger and I had to stop making love to you before any of us climaxed. As long as we all feel like we have unfinished business, we'll stay free and alert. But if any of us feels satisfied, that person will let his or her guard down again and be trapped here. It would be so easy to let that happen. But we *can't* let it happen. We have a job to do."

"Let's get our clothes and find Hecate," said the Ranger, getting to his feet. "I think it's time to move on."

"While we still can," added Bryn.

CHAPTER SEVENTEEN

Hadad continued his search for the missing masks. He was now more certain than ever that the masks were the key to defeating Yam and restoring the sun. As a last resort, he planned to recreate the silver mask from memory, but it would take time to smelt raw silver from mines in the Andes, hammer that silver into shape, and imbue the silver mask with protective powers. He would then need to ask La Curandera to perform certain rituals during the night of the new moon that would give the mask power. That would mean waiting until after the new moon to confront Yam, and that was too long to wait.

The original mask already possessed all the power it needed, accumulated over centuries of ritual use. Hadad had doubts a new mask would have the same effect as the original, but it would be better than nothing. Plan A was to find the original masks, plan B was to create new ones, and he didn't have a plan C.

He and La Curandera had searched everywhere at Machu Picchu they could think of, but the masks they wanted continued to elude them. Hadad had gone back to the temple site, armed with a flashlight, but the area near the Urubamba had been picked clean of relics. He decided to try the foothills next.

"If I were the Moon Priestess," he said to himself, "wouldn't I find a place where no one else would look for the mask for thousands of years? Now, where would that be?"

He continued to climb. He checked crevices, caves, beneath rocks. Finally, he came to a place of cut stones, part of a quarry that had been abandoned for centuries. Some of those stones, twice as tall and twice as wide as a man, had been cut from the rock face of the sacred mountain.

"If I were the Moon Priestess," he told himself, "I would lift one of those stones and hide the mask beneath."

Had Hadad instructed the Moon Priestess in how to move mountains? Surely not. The last Priestess of the Moon lived long after Hadad had moved away from the sacred valley. He would have told her nothing.

But Ayar Uchu remembered instructing two of his sisters, Huaco and Uqllu, in the secret magics of the east shortly after he had returned from his first travels, and sister Huaco and sister Uqllu were Coya. They may have passed on the secret of moving mountains to other Coya.

Hadad stood in front of the cut rocks and raised his hands to the sky. He breathed in deeply, held the breath in for a count of ten, and breathed out. He continued this breathing ritual until both hands began to feel warm, and a bluish-white glow emanated from his fingertips.

Now he initiated the bellows breath. Instead of breathing deeply as before, he pumped up his lungs with a series of short intakes through the nose, followed by intakes through every opening and pore of his body, and the intake of prana in such a manner, aided by volition and specific intention, fired up the dan-tien—the athenor in the exact center of his body near the navel—and the fire in the athenor caused the water and the material elements in the belly to boil. And the precipitate of this distilling process manifested as pure energy.

As he lowered his hands and pointed directly at one of the rocks, he reversed polarity and his aura changed color. Instead of bluish-white, his hands glowed fiery red.

And now he moved his hands upward again, directing the stone to rise in much the same manner as a minister or priest might urge his congregation to rise with but an upward gesture of his hands. Slowly, the stone began to move, rising upward in short, jerky motions until it stood about ten feet above the ground. Hadad could easily see beneath the base of the cut stone, and the ground was undisturbed and empty of relics.

He reversed polarities, and the monolith slowly settled back into place. He repeated the process with the second stone, and the third and the fourth. He continued until he had examined the ground beneath each of the stones. None of the standing stones had hidden the silver mask.

He continued his search up the side of the mountain, climbing slowly enough to check for hiding places along the way but fast enough to already be half-way to the top. Trees, shrubs, weeds, and grasses made the search difficult, but Hadad was both patient and thorough.

He found a cave that he thought he recognized. It looked like the same cave in which Yam, then known as Ayar Manco, had imprisoned Ayar Cachi while Hadad, known then as Ayar Uchu, had wandered all over the far east in search of magic. When Hadad had returned, he removed the rocks blocking the cave entrance and freed his brother's spirit.

If this was Cachi's cave, then the copper mask of the thunderer might still be inside. He entered with his flashlight pointed at the far corner where the ceiling of the cave narrowed to a crawl space. Amid a pile of rocks and layers of dust, he glimpsed the reflection of light bouncing off something shiny.

Hadad crawled into the narrow tunnel and moved the fallen rocks out of the way. He picked up the copper mask and shook it free of dust. Then he crawled back out and examined the mask closely.

It was indeed the same mask he had seen his brother wear in battle. Made of pure hammered copper, the craftsmanship was astounding. The face of the mask was a simple rectangular copper plate, wider than it was tall, with rectangular slits for eyes to see through, an extension of copper to fit over the bridge of a nose, and what looked like a stylized beard around a grimacing mouth. Twenty-four jagged thunderbolts, each razor sharp like the blade of a kris, extended on top and along both sides of the mask. There were no joints and no seams. The entire mask had been shaped from one solid sheet of metal.

"One down, and one more to go," said Hadad as he left the cave.

*   *   *

Lokesvara sat in lotus on the bare floor of his meditation chamber and created a mandala from colored sands. Jon Fish watched in admiration as fine grains of sand dripped like tiny raindrops from the master's fingertips to form delicate patterns ten thousand times more intricate than any gossamer spider's web. It reminded Jon that time was running out as surely as sand slipped through an upended hour glass. Kisi, Kiyari, Bryn, and the Ranger had already been gone four days. If they didn't complete their journey through the underworld soon, their bodies would die of dehydration.

In the drawing's center was the bindu, representing the center of the world which was supposed to be Mount Meru. Around that circle was a perfect square, and around the square was another circle, and around that circle was another square, and so on. Worlds within worlds.

Lokesvara mixed sands of various colors to produce subtle hues of great complexity: a thousand shades of green, blue, red, yellow, and degrees of white that ranged from the pure snows atop mystical Mount Meru to greys that were almost completely black. It was said that one could look into the heart of the mandala and see into one's own heart, and Jon Fish knew that was true.

Different shapes and different colors called out to different people. Jon found resonance with the earth colors, rich browns, vibrant reds, lush greens. They pulled him into the sand painting and spoke to him as if they were alive.

Akashagarbha, too, responded to the shifting sands, and Jon was suddenly very much aware that his spirit was not alone in this body. Akashagarbha saw multiple meanings in the lines and colors, and the Bodhisattva shared some of what he saw with Jon Fish.

"He makes a kylkhor," spoke Akashagarbha inside Jon's mind. "It is to be a refuge for the yidam of Vajrapani until the Ranger is ready to receive Vajrapani's spirit again."

"I'm worried about them, Akashagarbha," said Jon. "If the Ranger, Kisi, Bryn, and Kiyari don't return soon, they may never come back."

"That may be so," said Akashagarbha.

"I'm not used to doing nothing."

"Then you should return to San Diego. Your leave is almost up, and you have responsibilities you should not avoid."

"You're right, of course. But I have a few days left before I have to report in. And I can extend my leave to the end of the month, if I have to. I'd like to stick around a while longer."

"Then allow your spirit to accompany me as we go on a quest."

"Where?"

"Back in time. Hadad searches for the silver mask of the Moon Goddess. Perhaps we can assist him."

"How?"

"We have the ability to see where it was hidden. Come. Let us go to the far side of the universe and watch for the light of days past to arrive. We may only need to travel eight hundred light years."

"We can do that?" asked Jon.

"Yes," said Akashagarbha. "We can."

* * *

Once again Hecate inserted her silver key, and once again a door opened wide for them to cross another threshold. After the five entered, the door automatically closed behind them and left them in total darkness.

"Here," came Hecate's voice, "there be monsters. They can sense you, but you will not be able to see them. You may smell them when they get close, for they smell foul. You will definitely feel them if they touch you, and if they bite you they can devour your spirit. Here there be no sea but a swamp, and the path through the swamp is perilous. Reptiles of all kinds, many poisonous, occupy that swamp, and to the sides of the path lie beds of quicksand and all manner of monsters. I shall meet you on the other side where another door awaits."

"Ladies first," said the Ranger. "I had my fill of swamps and snakes at Camp Rudder during Ranger School. If I never see a snake again, it'll be too soon."

"You were trained in negotiating swampland?" asked Bryn.

"Yeah," admitted the Ranger. "We were attached to the 6th Ranger Training Brigade at Eglin Air Force Base in Florida for a couple of weeks in the Everglades. It wasn't my favorite part of training, but I survived."

"Then you should be the one to lead us," said Bryn.

"Please," begged Kiyari.

"Yes, please," said Kisi.

"Okay, but let's get a few things straight right from the start. Stay close behind me every step of the way. If I go off the path, let me go and you go on the rest of the way without me. You won't be able to help me in the dark. I'll either make it back, or I won't. But you have to keep going. Understood?"

"Understood," said Bryn.

Although the Ranger had refined his night vision so he could function almost as well in darkness as in daylight under normal circumstances, he could see no light at all in this world. No moonlight. No stars. No nothing. His peripheral vision was useless. He had no way to orient himself. He had to depend solely on touch and on intuition, placing one foot directly in front of the other.

"Bryn, reach out and place a hand on my shoulder. Kisi, put a hand on Bryn's shoulder. Kiyari, a hand on Kisi's shoulder. We'll go slow, one step at a time. Okay now, let's go."

He felt for the path with his right foot, found the right edge where solid ground ended and swamp began, then the left edge. The path through the swamp was only about twenty-four inches wide, and there was no room for error. If any of them lost their balance or made a misstep, they would all be in trouble.

He put his right foot down in the middle of the path, touched heel to toe, and put all of his weight on his left foot. He moved his right foot forward, found he was too close to the right edge, and moved slightly to his left. Either the path was moving or he wasn't walking in a straight line anymore. He wasn't sure which.

He tried another step and discovered the path had moved again. He put the next foot forward and felt something moving beneath him. It slithered under his heel, wound around his ankle.

"Snake," he called out, trying to shake it off his leg. He felt powerful coils tighten around his right calf as the reptile inched its way upward, felt the creature pass his knee. He tried to gauge where it's head would be, not more than six inches immediately to his right if he were to judge from the turns he had counted it made circling his right leg, and his right hand shot straight out and caught the scaly neck just below the jawbone and he squeezed with all the strength he could muster, feeling the creature's neck muscles tighten as he kept applying pressure.

Now he felt some of the coils unravel and the creature's tail slapped at the Ranger's ankle hard, knocking him completely off balance. As he fell to his right, he lost his grip on the snake's neck. He felt it slither out of his hand and he heard it make a big splash as it dropped back into the swamp a moment before he fell in himself.

Not only did the swamp smell truly foul, it tasted even fouler. Swampwater flooded both nostrils as he fell face forward into the snake and insect infested water, came back up to the surface, and tried to swim his way back to where he thought the path should be. But it wasn't there.

He splashed around trying to locate solid ground, but there was none to be found. Had he become so disoriented that he was now swimming in the opposite direction? Was he moving farther away from, rather than closer to, the only path through this miserable swamp?

Now he sensed other creatures in the water with him, some large, some not so large. One clamped onto his left arm and he felt sharp teeth sink all the way through to the bone. He had no idea what it was that had his arm, but he envisioned a giant crocodile that wanted to drag him alive through the murky waters to finally finish him off in its lair. He felt other creatures coil about first one leg and then the other, and he thought for a moment he would be pulled apart as they tried to take him in three directions at once.

He struck out with his free hand and connected with the head that held his other arm in its teeth. He expected to feel pain run through his arm as the creature's jaws clamped tighter, crushing the bones in his left forearm. But there was no pain.

He struck out again, this time with the heel of his hand. He heard something crack, and he didn't know if it was the monstrous head or his own bones.

It must have been his bones, because the creature didn't let go of his arm. Instead, it dove beneath the surface and pulled the Ranger down with it. Other things wrapped around his body—snakes or tentacles or weeds, he couldn't tell which—and he was at the mercy of whatever held him imprisoned under water. His lungs ached for air, his left arm felt numb as if it had been chewed off above the elbow, and his legs felt bound by thick ropes.

But he was still conscious, and as long as he remained conscious he had a fighting chance. He willed himself forward, and he felt a subtle change in direction as if he were now dragging the beasts instead of the other way around, and the creatures of the swamp that had wrapped around his legs and midsection seemed to sense it, too, and they struck at him and sunk their fangs into his flesh and he felt their poison enter his body and seep through his system. But he wouldn't give up, he'd never give up, and if they wanted him they would have to hold on.

Now he was racing through the water and he breeched the surface, and suddenly he could breathe again. All but one of the creatures had loosed their grips on his broken body, and he pounded that one to a pulp with his only good hand, hammering at it incessantly until there was nothing left binding him.

But the poison was having an effect, and he had a vision of the poison changing him into something he didn't want to be. He saw himself becoming one of them, one of the swamp monsters, one of the enemy. He saw his legs mold together into a tail, his arms fall off at the shoulders. He felt his teeth elongate into fangs, and his skin turn scaly.

The last thing he remembered was crawling up out of the swamp and placing his triangular head atop tightly-wrapped coils to wait patiently for prey to come his way.

*　　*　　*

Bryn heard the insects coming before she felt them, and she tried to defend her face with her hands. But they hit her hard, thousands of flying hard-shelled creatures that swarmed over her body, and they stung every part of her and injected their poisons, and she felt her flesh fester and inflame. Kisi's hand dropped from Bryn's shoulder as Kisi let out a scream. Kiyari, too, screamed. But their screams were quickly choked off as thousands of insects invaded their mouths, ears, and eyes.

Bryn felt them inside her clothes penetrating her private parts, and she wanted to scream but knew she shouldn't. Instead, she turned completely around and grabbed hold of Kisi, keeping her from falling off the path. "Hold onto Kiyari," ordered Bryn. "I will hold onto you. Together we shall be strong."

Kisi couldn't speak because her throat had swollen shut from innumerable insect bites, but she did as she was told. Kisi had always been stronger than she looked, and Bryn could feel that strength returning as she held onto Kisi for dear life. Kiyari was thrown off balance by the barrage of insects, and Kisi had reached out to the girl barely in time to prevent Kiyari from toppling off the narrow path and disappearing into the swamp.

"They cannot kill us," said Bryn, "unless we let them. And we won't let them."

The insects continued to plague them, and so did a bevy of frogs that had been attracted by the insects. Bryn squashed frog after greasy frog and kicked them off the path, leaving the ground beneath their feet feeling slimy and slippery and even more perilous than before, but the three women, three ancient sisters of the weird who had endured much together in the past and who continued to draw strength from each other's presence, pushed forward through the darkness one step at a time. Their skin itched, their feet stank, their muscles ached. They mourned, each woman in her own way, the loss of the man they called their brother, their lover, their friend. They were determined not to lose anyone else.

Finally, the swarms of insects began to thin, dwindling to only one or two bugs buzzing about their heads. The frogs, too, had disappeared.

Bryn felt something long and fat slither past her right foot, and she kicked at its tail but it had already gone past her and she missed it entirely. Kisi let out a yelp and did a little dance, nearly dragging all three off into the swamp.

"Bit me," Kisi managed to rasp through her swollen throat. "Bit my leg."

Bryn felt something puncture her own ankle, just above the shin. It hurt like hell, but she kept going. She heard Kisi stumble behind her. She couldn't tell if Kiyari was still with them or not.

"Ignore the poison," said Bryn. "If you don't let it get to you, it won't."

How much farther? she wondered after a dozen more steps. *Does this swamp go on forever? How long can we last?*

Kisi stumbled again, and she fell forward and plowed into Bryn's back. Both women lost their balance and fell to their right.

And landed on dry land.

Bryn reached out and felt all around her for the swamp, but there was only solid ground beneath her probing fingertips.

"We made it through the damn swamp," said Bryn, barely believing it. "We made it to solid ground."

"You hear, Kiyari?" asked Kisi, her voice barely more than a whisper. "We made it."

Kiyari didn't answer.

Bryn reached out and touched Kisi, then moved past Kisi and felt for Kiyari. "Kiyari!" she called. "Answer me!"

"Oh, no!" cried Kisi. "She must have fallen into the swamp."

"Stay here," commanded Bryn. "I'm going back to find her."

Bryn tried to retrace her steps, but it was impossible in the dark. She did find the edge of the swamp, the place where land ended and swamp began. She felt for the path, moving her foot along the edge searching for something solid. She walked first to the right, certain that she had fallen in the opposite direction, and the path should be to the right of where she was currently standing. She walked for fifty paces before walking back and going fifty paces the other way, but she found no path in either direction.

"Kiyari!" she shouted. "Kiyari, can you hear me?"

No answer.

"Kisi! Can you hear me? Where are you?"

"Over here," came the faint reply.

"Keep talking. I need to follow the sound of your voice to get back to you."

"You didn't find Kiyari?"

"No."

Suddenly, Kisi screamed.

"Kisi, are you all right?"

"Snake," said Kisi. "Big snake. It's crawling up my leg."

"I'm coming," said Bryn, running in the direction of Kisi's voice. "Keep talking. What's the snake doing now?"

"It's wrapping itself around my waist. It's really big. It's...."

Kisi's voice stopped in mid-sentence, as if her last thought had been choked off.

"Kisi!" yelled Bryn. "Kisi!"

CHAPTER EIGHTEEN

H e sensed prey in the dark by flicking his tongue. It worked in a manner not dissimilar to the way infra-red night-vision devices worked, the kind the U. S. Army had issued him in Iraq and Afghanistan. By constantly scanning the environment for energy signatures and filtering out inert or irrelevant information, he was instantly aware of any movement in any direction. His jawbone picked up subtle vibra-tions in the ground to quickly and easily pinpoint the exact location and direction of movement. It was as deadly accurate as the guidance systems of a sidewinder missile or a predator drone, and the Ranger now knew why the military had named them such.

His new spirit body reflected what he had become, and he had become a predator like the creatures that had poisoned him.

When he sensed two warm bodies advancing toward him from the direction of the swamp, he waited. If they didn't come closer, he would wait patiently and observe. If they came to him, he would attack. If they didn't come closer, he would go to them. He was the predator. They were the prey.

His sensitive lower jaw picked up the vibrations of their speech, and he was amazed when his mind translated those vibrations into words he understood.

"Kiyari!" one of them called out. "Answer me!"

"Oh, no!" cried another. "She must have fallen."

"Stay here. I'm going back to find her."

He recognized those voices, and he knew those names. Kiyari, Kisi, and Bryn. His traveling companions in the underworld. His friends.

He uncoiled and began slithering toward them. He was glad they were alive and had made it through the swamp. Wouldn't they be surprised to find he was alive and had made it through, too?

He stopped when he sensed that one of them was moving again, this time away from him and back toward the swamp. He waited for more information to come to him before he began moving again. His reptile instincts warred with his human instincts. He didn't want to reveal himself until he was ready to strike.

Strike? At them? At his friends? Don't be ridiculous. They weren't prey.

Yes, they were. He had no friends. Hadn't he said that? His friends were dead, killed by Taliban in Afghanistan.

Yes, that was also true. Those friends had been killed by Taliban, and he had revenged their deaths by killing as many of the Taliban and all their blood relatives he could find. He was a lean, mean, green killing machine. The Army had trained him, and they had trained him well.

But he was no longer in the U. S. Army. He was no longer a human being. He was a reptile, a snake, and he had new ways to kill that were just as effective as the old ways. As his sensitive tongue darted about and tasted the air, he was acutely aware of the two long fangs and the bulging poison sacs located to the sides of that forked tongue. One bite, and his enemies were toast.

"Kisi! Can you hear me? Where are you?"

"Over here," came the faint reply.

"Keep talking. I need to follow the sound of your voice to get back to you."

"You didn't find Kiyari?"

"No."

He sensed a shape sitting on the ground right in front of where he was crawling, and he slithered next to that body and felt its warmth, its softness. He touched it with his tongue.

Suddenly, he heard a scream.

"Kisi, are you all right?"

"Snake," said Kisi. "Big snake. It's crawling up my leg."

"I'm coming," said Bryn, running in the direction of Kisi's voice. "Keep talking. What's the snake doing now?"

He nuzzled her warmth with his triangular head. He wrapped his tail around her and hugged her to him. He laid his head between her breasts.

"It's wrapping itself around my waist. It's really big. It's...."

Kisi's voice stopped in mid-sentence, as if her last thought had been choked off.

"Kisi!" yelled Bryn. "Kisi!"

He spoke to her, but he had no vocal cords. He breathed in, but only hisses came out.

She struggled with him, rolling on the ground as he wound himself tighter around her midsection. "Kisi, it's me!" he wanted to say.

He heard the other one approaching fast, running now, her feet coming straight for him. Every instinct in his reptilian brain told him she was an enemy and he should strike now before she was upon him. But part of him was still human, and the human part held him back.

"It's the Ranger," whispered Kisi. "He's changed. You won't recognize him. But I know it's him."

"It can't be!" said Bryn, trying to disentangle the reptile from Kisi's body. The serpent let go, dropped to the ground, and coiled as if to strike. But it didn't strike.

"Don't hurt him," said Kisi. "He didn't hurt me."

Bryn sat on the ground next to them and said nothing.

"What happened to you?" asked Kisi, caressing the top of the Ranger's pointed head. "It is you, isn't it?"

"Yesssssss," the Ranger tried to say. "It issssssss me." But the words came out as hisses, and they weren't intelligible to humans.

"I couldn't find her," said Bryn. "She's out there somewhere, but I couldn't find her."

"Maybe I can," said the Ranger, knowing they couldn't hear him. He unwrapped his coils and slithered away in the direction of the swamp.

But Hecate stopped him.

"You cannot go back," she said. "You can only go forward." She removed the silver key from between her breasts and inserted it into the lock of a door that hadn't been there before. She turned the key clockwise and the door creaked open.

"You have all been changed by your experiences," she told them. "You are not the same as you were when you entered this realm, and the next world may change you yet more. Come, now. It is time to move on."

"What about Kiyari?" asked Bryn.

"She, too, is changed," said Hecate." This is her world now."

"We can't just leave her here," said Kisi.

"You may choose to remain here with her. If you do, the door will be locked once I go through to the next world. You will remain here forever. Is that what you choose?"

"No," said Kisi.

"Then cross the threshold and enter the next world on your journey through the underworlds. The choice is yours."

Bryn went first, then Kisi. The Ranger slithered across the threshold, and Hecate followed. The door closed behind them, and they heard it lock.

* * *

Hadad reached the top of the mountain without finding the silver mask. He was reasonably certain the mask wasn't here anymore. If it had once been hidden here, someone had found it and moved it.

But his search hadn't been a complete waste of time. Not only had he found the copper raingod mask, he had eliminated this mountain from his list of places to search.

He returned to Machu Picchu and showed his prize to La Curandera. Her spirit now occupied the condor effigy in the Temple of the Condor. From there, she could guard the vortex and also protect the unoccupied bodies of Bryn, Kisi, Kiyari, and the Ranger which sat in lotus nearby.

"That is indeed Illapa's mask," confirmed the healer. "Why is it important?"

"The Ranger wore it into battle as Ayar Cachi. It made him a fearsome warrior."

"The Ranger doesn't need a mask. He *is* a fearsome warrior."

"True. But I am told Ayar Manco fled when he saw Ayar Cachi in the mask. He fled more than once as soon as he saw the mask. He is afraid of the mask."

"Yam is a coward," said La Curandera. "He will not stand and fight unless he is certain in advance he has power enough to win."

"Perhaps that is not cowardice but wisdom," said Hadad. "Is it not wiser to flee when there is no chance to win?"

"Sometimes," agreed La Curandera. "But how many times have you or I or the Ranger or Jon or Bryn or Kisi died in battle because we believed in the cause? How many times have we fought on despite overwhelming odds because it was the right thing to do? We stood our ground and fought to the finish. We were willing to sacrifice ourselves because of someone or some cause we dearly loved and believed in. But Yam will not do that because he fears death. He is afraid to die because he knows what retribution awaits him in the afterlife. His karma is heavy with debt. He has a reason to avoid death at all costs. And that makes him a coward."

"Yam seeks the power to control his own destiny. Is that wrong?"

"It is wrong when it hurts others."

"Yes," said Hadad. "I have to agree. I will no longer excuse my brother's actions nor ignore them as I have in the past."

"Where will you search now for the silver mask?"

"Kiyari retains a psychic connection to the mask. When she returns from the underworlds, perhaps Kiyari can help me find it."

"And in the meantime?"

"In the meantime I will wait here with you. How much longer will they be gone?"

"Not too long. If they do not return in the next few days, they will not return at all."

* * *

"Here there be demons," said Hecate. "This is the echanted forest. It be where nightmares come true and fears become real. Beyond the forest is another door. I will await you there."

Once again the Ranger went first, slithering between trees and underbrush, his tongue tasting the air. He heard Bryn and Kisi walking cautiously behind him. This world, too, was completely dark, but the Ranger's reptilian senses proved to be an asset in the darkness. He wound between tree roots, easily in and out of thickets, and crossed a bog that may have contained quicksand. He was about to go back to warn the others about the bog when he suddenly remembered he had no way to communicate.

He heard them coming, and he had to stop them before they walked straight into the quicksand. They couldn't see it the way he could. And they couldn't hear him shouting a warning.

Or could they? He remembered that Kisi had been able to sense his spirit inside his new body, and he had likewise sensed something inside her, a kinship with her that he hadn't known before. Kisi was obviously more in touch with her animal side than most modern humans, and maybe there was a way to communicate with that side of her now.

He stopped in his tracks and focused his thoughts, directing them at the center of her head where the pineal gland moderated input from visual and auditory centers, marrying it with memories resident in the hippocampus, and routing appropriate danger signals straight to the amygdala. "Hear me, Kisi. Quicksand bog ahead. Big enough to suck both of you in. Go around it."

She didn't stop.

"Danger! Quicksand!"

He heard their footsteps slow.

"What is it?" asked Bryn. "Why did you stop me?"

"There's quicksand ahead."

"How do you know?"

"I heard it in my head. I think it was the Ranger talking to me. I think he was warning us."

"Where is this quicksand?"

"I don't know."

"Ten feet ahead," the Ranger projected at her.

"Ten feet ahead," Kisi said.

"Walk around it to the right," projected the Ranger.

"This way," said Kisi. "We can go around it if we walk to the right."

The Ranger wriggled his coils and turned completely around, and he went ahead of them again, as if he were walking point for a Ranger recon patrol in Afghanistan. His tongue snaked out and twitched, sensing heat, odors, movement, shapes, textures, even colors. His jaw picked up vibrations coming from the ground that others couldn't hear.

Something was completely different now, something had begun changing—morphing, warping, corrupting—in the forest that surrounded them and it wasn't at all pretty. At first, it was merely a subtle change, the tiniest shift in energy that was barely noticeable even to him. By moving to the right, off their original path, they had plunged deeper into the heart of the forest where evil lurked. Here, the trees were no longer merely trees. They were moving all on their own. And it wasn't just leaves and branches moving with the wind, it was deliberate movement as if the trees possessed a mind of their own.

Besides, there was no wind. The forest was deadly still except for the two women walking behind him and the rustle the movement of the trees made.

Now the shifts in energy were no longer subtle. The trees seized Bryn and Kisi, and though both women fought ferociously, Bryn and Kisi were lifted from the ground and securely held by forces beyond their control.

A light appeared in the distance, an eerie glow that grew larger and larger and brighter and brighter as it approached from afar, becoming blinding as it came closer and closer to the two women.

"I am Udug Hul," spoke the light. "I am a Gallu, a toll collector and gatherer of sacrifices for the Queen of this under-world. I will receive your spirits and deliver them to the Queen."

"The Queen?" asked Kisi.

"Queen Ereshkigal, ruler of this underworld realm known as Irkalla. Bring them," Udug Hul commanded the trees. And then the light moved off, diminishing until it disappeared, and the trees moved forward carrying their human cargo tightly clutched in branches that acted like arms.

The Ranger followed, slithering along the ground as fast as he could. Other trees parted to allow the walking trees to pass with their captives. Eventually, they came to a clearing wherein stood a magnificent castle built of stone. Surrounding the castle was a moat filled with skanky water and hungry beasts of reptil-ian descent, some with long, pointed snouts and rows of sharp crocodile teeth, others with fangs. The only way in or out of the castle was a single wooden drawbridge that had been lowered over the moat to allow the trees and their prisoners to enter. No sooner were they inside than the drawbridge began moving up-ward.

The Ranger coiled and sprang across the gulf, barely catching the end of the drawbridge as it ascended above the moat. His tail dangled precariously over the mouths of the snapping beasts, and he narrowly managed to retract his tail before it would have disappeared and the rest of him, head and all, likely devoured with it. He slid down the rough-cut wood of the drawbridge and wormed his way into the castle without anyone inside noticing him.

The castle grounds were lit up with bonfires blazing high in open pits throughout the vast courtyard, and over some of those open fires the Ranger could smell the remains of human beings roasting slowly on spits turned by giant green-skinned demonic fire-tenders. Fat bubbled and boiled and dripped down from broiled human flesh, each drop of fat causing fierce flames to flare up and singe what flesh was left on the spit. But the condemned souls trapped inside that seared flesh screamed and screamed as if still alive, although human life in this environment was impossible. This was the land of the lost, the land of the dead.

Within the castle grounds, demons of all kinds stood guard, some holding huge double-bladed battleaxes, some carrying pikes on long poles. Four of the fiercest-looking demons surrounded a portico overlaid with gold leaf. Cuneiform wedges were engraved into the gold, as were images of Sumerian and Akkadian idols that represented deities. One looked a lot like Hadad.

Moving slowly so he wouldn't attract attention, the Ranger wriggled up the portico's steps and slithered between twin columns made of marble. No one was looking down, and he managed to crawl inside without incident.

Beyond the portico was a large chamber, partly temple and partly throne room, with high vaulted ceilings and no windows. Three of the walls were decorated with more of the cuneiform wedges and symbolic representations, and in the center of the room was a sacrificial altar made of basalt. The only light in the room came from torches in ornate golden sconces on the walls, and between two of the sconces was a golden throne with images of Hadad engraved on both sides.

Above the throne, suspended on threads as thin as a spider's web, was a double-bladed axe. It hung there like the sword of Damocles, a reminder that power was perilous.

Seated on the throne, wearing a gown of transparent material that showed off every part of her luscious body, sat a woman who looked exactly like Kiyari.

Only it wasn't Kiyari. The real Kiyari had an innocence about her that gave her face a glow and made her look like an angel. This Kiyari was dark and hard, angular instead of round. Her breasts were pointed like daggers, and the V between her legs was dark and dank and festering.

Kneeling before the throne were Bryn and Kisi, stripped naked and shackled in irons.

"I am told my sister entered the underworlds with you," said the woman on the throne, her voice as cold as ice. "Where is she?"

"We don't know," replied Bryn. "We lost her in the swamp a world or two back."

"Fools!" shouted the woman on the throne. "How could you lose her? Do you know how long I have waited for my loving sister to return? Almost forever!"

Bryn and Kisi remained silent as the Ranger crawled closer to the throne.

"Here hold I the spirit of Damu-zid, the late husband of my beloved sister, until her return to take his place as my... honored guest. Let me show him to you, so you may see the fate that awaits you." She called to her demon servants, "Bring in Damu-zid."

Two demons left the chamber and returned a few moments later dragging the broken body of a tortured soul. Damu-zid had once been a splendid youth, handsome and virile, strong and god-like, and that remained obvious though little was left of what he once was. Every bone in his body had been smashed repeatedly, and he could not stand or even sit up on his own. As the demons dropped Damu-zid to the ground, he plopped down, his legs akimbo, like an old rag doll that had long ago been discarded by its owner.

"He cannot die, though he has endured a hundred thousand deaths," said Ereshkigal. "I have grown tired of toying with him. But you, my pretties, will amuse me to no end."

Ereshkigal stepped down from the throne and approached the two women. "You are not unlike my own sister. Proud. Arrogant. Beautiful. I shall soon change all that." Her hand lashed out at Bryn, smacking Bryn's cheek hard enough to turn it red. Then she raked her fingernails across the other cheek, digging in and leaving blood-red trails like the parallel rails of a train track.

Bryn tried to rise, but the demon holding her chains jerked her back to the floor and placed a green clawed hoof in the middle of Bryn's back squarely between both shoulder blades.

"Feisty bitch," sneered Ereshkigal. "I shall enjoy watching you grovel and plead."

She walked to Kisi next, and Ereshkigal lashed out and connected with Kisi's upturned nose. The Ranger heard cartilage crunch. If Kisi had been in her own body instead of a spirit body, broken cartilage would have driven directly into her brain, killing Kisi instantly.

Instead, Kisi had to endure the pain.

"Take them to the torture chamber," directed Ereshkigal, reseating herself on her throne. "Chain them to the rack. I will join you momentarily."

After Kisi and Bryn had been dragged off, along with the remains of Damu-zid, Ereshkigal motioned to one of the demons to approach the throne. The demon bowed so low, his snout nearly scraped the floor.

"What of the man who entered the underworlds with those two?" asked Ereshkigal. "Where is he?"

"We do not know, my Lady," replied the demon. "There was no man with them when Udug Hul captured the two women."

"Then find him, you fool. And find my sister, too. If they be not here, scour all the other underworlds until you find them."

"We cannot leave this world, Your Majesty," replied the demon. "Only you, and Udug Hul, may enter and leave as you please."

"Then send Udug Hul to me," said the Queen. "And you begin the search of all Irkalla for the man and the woman. As a reward to the one who finds them, I offer what will remain of the man to do with as you please. After I have finished with him, of course."

The demon salivated and licked his lips. "It shall be done, Your Highness."

Unused to waiting, the Queen fidgeted and fretted, tapping her foot anxiously until Udug Hul appeared in front of her. His radiance was diminished in the presence of Ereshkigal, though he still glowed as if composed of swamp gas, which the

Ranger suspected might be true since he smelled worse than decomposing fecal matter.

"Why did you not bring me the man as well as the two women?" asked the Queen.

"I saw no man," said Udug Hul. "If there had been a man with them, I would surely have brought him unto you."

"You kept him not for yourself?"

"No, my Queen."

"Then find him. If he is not in my realm, search the other underworlds. Find him."

"I shall, my Queen."

"And find my sister. I want her most of all."

"It shall be as you bid, my Queen."

"Go now. And do not return until you have them."

Udug Hul did not reply but glowed bright as the sun and then disappeared.

"Good dog," said Erkeshigal the moment he was gone. "I may throw a bone or two in your direction when you fetch them to me. For a bone or two will be all that remains of my sister when I have finished with her."

Ereshkigal descended the throne and went in the direction the demons had taken Bryn and Kisi. The Ranger debated following. Instead, he crawled on his belly to the portico, slithering dangerously close to the clawed hooves of a demon standing guard at the doorway. When he reached one of the marble columns, he wound his coils about the column and slithered to the top where he remained patiently waiting for the Queen to return.

He made no move when he heard screams coming from the dungeons below the throne room. He made no move when he saw two of the demons return with the bloodied bodies of Kisi and Bryn. He made no move when both women were placed naked on the sacrificial altar and spread-eagled. He made no move as Ereshkigal violated their bodies in every manner imaginable. He made no move until Ereshkigal ascended her throne.

Then he threw himself at the spider-web holding the double-bladed axe above the throne, knocking the blades loose, falling to the floor as the axe swung down from the ceiling, suspended now by only one strand of silk.

It swung like a pendulum, the sharp blade slicing through Ereshkigal's skull as it swung all the way past her left shoulder, and decapitating the head entirely on the return swing.

Before any of the four demon guards could react, the Ranger had sunk his fangs into two of them, draining both of his poison sacs completely. Both demons dropped instantly, so powerful was the poison. For the first time since he had transformed, the Ranger wished he had arms and legs to fight with, and he found himself transformed again, as if by magic, into a man again with two arms and two legs and a body to match.

As he came up from the floor, his bare hands were ready for anything. One of the two remaining demons came for him with a battle axe, and the Ranger spun and planted a heel in the demon's midsection that sent him flying across the room. The other demon came at him with a pike, and he parried the shaft with his left hand and wrenched it away from the demon with his right. He reversed the pike and drove the point through where the demon's heart would be if the demon had a heart. It was enough to leave the monster wriggling on the shaft like those humans skewered over fires in the courtyard.

The Ranger found a key ring dangling from the demon's belt, and he removed the ring and ran to the altar and released Bryn and Kisi from their chains. Both women were hovering at the edge of consciousness, and the Ranger knew they would never be able to walk out of the throne room in their current condition. He could carry one, but he couldn't carry both of them.

"Bryn, Kisi, listen to me," he whispered next to their torn ears. "Both of you listen. Your bodies aren't real. They are only reflections of your spirits. Your spirits are pretty bruised up right now, but I know you have something left inside you that wants to get out of here. Take a deep breath and focus on getting up. You can do it. I know you can. Breathe in. Breathe out. Focus."

Slowly, Bryn responded. He watched the fingernail scratches on her cheeks mend, the ears reattach. The open wounds on her torso closed, and the blood on her thighs dried up and faded away.

Kisi, too, began to stir. Her eyes opened and closed, her breath became more regular. The nipples that had been sliced off grew back, and the broken bones in her arms and legs welded together.

He didn't see, but he heard, the demon he had sent flying come at him again with the axe, and he wheeled and kicked out and sent the demon flying back into the corner.

Bryn was standing now, testing her legs. Kisi was sitting up, looking wondrously at the body she now wore. It was bigger and stronger than the one she had before.

"Grab an axe," the Ranger said, wrenching the pike from the carcass of the skewed demon. "We have to get out of here before they mend themselves and come at us again."

"Where is the Queen?" asked Bryn. "I owe her."

The Ranger pointed to the severed head. "I beat you to it," he said.

Kisi picked up one of the double-bladed battleaxes, and her new muscles bulged as she hefted it in both hands. She walked to where the headless body lay bleeding on the ground, and she chopped off both arms and both legs.

"Now we can go," she said.

They fought their way through the courtyard, each sustaining wounds that healed almost as soon as they were inflicted. But the demons they slew stayed down, and eventually they reached the drawbridge and cut the ropes that held it in place. The drawbridge dropped over the moat and they hurried across.

Within minutes they were back in the woods, feeling their way in the dark.

Three demons attacked them before long, and they swung and chopped and thrust their way past. They floundered around in the dark for what seemed like an eternity until they heard Hecate's voice say, "What did you learn in this world that you did not know before?"

"I learned," said Kisi, "that no wound is so deep that it cannot be healed."

"Good," said Hecate.

"I learned," said the Ranger, "that our bodies are only tools. Whatever body we are in, we'll learn how to use the tools we have available when we need them."

"Very good," said Hecate.

"I learned," said Bryn, "to really, really hate. I really hated Ereshkigal, and I have never before hated anyone so much that I would be willing to permanently sacrifice my own life force to take hers away. But I think I hated her that much. I would do that. I would definitely do that. If the Ranger hadn't killed her, I would have."

"She isn't dead, you know," said Hecate. "She cannot die. She may lose power temporarily, but it always comes back to her."

"If she isn't dead, I will go back and kill her. I will do that right now."

"Hear me, child. She isn't dead because she cannot die. Not in this realm that belongs entirely to her and where she rules supreme. Not in any of the underworlds. You may destroy her body, but she will only grow a new one. Her spirit is eternal, as is yours. Though she is eternal, she is trapped here forever. Or, at least, until someone takes her place."

"Who could take her place?" asked Kisi.

"You could. Or Bryn. Or Kiyari. She would trick you into sacrificing your life force. She cannot leave her domain for long, and she cannot enter the upper worlds unless someone volunteers to take her place in this world. She depends on Udug Hul to do her bidding and bring her sacrifices. Udug Hul is a being with the power to move between worlds, and you should fear him."

Hecate removed the silver key, and she once again inserted the key into a hidden lock and turned it. An open doorway appeared out of nowhere and she gestured the three to enter.

"It is time to take the next step on your journey through the underworlds," she said. "Welcome to Hades."

CHAPTER NINETEEN

Akashagarbha showed Jon Fish wonders beyond anything he had ever imagined possible. "All actions have enduring effects," said Akashagarbha as they shot across time and space. "What was done ten thousand years ago on Earth is only now reaching other parts of the universe. They will continue on, eventually affecting all parts of the universe. And those effects will cause reactions that, in turn, affect earth thousands of years from now. As above, so below. Changes here cause changes everywhere, and changes everywhere cause changes here. Ancient civilizations had a clearer view of the heavens than modern man. They looked up at the heavens and they were able to grasp the fact that everything is connected. The Incas, for example, knew that they could affect the heavens by their actions on earth, and they created elaborate rituals to produce the kind of effects they wanted. And they knew that the heavens could affect humans, as well; so they sought to control the heavens, to manipulate what happened there to their advantage. They were surprisingly successful."

"I see," said Jon as he watched Manco Capac at the Inti-huatana. Manco wore the golden mask, and he held in his hands the tapac-yauri, the golden staff of Kon-Tiki Viracocha.

"He holds much power," said Akashagarbha. "But we have not come all this way to see Manco prance around the Inti-huatana. We seek the moon mask."

Jon felt a slight shift in perspective, and the Moon Temple came into focus. He saw the priestess take the moon mask from the west wall of the temple where it had served as a mirror. He watched as she fled toward the hills, clutching the mask to her bosom as if carrying an infant. Minutes after she vacated the temple, hundreds of armed men rushed in from the opposite direction, destroying everything in sight. They ransacked the temple, torturing and killing three of the women who were still inside.

Then they began taking the temple apart, stone by stone.

Akashagarbha and Jon followed the girl, the last priestess of the moon goddess in the sacred valley of the Urubamba, as she fled for her life with the silver mask. She climbed higher and higher, running through the underbrush, then climbed again until she came to a trail that led around the mountain, and she followed that trail for miles. She walked the ancient trail from Machu Pikchu to the taller Wayna Picchu, where she found an old trail with stone steps that led up the north side of what was known as "the young mountain." About half-way up, still well below where the temples of the sun rose on neighboring

Machu Picchu, she crawled into a slit in the rock face, the entrance to a secret cave or tunnel that went deep inside the mountain. In complete darkness, she felt with her feet until she found stairs carved into the rock beneath where another Temple of the Moon had recently been constructed on Huayna Picchu. She continued downwards until she came to an underground river, the waters rushing cold over her bare feet. She placed the silver mask into the river and released it. Then she began the perilous climb back up those slippery stone steps, her feet still wet. At first, Jon was certain she would make it all the way back up, but her left foot slipped from an outcropping of stone, and she lost her balance and toppled off the stairway. She fell back down to the river. Her body broke apart as it hit jagged rocks, bounced off, bounced again, rolled into the underground river, and the swift current carried her away as if she had never existed.

"Now we know," said Akashagarbha.

"But what happened to the mask after she placed it in the river?" asked Jon.

"It followed the flow and fell into the underworlds," said Akashagarbha. "For that river connects the upper worlds of Hanan Pacha with the underworlds of Uku Pacha, heaven with hell. It is the river that waters the roots of the World Tree."

"Where in the underworlds is the mask now?"

"Because there is no light in the underworlds, we are unable to see where the mask eventually ended its journey. That is the River Styx which flows through all nine of the underworlds. The silver mask could reside in any of them."

"How can we get to it? How do we retrieve it?"

"It will remain in the underworlds until one of us enters the underworlds and searches for it there. I am unable to enter the underworlds. But you may go, if you wish. After the Ranger, Bryn, Kisi, and Kiyari return."

"Why can't you go with me?"

"My spirit is made of light. My presence in the underworlds would disrupt the delicate balance between worlds. I dare not go there."

"Then I will go alone."

"Hadad would journey with you if you asked. Retrieving the mask is important to him."

"I'll ask him when I see him."

"Then let us go and see him," said Akashagarbha, and they were back at Machu Picchu in the blink of an eye.

*   *   *

Hades was pure hell.

Dark and dreary, misty and gloomy, it felt torridly hot and humid, and it certainly felt depressing. Besides being completely dark, there were no discernible landmarks. Nothing to see. Nothing to touch. Nothing to intuit. The place was barren and empty. Completely. No sound. No vibration. No energy. No nothing.

"It's like the Void," said the Ranger, but his words went nowhere.

If Bryn and Kisi were still there with him, he wasn't able to reach them with words. He stumbled about trying to reach them in other ways, to touch them or to reach them with his mind, but it was as if they weren't there anymore. It was as if they no longer existed.

Was he all alone in this underworld? Had he only imagined they had crossed the threshold with him? Or were they here, too, unable to hear, to touch, to communicate in any meaningful way?

Time passed, if there were indeed such a thing as time here, and he felt increasingly more alone, more abandoned, more helpless and hopeless with every passing moment. He was alone with his thoughts, and he didn't like what he was thinking.

It *was* hopeless, wasn't it? They had lost Kiyari two worlds back, and now he had lost Bryn and Kisi. What could he do alone?

Nothing. He could do nothing. He was the Lone Ranger, and he was all alone.

So alone.

Loneliness seeped into every atom and molecule of his being and permeated his soul. He was separated from everything that had ever mattered to him—the Army, the Lamasery, his friends—and he could think of no reason why he should continue to struggle, to continue on, to think about anything ever again. Thinking was such a damn bother! Wouldn't it be far better to stop thinking and just lie down and die?

He remembered another time when he had felt that way. It was when he and Bryn and Jon and Kisi tried to stop Yam from sacrificing women in Missouri, and Yam had hit him so hard he had slammed into a tree and his head split apart, spilling his brains all over the place. Then Yam had hit him with a double whammy that broke every bone in his body. He was in agonizing pain, and Yam had promised to end that pain if he would give up. "Give me your life force," the man in the golden mask had offered, "and I'll take the pain away."

And he remembered another time, the worst time of his life, when Taliban sympathizers had led him into an ambush and all his men had been killed, blown to bits by improvised explosive devices and a barrage of gunfire that riddled their bodies and made them dance like marionettes on strings. He had been hit by dozens of rounds and pieces of shrapnel. They had penetrated his stomach and destroyed his spleen, some ruptured his ribs. Pain had penetrated every part of his body, and pain had corrupted his soul. He had nearly bled out on the ground, helpless for three long days and nights, before other Rangers found his body so broken they all thought he was dead. Unable to speak, going in and out of consciousness for three days and nights, his mind focused on surviving so he could extract revenge on all those who had betrayed him. And he had survived. And he had taken his revenge.

He could have quit. Maybe he should have quit. But he hadn't. He had a job to do, a mission to accomplish, and he had always finished his assigned job and accomplished his mission. And he would again. He had never let anything stand in his way before, and he wouldn't let anything stand in his way now.

"Focus," he told himself. "Focus on the mission."

They had entered the underworlds to find Yam Elman. Yam was here, somewhere, maybe not in this world but in one of the others, and they had to find Elman and stop him from returning to the Seita with allies from the underworlds. That was the Ranger's assigned mission now, and he would complete his mission even if it killed him.

That struck him as funny, and he laughed and laughed and laughed. He was already in the land of the dead, ha ha, and his spirit couldn't die. Not here. Not ever. But his body could. His real body. It would sure as hell—ha ha—perish if he didn't return to it soon. Ha ha. But he wasn't going to let that happen. Ha ha. He was going to complete his mission. Ha ha. And he would laugh in the face of death. Ha ha ha.Take that, death. Ha ha haaaaaaaa.

He moved forward again. He couldn't tell which direction he was going, but he was on the move now and he wasn't going to stop until he got all the way through this underworld, found Elman, fixed Elman, fought Elman, and finished Elman for good.

Somewhere ahead, there appeared a light, a tiny light that seemed to grow larger and brighter as he got closer to it. Udug Hul? No, it couldn't be!

It was a bonfire, a huge fire that burned out of the very ground itself, flames leaping high into the air above his head. The Ranger could see no source of fuel—no wood, coal, or petroleum—feeding the flames. The dancing red and blue flames were just there, as if they were alive, as if they had a mind of their own.

And dancing around those flames were three giant women, naked except for huge hooded serpents draped about their waists and cascading over their shoulders. One had black hair, one had blonde hair, and one was a natural red head.

They looked like Kiyari, Kisi, and Bryn.

"How did you get here before me?" he asked, and the women turned to face him as if they had heard him speak. "And where did you find Kiyari?"

"We are the Erinyes," said the blonde one who looked like Kisi. "I am Alecto, and these are my sisters, Tisiphone and Megaera. This is our abode. Who is Kiyari?"

"She looks like your black-haired sister."

"Tisiphone, have you ever heard of Kiyari?"

"Nay, my sister. I have been accused of resembling Persephone, our most beautiful and gracious Queen. But I know no Kiyari."

"Why have you come to the gates of Tartarus, mortal? asked Megaera. "What oath have you broken that you should dwell in this place?"

"I vowed not to take the lives of sentient beings," replied the Ranger. "It is a vow I regret breaking."

"Then you are in the right place. Tartarus is where oathbreakers receive their just punishments. You will remain here, in Tartarus, for nine years before drinking water from the Lethe. Then you be judged by Queen Persephone and King Haides in the Palace of Hades. If you have truly repented, you may be reborn to the land of the living."

"I can't stay here for nine years," said the Ranger. "I have been sent here to accomplish a mission."

"Oh, but you must stay here," insisted Alecto. "Unless the oath you took to accomplish your mission outweighs the oath you broke. Only the Queen may decide if that be true."

"Then take me to your Queen and let her judge me."

"This," said Megaera, "we cannot do. For the Queen is absent three-quarters of the year. She will not return until solstice."

"Then take me to the King."

"Haides is in mourning while the Queen is away. He sees no one."

"Sisters," said Alecto, "do you hear? Beware. Others approach."

Bryn and Kisi materialized out of the dark like ghosts. "We thought we had lost you again," said Bryn.

Alecto and Megaera looked at their twins as if they had seen their own reflections in a mirror. "You are me," said Alecto to Kisi.

"And you are me," said Megaera to Bryn.

"In another life, perhaps," said Bryn.

"This cannot be," said Alecto. "You should not be here. We must take you to the King. He shall decide what must be done with you."

"Come, sisters," said Megaera. "We shall all see the King. Bring the man with you."

They danced their way across the River Styx to ascend the top of a nearby hill where lay the pool of Lethe and beside that pool of crystal-clear waters rose a magnificent palace, opulent beyond belief, constructed of the purest gold and silver, hardened by fire and ice. Precious jewels of every description decorated the façade, and each of those jewels emitted a light of its own so the palace dazzled with colors, blinking violet, red, orange, yellow, green, blue, and white before visiting every hue in between. They reminded the Ranger of the bright neons and brilliant digital billboards that blinked above the busy streets of Tokyo.

As the three dancers escorted Bryn, Kisi, and the Ranger into a magnificent hall lined with tables full of luscious fruits, roasted meats, nuts, berries, and intoxicating drinks, the hall grew silent. Two thrones, each magnificently carved of solid gold and inlaid with jewels, sat in the middle of the room. Both thrones were empty.

"O, Aidoneus," Alecto addressed the empty throne on the left, "whose true name may never be spoken, we bring to you the spirits of three mortals for judgment."

"Go away," came a voice from the empty air above the throne. "Can't you see I am in mourning?"

"We cannot see you, O Aidoneus, for you wear the helmet of invisibility."

"I will not be seen until Persephone returns. Bring you news of her?"

"Perhaps," said Alecto, "these three may have news of your bride."

Aidoneus removed the helmet from his head and he suddenly appeared, seated on the throne. He was a big man, more than seven-feet tall with a massive chest and broad shoulders. He wore a sandy-brown beard that was neatly-trimmed, but his hair was long in the back and shimmered like sunlight on the sea. He reminded the Ranger of a younger version of Biegolmai.

"Have you news of the beautiful Persephone?" boomed the voice.

"We know her as Kiyari," answered Bryn. "She convinced Hecate to aid us on our journey."

"My beloved is Hecate's god-child," said Aidoneus Haides.

"So we understand," said Bryn.

"Where is this Kiyari? Where is my Persephone?"

"We lost her two worlds back. She didn't make it across the swamp with us. She may be dead."

"You left her there? To die alone?"

"We had no choice but to leave her behind. Hecate opened the door to the next world, and we could not go back."

Aidoneus seemed to see them for the first time. He did a double take. "How be it you look so much like Megaera and Alecto?"

"We don't know."

"This cannot be. Two manifestations of the same spirit cannot exist in the same place at the same time without one destroying the other. You must leave here at once."

"How is it then that Tisiphone and Persephone both reside here?"

"When the Queen is present," replied the King, "Tisiphone visits other worlds."

"Then send our doubles to other worlds to search for Kiyari. Or send us on our way. That will eliminate any chance of conflict between us. But we won't leave without the Ranger. He goes with us, or we don't go."

"Why are you here in my kingdom? Your bodies have yet to perish in the world above, but your spirits freely wander through the land of the dead. Not many mortals know the ways to reach my kingdom, and even fewer come here of their own free will. Most plead and beg and have to be brought here kicking and screaming, pleading for mercy. But there is no mercy in the underworlds. So I ask you now, what brings you three to Hades?"

"There were four of us when we began," explained Bryn. "We came to find Yam Elman, force him to return the sun to visibility, and trap him in the underworlds forever."

"Yam Elman? He who is also known as Yaw or Yah? The one we call Rahu?"

"Yes."

Aidoneus Haides laughed, a great big raucous belly laugh that wouldn't cease. "Who do you think you are," Aidoneus managed to say between guffaws, "that you might have the power to defeat Rahu in his own kingdom? Besides being leader of the Nagas, Rahu is a master of illusion. He alone has the power to hide the sun and the moon."

"That is why we must find him. He has hidden the sun from mortal eyes."

"Is this true?" Aidoneus asked Tisiphone.

"It is true, my King."

"Why has no one told me?"

"You did not wish to be disturbed by trivialities, my King."

"Trivialities? You call the lack of sunlight on earth a triviality? This man—this demon, this demigod—has turned all of earth like unto hades by taking away the light of the sun and the moon. This cannot be! It is an abomination! Here mortals may be punished for misdeeds simply by being deprived of all light. How will mortals fear entering my dark kingdom if earth is equally dark? Yam violates the laws of karma by his actions! It is an abomination that cannot endure."

"My sentiments exactly," said the Ranger.

"And you," said Aidoneus, pointing a finger at the Ranger, "what do you propose to do about it?"

"Stop him," said the Ranger. "Find him and force him to return the sun."

"How? What magic do you possess that is the equal of his?"

"I possess no magic."

"And the others?"

"Yes," said Bryn. "Kisi and I know magic. But our magic is grounded in earth magic, and earth magic is of no use to us in the underworlds. Kisi and I are also proficient in Vril. Unfortunately, we cannot access the power of Vril outside of our physical bodies."

"So you possess no magic either?"

"I guess we don't. Not here, anyway."

Aidoneus laughed again. "You came here with no magic? And you expect to confront Yam in his own domain? And you expect to be victorious? Did I hear you correctly? You expect to win without magic?"

"Yes," said the Ranger. "We do."

Aidoneus couldn't stop laughing. He tossed his head back and roared and roared.

Finally, when he had regained some control of himself, he said, "I have never laughed so much. Never. When my Queen is not here, mirth is absent and laughter is not part of my kingdom. But you have made me laugh. Perhaps you can make Yam laugh. Perhaps you will kill him with laughter."

"Perhaps," smiled the Ranger.

"Then go, with my blessing. I shall send Tisiphone with you to observe your feeble attempts, and she shall report back to me of the outcome. Perhaps it may make me laugh even more."

Aidoneus placed the helmet back on his head and he disappeared. But his laughter continued to fill the air until the three mortals and the three Erinyes had departed the Great Hall.

Hecate was waiting for them near the banks of the River Styx.

"What have you learned this time?" asked Hecate.

"The importance of laughter," said the Ranger. "Even in the land of the dead, laughter has a place."

"And you?" Hecate asked Bryn.

"That we can survive without magic to aid us," replied Bryn.

"And you?" she asked Kisi.

"That there are others who look exactly like us but are not us," answered Kisi. "Or if they are us, they exist independently of us."

Alecto and Megaera bid their sister well on her journey, and the two sisters remained on the hill while the three mortals, Tisiphone, and Hecate crossed the River Styx by walking upon the water. They watched as Hecate removed the silver key from her bosom and inserted the key into a brass lock, turned the key clockwise, and the five disappeared behind the door into the next world, the Land of Patala, the seventh underworld, and the Kingdom ruled by Rahu, Lord of the Nagas, King of Serpents and master of illusion.

CHAPTER TWENTY

All of Patala was ablaze with light. A hundred thousand jewels, not unlike the jewels of Hades where each gem possessed a brilliance of its own, lit up the landscape. Patala, unlike the other underworld realms they had seen, looked modern, not too different from a miniature Las Vegas or Reno. There were paved roads with posted speed limits which none of the fast-moving sports cars bothered to obey, ornate bridges carved of stone spanning the rivers Styx and Oceanus, even jewel-encrusted streetlights that glowed brightly in a variety of colors. A seventeen-story hotel, a smaller version of Caesar's Palace or MGM Grand, with an "All-Night Gaming" sign made of opals and emeralds, stood near the banks of the River Styx, next to a Chinese restaurant and a mini-mall of boutiques and gift shops. There were gas stations, car rentals, a strip club called "The Snake Charmer" advertising "Dancing Girls," several pawn shops, and a McDonald's-style fast-food restaurant with a drive thru.

"Not everything is always as it appears to be," warned Hecate "I shall wait for you beyond the city. Tisiphone may accompany you, but she must not interfere with your progress—or lack thereof—in this realm or any of the realms beyond. If she attempts to do so, she will receive swift and appropriate punishment."

"I will not interfere," said Tisiphone.

"Do I have your oath?'

"I swear I will not interfere."

"Then I take my leave," said Hecate, and she disappeared.

"This doesn't look too bad," said Bryn. "Nothing like I thought it would be."

"Rahu spares no expense to entrap visitors," said Tisiphone. "He welcomes all who would come here willingly. Few who enter his kingdom ever leave, however."

"Can any enter here without first passing through Hades?"

"Yes. Each of the underworlds sends emissaries to the worlds above. They may enter or leave by means of the rivers. Emissaries, such as Udug Hul, escort spirits and willing sacrifices into the underworlds. Rahu, too, has emissaries. They appear mortal when walking among mortals. You would be surprised by how many mortals come here of their own free will to gamble their lives away."

"Nothing surprises me anymore," said the Ranger. "Where will we find Yam?"

"Rahu frequents the gaming tables in the hotel. He also is said to visit one of the girls at The Snake Charmer. Her name is Mohini. He is enchanted by her."

"And is she enchanted by him?" asked Bryn.

"I have said too much already," said Tisiphone. "Some things you must discover yourselves."

"Should we split up?" asked Kisi. "Bryn and I can check out the gambling halls while the Ranger looks for Yam in the strip club. Tisiphone can go with whomever she wishes."

"I will accompany the Ranger," said Tisiphone. "I am already dressed to fit in at The Snake Charmer. I might appear out of place in the hotel."

No one seemed to notice when the Ranger and Tisiphone walked into The Snake Charmer. The place was dark, the only lights were focused on a stage in the far corner where two women danced to the rhythmic beat of drums and the lilting melody of reed pipes. Both women on stage were naked except for eight-foot-long pythons wrapped around their waists and breasts. Both women held the pythons' heads in their hands and moved the heads erotically in and out of their open mouths. No one paid any attention to the new arrivals. Tisiphone, too, was naked except for the serpent still coiled around her midsection.

Fourteen tables surrounded the stage. Each table seated two men and two women. From time to time the men and women would take their drinks with them and leave the table to visit the "The Snake Pit—VIP Room" located to the left rear of the stage. The women returned after a few moments in the VIP Room, drinks in hand, but the men didn't return with them.

"They lure unsuspecting men into that room and feed the men to the Nagas," Tisiphone said. "It really is a snake pit, but no one believes it until it is too late. Behind that door lies the land of the Nagas. Any man who enters that room voluntarily, loses his right to be reborn. His spirit is devoured by the Nagas.
"

"Where is Mohini?"

"She is busy behind the bar. Mohini works here as the sole bartender and cocktail waitress. If we take a table over there close to the stage, she will quickly come to us to fulfill our drink orders. You should order but not drink."

Mohini was incredibly beautiful, raven-haired, full-breasted, slim-waisted, most men's wet dream come true. She wore a simple sari, yellow in color, with blue lotus flowers embroidered in the fabric. "What's your poison?" she asked sweetly.

"What do you have?" inquired the Ranger.

"Toxin or venom?" asked Mohini.

"What's the difference?"

"Toxins take longer to work. Venums get right into your blood stream and kill you quicker."

"Toxin."

"On tap, we have hydrogen cyanide, carbon monoxide, botulinum, lye, formaldehyde, strychnine, and radioactive isotopes."

"Strychnine, I guess."

"And the lady?"

"Cobra venom cocktail, please. Unless, of course, you serve Amrita."

Mohini shot her a look. "Amrita, the elixir of life, is reserved for special guests only. I do not think you qualify."

"Then I'll have the cobra venom cocktail."

Mohini was back in a moment with the drinks. "I have no money," said the Ranger. "How do I pay?

Mohini laughed. "Drinks are on the house. Money is no good here. Rahu wants everyone to have a good time, and he foots the bill. So live it up while you still can."

"Sit with us for a moment," requested Tisiphone. "My friend is a stranger here, and he wants to ask you a question."

Mohini took one of the empty chairs. "What brings you to the land of the Nagas?"

"Yam Elman," said the Ranger. "You know him here as Rahu."

"I know him, yes," replied Mohini. "Elman's spirit now infests the same spirit body as Rahu. He is a hungry ghost. Things were better here before Yam returned to repossess Rahu."

"You don't like him?"

"No," said Mohini. "But I serve him. As I serve all who enter here. It is my job."

"Is he here now?"

"No. He is at the hotel engaged in sport."

"Do you expect him to come here?"

"He always does. It is here that he has his desserts. After he has fed at the casino."

"Dessert is in the VIP Room?"

"Yes."

"Then we'll wait here for him."

"Drink up. I will bring you more when you finish those."

The Ranger picked up his cup and drained it. Tisiphone's eyes went wide. "No!" she shouted. "You'll die! It really is poison."

"No," said the Ranger. "I won't die, because I won't let myself die. Now, I'll have a cup of Amrita, if there is any left. And if you'll serve me."

"I think," said Mohini, sounding impressed with the Ranger's act of defiance of death, "you qualify. I'll see if I can find some."

She was back in a moment carrying a cup of immortality. "Here," she said. "Drink this. It will make you into a god."

"I don't want to be a god," said the Ranger. "I only want to live long enough to complete my mission."

"What is your mission, O Brave One?"

"To find Yam Elman. To get him to return the sun. And to kill him if I can't stop him from returning to earth to carry out his plans."

"He cannot be killed. Rahu, too, has consumed the elixir of life. Cut off his head, and he will yet live. His spirit is strong, and it grows stronger."

"Then how can I force him to return the sun and the moon?"

"You cannot. Only Ketu can force Rahu to return the sun. Ketu is his twin."

"Is there no way to keep Yam in the underworlds forever?"

"None that I know of. If his mortal body is slain on earth, his spirit will be sent to the underworlds for cleansing. But do not expect him to repent. Eventually, of course, he will be reborn. Even he shall be reborn."

"Unless," suggested Tisiphone, "his body is slain on earth while his spirit is in the underworlds. Then his spirit will be trapped here."

"Or unless," added Mohini, "he voluntarily remains here. But I don't see a reason why he would do that. Yam comes here only to feed. When he is satiated, he returns to the land of the living."

"Maybe I can keep him here long enough for his human body to die."

"No," said Tisiphone. "Your body would die, too."

"I know," said the Ranger. "But it might be worth it to keep Yam away from mankind forever."

"He would only thrive here," said Tisiphone. "But you, I think, would be lost here. Good men do not belong in the underworlds."

"Then what are *you* doing here?" asked the Ranger. "Neither you nor Mohini is evil."

"We work here," said Mohini. "Though we may leave at any time, we choose to remain here. We have jobs that require our continued presence in the underworlds."

"What is your job exactly?"

"To serve drinks."

"That all?"

"Isn't that enough?"

"I suppose. Tisiphone, what is your job?"

"Right now, it is to observe you."

"But what keeps you in the underworlds?"

"My sisters and I punish certain kinds of sinners. We punish murderers, especially those who kill their fathers, mothers, brothers, or sisters; those who kill or make others suffer because of vanity, jealousy or anger; and those who despair and commit suicide. We also punish oathbreakers. We bring them to Hades and imprison them in the total darkness of Tartarus for nine years. Once they have suffered enough and agree to repent, to go forth and sin no more, the Queen may judge them worthy of rebirth. She sits in judgement only from the winter solstice until spring equinox."

"Then you and your sisters are emissaries of Hades?"

"Among other things. We pursue those who continue to commit heinous acts even after they are reborn, those who swear to repent and violate their oath. Our job is to remind them of the suffering that awaits them in Hades so they might change before it is too late. We may appear on earth as winged creatures known to the Romans as Harpies. Sometimes we are seen wearing long black robes such as human magistrates or judges might wear to court. Sometimes we are seen as ordinary women."

"Are you judges?"

"When need be. We have been empowered by the King to act as judge, jury, and executioner."

"Executioner?"

"When all three of us are in concurrence, or when ordered by the King or Queen."

"You kill humans?"

"Not directly. We torture them and drive them mad with guilt. They kill themselves, thinking they might escape us by dying. After their bodies perish, we bring their spirits to Tartarus for nine additional years of punishment."

"Do all emissaries have such power?"

"Yes."

"Why don't you punish Yam? He has killed his brother in several incarnations."

"We have indeed punished him in the past. But he is now an adept, and he is beyond our reach as long as he lives. We Erinyes are unable to touch his spirit. I am not even certain the King and Queen of Hades together have the power to punish Yam while he lives."

"Now I know why the King laughed when I told him I intended to confront Yam."

"What chance has a mortal with no magic?"

"If you have no magic," asked Mohini, "how did you enter the underworlds? Were you not brought here by an emissary?"

"No," said the Ranger. "We four entered a tunnel at Machu Picchu. Then we were carried to the first underworld by a river."

"And you passed through six of the previous underworlds without a guide?"

"Hecate guides them," said Tisiphone. "She opens the doors that allow them to pass from one underworld to the next."

"But why would Hecate aid mortals?"

"They were accompanied by an incarnation of my Queen," said Tisiphone. "She is Hecate's god-child."

"I see" said Mohini. "Where is your Queen now?"

"We lost her in the fourth underworld," replied the Ranger. "We wanted to go back for her, but Hecate wouldn't let us."

"Us? Where are your other companions?"

"At the hotel. They are looking for Yam."

"Do they know him? Does he know them?"

"Yes."

"Then you must pray, Brave One. Pray that they do not find him. For this is Rahu's world, and here Yam and Rahu act as one. Rahu will surely devour them."

"But they cannot die here. They are here in spirit only."

"That may be true," said Mohini. "But there are worst things than death, mortal. Pray your companions do not learn what those things are."

*   *   *

Bryn and Kisi entered the hotel, and they were surprised to see a large lobby filled with slot machines and hundreds of mortal-looking men and women sitting glassy-eyed in front of those machines, totally mesmerized by the spinning dials and flashing lights. They smoked cigarettes and consumed intoxicating beverages. A very long line of impatient men and women waited their turn to gamble their very souls away when the current player ran out of available credit. This was the underworld where compulsive gamblers went when they died, that they might learn to value what they already had rather than what they might gain. Here they could mortgage their souls for a chance to win big. Though they knew the odds were with the house, they didn't care. Win or lose, they were having the time of their lives and they expected the good times to go on forever. They had mistakenly thought they had died and gone to heaven. For most of them, this was as close to heaven as any of them would ever get.

So, too, was this the underworld for lechers and adulterers and those who coveted their neighbor's possessions. There were rooms in the hotel for liaisons of all sorts, and there was even a huge banquet room devoted to Roman-style orgies where togas were optional.

Everyone seemed to have a burning cigarette in their hands, or a cigar, or a joint, and scantily-clad cocktail waitresses passed among the crowds with trays of drinks and hypodermic needles and vials of pure heroin and crack pipes and hash pipes and all manner of indulgences. Though everything here was free, a gift of Rahu, there would be a terrible price to pay for every drink, every puff, every hit, every wager. Someone, after all, had to pay the piper, and Rahu and his minions intended to collect with interest for each and every indulgence. If that didn't teach one to mend his wayward ways before entering the next life, nothing would.

Beyond the hotel lobby was the diamond-studded entrance to high-stakes casinos, with separate rooms for blackjack and seven card stud, roulette, banco, and craps.

"Where do you suppose Yam might be?" asked Kisi.

"I bet he's playing poker," said Bryn.

They entered the casino, searched for the card tables, and seated themselves in leather recliners near the cocktail lounge where they could watch the action at the tables without being too obvious.

"I don't see him," said Kisi. "Do you?"

"No. I was sure he would be here."

A waitress came by and asked them to name their poison. "Just water," said Kisi.

"We don't serve water here," snapped the waitress and walked away looking thoroughly disgusted.

Two men, big burley bruisers wearing tuxes, removed one of the female players from a blackjack table, and the woman screamed and pleaded as she was dragged off the playing floor. "One more hand," she begged. "I'm good for it. Just let me play one more hand. My luck will change. You'll see. My luck will change. Just one more hand. Please! I'll do anything! Please!"

Bryn and Kisi watched as the men dragged the woman, still begging and pleading, to a door on the far side of the room. They opened the door, shoved the woman inside a dark room, slammed the door, and locked it.

Now the woman screamed in earnest, her pleas forgotten. Then the screams suddenly ceased.

No one else paid any attention. Another warm body filled the seat the woman had so recently vacated, and the other players continued to place bets as if there were no tomorrow. When their chips eventually ran out, they would surely face the same fate as the hapless woman. And who knew? Perhaps their luck would change and they would break the bank and then they could play forever.

More men in tuxedoes appeared to drag losers away from the tables, depositing the screaming bodies behind the same door.

"I'll bet my left tittie Yam is in that room," said Bryn.

"Sounds like a sucker bet to me," said Kisi. "Follow the sacrifices, and you'll find Yam holding a knife."

"He doesn't need a knife here, dear. Rahu is the king of serpents and ruler of the Nagas. Rahu has fangs. Lots and lots of fangs."

"So will Yam look like Rahu or like Yam when he comes out of that room?"

"We will see both, I suspect. He'll put on a pleasant face before he comes out so as not to prematurely frighten the tourists. Rahu wants the visitors to this kingdom to have one last fling to seal their fate. But we're not like any of the regular visitors they usually get in this place, and I'm betting we'll be able to see through whatever face he wears tonight because we've been trained to recognize the energy signature of Yam's true spirit hidden behind any kind of mask."

"But he'll sense our spirits, too," said Kisi. "He already knows we're coming for him. He'll be looking for us, just as we'll be looking for him."

"True," said Bryn. "Are you scared?"

"Yes," said Kisi.

"Good. Then you'll have a fighting edge when we face him. The only magic Yam will be able to use here is the power of illusion. Rahu is a master of deception, and so is Yam. They will both try to trick us. All we have is the power of our combined wills and determinations. Once we grab Rahu, Yam will attempt to flee. His spirit will leave Rahu's body and one of us needs to grab on to Yam's spirit body while the other holds onto Rahu. Think we can do that?"

"I wish the Ranger were here to help us," said Kisi.

"I do, too. But he isn't. So put that thought entirely out of your head, girlfriend. This is something we'll have to do without any help from a man."

"What if Yam doesn't come out of that room?"

"Then we'll go in there after him."

"How? How do we get in when the door is locked?"

"We'll take the key away from those bullies in the fancy suits."

No sooner did the bullies in tuxes drag one person to the back and shove him into that back room to simply disappear in the darkness, than another person came in from outside to take his place. The casino constantly remained much fuller than capacity, every seat at every one of the tables occupied by crazed gamblers laying down losing bets. The room so thoroughly reeked from thick clouds of cigarette and cigar smoke that hung above each table like a guillotine blade poised to drop on naked necks, that Kisi felt nauseated. Obviously, there were no Fire Marshalls in this underworld, nor clean air ordinances. This was the kind of thing that hadn't been allowed on earth since the nineteen-eighties when warnings began appearing on cigarette packages. Didn't anyone here worry about getting cancer?

Bryn focused on the men in the tuxedoes, watching them like a hawk. They moved briskly from table to table, picking up losers and dragging them to the back room like bags of garbage dragged to the curb on trash collection day. Bryn had lost count of how many spirit bodies had disappeared into the back room, and none ever came out. Either that room was filling up, or Rahu's stomach was, unless one or the other was a bottomless pit. Here, anything was possible.

There were three pairs of men in tuxedoes, and each pair possessed a key to that special room. All of the casino's bouncers were big, and she could see familiar bulges under their coats where they carried large-caliber automatics. They were probably ex-cops or former military, or maybe both, in at least one or more of their previous lives on earth. Getting the keys to that room away from any one of them would be difficult, if not impossible.

But she had to try. She selected one of the pairs that looked bored and seemed a little sloppier than the other pairs, and she signaled Kisi to be ready to make a move.

Before they could move, however, the door opened from inside, and Rahu stepped out. He appeared as a short, fat man with a curly beard, not unlike the way Yam Elman had looked the last time Bryn saw him at Machu Picchu. Unlike Elman, however, Rahu had two larger-than-normal eyes that practically bulged out of their sockets, and the pupils were not round like human eyes but vertically-slitted like the eyes of a snake.

Rahu closed the door, locked it, and turned to survey the tables.

Bryn gave Kisi the go signal, and both women raced toward the back of the room where Rahu stood. Bryn hit him first, smashing her head into his soft gut while grabbing his arms and forcing him to the floor. He writhed in her grip, struggling to free himself. When he found himself pinned to the floor, he began changing.

Now it felt like Bryn was trying to hold onto a dozen wriggling snakes. Rahu's solid humanoid body had dissolved, and in its place were several dozen king cobras, their dark hoods fanned out like an elephant's big ears and their backs arched to strike. And now they were striking, and she could feel their fangs sinking into her flesh, sense the poison entering her bloodstream, feel the venom beginning to have an effect.

But she knew it wasn't real. It couldn't be real because her spirit body wasn't real, though it certainly felt real. She existed in this realm as pure spirit, and her spirit body was merely a combination of her own imagination and her will. She had learned that fact in one of the previous underworlds when she had been bitten by a poisonous snake while walking across a

swamp. That snakebite had seemed real, too, but she had continued on and suffered no long-term ill effects. She allowed the
king cobras to strike again and again, but she held onto Rahu
with her will and Bryn didn't let the snakebites bother her and
they didn't.

And now she saw Yam Elman's face and insubstantial
form rising up out of the mass of writing reptiles, as Yam separated his spirit from all that was Rahu and attempted to escape.
But Kisi was waiting for him, and she clamped onto Yam's spirit form and held on with both hands and her iron will.

Bryn was vaguely aware of all six tuxedoed thugs rushing toward them at the same time, and she held onto Rahu with
her will while she grabbed a handful of poisonous snakes and
hurled them in the direction of the bouncers. The snakes looked
real enough to the thugs that they reached inside their jackets,
pulled out their guns, and began shooting at the floor.

The sound of gunfire and bullets ricocheting from the
floor seemed to snap some of the card players out of their tranc-
es, and a few dozen people began scrambling for the exits,
blocking the aisles and keeping five of the bouncers from getting close enough to interfere. Most of the players remained at
their hallowed places at the tables, however, eagerly anticipating
the next turn of the cards, completely oblivious to the pandemo-
nium erupting all around them.

Bryn heard footsteps behind her, and she felt one of the
burly men grab her by the hair and pull hard, jerking her head all

the way back, trying to snap her neck. She instantly reacted by jabbing her left elbow rearward as hard as she could into the man's groin area, and the pressure on the top of her head ceased as the man released her hair to clutch at his lower abdomen with both hands.

She felt bullets pass through her spirit body, and she instantly willed the pain away. But she had been distracted and lost her focus on Rahu, and she felt him slip out of her tenuous grasp.

She heard Kisi cry out, and she knew Kisi had also been shot. "Ignore the pain and hold onto Yam," Bryn shouted. "Don't let go!"

"I lost him," Kisi said. "He pulled away from me. I don't know where he went."

Bryn jumped to her feet, spun, and kicked one of the tuxedoed men squarely in the face. She whirled and caught one of the other men with a blow to the solar plexus, shattering the breastbone and driving shards of broken bone into his heart. She saw another coming directly for her with his gun aimed at her own heart, and she threw herself at him and wrestled the pistol out of his hands. She smashed the gun against the side of his head, and she heard a satisfying crack as metal met bone.

Now she was firing the gun at the remaining two men, hitting one in the gut and the other in the chest. Both men went down.

But Rahu had pulled himself together, and he emitted a mighty hiss as he changed again into a serpent. This time he was no paltry ordinary snake, but the king of all snakes, thirty-feet long and a full foot or more in thickness, his head towering high above Bryn and Kisi, his fangs dripping venom. He opened his jaws wide, and Bryn knew he intended to swallow her whole. She emptied the gun into his head, but the bullets had no effect.

Just at the very instant Rahu intended to strike, something very powerful and very sharp spun through the air and completely, neatly and cleanly, severed Rahu's head from his body. Rahu's head fell to Bryn's right, and his body simply dropped to the floor.

Bryn turned around and saw the Ranger and Tisiphone running toward her. "Bring Kisi," shouted the Ranger. "We need to get out of here now."

"How did you do that?" Bryn asked.

"I'll explain later," said the Ranger. "We want to be as far away from here as possible when Rahu pulls himself together again. C'mon, let's go!"

CHAPTER TWENTY-ONE

H ecate was waiting for them at the city limits. "What, pray tell, did you learn in Nagaloka, known to you as Patala or Nagaland?"

"I learned to awaken and release the power of the Kundalini spirit within me," said the Ranger.

"And how did you do this?"

"Coiled about the base of the spine like a snake, the Kundalini resides within every spirit body as a subtle energy. Most of the time, as we mindlessly move through the mundane world, Kundalini sleeps to store energy. But when we awaken the sleeping serpent through will or desire, it rises up from the center of our being and ascends the various energy channels of the subtle body to release unbelievable energy, setting the chakras to spinning like wheels of light, firing the dan-tien, opening all the subtle centers. As the Kundalini rises, it becomes a powerful force. I was able to direct that force at Rahu, severing his head from his body."

"Who taught you to do this? One needs a guru and many lifetimes of meditation to release the Kundalini."

"Lokesvara Sailendravarman taught me the Tummo and the red and white bodhicittvas."

"I know of Lokesvara Sailendravarman. He is indeed a master and worthy of respect. But why did you choose to use the Kundalini power against Rahu at his time?"

"Mohini suggested it. She said serpent power was the only power that could stop Rahu. And she was right. It worked."

"And how did you meet Mohini?"

"I found her working in a bar called The Snake Charmer."

Hecate looked disapprovingly at Tisiphone and shook her head sadly, but she said nothing.

"I learned," said Kisi, breaking the awkward silence, "that Yam is slippery. He can be impossible to hold onto. He slips through one's fingers like smoke."

"It has been said that Yam is all smoke and mirrors," said Hecate. "And that is obviously true."

"And I learned," said Bryn, "that pain exists only in the mind. One may will it away if one can stay focused."

"Where did Yam go?" asked the Ranger. "Is he still here in Patala?"

"He fled to the next world where he plans to entrap you," said Hecate.

"But how did he leave? Does he have a key?"

"He employed one of the emissaries of Rahu to take him by river. Two great rivers, the River Styx and the River Oceanus, flow through all of the underworlds. He uses the rivers to travel from one world to another. It is the River Oceanus that nourishes the roots of the World Tree. From that river, he can access all worlds here and above."

"Why don't we use the rivers?" asked the Ranger.

"Because," said Hecate, removing her silver key and opening another door, "this way is much easier."

After they stepped through the doorway into darkness, Hecate said, "Here be Rijisha, which some call Rasatala. It is the land of pure selfishness, where one forgets about all others, forsakes all others, and is only interested in the I. It is a land of opposites, of polarities, of twins. A land of dopplegangers and shadow selves. It is a land not unfamiliar to Yam Elman."

"Is there no light in this world either?" asked the Ranger.

"Have you so soon forgotten the Kundalini?" replied Hecate. "Do you not carry your own light within you?"

"I do," agreed the Ranger. He remembered Lokesvara telling him not to hide the light within, but to allow Kundalini light and warmth to shine forth like a beacon to the unenlightened. He went inside himself, stirred the Kudalini from slumber, and slowly began to glow. As he fanned the fires of the dan-tien with the Tummo breath, he emitted a light and a warmth that rivaled the sun.

"Lokesvara has taught you well," said Hecate. "I leave you now to continue your journey. May fortune smile upon you until we meet again."

And then she was gone.

They walked the barren land for what seemed like miles. This land, they saw, had rich, black soil, the kind that grew great crops. But without sunlight, nothing seemed to grow here except worms and insects. The land looked flat as a board, and the horizon stretched unbroken as far as their eyes could see. Nothing interrupted the monotony: There were no trees, no hills, no valleys, no rivers, no creeks, no trails, no footprints, not even a rock.

"We know there are two rivers somewhere in each underworld," said Bryn. "We'll keep walking until we find one of the rivers in Rasatala."

"I need to rest," said the Ranger. "My batteries are getting drained. I'm going to put the Kundalini to sleep."

They sat on the ground, and when the Ranger's light went out the ground turned bitterly cold. Within minutes, they felt that cold seep into their spirit bodies.

"Turn it back on," pleaded Kisi. "I don't like this cold."

"I can't." said the Ranger.

"Then teach us how to do it. You can do that, can't you?"

"Okay," said the Ranger. "I will. You already know how to meditate, so you might be able to learn how to do this quickly enough. First, go inside yourself. Go deep inside yourself. Find the very center of your being. Now place yourself in your exact center and begin silent meditation. Focus all of your awareness there at that center, about four fingers below the navel. Ignite the fire in your belly by holding your awareness there until you see flames flare up. Begin repeating a single *Bija* or seed syllable inside your mind like a mantra. You can use Om, or Ah, or Dhih, or Hum. They all work, so pick the one that feels most comfortable to you. Repetition is the key. Allow one part of your mind to continue the mantra as another part focuses on the breath. Breathe in. Hold the breath inside for a count of five. Breathe out. Picture prana—the sacred energy resident in air—entering your body through every pore. See prana as a color. White, red, blue, yellow. Once again. Breathe in. Hold the breath in for a count of five. Breathe out. Feel the *Drod*, the fire in the belly, grow hotter and brighter with each and every breath. Begin the Tummo exercises. Tummo fans the flames of the fire with the bellows breath. Take quick, short intakes of breath through both nostrils as if you were pumping a bellows, which is what your lungs are. Feel the flames rising from your center. As you continue the bellows breath, the flames rise higher and higher, hotter and hotter, brighter and brighter. Now the intense heat you are generating awakens the sleeping Kundalini. The serpent uncoils from around your center and rises up with the flames. As the serpent's head and the heat of the flames pass each of your chakra centers, those chakras become infused with Kundalini energy. Each chakra, in turn, begins to spin. Faster and faster. Faster and faster. Faster and faster. Feel the heat expanding now. Feel the glow increasing. It begins in the belly and rises all the way to the top of the head. But don't release it yet. Circulate that heat and light through the Ida and Pingala, the male and female meridians on each side of your spine. Keep that heat circulating in your body like a modern heat pump. Keep it circulating. Now open up your third eye—the Ajna—and allow the light to shine forth."

"It's not working," said Bryn.

"It takes practice, Bryn. Keep at it. The fire will come."

"I can feel the fire in my belly," said Kisi.

"Good," said the Ranger. "Now fan that fire with the bellows breath."

"I give up. I can't do it," said Bryn, sounding frustrated and angry. "And I'm getting colder. I'm shivering. Can't you light your fire again and warm us up? Please?"

"I suppose I could," said the Ranger. "But I want to save my energy. I don't want to burn myself out."

"We could freeze to death out here," said Bryn. "You have the power to warm all of us up. Why won't you do it?"

"You won't freeze," said the Ranger.

"How do you know? It's getting damn cold. I'm shivering. Why aren't you cold?"

"Think, Bryn. You know you can't die. Your body here isn't real. You don't really feel the cold. You only think you do. Focus, Bryn. Focus on the mission. Ignore the cold. It's not important."

"I can't focus. I'm too cold to focus."

"I can't focus, either," said Kisi. "I can't do this thing. I can feel the fire inside me, but I can't make it grow, can't make it bigger. I'm too cold to think of anything else right now. The cold gets in the way."

"See," said Bryn. "I'm not the only one who can't do it."

"Practice," said the Ranger. "It takes lots of practice. Try again. You already know how to meditate, and you're both accomplished hatha yoga practitioners. You've had several lifetimes to perfect deep breathing. Now add Tummo: Kindle the fire in the dan-tien, fan the flames with the bellows breath, and release the Kundalini. You can do it. I know you can."

"Damn it!" shouted Bryn. "Why the hell won't you just give us some heat?"

"Because I don't have any to give," shouted the Ranger back at her.

"It's because you want to keep it all for yourself. That's right, isn't it? You don't feel the cold because you have a fire burning inside you that keeps you warm."

"So do you," said the Ranger. "We all do."

"Well, mine doesn't work. And yours does."

"Yours will work. Just give it time."

"You don't understand," said Kisi. "We're too cold to make it work. But you can make yours work. So why don't you?"

"Yes," said Bryn. "Why don't you?"

"Because I can't," said the Ranger. "Not right now. I already used up most of my energy. Let me rest."

"You can rest when you're dead," said Bryn. "I need to get warm. You have the power to warm me up. Why won't you? You're just being selfish!"

"No," said the Ranger. "I'm just being practical. And I'm being smart."

"And I suppose," said Kisi, "you think we aren't?"

"No," said the Ranger. "You aren't."

"Asshole," said Bryn.

"What did you say?"

"I said you were an asshole."

"Because I'm being practical and you're not?"

"No. Just because you really are an asshole. I'm cold, and you have all that heat inside you that you want to hoard for yourself."

"Listen, Bryn, you're not thinking straight. Kundalini is like a battery. When it runs low on juice, you need to recharge it. If I had enough to share, I would. But I don't. So I can't. I'm not going to drain my battery completely just because you're cold."

"I don't care. All I know is I'm cold, and you aren't. That's not fair."

"Fair has nothing to do with it. If I had any energy to spare, I would certainly share it with you. You know that, don't you?"

"No," said Bryn. "I don't."

"Me, neither," said Kisi.

"What the hell is wrong with you?" asked the Ranger. "Both of you are being real prissy over nothing."

"Prissy!" snapped Bryn. "Did you say prissy?"

"What else would you call it?"

Tisiphone cleared her throat loud enough to interrupt the conversation. "Listen to yourselves!" she said. "You're acting selfish. All three of you."

"No," said Bryn. "I'm not being selfish. It's just that I'm right, and he's wrong."

"Ha!" said the Ranger.

"It's the cold making you like this," said Tisiphone. "The cold in this place drives you crazy. It makes you see the faults in everyone else and blinds you to your own."

"I'm not crazy," said Kisi. "I'm just cold. Terribly cold."

"See?" said Tisiphone. "It's the cold doing this to you. If you don't come to your senses, you'll be at each others' throats next. Is that what you want?"

"Yes," said Bryn. "This selfish bastard deserves to learn a lesson."

"If you think you're man enough to take me on," said the Ranger, "go ahead and try."

Bryn lashed out and connected with the Ranger's jaw, knocking him back into Kisi. Kisi sprawled on the ground with the Ranger sprawled half on top of her, and the cold possessed her completely. Before the Ranger could manage to get to his feet, Kisi was on him like flies on excrement.

She pounded both fists into his face, releasing all the pent-up anger and aggression the cold could provide. He grabbed her wrists and held them with an iron grip, trying to flip her over with his legs, but Kisi kneed him in the groin and he released her hands.

Now Bryn was kicking them both and stomping down hard with her heel, smashing Kisi's windpipe and crushing the Ranger's right arm. She aimed her next heel stomp at where she thought his sternum should be, but her heel pounded dirt instead. He had rolled out of the way in the dark and rolled into a fighting stance ready for action.

When her right foot came for his face, the Ranger grabbed and twisted both the foot and ankle hard to the left. Bryn lost her balance and fell on top of Kisi, kicking and screaming.

As the two women tussled with each other, the Ranger withdrew into himself and found his fire. With the intent of destroying both Bryn and Kisi with a single burst of energy, he began Tummo. He fanned the flames until they reached the Anahata, his heart chakra.

Suddenly, he felt a change of heart. Tummo filled him with warmth and love instead of cold and anger. He felt the Kundalini rise up, and he could have struck out at Bryn and Kisi with what power he had remaining, but he didn't. Instead, he allowed the Kundalini to flood the central channel with heat and light, rising ever higher and higher, setting the Vishuddha spinning, the Ajna to open, and the Sahasrara to vibrate.

Bryn and Kisi froze. Now that they had light so they could see each other again, they were horrified by what they had done.

Bryn's nose was broken, and huge chunks of her hair were missing. Kisi had two broken teeth, and another was loose in her mouth. They looked terrible, and they felt even worse.

But the heat and light instantly changed them. Even as they stared at the damage they had wrought, healing had begun. Tummo wasn't magic, but like magic it had the power to change things.

Already, the Ranger had significantly changed. His fractured arm had healed completely, and the bruises and shallow cuts on his face disappeared. His face glowed with the same vibrant light that surrounded his entire head like a halo.

If he had been in his own body—the human body that he had left behind at Machu Picchu—the chemical changes caused by Tummo fire would have altered his immune system to make the same kind of rapid repairs happen. When the Kundalini reached the Sahasrara, the crown chakra, he would have experienced pure ecstasy as serotonin flooded his brain, as acetylcholine lowered his heart rate and rushed to strengthen the muscles of his arms and legs, and as every neural connection fired simultaneously to send signals flowing from axons to dendrites to new axons. His eyes would have been able to focus on the minutest detail, and his memory would have been enhanced exponentially.

Similar changes were taking place within his subtle body. He offered a hand up to both Bryn and Kisi, and he hugged them close, sharing his warmth, completing their healing. He smiled at Tisiphone and nodded thanks.

Tisiphone returned the smile and acknowledged the Ranger's nod with a nod of her own.

"I'm sorry," said Bryn. "I don't know what came over me. I'm so sorry. I'm really really sorry."

"It's this place," said Kisi. "This damn place. The dark and the cold get under your skin and make you think and do things you ordinarily wouldn't think or do. None of us could help what we said or did."

"I can't believe how much difference light makes," said Bryn. "We might have overcome the cold if we had light. But the absence of both heat and light was intolerable."

"I can't keep my Kundalini active forever," said the Ranger. "I'll need to rest again in a few minutes. But while we have heat and light, would you like to try to light your own fires? Kisi, you came close before. Please try."

Kisi sat in lotus and went inside. Bryn, too, sat in lotus and began the breathing exercises. They continued until the Ranger's light began to fade.

"I've got to rest," he said, as his light began to flicker. And then his light went out.

But Kisi's light began to glow, and she opened her third eye to dispel the darkness. "I did it!" she announced, sounding excited by her new-found ability. "I finally did it!"

"Let there be light," said Bryn, and she began to glow, too. "And behold, it was good."

"Thank you," said the Ranger.

"One of us can provide light and heat while the other two rest," said Bryn. "Now let's see if we can find those two rivers and Mr. Yam Elman."

They began walking again, Kisi lighting the way. When Kisi got tired, Bryn took over. Then, when Bryn's light began to fade, the Ranger fired his dan-tien and released the regenerated Kundalini. Finally, they saw in the distance what looked to be a single tree. It had no leaves, and the twisted trunk had only four branches, two of which were broken. From this distance, it was impossible to tell if any part of that tree were alive or if all of the tree were completely dead. And just beyond that tree ran a river.

"Oceanus," spoke Tisiphone. "Beyond Oceanus lies the end of this world and the doorway to the next."

"Still no sign of Yam," said Bryn. "If he plans to trap us in this world, we should expect to see him soon."

As they approached the tree, Kisi said she thought she saw movement in one of the broken branches.

"It may just be the wind," said Bryn.

"There is no wind here," said the Ranger.

He had been so focused on the tree that he hadn't noticed how dirt for a mile or more behind them rippled, swelled, and then bulged up like the ground itself was about to explode. When he did notice, it looked as if something huge was buried beneath the ground and burrowed toward them. Whatever it was, it was coming at them incredibly fast.

The black soil erupted like a volcano, and some kind of monstrous serpent with four fierce-looking heads on separate necks attached to a single serpentine body nearly a mile long reared up to strike. As the ground split open around it, all four walking companions lost their footing and sprawled face-down in the dirt.

"Vasuki," gasped Tisiphone as she looked up at the four-headed monstrosity.

"It's a fucking dragon!" shouted the Ranger. "A fucking dragon with four heads!"

One of the heads targeted Tisiphone, another Bryn, another the Ranger, and the fourth aimed for Kisi. But the Ranger had already rolled into a fighting stance, and his Kundalini was all fired up and ready. He unleashed the awakened serpent from within himself and sent forth a blast of light so bright and powerful that the nagaraja was blinded. All four heads missed their targets and slammed into the dirt, throwing up a cloud of black particles that rained down and partially buried the humans and Tisiphone.

And the Ranger felt his fire fizzle out. He was completely out of juice, his energy depleted.

"Kisi!" he called. "Begin Tummo now! Fire up your Kundalini fast! I'm all used up!"

Kisi began to glow. She dug out quickly, but not quickly enough to avoid Vasuki's writhing body. One coil slammed into her like a Mack truck doing sixty on a freeway straighaway, and her glow faded fast as she lost consciousness.

Bryn reacted instantly. Though less experienced in meditation than Kisi, she knew how to remain calm under fire. She went inside herself, fired up the internal athenor, breathed life into the serpent sleeping inside her center, and unleashed a barrage of firepower that split Vasuki wide open.

The giant serpent thrashed about, and the ground shook and quaked. Bryn hit it again with another blast of pure white light. This time the scaly flesh burst into flames, and the entire mile-long length of the serpent's body was ablaze.

"Save some," shouted the Ranger. "Don't use up all your juice."

Bryn's light dimmed.

In the firelight from Visuki's burning skin, they could see thousands of wriggling forms emerge where the monster had split apart. Visuki's offspring fled into the river where they sought protection from the flames.

Among them, the Ranger thought he saw the subtle form of Yam Elman, but the Ranger's fire was not strong enough to send a blast at any of the fleeing forms. By the time he alerted Bryn, Elman had disappeared.

"Where does that river go from here?" the Ranger asked Tisiphone.

"It floweth into the next world—Nifelheim, the land of giants—the ninth and last of the underworlds you must pass through."

"Then that's where we'll find Elman," said the Ranger. "Let's see if Kisi needs our aid. Then we'll go after Elman."

Kisi's broken body lay in the dirt near the long neck of one of the sea serpent's heads, and the Ranger now recognized that head as resembling the head of Ao Guang, the Dragon King of the South Seas. He suspected the other heads were Ao Guang's three brothers, Ao Qin, Ao Run, and Ao Shun.

Bryn cradled Kisi in her arms, and Bryn's glow enveloped both of them. Within seconds, Kisi's eyes opened and she smiled up at her friends. "Did you find Yam?" she asked.

"He was inside the dragon," said the Ranger. "He escaped into the river."

"Let's go after him."

"Are you well enough to walk?"

Kisi stood up and tried her legs. "I'm a little shaky," she said. "But I can walk."

"Then let's go," said the Ranger.

CHAPTER TWENTY-TWO

H adad and Jon paced back and forth in front of the empty shells that Kisi, Bryn, Kiyari, and the Ranger had left behind, waiting impatiently for those four slack sacks of bones to return to life. More than a week had passed since Bryn, Kisi, the Ranger, and Kiyari had left their bodies to journey to the underworlds. Though normal metabolic processes, as well as heartbeat and respiration, had slowed to a minimum, dehydration had begun to take a toll. If the travelers didn't return soon, it would be too late.

"I'm going down there after them," said Jon. Earlier that day Jon had telephoned the Corps and asked to extend his leave until the end of the month. Because he had friends in G-1, and because he had earned leave on the books that he had to use before the end of the year or lose it, the extension was granted.

"You can't," said Hadad. "Biegolmai wants them to complete this journey on their own."

La Curandera spoke from the stone: "Waiting can be difficult. But you must wait. They still have time to return."

"We need to find the moon mask," said Hadad. "And we need Kiyari to wear it."

"She will return," said La Curandera confidently. "And so will the others."

"How can you be sure?"

"Have you learned so little of trust in all of your past lives?"

"I don't trust my brother," said Hadad. "He wanted us to follow him into the underworlds. He went there for a reason, and I suspect it was to trap us there. I think he expected I would be one of his pursuers."

"Won't he be sorely disappointed to learn you were not?"

"He'll be madder than hell."

"I know you hate to disappoint your brother, but this time it may be better if you did."

"Where do you think the silver mask ended up?" asked Jon.

"If it was placed into Styx or Oceanus, it could come to rest in any of the nine underworlds," said La Curandera. "It may be impossible to find."

"Kiyari can find it," said Hadad. "She still has a psychic link to the mask."

"If they aren't successful at forcing Yam to return the sun," said Hadad, "we cannot afford to wait. Our last chance may be to have Kiyari wield the power of that mask. You haven't seen what darkness is doing to people, have you? It's driving them absolutely crazy. All over the world neighbor is turning against neighbor, brother against brother. No one trusts what they cannot see."

"Things have really gotten so out of hand?"

"Yes. If darkness continues, there will be devastating wars. Sooner or later someone is going to push the button and drop nuclear bombs on someone else, and that someone will retaliate with more bombs until the whole world goes up in smoke."

"We will wait another day," said La Curandera.

*　　*　　*

"What did you learn in Rasatala?" asked Hecate on the other side of the river.

"I learned how to awaken the Kundalini," said Bryn. "I learned that power can be used to heal or to harm. I learned that either or both can be draining, and one must choose how and when to use the Kundalini power or it won't be there when we need it."

"Very good," said Hecate.

"I learned about the power of darkness," said Kisi. "I learned that we each carry darkness as well as light inside us, cold as well as heat, anger as well as peace, hate as well as love. Sometimes we let one blind us to seeing the others."

"A valuable lesson indeed," said Hecate. "And, Mr. Ranger, what did *you* learn?"

"I learned to trust. And to share. I learned the benefits of working together with others. One person alone may have very limited resources. But when we work together, one is able to share resources and help others survive when those resources begin to run out."

"And you, Tisiphone, have you learned your lesson yet?"

"Yes, My Lady," said Tisiphone, bowing her head.

"Then it is time for you to complete your journey." Hecate took out her key, inserted the silver key in a brass lock that suddenly appeared, turned the key clockwise, and held the door open for them to cross the threshold. As the door slammed shut and locked, Hecate said, "Here be Nifelheim, land of mist, ice, and giants, the ninth of the nine underworlds. I leave you now, for I must return to my duties. From here, you may be able to return to your own world, the land above, by climbing the World Tree. If you survive, that is. Fail to meet the challenges of this world and you will remain here forever."

"Thank you," said the Ranger. "Thank you for helping us. We couldn't have done it without you."

"I did it not for you, mortal, but for the sake of my god-daughter."

"You abandoned her in the swamp, but you stuck with us all the way through the underworlds. Why?"

"I promised her I would be your guide through all nine of the underworlds. I have kept that promise and met my obligations to her. More than that, I cannot say. Fare thee well."

And then she was gone again.

"I've been to this land before," said Bryn. "Not in this life, but a long time ago in one of my past lives."

"What do you remember of Nifelheim?" asked the Ranger.

"I remember that it's cold."

"Like in the last place?" asked Kisi. "At least it isn't dark, too. Just filled with mist. We can see, but we can't see far."

"This is the land where fire marries ice," said Bryn. "That's what creates the eternal mist. Fire meeting ice."

"How did you get here when you came here before?" asked the Ranger. "And how did you get out?"

"The Seita," said Bryn. "The roots of Yggdrasil, the World Tree, extend straight down from the Seita into Nifelheim. You can climb down and back up on those roots the way Jack climbed up and down the magic beanstalk."

"Where do we find these roots?"

"There is a bridge over the blue-black waters of the River Oceanus not far from here. The eternal mists make the bridge appear all of the colors of the rainbow. North of that rainbow-colored bridge, the waters freeze into a solid block of ice. But south of that bridge the waters run over rapids that heat them to keep them liquid. There Oceanus is called <u>Gjöll</u>, which means noisy, and the bridge over the river is called the <u>Gjöll</u> Bridge. To the south of that same bridge we shall find the roots of Yggdrasil, the World Tree, bathing in the warmed waters. There the waters are called Uroar's Well. Next to the roots of Yggdrasil is a magnificent ice palace called Éljúðnir, the domain of Hel, the Snow Queen."

"Hel?"

"Yes. This is her land. The land of Hel. Hel is not a land of fire and brimstone, but a land of fire and ice. Hel has indeed frozen over."

"You aren't kidding, are you?" asked Kisi.

"No," said Bryn. "I'm not. Nifelheim is one of the places bad people go after they die. It is the opposite of Valhalla, Oddin's Hall in Asgaard, where valiant warriors claim their reward. The land of Hel is a place for cowards, thieves, liars, and cheats."

"Then I'm sure," said Kisi, "Yam Elman feels right at home here."

"He will find plenty of allies in Nifelheim," agreed Bryn. "Not only among like-minded spirits of deceased mortals, but among frost giants and trolls. He will try to persuade Hel to release them all, first to fight against us, and then to ascend the roots of the World Tree and invade the land of the living. The spirits here cannot endure the light of the sun, but Yam has hidden the sun. Imagine what will happen if earth is overrun with disembodied spirits, frost giants, and trolls!"

"We've got to stop Yam before that happens," said the Ranger. "C'mon. We're heading for Hel's palace."

So the four set out across the frozen land, kindling their internal fires to keep warm as they walked.

BOOK IV

Brothers will fight
and kill each other,
sisters' children
will defile kinship.·
It is harsh in the world,
whoredom rife
—an axe age, a sword age
—shields are riven—
a wind age, a wolf age—
before the world goes headlong.
No man will have
mercy on another.

-------Voluspa. The Poetic Edda, Volume II.

CHAPTER TWENTY-THREE

"What would you have us do?" asked Biegolmai.

"Destroy Yam."

"If we do destroy Yam, will that return the sun? I think not. Only Yam can remove the spell he has placed on men's vision, and destroying Yam could make that spell permanent. Believe me, we are doing all we can without making matters worse."

"This has already progressed from bad to worse," said La Curandera. "All hell threatens to break loose over the entire planet, yet we do nothing to stop it."

"We are doing all we can do."

"I refuse to accept that, Grandfather. At least allow me to aid Bryn and the others in the underworlds. They should have returned by now, and they may desperately need my help."

"My Fenriswulfr inform me they have reached Nifelheim. Soon they shall confront Yam at the Gates of Hel. If they emerge successful, they may yet prevent Yam from sending diseased spirits back into the middle worlds where those depraved spirits might wrought untold damage. If our friends are unsuccessful, we will have no recourse but to intervene."

"But that might be too late!"

"There is more at stake here than you know, granddaughter. Lives may be lost, true; but lives are lost all the time and yet the cycles of life continue, the dead are eventually reborn, die, and are reborn again. Yam's actions may already have set in motion repercussions that could disrupt the very cycles of existence, and because of that we must tread carefully. Our job is to restore balance and harmony, and to restore balance we must first deplete Yam of all the accumulated power already at his disposal. Once he is drained, he will be vulnerable. Only then might we be able to force him to reverse his actions."

"And you expect Kisi, Bryn, Kiyari, and the Ranger to drain him?"

"The coming battle in Nifelheim is but a first step. If our people are successful in defeating Yam, we may be able to take a second step."

"And if they aren't successful?"

"Then Ragnarok," said Biegolmai. "Then all Hel really does break loose."

*　　*　　*

The gates of Hel stood wide open, as if Hel were expecting them. Inside the gates they saw a number of small villages surrounding the giant palace of ice, and each of the villages had craftsmen busily working to produce armaments. There were blacksmiths toiling at forges, producing broadswords and shields and battleaxes and a variety of other armaments. There were groomsmen hitching giant steeds to chariots or saddling mounts. Many of the craftsmen were dwarves.

No sooner had they passed through the massive iron gates than those gates slammed shut, trapping them within the high walls surrounding the ice palace.

"I guess they were waiting for us," said Kisi. "They wanted to trap us as soon as we got inside."

"Either that," said Bryn, "or we got here a lot sooner than they expected. They may have closed the gates to try to keep us out."

"Bryn may be right," said the Ranger. "It looks like they're just now finishing their preparations to welcome us. Shall we enter the palace and pay a surprise visit to the Queen?"

"She will not be pleased to see us," said Bryn.

Two frost giants stood guard at the palace entrance. They were armed with broadswords, but they looked big enough that they wouldn't need to use weapons. They could tear a man apart with their bare hands.

One of those guards stepped forward to block their way. "State your business," said the giant.

"We come from afar to pay respects to the Queen," said Bryn.

"She did not say she was expecting you."

"Believe me," said Bryn, "she *is* expecting us."

"I do not believe you."

"Tell the Queen that Brynhildr Helgasdottir is here. I am certain she will remember me."

"Watch them," the guard told the other giant. "If they try to enter the palace without the Queen's permission, cut them to pieces and feed them to the wolves."

After the guard went inside, Kisi whispered, "You know the Queen?"

"We've met," said Bryn.

"Favorably?"

"Not always."

When the guard returned, he stepped to one side and held the door open. A tall, thin man in a heavy fur coat appeared in the open doorway. "The Queen will see you now," the new man growled in a gruff voice. "Please follow me."

The ice palace was huge. It looked like it had been carved from one solid block of ice. But the Ranger suspected some brilliant architect had first designed and constructed wooden frames twenty feet tall for the walls and roof, poured tons of water into the spaces between those frames, and waited for the water to freeze. Then he had employed hundreds of artisans to remove the wooden frames, cut openings for doors and windows, and engraved ornate designs above those openings. It must have taken years to complete, and it must have been a labor of pure love.

Or, perhaps, a labor of penance.

On either side of the entrance, long hallways stretched the entire length of the building and branched off into other hallways like an elaborate labyrinth. The tall, thin man escorted them through the maze to a massive oaken door in front of which stood two guards that looked even bigger and uglier than the two that had stopped them at the front entrance.

As the guards bowed and stepped aside, the tall man pushed the doors inward and they entered an enormous hall that eclipsed, in size and in splendor, even Haides' hall in Hades. Colored engravings depicting human sacrifice had been etched into the ice walls, and the ceiling glowed blue with a natural phosphorescence that provided the only light. There were no torches nor fires anywhere in that great hall, and the room was dark and cold and foreboding.

At the other end of the great hall was a throne made entirely of ice. Seated on that throne was the most beautiful woman any of them had ever seen. Beautiful, yet cold. Distant, as if she might melt if anyone touched her.

She was not only beautiful, she was literally bigger than life. Even sitting down, she towered well above everyone else in that hall, even the giants. Yet, her proportions were so exact, so perfect, that one noticed only her beauty and not her size. Her long hair was pure white, and her skin was pale as though it had never seen sunlight.

Standing next to her, and surrounded by more than a dozen giant armed guards, stood a grinning Yam Elman.

The tall man in the fur coat bowed at the waist, and the Ranger and his companions quickly did the same.

"Your Highness," growled their escort, "May I present Brynhildir Helgasdottir, Kisikil Lilake, Tisiphone, and a man whose name is unknown."

"We know Bryn only too well from previous encounters, not all of them pleasant," said the Queen, and her icy voice echoed through the chamber like the sound of icicles shattering on the ground as they hit the ground on a cold winter's eve. "We have heard the names of Kisi and Tisiphone also. But we are most intrigued by the man. Do you not have a name?" Her eyes bore into his as if searching for the answer to her question inside his mind.

"I have many names, Your Highness," said the Ranger.

"But how shall we address you? What is your birth name?"

"My driver's license and passport say my name is Albert Schweitzer. You can call me Al, if you want."

"That is not what we asked," said the Queen.

"I know," said the Ranger.

A look of amusement passed over the Queen's countenance. "You would play games with *me*?" It was the first time she had used the personal pronoun instead of the royal "We." The word sounded foreign to her, and the Ranger wondered if this was the first time she had ever used it.

"If it pleases the Queen."

"No man has ever pleased this Queen," she said. "Would you be the first?"

"I would if I could," said the Ranger. "What did you have in mind?"

"We shall show you our mind in good time. But first let us introduce our other uninvited guest. This is Shalim Yam Elman, whose many names we also know well. He came to us this day on the river you call Oceanus as the serpent we call Jörmungandr. He is brother to the wolf, and he would be our brother as well."

Elman's spirit body was short, fat, and bloated. His face was scarred, and he had only one eye, the other missing from the left side of his scarred face. He grinned at them like a Cheshire cat about to pounce on an unwary canary.

"Your Highness," Bryn addressed the Queen, "he deceives you. This man is a snake, a jackal, a thief. He has stolen the sun from mankind, and would steal your throne. Join with us, and put an end to his treachery."

"Is this true?" the Queen asked Elman.

"It is indeed true, Your Majesty, that I hid the sun and the moon. It did it for you, to pave the way for you to enter the upper worlds. I have freed you from eternal exile in the netherworlds so you may walk freely among men, and men will quake in fear at your passing."

"And you did this out of the kindness of your heart?"

Elman laughed, but it sounded so much like a cackle that even the Queen looked at him with distrust. "No, Your Majesty," Elman hastened to clarify. "I did it because I, too, feed on fear. I will take only what you reject. I would put the fear of Hel in men's hearts, so some may flock to what they perceive as the lesser evil. When you walk on earth, Your Majesty, you will bring winter with you. People will volunteer to sacrifice themselves as their only escape from the cold and the dark and the fear. There will be enough sacrifices to satisfy both you and me."

"And why do you want this?"

"Because I want to live forever, as you live forever, without fear of retribution for my sins. Is that so much to ask?"

"We perceive that you speak truly, our brother. It would amuse us greatly to walk among men again, to feel their fear and to receive their sacrifices."

"Then kill these four," said Yam Elman. "They would stand in our way. Imprison them here in your kingdom until their mortal bodies perish. Then you may toy with their spirits as you please."

"Guards!" ordered the Queen. "Seize them and put them in the dungeons."

Before the guards could reach them, Bryn and the Ranger rapidly fired up their dan-tiens. They had already begun Tummo breathing. Kisi and Tisiphone fought off the guards long enough for the Ranger's Kundalini to reach his Ajna. He opened his third eye and light poured forth, blinding the guards. The giants thrashed about blindly, swinging swords at empty air.

Bryn, too, had awakened her sleeping Kundalini, and she sent a blast of power straight for the Queen, melting the throne. The Queen fell unceremoniously to the floor where she lay in a pool of water.

"Guards!" shouted the Queen, picking herself up from the puddle of water. "Alert the army and bring reinforcements. Quickly!"

The Ranger spun at the sound of the massive oak doors opening inward, and he saw the tall, thin man bound across the threshold, changing form even as he leaped for Kisi. Where the tall, thin man had been but a moment before there was now a scrawny beast with a long snout and rows of sharp teeth, and the beast was raking razor-sharp claws into Kisi's back. His jaws snapped at Kisi's neck and would have torn out her throat if Tisiphone hadn't intervened. Tisiphone plunged her hand into the monster's mouth and the jaws snapped shut on Tisiphone's arm instead of Kisi's neck, severing the arm between wrist and elbow.

The Ranger sent a blast of pure Kundalini energy at the man-sized wolf, and the beast dropped Tisiphone's arm and ran from the room, yelping in pain, his pelt smouldering. The Ranger picked up the arm, brought it to where Tisiphone lay in a pool of blood, held the severed piece next to the rest of the arm, and welded the two parts together with Kundalini fire and Tummo healing energy.

More guards poured through the door, and the Ranger blinded them with another blast of light and heat that seemed to stop them in their tracks. It was as if the light had frozen them as solid as the walls of the ice palace.

"We don't want to harm anyone," the Ranger announced loud enough for the Queen to hear. "All we want is to take Elman with us and leave in peace."

"It is too late, Mr. Albert Schweitzer," said the Queen. "Our brother has already fled. Nifelheim is a land of cowards, liars, and diseased souls, and Yam Elman felt very much at home here until you arrived. But your bravery has unnerved him. He will not face you in a fair fight."

"And you, My Queen? Will you face me fairly?"

"No," said the Queen. "It is against our nature to be fair. Certainly never in a fight."

"I don't want to fight you."

"We have met men like you only rarely in all of the eons we have been Queen," she said. "We have not been successful in keeping any of those men here with us for long. Is it any wonder that I yearn to walk among men where I might find one like you who would give himself voluntarily to be with me?"

As the Ranger watched, tears filled the Queen's eyes and ran down the Queen's cheeks like melting ice. The Queen quickly turned her face away and said, "Go now. Leave my land before I change my mind and keep you here forever."

The Ranger grabbed Tisiphone by the hand and pulled her toward the doorway. Kisi and Bryn backed out slowly, keeping their eyes on the Queen and her guards.

Once in the hallway, Bryn touched Kisi's back with healing energy. Then the four ran down the hallway and out the front door, past the surprised guards, and were out the gates which had been opened to allow Elman to exit only moments before and hadn't yet closed.

They could see Yam in the distance, scurrying across the rainbow-colored bridge. He stopped in the middle of the bridge as a troll emerged from the far end and came toward him armed with a battleax. Elman changed from human form into the serpentine Jörmungandr, and he quickly slid off the bridge into the icy waters and swam the rapids toward the roots of the World Tree. The troll fled in terror.

The Ranger stopped, raised his hands, and directed a barrage of Kundalini energy at the fleeing Jörmungandr, causing the waters around him to boil. The serpent immediately changed directions, dove beneath the waters, and disappeared.

"You missed," said Bryn.

"I wanted to stop him, not kill him," said the Ranger. "We still need him to return the sun."

"Where did he go?" asked Kisi.

"He hides beneath the bridge," said Tisiphone.

"Can we reach the roots without crossing the river?" asked the Ranger.

"It's a stretch, but we can do it from this side," said Bryn. "Come on. I'll show you where."

They walked south on the east side of the river, past the rapids, to Uroar's Well. There, descending from the mist, were the giant roots of Yggdrasil, the World Tree.

"Ladies go first," said the Ranger.

Bryn leaned over the rushing waters and reached for the thickest root. She grabbed on, and swung both legs around the root. Then she shimmied up until she disappeared into the mist.

Kisi went next. She was barely able to reach the roots, but she stretched until her fingers touched and then encircled a single root. Her spirit body had grown stronger and taller since entering the underworlds, and she flexed her new-found muscles to hold tightly to the nearest root with both hands until her shapely legs also wrapped around it and she could climb the root like climbing a rope.

After she entered the mist, the Ranger said to Tisiphone, "Your turn."

"I cannot," said Tisiphone. "Though I have visited your world many times, it was usually in the company of my sisters. I would be lost there without them. I must return to Hades."

"I want to thank you," said the Ranger, touching the side of her face with fondness. "We would not be here now without your help."

"No," said Tisiphone. "It is I who must thank you. You have taught me much about human beings I did not previously know. And you saved my arm."

"And you saved Kisi. Will you be in trouble for that?"

"Perhaps. I gave my word that I would not aid you and I have broken my oath. For that I am not yet sorry, but I am sure I soon will be. Nevertheless, I will remain here and take my punishment. I wish you well."

Before the Ranger could say another word, Tisiphone had disappeared. The only trace that remained of her was an after-image in the Ranger's mind that reminded him of Kiyari, the woman he loved and cherished.

The Ranger reached out with both hands and took hold of the biggest root, and he pulled himself up as he had first learned to do in the Army's confidence course in basic training. Within moments he was through the mist and clinging to the trunk of a scrawny birch tree near a pile of rocks in what seemed a winter wonderland. Snow pelted his face and winds whipped through his hair. He could see starlight between the clouds, and those stars reflected off the snow on the ground, producing almost enough light to see.

A flock of ravens appeared in the sky, cawing loudly. One of those ravens, larger than any the Ranger had ever seen before, separated from the others to land on the ground directly in front of him.

"Return quickly to your bodies," said Biegolmai as the raven changed form and grew a white beard. "I will guard the Seita."

"Yam is still down there," said the Ranger. "We couldn't capture him."

"But you did prevent him from unleashing Hel's haints on an unsuspecting world," said Biegolmai. "I will seal the Seita so the denizens of the underworlds cannot climb the World Tree. You have done well. Now return to your body while there is still time."

As soon as the Ranger thought about his human body, his spirit flew home. He opened his eyes in Machu Picchu, took a deep breath, filled up his lungs, and stretched both arms.

Kisi and Bryn had also returned to their bodies. Jon and Hadad were handing them ladles of fresh water which they gulped down greedily. Kiyari's beautiful body sat next to the Ranger, looking lifeless and forlorn in the flickering torchlight.

"Where is Kiyari?" asked Hadad. "We need her."

"She is still in the underworlds," said the Ranger, finding his voice. "We lost her in a swamp in the fourth world."

"Go get her," ordered La Curandera from the stone. "Go now, and bring her back. Quickly, before it is too late."

"I'll go," said Jon. He sat in lotus and began deep breathing.

"And I," said Hadad. He, too, sat in lotus and inflated his lungs.

"I'm going back with them," said the Ranger.

"It is much too soon for you," warned La Curandera. "Your body has not sufficiently recovered. Wait an hour. Two would be better. Then you may join them."

"I'm going now," said the Ranger, "and you can't stop me." He closed his eyes and began resealing all the openings to his body. His breathing slowed, his heart calmed, slowing his circulation to a crawl; he focused his thoughts, and he separated his spirit self from his physical self.

Because he had already sealed himself to the outside, he did not hear La Curandera's warning that he would surely die if he left his body for more than a day, two at the most. But he would have gone back to search for Kiyari even if he had heard those words, because he loved Kiyari more than life itself and he didn't want to live in any world without her.

It would be far better to be dead and together with Kiyari's spirit in the underworlds than to be alive and living on earth with only her memory.

CHAPTER TWENTY-FOUR

T he Ranger caught up with Jon and Hadad at the river. This time, he knew where he was going and how to get there. He dove into the River Styx deliberately, letting the river carry him headlong into the depths of darkness, and Jon and Hadad followed him to the underworlds.

He remembered Hecate telling him that emissaries traveled the rivers Oceanus and Styx to journey between all nine underworlds, and instead of exiting at the first underworld as he and his friends had done the last time, he urged Jon and Hadad to remain in the river with him, bypassing the first three worlds. He knew now that Styx and Oceanus reached into all of the underworlds, and they rode the turbulent river to where the Styx fed into the brackish waters of the swamp. Then the Ranger and his companions exited the river and searched until they found a sliver of dry land.

"I can't see a blasted thing," said Jon. "Is this whole place pitch black?"

The Ranger fired up his dan-tien. Within minutes, he emitted enough light for them to see their immediate surroundings.

They were standing at the far end of the dismal swamp, near the door to Irkalla. "This is where," said the Ranger, "we noticed Kiyari was no longer with us. She's got to be back there in the swamp somewhere."

"She may be dead," said Jon.

"If there's one thing I learned on my first pass-through, it's that we can't be killed in any of the underworlds. Our bodies here aren't real. Our spirits are, but our spirits are eternal. If Kiyari is here, her spirit's still alive."

"Then let's find her," said Hadad.

"Do either of you know Tummo?" asked the Ranger.

"Lokesvara taught me," said Jon. "I know how to raise the Kundalini."

"I watched a Bon shaman raise the Kindalini long ago in Tibet," said Hadad. "I understand the principle involved, but I have never practiced."

"Now is the time to practice it,".said the Ranger. "Both of you fire up your dan-tiens while I change into something more appropriate for this environment.

As Jon began to glow, the Ranger allowed his light to dim. He focused his will, remembering what it felt like to be a snake, and wished he were back in a reptilian body. His arms fell off, his legs melded together, his head became triangular. He flicked his forked tongue and tasted the air.

Then he crawled to the edge of the swamp and slid into the murky depths, diving deep, wriggling his powerful tail as he headed straight for the bottom.

Only there was no bottom. He continued downward for what seemed like forever, passing creatures big and small, predator and prey, but there was no end to his downward descent. Kiyari could be anywhere.

He came back up to the surface and tried to sense her presence. "Kiyari," he called to her with his mind. "Where are you?"

If he had a psychic connection with Kisi and Bryn, he surely had a psychic connection to Kiyari. Something had brought them together time after time, regardless of what skin they were in, and he went deep inside himself and found the love he had felt for her when she was his sister, his wife, his lover. The connection resided in the anahata chakra, the heart chakra. He saw himself as Shiva, and Kiyari was Shakti. The yin and the yang united. The conjunction of the animal and the spiritual selves. He visualized her face, her breasts, her vulva. He saw her as Uqllu and himself as Ayar Cachi, Kiyari as Kripi and himself as Drona, Kiyari as Helen and himself as Paris, Kiyari as Gwenevere and himself as Lancelot. He reached out for her in spirit and he felt their spirits reunite.

"Kiyari, where are you?"

"I am here," she said.

"Where?"

"Right beside you."

Kiyari, too, had changed form. He never would have recognized her in the body she now wore if he hadn't sensed her presence next to him.

Kiyari was a bug, a beetle. Not just any beetle, though; Kiyari had transformed into a giant dung beetle, better known as a scarab, the sacred symbol of the ancient Egyptians. She was at least three feet long and nearly as wide.

And she carried in her mandibles a hunk of hammered silver.

"I thought we had lost you," said the Ranger.

"You did," she said in his mind. "But I knew you would come back for me. I knew you would find me."

"Jon and Hadad await us on the shore. We have little time left. We must return to our own bodies while we still can."

The Ranger led the way, swimming through the foul waters as only a snake can, and the beetle followed, though carrying the silver mask made swimming difficult. It wasn't long before they saw lights ahead, and the Ranger crawled up on shore and changed back to human form.

He took the mask from Kiyari, and she scrambled up to solid ground, frightening Jon and Hadad with her appearance. Both men had their Kundalinis fired up, and they were about to blast the beetle when the beetle transformed into a more human-looking Kiyari.

"I have the silver moon mask," said Kiyari. "I heard it calling to me from the depths of the swamp, and I went to fetch it from the roots of reeds. When I returned to the path, Bryn and Kisi were already gone. I waited for you here, knowing the Ranger would eventually come back for me. I'm happy to see all of you again."

"And we are very happy to see yo u," said Jon. "Although we thought the giant bug was going to attack us. You scared the crap out of both of us."

"That was appropriate," said Kiyari, smiling. "It was a dung beetle. It feeds on excrement."

"Let me see the mask," asked Hadad. He took the silver mask from the Ranger's hands and examined it closely. "Yes," he said. "It is as I remembered."

"We're running out of time," said the Ranger. "We need to get home to our bodies. C'mon, back to the river. We'll walk on water the rest of the way. We have five more worlds to pass through before we can get home."

The Ranger and Kiyari showed Jon and Hadad how to walk on water, and they followed the river into the next world.

And found Udug Hul waiting for them.

Hul hit them with a power blast that knocked them from their feet, and a dozen demons were upon them before they could recover. The Ranger felt a blade pass through his left arm and another sever his right leg. Then an axe chopped off his right arm, and pain hit him from all directions.

Jon and Hadad received similar treatment, and the Ranger saw their arms and legs float down the river leaving a trail of red in their wake. Kiyari was roped head and foot, bound up like Christmas package ready to be placed under the tree.

Demon claws picked up their bodies by each of their remaining legs, and dragged the bodies through the forest toward the castle. Kiyari, too, was dragged.

As they passed through the courtyard, the Ranger noticed there were fresh human bodies roasting on the spits, and he wondered if that was where he would end up after the Queen finished with him.

If there were anything left of him, that is, after the Queen finished.

They were dragged into the Queen's hall and dumped unceremoneously in front of the throne. The Ranger looked up to see a reconstituted Ereshkigal seated on the throne. Next to her stood a grinning Yam Elman, rubbing his hands together in glee.

"So the prodigal sister returns after all this time," said Ereshkigal. "I have waited an eternity for this day."

"Nice to see you, too, Ereshkigal," said Kiyari.

"Bring Damu-zid that my sister may behold what has become of her beloved and also to see what fate awaits her when she takes his place in my dungeons."

Two demons entered dragging Damu-zid, depositing the battered and beaten and broken body of Ishtar's former husband at the feet of the Queen.

Kiyari said something that sounded like "Oh, no," and a single tear formed in her right eye.

"I have toyed with him enough," said the Queen. "Feed what is left of him to the dogs."

"May I have him, My Queen?" asked Udug Hul. "You promised a reward for finding your sister."

"You have been a faithful servant. Take him as my reward to you."

Udug Hul's light grew brighter. Soon it seemed to consume the body of Damu-zid, and then the two disappeared together in a blaze of light.

"Now you may watch your friends suffer," said Ereshkigal. She rose from the throne and took a battleaxe from one of the demons.

Then she hacked the remaining legs off the men.

Pure agony ripped through the Ranger's spine and disturbed the sleeping Kundalini. The serpent raised its hooded head and spit fire into the dan-tien. Flames flared up, and the Kundalini power erupted uncontrolled.

Pure qi poured from the Ranger's crown chakra like lighning bolts from a thunder cloud, striking randomly at everything standing in the room. One bolt tore into Ereshkigal, ripping her beautiful body apart, pieces of her flying around the room to cover demons in gore. Several of the demons were similarly struck, and they exploded like firecrackers on the Fourth of July. Yam, covered in blood and slime, ducked behind the throne as the walls and the ceiling caught fire, filling the room with smoke and flames.

All of the Ranger's chakras were spinning like mad, some clockwise, some counterclockwise. He fought to regain control, sending them spinning in the same direction. Now the pain was gone, and he felt a tingling where his arms and legs had been. As he watched, new arms and legs sprouted from the bloody stumps.

Now there were more demons rushing to aid their Queen, and the Ranger met their charge with a charge of his own. He sent a blast of pure Kundalini power into the herd and they went flying like bowling pins hit by a strike ball that curved right into the pocket.

As soon as he had hands and feet, the Ranger rushed to Jon and immersed him in Kundalini healing. Then he attended to Hadad. When both men showed signs of recovery, the Ranger jumped to his feet. He fired another blast at the doorway, then he ran toward the throne.

"Kindle your dan-tiens," shouted the Ranger. "Fight off the demons while I go for Yam."

He had seen Yam leap behind the throne as soon as the fireworks started, but Yam was no longer hiding there.

Since there was no way in hell Yam could have gotten through the front doorway piled high with smouldering demon carcasses, so he must have gone in the opposite direction, toward the dungeons. Taking the stone stairs down three at a time, the Ranger plunged into the dark, dank foundation beneath the palace. He opened his Ajna and projected just enough light to see where he was going. If Yam was waiting somewhere ahead, he was waiting in complete darkness.

The dungeons consisted of one big room with every torture device imaginable on open display and ready to use. An iron maiden stood open, sharp spikes pointing outward; a rack long enough to break a large man in two stood in the middle of the floor, iron chains attached to wheels, rollers, and cranks. Various smaller devices hung from pegs on the wall: iron pokers to heat and sear flesh; a Spanish spider with sharp metal claws to rip a breast off a woman with a single squeeze of the handles; various whips, scourges and knittles; thumb screws of all sizes and varieties; every manner of garrotte imaginable; axes, swords, carving knives, and screwdrivers; hammers and sledge-hammers. There were iron rings and chains hanging from the ceiling, and a gallows rope.

But no Yam Elman. Around the big room were dozens of cells containing prisoners, but all of the cells appeared locked. If Elman had come this way, he must have found some way to escape that wasn't readily evident.

The Ranger ran back up the stairs. Hadad had freed Kiyari, and the three humans were fending off demons with Kundalini fire and battleaxes. A demon yelped as Kiyari brought the blade of an ax down on his head, practically splitting him in two.

"Did you get Yam?" Jon asked when he saw the Ranger.

"Slippery bastard must have changed into a snake and slid between cracks in the foundation stones," said the Ranger. "What say we get the hell out of here before they send in reinforcements."

"Just how do you plan to do that?" asked Jon. "There's a pile of green puke blocking the door, and there are probably a hundred more trying to get in or waiting out in the hall to carve us to pieces when we try to leave."

The Ranger pointed his finger at the rock wall behind him, and beams of light shot out of his fingertips like lasers, melting the solid stones and leaving a hole big enough for them to get through one at a time. "We go thataway," said the Ranger. "Take Kiyari and Hadad and go. I'll hold them off as long as I can."

Jon motioned Hadad and Kiyari toward the hole in the wall, and they disappeared into the night. The Ranger fired one last blast at the demons trying to get in the door, then he turned and ran as fast as he could through that same hole.

There were few demons left in the courtyard, and Jon and Hadad were able to neutralize them with swipes of their battleaxes. They ran over the drawbridge and through the woods without encountering any resistance.

They were almost to the river when a dozen trees moved into their path and blocked the way.

The Ranger hit one of them with a weak blast of Kundalini energy, but when he tried to fire again, he couldn't get the serpent to rise up within him. He was spent, out of juice, and dead tired.

This time Jon responded with a blast that set the trees aflame, their leaves and limbs ablaze. A horrible howl filled the forest as the flames spread from tree to tree, and the night filled with bright light and woodsmoke.

"This way," yelled Kiyari, and she ran through the flames toward the river. Her hair caught fire as did the rest of her remaining clothes, but she kept running until she reached the river and she dove straight in, extinguishing the flames. Hadad followed, with Jon and the Ranger close behind. When they reached the river, they submersed themselves completely.

When Kiyari surfaced, her hair began to grow back and the burns on her face and hands faded away. She turned around and began walking upstream toward where they had been captured. When she got close to the spot she was seeking, she stopped and listened.

Then she dove into the river. This time when she resurfaced, she held the silver moon mask in both hands.

"I dropped it when we were attacked," she said when she got back to the others. "I was afraid one of the demons might have found it. But I guess they aren't interested in silver."

"Let's go before Udug Hul comes looking for us," said the Ranger.

As they passed through Hades, they heard horrible screams. Some of those screams sounded like they were coming from Kiyari. The Ranger jumped on shore and ran through the dark, following the sounds of screams.

They were coming from the fire where he had first met the Erinyes dancing around the flames. Now he saw two of the same women, Alecto and Medaera, dancing.

And he saw Tisiphone hanging upside down over the flames. She was being slow roasted, tortured like the humans in Ereshigal's world, only this time it was her very own sisters doing the torturing instead of demons.

"Take her down!" ordered the Ranger. "Take her down now!"

"She broke an oath," said Alecto. "She must be punished."

"She's been punished enough."

"Oathbreakers must be punished for nine years. Her punishment has only begun."

"But she's your sister!"

"And she broke her oath. Would you have us punish some oathbreakers and not all? Where is the justice in that?"

"But she saved our lives. She saved my life. Doesn't that count for something?"

"Of course. But she must still be punished for breaking her oath. It is the law of Karma. All actions have consequences. Tisiphone knew that. She was willing to accept the consequences."

"How can you punish Tisiphone and let Yam Elman run free?"

"He has not yet been judged. Tisiphone has."

"Who judged her?"

"We did."

"You and Medaera?"

"Yes."

"I can't let you do that to her. She saved my life. I owe her. Punish me, and let her go."

"You would be punished in her stead?"

"Yes," said the Ranger. "I would."

"But would not your mortal body perish on earth while you received our punishment here? And would you not forfeit the possibility of rebirth?"

"Yes," said the Ranger.

"And still you would do this?"

"Yes," said the Ranger.

"We cannot allow you to sacrifice yourself for her," said Medaera.

"Then cut her down and let her go."

"We cannot."

"Then I will cut her down," said the Ranger. He reached inside for what little Kundalini force he had remaining.

"We cannot allow you to free her," said Alecto. She stood between the Ranger and the dangling Tisiphone.

"Maybe you can't," said a female voice behind them. "But I can."

"Your Majesty!" said both Alecto and Medaera at once, prostrating themselves in front of Kiyari.

"Cut her down immediately," ordered Kiyari. "Then bring her to the court. I would have words with the King."

"Yes, Your Majesty," said Alecto. She snapped her fingers, and the rope holding Tisiphone's ankles came apart. Tisiphone dropped toward the fire, but the Ranger reached out, grabbed her just in time, and cradled her in his arms.

On the way to the hall of the King, the Ranger released the last of his Kundalini energy to heal Tisiphone's burns.

When the King saw Kiyari, he immediately removed his helmet of invisibility and jumped from the throne to take her in his arms. "Persephone, you have come back to me! And you came back early! You truly love me!"

Kiyari kissed him. She genuinely seemed happy to see him. "I always do come back to you, don't I?"

"Only because you must," the King said. "But this time you are early. Nearly two months early."

"O Aidoneus, a terrible injustice has been done. I cannot return to you until I help to rectify it."

"What? An injustice? We shall rectify it together, for we suffer no injustice to continue when we have the power to end it. What is this injustice?"

"The sight of the sun has been taken away from mankind," said Kiyari.

"So I have heard," said the King.

"Is there nought you can do to return the sun?"

"I have the power to do many things, Aidoneus said. "But that is not among them."

"There is another injustice," said Kiyari. "This you do have the power to rectify."

"What is it, my love?"

"Tisiphone is being punished for helping my friends. She prevented Yam Elman from killing them."

"Is this true?" Aidoneus asked Alecto.

"Yes, my Lord," said Alecto. "It is true."

"Did I not send Tisiphone with them?"

"Yes, my Lord. But only to observe."

"And have I not given her, as well as you, the power to intervene in the affairs of mortals when you see fit to intervene?"

"Yes, my Lord. But Hecate made Tisiphone promise not to intervene. Tisiphone broke her promise."

"Hecate! Again she intervenes in my affairs. If it weren't for Hecate, my love would remain here with me year round, instead of only three months. If Hecate weren't my beloved's godmother, I'd curse that old witch!"

"Tisiphone must still be punished for breaking her oath, my Lord. It is the law."

"Yes, of course. And punished she shall be. But on my order, not yours."

"As you wish, my Lord."

"Then hear my decree of punishment. For six months of every year for nine years, Tisiphone is banished from my kingdom. She will reside in the land above, walking the earth as a mortal woman. For the other six months of every year for nine years, Tisiphone will resume her duties here in Tartarus."

"But, my Lord," protested Medaera, "what about the Queen? She and Tisiphone cannot both reside on earth for six months of every year."

"Oh," said Aidoneus, hiding a smile. "I forgot. In order for my decree of punishment to replace yours, Persephone would need to agree to spend those six months here with me." He looked Kiyari in the eye. "Would that be so terrible, my dear? You already spend three months of every year here. What is three more months?"

"You never change, do you, Aidoneus?" said Kiyari.

"Isn't that what you love most about me?" asked the King of Hades. "The rest of the universe changes constantly, but

my love for you only grows greater with every passing moment."

"One of the things," admitted Kiyari.

"Then you agree?"

"Yes."

"Wonderful!" laughed Aidoneus. "Then it is settled."

"But two months remain before the solstice, and I would
have until then to help my friends rectify the other injustice. Is
that agreeable?"

"But you just got here," said Aidoneus. "And already
you want to leave?"

"It is something I must do, my Lord. Would you deny
me such a small favor?"

"I would not deny you anything," said Aidoneus.

"Except my freedom," said Kiyari.

"You have always been free, my love," said Aidoneus.
"You are free to come and go as you please. I would not hold
you here against your will."

"You made me love you," said Kiyari. "And now I can
not help but return to be with you."

"Then go, if you please. And return when it pleases
you."

Kiyari kissed Aidoneus ardently, and the two clung to
each other as if they were one.

And then Kiyari pushed Aidoneus away. "Until the solstice, my Lord. I shall return."

Tisiphone seized the moment to kiss the Ranger full on the lips, as Kiyari had kissed Aidoneus, and he felt her tongue snake into his mouth to dance around his. Then she, too, pushed away.

"Thank you," she said. "And thank Persephone for me also."

"Ready?" asked Hadad. "We need to get back. Time is running out."

The three Erinyes escorted them back to the river, and there they said farewells and parted. All three waved goodbye as the four mortals walked northward.The Ranger could still see them standing there, waving, until he crossed into the next underworld. The Ranger took them quickly through Patala and Rasatala without stopping. When they reached Nifelheim, the river became more turbulent. Currents ran faster and faster, tumbling over rocks and boulders and huge chunks of ice suddenly appeared from nowhere like icebergs floating in the north Atlantic, only to melt away and make the river swell its banks. The four continued on until they reached the calm of Uroar's Well where the roots of Yggdrasil extended from the nurturing waters up into the mist.

"I'll take the mask," said Jon. "I can climb with one hand. Kiyari, you go up first."

Kiyari made the arduous climb into the mist, and Hadad followed her. Then Jon went up one-handed, carrying the silver mask. Finally, the Ranger grabbed hold of the roots and was about to begin his ascent when Udug Hul appeared out of the mist south of the rapids. Hul's brightness blinded the Ranger, and the Ranger nearly fell into the river. But he ignored the pain shooting through his eyes by going inside himself to awaken the sleeping serpent within. He had depleted the last of his Kundalini energy while healing Tisiphone, however, and the serpent was sound asleep. No matter how hard the Ranger tried, he couldn't get the serpent to rise. He was all out of ammunition and the enemy was almost upon him.

Even with his eyes tightly closed, he could feel the incredible intensity of Udug Hul's power. The light grew even brighter as Hul drew closer. If Hul touched him, he had the distinct feeling his life would be over in a flash. Or, maybe, Udug Hul would withhold some of that awesome power and only incapacitate the Ranger. Maybe Hul wanted to watch Ereskegal torture the Ranger the way she had tortured Damu-zid. The Ranger really didn't want to know what Hul had done with what little had remained of Damu-zid when Ereskegal had finished with him. It probably wasn't pretty. The Ranger sure didn't want the same thing to happen to himself.

The Ranger felt his muscles flex automatically as he grabbed onto the roots and hauled himself, hand over hand, higher and higher. He had practiced climbing up and down ropes a thousand times in training, and one hand followed the other, lifting him into the mist, pulling his weight upward, his eyes still tightly closed, right hand, left hand, right, left, right, left.

His mind remembered some of the marching songs he had sung along with the other troops in training, and he sung them now. "I want to be an Airborne Ranger, I want to live a life of danger...left, right, left, right...If I die in a combat zone...left, right, left, right...box me up and ship me home...left, right, left, right...lay my rifle across my chest...left, right, left, right...tell them all I did my best...left, right, left."

And then he felt Jon Fish grab his shoulders, pulling him the rest of the way up the World Tree, felt the wind in his hair, the snow on his face.

And then he thought about his own body waiting for him at Machu Picchu, and he felt his body pulling him home, and he let it.

And he opened his eyes and saw Kiyari sitting next to him and smiling at him, and he knew he was back in the real world and it felt really good to be alive.

CHAPTER TWENTY-FIVE

Two sheriff's deputies served the eviction notice at 2:30 PM on October 29. They drove up to the house in a marked police car with the MARS lights flashing red and blue. Sheila Ryan met them at the door and accepted the notice on behalf of her client, one Ms. Diane Groves, who was so named on the eviction notice.

They had twenty-four hours to leave the property. Then the police would be back and Yam would be with them. As Sam Elman, Yam would legally take possession of the house, the trees, the sacred circle, and the vortex. And, Sheila said, there was nothing they could leagally do to stop him.

"He doesn't give up, does he?" Diane said.

"Nor do we," said Sara.

"He has the law on his side," said Sheila. "I have appealed the old court ruling, but it will take months, maybe years with the courts bogged down the way they've been since the darkness, to get a hearing. We don't have any recourse but to vacate."

"We have a higher law on our side," said Sara. "We can't let Yam have the vortex. We'll fight, if we have to."

"Fight the police?"

"Yes."

"They'll have guns. What can we do against guns?"

"We have fought men with guns before."

"I remember," said Sheila. "And guns killed Diane's sister and nearly killed Lokesvara. There must be a better way."

"I thought Hadad had a plan," said Diane. "What's going on with that?"

"He has to wait until the night of the new moon," said Sara. "That's on the thirty-first."

"That will be too late," said Sheila. "Yam will have taken control of the vortex by then."

"Then we'll have to ensure he doesn't take control," said Sara. "Come, sisters. We have preparations to make."

*   *   *

When Hadad handed the Ranger the copper mask of Illapa, the Ranger's mind flooded with previously-forgotten memories. He saw himself on the banks of the Urubamba River wearing that mask as he fought against Ayar Manco's minions in the sacred valley. Urubamba meant "flat land with spiders" in Quechua, and there indeed were spiders in the valley: the Chilean recluse, huge tarantulas, and hundreds of other arachnids.

Though the Ranger hated spiders and snakes with a passion, they were always strangely attracted to him. As he marched against Manco, thousands of spiders marched with him. The damn things seemed to follow him everywhere.

Perhaps it was because of the fierce Illapa mask, or perhaps it was because of all of those spiders or the stone soldiers that wouldn't die no matter where they were hit with arrow, axe or sword, the enemy had fled that day in panic. Manco, of course, had fled first, and his troops followed their leader, running away like the frightened dogs they were.

Hadad was certain the copper mask inspired great fear and was entirely responsible for the rout of Yam and his lackeys, and it probably did play a part, although minor. After all, who in their right mind would stand to fight the god of thunder? But the Lone Ranger knew it was the fighting skills of the man behind the mask that made the real difference, not the mask. If a man didn't know how to fight or didn't have the guts to stay in a fight to the finish, no mask in the world would help him win.

If there was one thing the Ranger knew, it was how to fight. He had fought enemies with broadswords, battleaxes, bayonets, muskets, Mausers, Garands, M16s, and M4s. He had lived and died by the sword in many lifetimes, and this lifetime wasn't any different.

He had enlisted in the Army at eighteen, just out of high school. He didn't mind school while he was there, and he had excelled in history and geography. Math and English held little interest for him, but he passed them anyway with mostly As and Bs. Though his grades were good enough to get him into most colleges, he had never considered going to a college or university. What he wanted more than anything else was to be a soldier.

And he had been a soldier, one of the best in this man's army, for almost twelve whole years. He had served with honor in Iraq, and he was made the leader of a select Ranger team in Afghanistan. It was during his second tour in Afghanistan that his elite Rangers had been betrayed by Taliban sympathizers and ambushed by Taliban fighters in the hills. His entire team had died in that ambush. All except him.

After that, he went more than a little mad, killing Afghans indiscriminately. He blamed the Army beaurocracy, and the politicians that made Army policy, for trusting Afghans and allowing the ambush to happen, but he blamed the Afghan people most of all. He crawled out of camp at night, snuck into Afghan villages, and slit the throats of every Afghan he could find.

During the day, he was relentless in his pursuit of enemy soldiers, killing more than all of the rest of his unit combined. He was commended for his aggressive actions, rewarded for his uncanny ability to ferret out and destroy enemy combatants, even earned a medal or two and was promoted ahead of his contemporaries. He was a one-man killing machine, and he killed hundreds of people before the Army sent him for psych evanuations that got him cashiered out of the service with a medical discharge. He was considered unfit for further duty, and he might have collected regular disability payments for a service-connected disability except he never applied for them. As soon as he left Fort Benning, he seemed to drop off the face of the earth as if he had never existed. Neither the Army nor the VA ever heard from him again.

He went to work for a security firm that hired ex-military to do odd jobs that weren't always legal and sometimes involved torture and murder. The firm provided him with several new identities, and he managed to impress his employers with his abilities and his apparent fearlessness. It was as if the man he was had died in that ambush in Afghanistan, and the man he had become bore little resemblance to the man he had been.

Then the firm sent him to do wet work for a screw factory in Rockford, Illinois, that was nothing more than an elaborate cover for a secret Chinese military operation, and the factory tried to kill him when he failed to carry out their orders in a timely manner. He had teamed up with Lokesvara and Jon Fish and a handful of others, and they had fought a Chinese general and his supernatural allies in an epic battle that turned the world upside down and back right side up again.

Meeting Lokesvara had been a life-saver, changed the Ranger's life so completely and profoundly that he became a monk. He learned how to remember all he had been, and he learned how to become all he could be. He learned that he was an avatar of Vajrapani, one of eight great Bodhisattvas, and he learned to call forth that part of him that manifested the awesome power of Vajrapani. There were times when he and Vajrapani seemed one entity, and times when they were completely separate consciousness. This was one of those times when they were separate.

Because something had happened to him back in Missouri when Yam double whammied him that separated them, sent Vajrapani elsewhere while the Ranger plunged into the abyss of despair. He had lost all connection with the sworn protector of the Buddha, the dharma, and the sangha. But now, as he put the copper mask up to his face, he felt the power of Vajrapani return to him once more. For the first time in several weeks, he felt complete.

Kiyari, too, was trying on a mask. He remembered seeing her in that mask a long time ago. Kiyari had been his sister then, the Coya Uqllu, a priestess at the Temple of the Moon. Though her body was different, her spirit then had been as beautiful as it was now.

Had he felt a definite pang of jealously when Kiyari kissed Aidoneus in Hades? Yes, he certainly had. But then Tisiphone had kissed him, warmly and deeply, and his jealousy had faded away as if it had never existed.

He was confused. Both women were so alike he sometimes forgot which was which. Was it possible to love two women at the same time? And were either of the women real?

Were they human or were they goddesses?

Did it matter? He still had a mission to accomplish, and love would have to wait. It always did, because true love was eternal. It endured despite the vicissitudes of time. For there was time for everything under the sun.

But now was not the time for love. Now was the time for action.

Hadad's plan was to have the Ranger scare Yam with the copper mask and the power of Vajrapani, knowing that if Yam was scared and backed into a corner, he would don his golden mask and call upon the power of the sun to protect him from the thunderbolts. Then Kiyari could approach him wearing the silver mask, and any power Yam expended would be reflected right back at him. The idea was to immobilize Yam but not kill him. Kiyari said that might be possible if she could angle the mask just right. And only if they confronted Yam on the night of the new moon when moon magic and earth magic were married.

Though the Ranger had doubts Hadad's plan would work—too many variables, he had told Hadad—it was the only plan they had. Yam had eluded them every time they had tried to capture the slippery son of a bitch, and it seemed unlikely he would allow himself to be backed into a corner.

And right now they didn't even know where Yam would be on the night of the new moon. He could be anywhere two nights from now, and they would have to find him first before they could confront him.

La Curandera was glad to have Kiyari back. Once again, both spirits cohabited the same human shell. They freely shared thoughts, and it was sometimes difficult to determine which woman was in control at any given time.

"I have just spoken with Sara," said La Curandera in Kiyari's voice. "Yam served an eviction notice on Diane's property. They have until tomorrow to turn the place over to Yam."

"Then we know where Yam will be," said the Ranger. "He'll be in Wisconsin tomorrow. He won't want to wait to take possession of the vortex. He's probably in Wisconsin now. We can go there right now and confront him."

"But now is too soon," said La Curandera. "Moon magic and earth magic need the dark of the moon to produce the combined effects we want."

"But the moon is already dark," said the Ranger. "It's been dark since Yam hid the sun."

"And that's all Yam did," said La Curandera. "He hid the sun from mortal eyes. But the sun and moon are still there. Their effects haven't changed. The only thing that's changed is our ability to see them."

"I don't understand all this magical mumbo-jumbo," said the Ranger. "How can the sun and moon still be there and I can't see them?"

"Yam is using a powerful spell that causes negative hallucinations," said La Curandera. "He doesn't have the power to actually move the sun or the moon. And even if he did have that power, as Akashagarbha has, he wouldn't want to use it. Moving the sun and moon would disrupt the balance of the universe so badly that powers beyond any of us to control would intervene to restore balance. As it is, Yam is pushing the envelope. He has caused shifts in the delicate balance of power—shifts in the karmic balance—that will soon require intervention. If we can't handle it, someone bigger than you or I will have to step in. Yam hopes to acquire enough power using chaos magic, human sacrifices, and the power of a vortex to survive if and when that happens."

"Someone bigger than you or I? You mean like Haides? Or Hecate?"

"Bigger than that."

"Who or what is bigger than that?"

"Someone with the wisdom not to interfere directly unless there is no other alternative, no other choice."

"I still don't understand," said the Ranger.

"You and I don't have to," said Jon. "We're just foot soldiers. Ours is not to wonder why, ours is but to do or die. Got that, soldier?"

"So what can we do now? Right now?"

"Go to Wisconsin," said Hadad. "That's where Yam is, and that's where we'll contront him on the night after next. Kisi and Bryn have already gone there to prepare."

"I'll stay here and hold down the fort," said La Curandera. "Kiyari needs to go with you, and I'll make do in the Condor stone. From there, I can keep in touch with the condors in the sky through the stone, but I will be out of contact with you once you leave."

Kiyari blinked out of existence at Machu Picchu. Jon, Hadad, and the Ranger followed her to Wisconsin. Time was running out, and they all could feel it.

*   *   *

Lokesvara continued to construct the mandala, and the sand painting had now expanded beyond the walls of his private meditation chamber into the halls of the main temple. Monks and students, maintaining a respectful distance, watched the sands sift silently through the master's fingers.

"Never before have I seen anything so beautiful," said one of the monks.

"Nor as intricate," said another.

"Nor as complex," said yet another.

"It is as if he were encompassing all of time and space within the frame of this one mandala," said one of the older students. "What is his purpose in doing so?"

"He adds the Sri Yantra," said the first monk. "See, he marries Shiva and Shakti in eternal triangles, surrounds them with lotus blossoms, and constructs the four portals to the infinite to protect the sacred union of opposites. Worlds within worlds within worlds, opening to other worlds within worlds."

"He chants," said the second monk. "His breath, like the breath of Manjusri, is as soft as the whisper of the winds through the trees. Listen closely, and you may hear."

"Om Ra Pa Tsa Na Dih," said Lokesvara.

"Om Ra Pa Tsa Na Dih," said the first monk.

"Om Ra Pa Tsa Na Dih," repeated the second monk.

Soon the halls of the temple echoed with the sounds of all the monks chanting in unison, harmonic overtones blending, mixing, becoming one. "OM RA PA TSA NA DIH!"

As they chanted, the monks felt the painting fill with power, the symbols come alive. The colors and the shapes began to move, to merge. They knew now that the master had recreated from memory the Great Mandala, the wheel of life encompassing all things, and the wheel began spinning as if all of the chakras in the entire universe were spinning together, synchronized, spinning in the same direction. Faster and faster now, the chanting accelerating to match the spinning colors, and the great wheel turned, the enire building turned.

And, beneath their feet, they felt the world turn with it.

CHAPTER TWENTY-SIX

When the police arrived, Bryn and her friends were ready and waiting.

There were two squad cars this time, and both of those late-model cars stopped dead in their tracks halfway between the road and the house when both engines cut out at the same time. All attempts to restart the motors proved futile, and the headlights and flashing MARS lights dimmed, then died, plunging the driveway into darkness.

Four uniformed deputies exited the squad cars. One of the deputies carried a pump-action shotgun, and all were armed with huge pistols in leather holsters and they carried overized flashlights in their hands. They managed to advance no more than ten paces before they were attacked by birds.

Kisi, Bryn, and Diane swooped down on the unsuspecting men from perches on treetops where they had patiently observed the deputies' arrival, waiting until the men were out of the cars and walking toward the house. Bryn knocked the shotgun from one deputy's hand, then she circled around and swiped at the back of the man's head with a talon. The deputy's hat went flying but his head wasn't touched.

Kisi and Diane both raked the hands holding flashlights, and the men yelped as long scratches on the backs of their hands filled with blood. The fourth deputy drew his sidearm and fired at shapes that flittered around in the darkness. One of the rounds winged Kisi, and she quickly transferred her consciousness to another bird as the one she had formerly occupied crashed into the ground.

Bryn hit the fourth deputy on the side of his face, raking her talons across his forehead before she flew away. Blood streamed from the open wounds and flooded his eyes, blinding him. He staggered backwards, trying to wipe blood from his eyes with his uniform sleeve.

All four men quickly retreated to the safety of their squad cars and tried to radio for help, but they instantly learned that electronics were useless this close to the vortex's electromagnetic field. None of their radios or cell phones produced anything but static.

When they couldn't restart their cars after numerous attempts, they abandoned the cars and began running toward the highway. Though none of the men saw the hawks flitting overhead, they did hear the flapping of wings following them relentlessly until they reached County trunk O and turned left toward the nearest town.

Once they were sure the four men were leaving, all three women returned to their human bodies on the living room floor in front of the fire.

"They'll be back," Bryn said as soon as she was ensconced in her own body.

"And they'll bring reinforcements," said Diane.

"It will take them an hour or two to get people out here," said Sara. "You bought us some more time."

"I lost one of the Hawks," said Kisi. "I don't think it survived."

"I'm sorry," said Sara. "Hawks have always been our good friends. They will watch the roads for us and alert us when the men come back, and they will allow us to join them again in driving the men away."

"Was Yam with the deputies?" asked Hadad.

"No," said Bryn. "Yam employed one of the emissaries of the underworld to return him to Wisconsin. We can assume Yam watched what happened in spirit, but he will show his face here only after we have been driven away by police. He is as much a coward as he has always been, and he will make others do his dirty work for him."

"I did not sense his spirit anywhere on the property," said Kisi.

"Yam can't come on the 1800 acres in spirit form while our wards hold," said Sara. "He was probably watching events from the other side of the highway. He saw us escort the police off the property."

"So how do we corner him?" asked the Ranger.

"By tomorrow night he'll be desperate enough to try to get past our wards or look for ways to counter or take them down, and he'll have to do that by physically stepping onto the property. That's when we can confront him. But we'll have to stand off the police until then, and that may not be so easy next time. We don't want to harm innocent people who are only do-ing their jobs, but they'll try to harm us if we let them. So we won't let them, will we?"

"How long before the cops come back?" asked Hadad.

"Three or four hours, maybe less if they discover their cell phones work just fine once they're out of range of the vor-tex's interference."

"They'll probably call in the state police to assist them before morning," said Diane. "When the state boys get here, we'll have a real battle on our hands."

"Nothing we can't handle," said Bryn. "Let them come."

"Don't be so sure," said Diane. "They'll bring lots of firepower. Of course, they'll probably try to negotiate before shooting at us. But when we refuse to leave, they'll try to come in or try to force us out."

"The house is protected," said Sara. "I've got spells in place to repel bullets. And they won't be able to physically enter the house uninvited."

It took the police longer than they thought to come back with reinforcements. This time there were six deputies, and they all had assault rifles and body armor.

They parked the two new squad cars behind the stalled cars, and two of the deputies approached the house on foot while the others took cover behind the cars. The two who approached the house tried to open the front door, then they tried to kick it in with their boots. But the door resisted their feeble effors as if it were made of solid steel instead of sturdy oak.

One of the deputies made the mistake of firing his assault rifle at the brass lock, expecting the lock to break or at least the wood around the door to splinter. Instead, the 5.56 millimeter round ricocheted off the door and struck the other deputy squarely in the chest, knocking him to the ground.

The bullet embedded in the man's shirt after flattening against the deputy's Kevlar vest.

Now the other deputies opened fire at the windows on the front side of the house from behind the cover of the squad car, but their bullets only ricocheted off the thin glass as if it were bullet-proof and shatter-resistent.

"The damn place is a fucking fortress!" swore one of the deputies.

The man on the porch and the man on the ground backed away from the house as if they expected someone inside to return fire. They made it all the way back to the squad car before a flock of birds came out of nowhere and snatched the assault rifles from their hands.

"Where the hell did all those fucking birds come from?" asked the deputy who had shot at the door.

"The trees," said one of the others. "The trees are full of birds. Someone must have trained a few. Did a good job, too."

"There's at least a half-dozen of the damn things," said another. "They hit all of us at the same time."

"Ain't natural," said yet another.

They all had their handguns out now, and they waved their flashlights at the sky trying to find a bird to shoot at. But there wasn't a single bird visible. After a while, they switched off their flashlights.

"What you want us to do, Jake?" one of them asked.

"Sit tight. We ain't getting in, but we ain't letting them out either. We'll stay right here till hell freezes over."

"I already worked a double shift today," complained the one who had been shot in the vest. "You think the county will pay triple overtime for an eviction?"

"This ain't just an eviction anymore," said Jake. "They scratched the fuck out of Dan's face, and they stole our rifles. You gonna let them get away with that?"

"Lots of weird things happening around here since the sun went away," said the guy with the bullet in his vest. "We don't have enough people on the whole damn force to handle half of it. I say we go home and get some sleep, then we can come back tomorrow and see if they're still here. If they are, we'll haul 'em in."

"And if they're gone?"

"Then good riddance to them."

"You go," said Jake. "I'm staying. When you get back to the station, call the state police again and hurry them up."

Jake and another deputy remained squatting behind the stalled squad cars while the other four took the two cars that worked and backed the squad cars up the firebreak to the highway. As soon as their headlights faded from sight, Jake stood up and shouted at the house, "All of you in there come out with your hands up or we'll come in and get you."

When he got no response, Jake added, "Okay. We'll wait you out then. The sooner you give yourselves up, the easier the law will be on you. If this goes on, I'll see the book thrown at you. Come on out!"

Four state police cruisers and an armored swat team truck arrived shortly before noon on October 31. Two of the troopers conferred with the deputies, and then one of the troopers approached the house and knocked on the door.

Sheila opened the door but did not invite the officer into the house. She identified herself as Diane Groves' attorney, and she told the trooper Ms. Groves did not intend to leave the property until her appeal was settled in court. She said Ms. Groves was a respectable citizen, a tenured professor at the state university, and Ms. Groves would surrender to the court only after her appeal was heard.

The trooper insisted that the police be allowed to enter the house, and when he attempted to step across the threshold his legs locked up and he was propelled backward off the porch as if he had just touched a live electrical wire. He lay stunned in the dirt at the bottom of the steps.

Two swat team officers in full body armor rushed in and dragged the man away from the porch, then carried him to the SWAT truck. Other swat team members were busily setting up flood lights to bathe the whole house in bright light. They strung thick cables from the lights to a 10 kilowatt gas generator near the back of their truck. But no matter how hard they tried to start the generator, it wouldn't kick over.

They brought out a public address system, but that wouldn't work either. Finally, one of the men shouted, "Come out now with your hands up. Or we'll come in and forcibly evict you."

After they waited what seemed like a long time, they assembled two squads of four men each to attack the house. They carried smoke bombs and concussion grenades and tear gas canisters, assault rifles, and flashlights. They wore gas masks over their faces. They charged at the house from different directions, but no one shot at them and they were trained not to fire unless fired upon. Nevertheless, they were ready to be shot at and to shoot back.

One team had a compact battering ram designed to break down any door, including one made of four-inch thick steel. They hit the door hard, but the door didn't budge. They hit it again. This time the battering ram broke.

One man tried to smash a window with the butt of his rifle, but the glass didn't shatter as he expected it would. He fired a shot at the glass, but it still wouldn't break.

Both teams withdrew to the SWAT truck and waited. The people in the house, and the people sharing consciousness with the birds in the trees, began to relax.

But the police didn't relax. They formed into new teams, and they set up something that looked like a mortar. Two of the SWAT team members carried M-72 light anti-armor weapons called LAWs, and the Ranger suspected they had armor-piercing rounds loaded in their assault rifles.

"Can your spells stop armor-piercing bullets?" he asked Sara.

"We will soon find out," said Sara. "They're aiming at the house now."

When the mortar lobbed the first shell at the house, there was a big boom, not unlike the sound of thunder when lightning split a nearby tree. Simultaneously, they heard hundreds of pit-pats against the side of the house like hailstones pitting the wooden boards each time one struck. They saw dozens of bright flashes outside the windows, and the Ranger was sure the house would catch fire.

But the spells held, and not a single bullet entered the building. Rockets exploded, but they did little damage to the house itself. A few of the trees nearest the building were blazing, but it didn't look like the fires would spread to the old-growth forest where Bryn, Kisi, and Diane waited in the pines.

The police kept up the barrage for nearly fifteen minutes. Then, either out of ammunition or out of patience, they ceased fire and conferred about what to do next.

At 6:43 PM, the SWAT vehicle backed out of the firebreak, followed by a state police squad car. A few minutes later, the SWAT truck pulled back down the firebreak and parked.

"Someone went out in the squad car to radio for instructions," said Sara. "I don't think they'll do anything more until he gets back."

"Yam hasn't showed up yet," said Hadad.

"Afraid he won't show?" asked the Ranger.

"No. He'll definitely show up here tonight. He needs to take possession of the vortex before midnight. He's using the cops as a diversion. He knows we won't surrender the property without a fight, so he's making the cops do the fighting for him while he sneaks around behind our backs."

"Why midnight? What's so important about midnight tonight?"

"Because midnight on October 31st—All Hallows Night, All Soul's Night, Halloween, Samhain, the Day of the Dead—is a seventy-two hour period when the doors to the underworlds are opened and the dead can come back to earth without being reborn. All they need is a way out of the underworlds, and that requires access to one of the four primary vortexes with direct connections to the World Tree. Biegolmai has secured the northern portal at the Seita, so that vortex is useless to them this year. La Curandera has secured the southern portal at Machu Picchu. Lokesvara guards the eastern portal. That leaves only the western portal. As long as we're here and physically in possession of this vortex, the dead can't escape. Rahu and his nagas, Hel and her trolls and frost giants, Ereshkigal and her demons, and all the other monsters of the underworlds have no way to run rampant here on earth. But if we leave the vortex unattended, if we're driven off this property or so preoccupied that we lose focus and let our wards lose power, Yam will open the vortex and all hell will break loose. That will be pure chaos, and Yam feeds on chaos."

"Sara is the key," said Kiyari. "It is her will—and her will alone—that strengthens the wards and spells that protect this vortex. As long as her body remains in physical contact with wood, she was the power to control the vortex. For the vortex here is not made of stone but of wood. This vortex is unique because the vortex here is caused by the trees still growing in the old-growth forest on this ancient land, trees whose roots reach all the way to the waters of Oceanus, roots that extend down through the body of the earth mother herself and draw strength and power from her nature and nurture, roots that can heal the sick and the maimed, roots with the power to cure or kill, roots that lead between worlds, roots that may provide a means by which Yam would release his minions if we allow it."

"It is bad enough that Yam has hidden the sun," said Hadad. "Think of how bad it will be if those hellish hoards run free, what chaos that might cause. We cannot let that happen."

"That squad car is coming back," said Jon who was watching out one of the windows. "And he's bringing a dozen other cars with him."

As they watched, local police officers and deptuties from surrounding counties disembarked, unloading weapons, ammunition, and door-busting battering rams. The make-shift task force now looked like a small army.

Accompanying the new arrivals was a short, fat man with a scarred face and only one eye. His new body had taken the form of the old, reflecting the spirit that occupied it.

"I told you he would come," said Hadad. "The only way onto the property is the firebreak. The rest is protected by the trees."

While the newcomers suited up with body armor and weapons, Elman conferred with the state troopers about something. He pointed to the trees.

"I'd give my eye teeth to hear what they're saying," said Jon.

"He's telling them to set fire to the trees," said Sara.

"How do you know?" asked the Ranger.

"Diane's hawk overheard them."

"You're in contact with the hawks?"

"Yes. And with Diane, Bryn, and Kisi."

"Will they do it? Set fire to the trees?"

"The state trooper doesn't want to. He says the Department of Natural Resouces would hold him responsible for a fire that destroyed the trees. But Yam argues that he is the legal owner of this property and he has a right to burn down the trees. And the house, too."

"Can he do that? Isn't the house protected?"

"Yes. But if the trees are destroyed, my spells will lose power. I depend on the trees to make my magic work. The trooper is sending one of his men to call in volunteer fire departments to control the blaze. Yam doesn't want to wait, but the trooper refuses to start the fires until there are firemen present to prevent the flames from spreading beyond Yam's property line."

"What time is it?" asked the Ranger. "I don't wear a watch anymore."

"Almost ten o'clock," said Jon.

"Do we have to wait until midnight to confront Yam?" asked the Ranger. "Can't we go after him now?"

"The moon won't pass out of the earth's shadow before then," said Kiyari. "It must begin waxing to have the effect we need to subdue Yam. If we want to force Yam to return the sun, we must wait."

"How long before the firemen get here?"

"At least an hour," said Sara. "Perhaps longer. They are all volunteers, and they need to assemble at the station before they can respond."

"That's cutting it close," said the Ranger.

"Too close for comfort," agreed Jon.

CHAPTER TWENTY-SEVEN

B egolmai began playing his drum. The tap, tap, tap of his fingers on the drumhead soon escalated to ratta-tap-tap. Then it became. boom! ratta-tap-tap boom! Boom! boom! ratta-tap-tap boom! Boom! boom!

He began at exactly midnight in Lappland, seven hours before Midnight in Wisconsin, and six hours after Lokesvara began chanting in Cambodia. They would continue chanting and drumming for seventy-two hours, or until the battle was done, whichever came first. It was the least they could do.

And, for the moment, it was the most they could do.

As the sounds of the beating drum stirred the night air the way sounds of a mother's heartbeat stirred the soul of a re-born while in utero, subtle shifts in the energy of the universe took place which ordinary mortals couldn't sense and wouldn't be able to process. Vibrations in the wood of a simple hoop drum formed from the wood of the World Tree, amplified by sacred symbols carved into that wood by Biegolmai himself, spread out from northern Scandinavia and paved the way for other subtle changes to take place.

Biegolmai continued tapping, and as the rhythms increased in tempo he added his voice to the mix. He sang the
jojks, ancient wordless chants called "leudd" that were old before the first glaciers spread across this land millennia ago.
Because the language of leudd was universal, a native shaman in
the stepps of Russia or in the highest mountains of Tibet or in
the Andes of South America or the Rocky Mountains of the
Western United States would have recognized the intent.

For on this night Biegolmai knew there would be shamans all over the world beating their drums and joining the
vibration of their own living voices with his. Not only was this
the eve of the Day of the Dead, it was also the time when the
earth moved between the sun and moon, the planets Venus and
Mars aligned, and the energies of the universe shifted. It was the
most auspicious time imaginable.

What happened tonight, and in the two days that followed, would have a profound impact on the futures of this
world and many others. Whether order would be restored or
chaos would rule the entire universe would depend on a small
group of humans in Wisconsin.

Plus a little help from their friends.

*   *   *

The firetrucks arrived at 11:35 PM, two pumpers towing
water trailers and a big red hook and ladder. They blocked the

firebreak all the way back to the county highway, and the trucks lit up the night sky with their headlights and the red and blue flashing signals atop their cabs.

It took the fire chief a good fifteen minutes to confer with the troopers and look over the situation. He argued with Elman and shook his head angrily. He wanted to put fires out, not start them.

Finally, the state trooper directed his men to load incendiaries into their mortars and shoulder-fired rocket launchers. It was already after midnight when they fired the first shots.

Three dark shapes darted out of the trees and swooped down on the men with the rocket launchers. This time the birds didn't hold back. They flew with their talons outstretched and they drew blood. But there were enough men that the three birds had to repeat the maneuver multiple times, and several of the incendiary grenades reached their targets. The men with assault rifles declared open season on birds. Two of the birds were hit, but two others quickly took their places.

"Now is the time," said Kiyari, holding the silver mask up in front of her face. Before the Ranger could stop her, she walked to the door, opened it, and stepped out to the porch.

The Ranger put on his own mask, and called on Vajrapani to help. He ran out on the porch and stood next to Kiyari. Clouds in the sky began filling with energy, and thunder boomed, drowning out the sounds of gunfire and more rockets being launched at the trees.

Sara's spells must have held. As long as the Ranger and Kiyari remained on the porch connected to the house, bullets stopped a few inches from where they were standing, bouncing off an invisible energy shield and falling to the ground where copper-jacketed bullets began to pile up like pennies in a piggy bank.

But several of the trees were already ablaze, and the fire was speading to other trees nearby. Vajrapani opened up the heavens and called forth a torrential downpour. One of the fires went out and the others began smouldering.

Suddenly, a faint glow began to materialize next to where Yam stood urging the police to continue firing at the trees. Within seconds the glow became a bright light that was blinding. Udug Hul appeared on earth. And the emissary of Ereshkigal had brought a bevy of demons with him from the underworld.

Hul's light flared even brighter, and he raised his hands and pointed at the trees. Flames lept from his fingertips and shot into the forest, igniting the needles and branches of a dozen or more old-growth pines.

Vajrapani unleased a thunderbolt at Hul, but the only effect it seemed to have at all was to make Udug Hul glow even brighter than before.

Hul barked laughter, and his laughter sounded worse than a thousand fingernails dragged across chalkboards. Hul was beyond ugly, he was absolutely hideous.

"I have come for my Queen's sister," he growled, advancing toward the house. "Let me take her, and I may let you live. Then, again, I may not."

Each blast of lightning Vajrapani threw at Udug Hul only increased Hul's power. He grew visibly taller and bigger with every lightning bolt that touched him. He was twenty paces from the porch when Jon Fish stepped out onto the porch and called upon Akashagarbha for aid. The Boundless Space Matrix materialized and charged at Udug Hul, wrapping his huge arms around both the being from hell and encompassing also the weird light emanating from Hul, and both Akashagarbha and Udug Hul disappeared in the blink of an eye. The world suddenly seemed dark and empty. And a whole lot safer.

Yam directed Hul's demons to rush the house, and the Ranger hurled thunderbolts at them, setting them on fire. They emiited hideous screams as burning demonflesh fouled the air, but they kept on coming toward the house until they crumpled into ash.

More demons appeared, and now the Ranger could see a frost giant and a troll among them. The fires destroying the forest was slowly destroying the protection of the vortex, and the way between worlds was now wide open.

Kiyari flinched as a single bullet penetrated the shield protecting the house. Fortunately, the bullet had lost most of its momentum before striking her chest. It barely broke her skin, though a blotch of blood appeared on the front of her blouse.

Panicked state troopers and sheriff's deputies were firing guns at anything and everything in sight. One of the big green demons, angered by the pin-pricks of rifle bullets bouncing from his thick hide, tore the head from a tropper and swallowed it whole. Tiny trolls, armed with broadswords and battleaxes, charged into the remaining troopers and tore them apart.

"Put the forest fires out," directed Hadad from behind them in the doorway. "I'll take care of the demons."

Vajrapani waved both hands at the clouds, and the torrential downpour increased until it seemd like huge buckets of water spilled from the sky. Or perhaps the gods were openly weaping at the loss of the trees, and it was tears of the gods, not rain, that fell on the flaming forest. Black smoke billowed skyward as the flames smouldered, smoked, smothered, and then went out. Some of the trees were badly scorched, but most were still standing. A few looked untouched.

Once the flames were gone and the trees could breathe again, they began to flesh out, to branch out. Some even sprouted entirely new limbs while the Ranger watched. Green appeared on those branches, and fresh growth sprung from the ashes. Mother Earth possessed miraculous healing powers.

Yam was still able to bring in reinforecements from the underworlds in droves, and Hadad's Kundalini power was rapidly being used up fighting off demons. Vajrapani joined Hadad and unleashed another series of lightning flashes that cut down a frost giant, two trolls, and a handful of demons.

Kiyari had bravely stepped off the porch and was slowly walking toward where Yam cowered behind the police cars. She held the silver moon mask in front of her face, and it looked like she was having a hard time seeing around it because she stumbled and nearly fell. When Yam saw her coming, he smiled. He reached inside his suit coat and brought out the golden sun mask. He slipped it over his face.

"I looked for you at Machu Picchu," he called out, still hiding beind the cop cars.

"I was there," she said.

"You have the mask and I want it," said Yam. "I knew you had knowledge of the mask's whereabouts, and I would have sucked that knowledge out of your brains if I'd found you before the healer possessed you. I need the moon mask to make my power complete—to marry the sun and the moon—and I shall have the mask. Once I have both masks, I will become like a god and be able to command the heavens and the earth."

"Come and get it then," said Kiyari.

One of the demons reached his claws for Kiyari, and Vajrapani sent a lightning bolt to take off the demon's arm before it could touch her. A frost giant loomed over her with a broadsword, and lightning struck the sword and electrocuted the giant, frying him to a crisp. Kiyari kept walking as if nothing had happened, completely focused on the adversary in front of her.

"Are you afraid to face me, brother? Are you so frightened by one little girl that you hide your face behind a mask and your body behind the wrecks of automobiles?"

Now Yam's golden mask began to glow with the power of the sun, and Vajrapani could sense the incredible power behind that mask. Yam's power had grown exponentially with every day of darkness, and it would double overnight if he got possession of the vortex, possession of the masks, and opened the doors to the underworlds permanently. Chaos would rule, and Yam would be in his element.

And all that stood in his way was a girl in a silver mask.

Though the number of demons coming through the veil began to diminish once the fires went out and the trees began to regenerate, demons and giants still kept coming. Hadad and Vajrapani were kept too busy to aid Kiyari directly.

Yam's mask grew brighter and brighter, and the two faced off like gunfighters facing each other in the street in some old black and white western movie on late-night television. Yam drew first, firing a blinding burst of energy directly at Kiyari's face. The blast hit the silver mask and bounced straight back at Yam like a ricocheting bullet.

Yam dodged the bullet and fired again. He remembered Ayar Manco dying the last time he had faced that silver mask, so this time he aimed at the center of Kiyari's vulnerable body instead of her face.

And the blast of energy Yam unleashed hit Kiyari's midsection and ripped out her guts. The silver mask flew out of her hands as intestines flew out the twelve-inch hole drilled through her back to splatter the ground like a tipped-over plate of steaming-hot spaghetti in a busy Italian restaurant.

The Ranger saw red. Thunder boomed as Valrapani shot a dozen lightning bolts at Yam Elman, catching Yam completely by surprise, and splitting Yam's body in two before frying both parts like a beefsteak forgotten too long on a hot backyard grill. Yam had no chance to transfer his spirit before his body perished, no time even to scream. If there were one consolation, it was that Yam Elman would get his just reward in the afterlife. Whether his spirit went up or down, he had lots of lessons to learn before he would be reborn in a new body. Every pain he had inflicted on others through the centuries would now be inflicted on him.

Hadad finished off the last few demons and giants, and he ran to his brother's corpse and removed the golden mask. What was left of the face beneath that mask was totally unrecognizable.

"Now we'll never be able to learn how to return the sun," Hadad lamented as he looked at the charred body of his brother.

"Sorry," said the Ranger. He *was* sorry, though he didn't sound sorry. He was sorry that Kiyari had died needlessly. If he had it to do all over again, he still would have fried Yam Elman without blinking an eye or thinking twice. Yam deserved to die, and the Ranger was strangely pleased to have been the agent of Yam's destruction. To hell with his vow of ahimsa. What was one more death to answer for in the afterlife? Yam had killed Kiyari, so Yam deserved to die.

As the Ranger knelt by Kiyari's lifeless body, he noticed the ground around her begin to shimmer and coalesce into something solid. Suddenly, there were three naked women standing right there next to him looking down at Kiyari.

"Aidoneus sent us to help," said Tisiphone. "But I see we arrived too late. I'm sorry."

The Ranger looked at Kiyari, then at Tisiphone, then back to Kiyari. Then he held Kiyari's body in his arms and stared to cry.

*   *   *

Akashagarbha took Udug Hul all the way into the void and simply dumped him there.

But Hul didn't stay there. Fortunately, Akashagarbha suspected Hul had more power than anyone gave him credit for, and Akashagarbha waited at the edge of the void for Hul to reappear.

"I don't want to destroy you," Akashagarbha told Hul as the demon emissary emerged from the darkness.

"You can't," said Udug Hul.

"Then what am I going to do with you?" asked Akash-agarbha.

"Allow me to return to the underworlds."

"That I will do, but only if you return directly to the un-derworlds. Do not pass go and do not collect two hundred dollars."

"I was sent to fetch the Queen's sister. I will not return without her."

"Then you will have a fight on your hands."

"So be it," said Hul. He unleashed a blast of energy at Akashagarbha that would have scattered the remains of anyone else among the stars, but Akashagarbha barely flinched. He hit Hul with a blast even more powerful, but Hul only laughed.

"I feed on energy," said Hul. "Each time you attack me, I grow stronger."

Akashagarbha grabbed Hul and dragged him back into the void. The two grappled and fought for what seemed like an eternity.

Suddenly, Udug Hul gave up struggling. It was as if all the fight had gone out of him and he simply gave up. He stood completely still as if seeing something far away, something even Akashagarbha couldn't see.

Akashagarbha took pity on Hul when he saw the forelorn look on the demon's face. Hul seemed almost human. "Are you ready to return to the underworlds now?" Akashagarbha asked.

"I am," said Hul.

"Without another fight?"

"I have failed in my mission," said Hul. "I must go back and inform the Queen that her sister is dead."

"Kiyari is dead?"

"Even in the void I felt her passing."

"How is that possible?"

"You are mighty, O Akashagarbha, but there is much you have yet to learn. Among other things, I am an emissary of the underworlds. I possess an uncanny sense of connection with the spirits of the recently departed. It is part of my job, and I am good at my job. Kiyari's body is dead and her spirit has departed. What happens to her spirit now is out of my hands."

"How did Kiyari die?"

"She was killed by Yam Elman."

"She's really dead?"

"You doubt my word? Her body is deceased and her spirit has left her deceased body. Of that I am certain."

"What will you do now if I let you go?"

"I will return directly to the underworlds, as I must, and tell my Queen. She will be very angry, but then she is always angry. It is part of her nature."

"Before you go, Udug Hul, tell me more of who you are and what you do. The workings of the underworlds are a mystery to me."

"And they must remain a mystery," said Hul. "You are a being of the pure lands, and your enlightened spirit need not be burdened with things that do not concern you. To tell you more would taint your spirit, and that I will not do."

"I did not expect honor from one such as you," said Akashagarbha.

"Honor has nothing to do with it," said Udug Hul. "We all have our limits, even the Boundless Space Matrix and Udug Hul. Limitless power does not exist. Not even for you or for me. There are boundaries for both of us. With that said, I wish you farewell."

Udug Hul disappeared, and Akashagarbha didn't try to stop him. Though they would always remain worlds apart, Akashagarbha couldn't help feeling that he and Udug Hul were but opposite sides of the same coin.

An instant later, he was back in Wisconsin.

*　　*　　*

"We're out of luck," said Hadad. "When Yam died, he took the secret of how he masked the sun from humankind with him down to the underworlds."

"Then we'll just have to go down there and get it from him," said the Ranger. "We'll find Yam's spirit and make him take the mask off the sun or tell us how to return the sight of the sun ourselves. I'll volunteer to go. Who will go with me?"

"That we cannot allow," said Tisiphone. "Whichever of the underworlds now holds Yam Elman prisoner will punish him appropriately and most severely, but he cannot be allowed to speak to anyone not of that underworld. The secrets of the dead must remain a secret."

"Can't you find him and question him?"

"Even if I could do that," said Tisiphone, "I wouldn't."

"Why not?" demanded the Ranger.

"Because I have sworn an oath," said Tisiphone. "I have broken one oath. I will not break another."

"Then we are out of luck," said Sara. "We lost Kiyari. And we lost the means of uncovering the sun."

"But Yam didn't get the vortex," said Kisi, "and the door to the underworld has closed again. The rest of us are alive. The forest survived. We are both unlucky and lucky."

"And Kiyari will be reborn," added Bryn. "She has not been lost forever. We shall all see her again in our next lives."

"Our job now," said Sara, "will be to teach mankind to live in darkness. That will not be easy. I must confer with Biegolmai, Lokesvara, and La Curandera. If there is nothing more we can do to restore the sun, then we'll find another way to provide light to the world."

"What do we do about the dead police and firemen in the front yard?" asked Diane. "How will we explain their deaths to the state police that are bound to come looking for them?"

"Nothing remains of the demons and giants," said Bryn. "Their rotting corpses disappeared when the doors closed to the underworlds. It is as if they were never here."

"Tell the police," suggested Sheila, "that Sam Elman went crazy. He attempted to torch the whole place, and when the police and firemen tried to stop Elman, he killed them all. He went beserk. He used the police weapons to set fire to the forest and he must have made a mistake with launching an incendiary device and burned himself up in the process. That's as close to the truth as we need to get. This whole house, and everyone in it, would have gone up in smoke too, if a freak storm hadn't put out the fires. I'm willing to swear to that in court, and so should you."

"What about the vortex?" asked Diane. "What about Elman's claim to the land?"

"It will pass to the next of kin. That's Hadad. I'm sure Hadad will keep the place safe until we can win on appeal. Hadad can tell the police he has taken possession of his brother's property as the sole heir. I think that will get the rest of us off the hook, and Hadad can allow you to remain here as caretakers of the estate while the estate goes through probate."

"We must return to Hades," said Medaera. "Our King will be sad when we tell him his Queen died, but he will be pleased to learn that Yam Elman has gone to his reward. Time does not mean the same to immortals as it does to humans, and Aidoneus shall be pleased to see his Queen again when she has been reborn and reaches maturity."

Tisiphone gently touched the Ranger's cheek, and he kissed the back of her hand. "Goodbye," she said. "I am truly sorry for your loss."

"Will I ever see you again?"

"The King has decreed that I must walk the world as an ordinary woman for half of each year. I shall return on the winter solstice and depart on the summer solstice. Perhaps our paths may cross."

The feel of her touch remained long after she was gone. The Ranger stared into the fire in the huge fireplace in Diane's lving room and tried to see the future. He couldn't imagine a future without Kiyari in it in one form or another, and the future looked bright despite the lack of sunshine. The Lone Ranger was still alone, but he knew he wouldn't remain alone forever. He would see Tisiphone after the solstice, and someday he would see Kiyari again, too.

"I must get back to the Corps," said Jon Fish. "My extended leave has expired, and I'm scheduled to report in at 0700."

"Thanks, Jon," said the Ranger, looking away from the fire. "You were a big help."

"Sorry I didn't do more."

"You took care of Udug Hul. That turned the tide of battle in our favor. I don't know what we would have done without you."

"You met Udug Hul in the underworlds. Tell me all you know about Hul."

"Hecate says he's dangerous, and I'd have to agree. He's one of the few underworld beings that moves freely between worlds. Ereshkigal treats him like a dog, and sometimes he looks and acts like one. But he is very powerful, and there is something about him that makes him more than just a demon. He said he is a Gallu, whatever that means."

"A Gallu?"

"A Gallu means supreme servant in Akkadian," said Kisi. "A Gallu is a demon formed from fire. He is a devil, a jinn, an Iblis, a ghoul."

"A ghoul?" asked the Ranger. "A Gallu is a ghoul?"

"One who devours the dead," said Kisi. "Udug Hul is formed of fire, and he devours the dead."

"That explains why he can appear as bright as he sometimes does," said the Ranger. "He is made of fire."

"And," added Jon, "it also explains why he fed on energy when we fought. Every time I hit him with a blast of energy, I was only feeding more fuel to the fire."

"Gallus are said to devour spirits that cannot be redeemed," said Kisi.

"Ereskigal gave Damu-zid to Udug Hul when she was through with him," said the Ranger. "I assume Damu-zid was beyond redemption. Did Udug Hul consume him with fire?"

"From what I saw of Damu-zid," said Bryn, "it may have been the merciful thing to do."

"It is difficult to believe that Kiyari and Ereshkigal were sisters," said the Ranger.

"No more difficult to believe than Yam and Hadad were born brothers," said Bryn. "There is a shadow side to each of us. Sometimes that shadow side remains inside us. Sometimes it is a separate entity. Sometimes we have more than one shadow."

"I wonder if the Erinyes are our shadow sides," said Kisi.

"Whatever they are," said Bryn, "they are not evil. They have a code of honor that seems alien to us, but they do have a code of honor."

"So does Udug Hul," said Jon. "Akashagarbha learned about that in the void. Hul may be a demon, but he is bound by rules like the rest of us."

"You sound like you like the bastard," said the Ranger.

"Like is the wrong word. Respect may be more accurate."

"How can you respect a demon?"

"You, of all people, should know the answer to that," said Jon Fish. "When you became a Buddhist monk, didn't you learn to respect the divine in all sentient beings?"

"Yes. But a *demon*? How can you see anything divine in a demon?"

"He has his purpose in the scheme of things," said Jon. "We don't know everything, do we? Nothing exists that does not have a place in the great chain of being. Udug Hul has a place. Maybe we can't see it yet, but he does have a place and a purpose."

"I'll take your word for it," said the Ranger. "Maybe it's time for me to return to being a monk. I have a lot to atone for, and a lot yet to learn."

"Then let's go," said Jon. "I'll go with you back to Angkor and pick up the rest of my uniform. Then I'll be off to San Diego."

CHAPTER TWENTY-EIGHT

Lokesvara was still painting with sand when Jon stopped by to say farewell. Now the mandala had grown to gigantic proportions, filling several rooms and hallways with shapes and colors.

"I need to get the rest of my uniform," Jon said. "But you've blocked the way to your chambers with your painting. How do I get through?"

"You were meant to walk through the sands," said Lokesvara. "Nothing is permanent, everything changes. Your footprints become part of the painting. It is as it should be."

Jon felt a tingling in his toes as he stepped on the sands. Each step he took caused sands to mix, swirl, fill in. Jon reached the inner chamber and found his uniform hanging where he had left it, changed clothes, and came out looking like a Marine.

"I need a shave and a haircut," he told the Ranger. "If I report in looking like this, I'll set a bad example for the troops."

"You do look like you've been through hell," said the Ranger. "I'll show you to the bathrooms and I'll lend you a razor and soap."

After Jon showered and shaved, he made sure he was high and tight. He took off all the hair on the top of his head except for an eighth of an inch covering the crown.

"Now you do look like a Marine," said the Ranger when Jon donned his battledress blouse and insignia.

"I wish I could say it's been a pleasure," said Jon, shaking hands with the Ranger.

"We'll meet again."

"Next time I hope it's over a few beers in the NCO club," said Jon. Then he blinked out of existence in Cambodia and blinked back into existence in California.

He reported in to the First Sergeant at the Headquarters Company of the Headquarters and Service Battalion at 0600.

"You picked a hell of a time to go on leave, Gunny," said the First Sergeant, a guy who stood six inches shorter than Jon but was all muscle. The topkick's name was Benjamin Nathan, and they had served four tours together, three in Iraq and one in Afghanistan. Now they were training the next generation of combat Marines together. "We've been on alert since the day you left. If we could have contacted you, we would have called you back."

"Family emergency," said Jon. "I lost a sister who was killed by some weirdo. I've been trying to track down the killer. We finally got him this morning."

"Things are tough all over, Gunny," said the top sergeant. "Don't expect me to cry over your family problems."

"What's been happening while I was gone, Top? Anything I need to know?"

The topkick shuffled some papers before answering. "Everyone's gone crazy except me," said the topkick. "And sometimes I ain't sure about me. It's dark out there, in case you haven't noticed. New recruits started acting crazy after the first day or two. Things have gotten so out of hand we had to suspend weapons training and lock down the post. We had fourteen suicides here yesterday, and one of them was Charlie Goodman."

"I served with Charlie in Iraq," said Jon. "He wasn't the type to take his own life."

"Well, he did. It's this damned darkness. It makes people do things they wouldn't ordinarily do."

"I thought it would be over by now," said Jon. "But it doesn't look like it will be anytime soon."

"You don't want to hear about my problems, and I don't want to hear about yours. That's what chaplains are for. Go on back to your unit and whip those boys into shape. Randolph can't handle it anymore."

"Roger that. I'm on my way."

"And Jon?"

"Yeah, Top?"

"I'm glad to see you're still sane. Don't let the darkness get to you. I don't want to lose any more men."

*　*　*

The Ranger watched Lokesvara continue to paint. "Can I help?" he asked.

"You have done enough already," said the old man. "Someday I will teach you to do what I am doing, but today I must do this alone."

"We didn't get him," said the Ranger. "I had to kill Yam before we could learn how to restore the sun."

"I know," said Lokesvara. "You did what you had to do. The rest is out of your hands."

Then whose hands is it in? the Ranger wanted to ask. But he bit his tongue and watched the old man work. Monks brought new sand to refill the bowls as Lokesvara grabbed handsful of the colored silica and continued to make shapes that interlinked, some touching, some separate. If there were a pattern evolving, the Ranger couldn't see it.

The old man never stopped working. Anyone else would have tired long ago, but Lokesvara kept working like a man less than half his age. The Ranger had no idea how old Lokesvara might be in this incarnation, but some of the monks said he was older than the hills. Lokesvara had looked old when the oldest monk among them had been a novitiate, and that was more than fifty years ago.

Finally, Lokesvara dripped a last handful of sand onto the floor and said, "Sadhu, it is finished." The old man tried to stand up, but he had sat in lotus so long that his muscles refused to obey his will. It was the first time the Ranger had ever seen the old man seem weak.

He helped Lokesvara to his feet, and practically carried him to the sick room. He laid the frail form on the sick bed and called for assistance.

Within minutes, the room was filled with monks and students fretting about their master. Monks brought water and bread, hot broth made of many vegetables. Incense was lit, and prayer flags flown.

"Light will return soon," predicted Lokesvara. Then he closed his eyes and smiled a satisfied smile.

CHAPTER TWENTY-NINE

U dug Hul appeared in the squad room of the U. S. Marine Corps barracks at 7:05 AM Pacific Time, and he brought the sight of the sun with him. Sunlight streamed through the windows for the first time in more than a month.

All of the men rushed outside the barracks to see if the sun were really back in the sky where it belonged. When they saw that it was, they jumped up and down for joy. None of them wanted to go back inside, so they missed seeing the brief meeting between Gunnery Sergeant Jonathan Roy Fish and a being made almost entirely of light.

"I wanted you to know that I have taken possession of the spirit of Yam Elman," said Udug Hul in a voice that barely approximated human speech. "When my Queen heard that Yam was the cause of her sister's death, she demanded that I fetch him for punishment. I fulfilled the Queen's request, and I can assure you that Yam is quite unhappy."

"Then I have you to thank for returning the sun?"

"Was it not you who allowed me to return to the under-worlds?" asked Udug Hul. "It seemed only fitting that I repay you by returning something you value."

"You tortured the secret from Yam?"

"He has already told me many things," said Udug Hul. "How he used magic to bend light was but one of them."

"How did he do it?"

"Would that I could tell you, but I cannot. The secrets of the dead stay with the dead."

"So I have been told before."

"Bear it to heart. I would hate to come after you for stealing knowledge from the dead. Now I must go."

"Before you leave, I must know one thing more. If the secrets of the dead remain only with the dead, does that mean you are dead?"

"I have never been alive," said Udug Hul. "I was born of the flames of hellfire, not the flames of desire, and I am neither alive nor dead. I am something between life and death. I do not cherish life as you do. Nor do I despise it."

"How did you come to serve Ereshkigal?"

"One question is all you may ask and all I will answer. Farewell, mortal."

Udug Hul departed, but bright sunlight remained even after he had gone. Jon heard laughter erupt outside the barracks, filling the company area for the first time in much too long. Jon went outside to join his men in celebration.

"Ain't it wonderful, Gunny?" asked a private, his face grinning from ear to ear. "We all knew things would be better when you got back. You're our good luck charm."

At the end of the company street the Top Sergeant and the Major stood looking up at the sky in wonderment, not believing their eyes. The First Sergeant removed a pair of aviator sunglasses from a pocket of his blouse and put them on.

Then the First Sergeant growled down the street: "Today's a training day, you yahoos. Get your asses in gear and bust butt over to the armory. You're due on the rifle range in fifteen minutes!"

Jon repeated the command. "You heard the First Sergeant. Fall in. We'll double time all the way."

The men immediately snapped to attention, though it did take some of them longer than others to wipe the grins off their faces.

The sun was back in the heavens, Gunnery Sergeant Fish was giving orders, and all was right with the world.

*　　*　　*

"What did you do, Grandfather?" La Curandera asked Biegolmai as they met on the World Tree.

"I sang," said the man who did look very much like Santa, especially now that a jolly smile had replaced the seriousness that had dominated the line of his lips for more than a month.

"Then who returned the sun?"

"We all had something to do with that. I played the drum and sang the jojks, Kiyari sacrificed herself, Akashagarbha took Udug Hul to the Void, Bryn, Kisi, and Diane became birds, the Ranger made it rain and saved the trees, Sara talked to the trees and closed the door to the underworlds, and Lokesvara painted a picture."

"Lokesvara painted a picture? What kind of picture?"

"A Great Mandala."

"And what did that do?"

"It brought two of the opposing foces of the universe together in harmony," said Biegolmai. "Mutual respect often brings enlightment. That's what Loksvara believes, and he may be right. Lokesvara is very wise."

"How is Lokesvara? I heard he was ill."

"He was drained by his efforts," said Biegolmai. "None of us is as young as we used to be. We tire too easily these days. Perhaps it is time for some of us to seek reincarnation."

"Do you mean me?" asked La Curandera.

"You have been without a body of your own for more than a year. Wouldn't it be nice to be a child again?"

"Yes," admitted La Curandera.

"Then go. Climb the World Tree to the top and enter the spirit realm. You have earned a time of rest and reflection. I may join you soon."

"You, Grandfather? I have never known you to require rest."

"All of us do from time to time," said Biegolmai. "Farewell, Granddaughter. We shall meet again."

Biegolmai watched La Curandera's spirit ascend the World Tree and disappear into the spirit realm.

Then he picked up his drum, sang the jojks, and the sun rose and set on time.

* * *

Though some of the sands had shifted with the passage of time, enough of the colors and shapes remained for the Ranger to discern the pattern of Lokesvara's intention.

Everything was balanced. There were an equal number of male and female triangles, and for every circle there was a square.

Light and dark were balanced, too, perfectly balanced, just as day and night were balanced at the equinoxes.

That a single human mind could conveive the immensity of the interrelationships was amazing, but that one man could paint such a picture so accurately was absolutely incredible. The Ranger couldn't imagine doing something similar in a million years, and yet Lokesvara had done it in days.

Of course, Lokesvara had Manjusri to help him.

Much of what he saw was beyond the Ranger's comprehension, especially a single set of footprints crossing the picture in two directions. Why had Lokesvara allowed Jon Fish to disturb the painting in any way? What difference had Jon's passing made to the grand scheme of things?

"Footprints are always important in intelligence gathering operations," an Army officer had lectured in Ranger school. "Footprints left behind in the sand or mud can tell us many things: the number of enemy or friendly combatants, the presence of civilians, the direction of troop movements, how much equipment the enemy is carrying, the interactions of events, even the time these things took place. Learn to pay attention to footprints. Footprints are important."

Following the footprints with his eyes, the Ranger saw where Jon's footprints crossed the bindu, the center of the universe. Then they continued on to the other side where the sands were scuffed. Then they returned, mixing light and dark sands together as they moved across the Sri Yantra to exit the east portal.

The sands surrounding the east portal of the Sri Yantra were bright, nearly pure white, as opposed to the west portal where the sands were dark, nearly pitch black. But Jon's passing had mixed up some of the sand, and there was a place in the east where a few grains of black were mixed in with the white.

As he watched, the Ranger thought he saw movement in the sands, as if Jon's passing had set something in motion that was still ongoing. Now the sands shifted to fill in the void left by Jon's footprints, and moments later the footprints were entirely gone as if they had never existed.

"Nothing is permanent," Lokesvara said from the hallway behind the Ranger. "Everything changes."

"Should you be out of bed so soon, Master?" asked the Ranger.

"I wanted to see the sunlight," said Lokesvara. "The sick room has no windows."

He stepped onto the mandala and walked across it without leaving footprints. When he reached the bindu point in the exact center of the painting, he placed a sandal on the bindu and began scattering the sand with his right foot.

"Join me," he said. "Help me break up the bonds with the past that we might begin again."

"Why would you want to destroy something that took so much time, so much work?" asked the Ranger.

"It has served its purpose," answered Lokesvara. "Now is the time for new beginnings. This is the first lesson in the Pho-wa, my son. You must learn to let go of the past or there can be no future."

Together, they scattered the sands. And when all of the sands were mixed together and the shapes and colors of the painting were no more, Lokesvara said, "Sadhu, it is done."

END

ABOUT THE AUTHOR

Paul Dale Anderson has written more than 27 novels and hundreds of short stories, mostly in the thriller, mystery, horror, fantasy, and science fiction genres. Paul has also written contemporary romances and westerns. Paul is an Active Member of SFWA and HWA, and he was elected Vice President and Trustee of Horror Writers Association in 1987. He is a current member of International Thriller Writers, Author's Guild, and a former Active Member of MWA.

Paul has taught creative writing at the University of Illinois at Chicago and for Writers Digest School. He has appeared on panels at Chicon4 and Chicon7, X-Con, Windy Con, Madcon, Odyssey Con, Minncon, the World Horror Convention, and the World Fantasy Convention. Paul was a guest of honor at Horror Fest in Estes Park, Colorado, in 1989. He is currently the chair of the 2015 HWA Stoker Awards Long Fiction Jury.

Paul is also an NGH Board Certified Hypnotist, an NGH Certified Hypnotism Instructor, a certified Past-Life Regression Therapist, and an IBRT certified professional member of the International Association for Regression Research and Therapies.

Notable suspense and horror fiction by Paul Dale Anderson:
(1984). *Love Till the End of Time*. Madison, WI: The Strange Company.
(1985). *The Devil Made Me Do It*. Madison, WI: The Strange Company. Available as a digital edition from Crossroad Press.
(1987). I'll Show You Mine. In D. B. Silva (Ed.), *The Best of the Horror Show*, (pp. 66-67). Chicago: 2AM Publications.
(1989). *Claw Hammer*. New York: Pinnacle Books. Available as a digital edition from Crossroad Press.

(1989). Better Than One. In J. N. Williamson (Ed.), *Masques III: All-New Works of Horror and the Supernatural (*pp. 68-73). New York: St. Martin's Press. Reprinted (2002) as *Darker Masques* by Pinnacle Books.

(1990). *Daddy's Home.* New York: Pinnacle Books. Available as a digital edition from Crossroad Press.

(1991). The Best. In J. Gelb & M. Garrett (Eds.), *Hotter Blood: More Tales of Erotic Horror* (pp. 161-171). New York: Pocket Books. Reprinted (2004) by Pinnacle Books. Available as Kindle edition.

(1992). Rites of Spring. In J. Gelb (Ed.) *Shock Rock* (pp. 121-126). New York: Pocket Books.

(1995). What You See. In J. Gelb & M. Garrett (Eds.), *Seeds of Fear* (pp. 219-235). New York: Pocket Books. Reprinted (2005) BY Pinnacle Books. Available as Kindle edition.

(2011). Better than One. In J. N. Willliamson (Ed) *Illustrated Masques: Masques Stories in Graphic Format.* Gauntlet Press. Reprinted (2012) as trade paperback by IDW Publishing.

(2015) *Abandoned.* Eldritch Press. March 2015.

(2015) *Icepick.* Crossroad Press. March 2015.

(2015) *Pickaxe.* Crossroad Press. March 2015.

(2015) *Meat Cleaver.* Crossroad Press. May 2015.

(2015) *Pinking Shears.* Crossroad Press.

(2015) *Axes to Grind.* Crossroad Press.

(2015) *Deviants.* Damnation Books.